Field of Lies: CW01632989 or series.

Guardian of aylor series.

The Nick of Time: a humorous account of John Pye's service with Staffordshire Police.

The Vampire of The Villas: a short story and the author's own true account of the death of a man who believed in vampires.

Some events as outlined in 'Endnotes' are factual.

Cover design by Chris Stone, Chris Stone Films.

ISBN: 978-1-9996535-0-7

This is a first edition paperback version of Cathedral of Lies

Couldn't have done it without you folks

Nick Tucker

Kevin McNulty

John Moss

Gladys Pye

Adam Pye

Chris Stone

Cathedral
Of
Lies

John Pye

ONE

Monday June 2nd 1986

THE GUNSHOT launched a flock of pigeons skywards. They had been dozing heavy eyed in the hot afternoon sunshine on a grey slated roof. The creatures flew in a sweeping spiral before settling back into the same spot, unperturbed by the minor interruption to their afternoon siesta.

That slight pressure on the gun's trigger had, however, catastrophically transformed the usual orderly procedures of the building below that roof.

The deafeningly loud blast propelled a copper nosed bullet into the ceiling of Exeter Crown Court at one thousand feet per second. It had been calculated correctly that the noise would carry to where a man sat waiting at the wheel of a Jaguar saloon some seventy yards from the building's historic gateway. This was the signal.

His bony shark's fin elbow jutted out through the open window. Timing was vital, there could be no waiting. His arrival outside the entrance must be neither too early nor too late. Fingers which had nervously drummed against gleaming black paintwork for the past hour finally came to rest.

The car sat kerbside, squat and menacing, its engine ticking over, a heat haze shimmering above the bonnet. His hand pushed the vehicle's auto shift lever into DRIVE.

Ten minutes before the gunshot the occupants of the court building were acting out the customary routines of arrogant pomposity so familiar within the annals of the British judicial system.

Black robed ushers moved, as if on wheels, across the chequerboard tiled foyer floor, calling names and checking lists. Police officers paced with notebooks in hand, eyes gazing ceilingwards, trying to memorise.

Courtroom number one was to be found on the first floor, and on this day boasted an impressive selection of barristers' wigs. Each wig nodded back and forth, tilted left or right, or moved up and down in accordance with the wearer beneath. The case against David Paul Sweeney was a serious one and now into its second week.

Jacob Bunn looked up at Judge Charles Golding from his seat within the defence council's enclosure. He was aware that the attention of the line of advocates and junior barristers either side had been directed towards him. He fanned his face briskly with a manila folder and rose to his feet.

A trickle of sweat crept from beneath his wig, zigzagging its way down his well-tanned cheek. He had attained the healthy glow courtesy of the sunlamps in his private gymnasium: *Jay's Health and Fitness,* a side-line business venture. Bunn's lean six feet physique was also down to extra sessions in his Taunton-based gym. The eighteen carat Rolex glint from his left wrist played twinkling games as he placed the folder down onto the dark oak desk in front and dabbed the sweat trickle with a large white handkerchief. He cleared his throat.

Shafts of afternoon sunlight rippled into the room through a domed ceiling window. Judge Golding stared down at Bunn in expectation.

At thirty-five years of age Bunn had several years of experience in his role of senior barrister. The defence of gangsters were his bread and butter and his current client, Sweeney, produced high earnings over a long period of time. Bunn had no qualms over such issues. Some would say: "No principles".

He leaned forwards, pressed his palms down onto the desk, and viewed the jury. His thick dark eyebrows were raised high as he pondered his words.

Sweeney gazed down from the dock. Dark gypsy features, black gelled hair, expensive charcoal grey suit. If you narrowed your eyes there was a certain film star look about him, but the Tenerife tan had gone. The weeks spent inside Exeter Remand Centre saw to that. There were handsome characteristics: strong chin, chiselled cheekbones. But warning signs of the truth of the man within had been posted. A swallow tattoo on his neck occasionally peeked above his shirt collar and a jagged five-inch scar adorned his left cheek. The man responsible for the scar was no longer alive; he lay buried in several locations.

Two huge uniformed constables sat in the dock, directly behind Sweeney They were the largest available within Devon and Cornwall's Constabulary. The courtroom joke was going around that they had been transferred from Gulliver's Kingdom. The Chief Constable was clearly taking the prisoner's reputation seriously.

A string of killings and disappearances preceded Sweeney's ascent to the position of the country's biggest importer and supplier of cocaine and cannabis. All the victims were major criminals themselves, top drug dealers and their henchmen. The police were initially delighted, as one by one names were crossed off their lists of most wanted.

It wasn't long before a certain *David Sweeney* replaced the deceased gang leaders. It took even less time to work out that he and his team had found the most efficient method of dealing with the opposition.

Sweeney had come a long way in his ungodly career since starting out as a schoolboy in the Midlands. Shoplifting progressed to burglary, car theft and robbery. He'd paid a small price over the years for this apprenticeship, with stints in children's homes and detention centres. The token prison sentence he eventually landed made him realise the error of his ways – getting caught, hence the move down south, close to the coast, where his enterprise could flourish unabated.

At a youthful twenty-nine years, Sweeney grew along with his empire. His terrifying use of violence quickly elevated him to the top of the criminal tree; all the more reason why he was so confounded at finding himself standing before this court, with his once massive organisation caving in from all sides. Assets were stripped away by the courts, property seized and record breaking jail terms handed out to all but a handful of his trusted criminal servants.

Sergeant Peter Lacey and Constable Reg Timson were the two detectives who featured prominently in all these cases. Having given their evidence the pair positioned themselves in seats behind the prosecution team to watch from close quarters as Sweeney's world crumbled under the mounting pressure of evidence.

Lacey, a nearing retirement CID veteran, loathed the crown court necessity for suits, but it was the new shirt his wife had purchased for him at the weekend that was literally rubbing him up the wrong way. He hooked a thumb between collar and neck giving it a tug. *Too bloody small*, he considered as he caught sight of Timson studying him.

Timson, at six feet two inches was taller, and at forty-two years of age, five years junior to Lacey. Suppressing a grin, Timson crinkled up around the eyes as he watched Lacey's discomfort. He dragged the palm of his right hand over his thinning, greying hair and mischievously whispered over: 'Got a problem?' He'd heard the shirt story several times that morning.

Sweeney sat in the dock, predatory eyes drifting from Bunn to Lacey and then to Judge Golding, expression oozing hatred and loathing in equal measure. The fingers of his right hand were curled over the edge of the brass rail that surrounded the dock, each one bearing its tattooed letter of the alphabet: ACAB.

It was an acronym all too familiar to police officers finding themselves fingerprinting some thug or other: *ALL COPPERS ARE BASTARDS*

Sweeney settled his stare upon Bunn. "His brief," as he liked to call him. He raised a hand to his mouth, touching his lips. It was a signal the court had come to understand meant that Sweeney 'wanted a word'.

Recognising the sign, Bunn cast his gaze back towards the judge.

'M'Lud,' the phrase crept from his lips. 'I feel at this stage that I must beg your agreement to a short adjournment whilst I consult with my client.'

The case was not going well for Sweeney, or indeed, for Bunn. Lacey's description: "Cut and dried", was perceived as accurate by most of those present in court. This likely included both Judge Golding and all twelve members of the jury.

Golding looked down at Bunn over the top of his spectacles. An indication of frustration given away with the sigh which accompanied his agreement to the request. 'Yes, Mr Bunn, we will take a thirty-minute recess.'

Lacey poked his glasses back up the bridge of his nose and glanced over at his colleague. A look of annoyance had taken over his face. 'What now,' he muttered under his breath. 'This is the second time today, why doesn't he throw the towel in? Perhaps that's it! Maybe he's changing his plea to guilty.'

Timson's half-open mouth portrayed his own bewilderment.

'All rise,' commanded the court usher as Judge Golding stood to his full, portly, five feet eight inches, turned on his heel and left through the green padded door behind him.

The constables escorted Sweeney from the dock, one either side, following Bunn towards the doorway leading to the cells and interview room.

Sweeney's attempts to elbow more space from his gargantuan escorts met with rejection and an even tighter closing of ranks. He turned and caught Lacey's stare. A sneer towards the detective sergeant was the best he could manage before being unceremoniously ushered through the door.

A smile of satisfaction lit Lacey's craggy features. 'Not all coppers are bastards,' was his softly spoken comment. 'Only some of us.' The smile persisted as he went over the events of the past eighteen months, a catalogue of revelations and priceless information which increasingly whittled away Sweeney's empire. It had culminated in this court case with Sweeney himself in the dock and looking at a life behind bars.

It had been a long time since Sweeney soiled his own hands by actual physical involvement in a drugs shipment. But he was so short on trusted manpower due to the police operations that he had to take the risk. The informant chuckled over the telephone as he told Lacey the precise details of what would take place, where it would happen and who would be involved.

"Squawk", Lacey's nickname for the informant finished off his conversation with: "This is the last call that you'll get from me, don't mess it up, you've got the boss this time."

Lacey didn't mess it up. He planned it in his usual meticulous way. The video footage showed Sweeney himself from two camera angles actually loading up a long wheel base Mercedes van with bales of cannabis and packs of cocaine. The film created hysterical, leg-slapping laughter in the operations room at the debriefing. There were many pats on the back and double malts provided for Lacey and Timson.

Squawk's identity, had never been established. He was just a voice on the telephone, a muffled, poisonous sounding individual who would speak only to Lacey. The conversations were straight and to the point, always ringing from a different payphone.

Looking up, Lacey shook himself from his thoughts as a sound of distant shouting grew louder. It created a: "SILENCE IN COURT", more quickly than any court usher could have accomplished it.

The indistinct noise became a strident torrent of echoing, verbal violence as the door through which Sweeney had been escorted crashed open, its handle smashing into the wall behind.

'Stay right where you are,' roared Sweeney. 'Or this useless bastard gets his fucking toffee-nosed brains blown out.'

Jacob Bunn stumbled pathetically into the courtroom, driven forwards by Sweeney's rough grip on the scruff of his neck. Sweeney's other hand pushed the barrel of a black handgun hard into

Bunn's temple.

The two constables looked in helplessly from the open cell corridor doorway, knowing that the situation was too dangerous to even think about intervening.

Sweeney hurled his hostage towards the exit door. His desperate glare scanned the anxious faces, whilst a cascade of threats and foul language exaggerated his intentions and warned potential heroes to think again. He jammed his knee hard against Bunn's backside, shepherding him forwards. The barrister staggered, half-crouching, vainly trying to pull his head away from the gun.

Lacey's stare fixed onto Sweeney, weighing up the situation as the gunman spotted him. Sweeney's face creased into a sneer as their eyes met. He jerked the blundering barrister to a stop and then swung the gun away to thrust it out at arm's length towards Lacey.

'And *you*, you bastard, Lacey.' His teeth were clamped together, only his lips moved. '*You* can have it now anyway.'

Lacey was halfway beneath the desk before Sweeney even got his words out. In the same instant Bunn forced Sweeney's gun hand upwards. 'NO,' he shouted as the shot rang out with a thunderous report.

Out in the street the Jaguar's driver pressed his foot down onto the accelerator.

Sweeney yanked Bunn back by the scruff of the neck, almost lifting him off his feet. He stuck the gun back into his temple and booted the double doors open with a mighty thrust of the sole of his shoe. Plaster and paint fragments fluttered to the floor from the damaged ceiling where the bullet had embedded itself.

Bunn toppled three steps at a time down the broad curving staircase, his black robe flapping like a flag in the wind as Sweeney propelled him forward. Police officers, court officials and members of the public vanished like smoke through any door that would open.

The fat tyres of the Jaguar juddered to a halt outside the court's main entrance as the ABS system struggled to control the wheels' cravings to lock. The balaclava-clad driver's arrival had been perfect.

Sweeney violently manhandled his hostage in though the rear door and pitched himself in after. The car took off with a roar from its giant engine, tyres pinching down onto the cobbled road surface and squealing. The door smashed shut under acceleration as the driver expertly weaved between parked vehicles and ripped around the sharp right-hand bend at the end of the street and out of sight.

TWO

Thursday June 5th

LITTLE STONELEIGH, Staffordshire. A quaint old market town. Two-way traffic, a cattle market, tobacconists, fruit and veg shops, small rustic pubs and a tiny little Woolworths. Many of the features which were disappearing in other small towns.

Closely hugging the town centre were a few streets of imposing Victorian villas. No doubt they had originally been homes to executives of the day when the town thrived on its diet of beer brewing and shoe making.

A little further out were the rows of two-up two-down terraces, which were followed in the evolutionary processes by streets and avenues of 1930's built homes. The locale of the town itself finally petered out perhaps a mile from the centre with a scattering of 1950's council estates.

The antiquated police station in Ford Street, near to the town's centre was responsible for a great deal more than the nearby neighbourhood. It took in a third of Staffordshire's one thousand square miles. This included swathes of open countryside, several villages, hamlets, stately homes and the sprawling green belt area of Cannock Chase.

Detective Inspector Doug Taylor positioned his coffee mug on the corner of his desk and looked up through the open doorway into the main office. The vast lofty space amplified the sound of several telephones competing against each other for someone to answer. The office had been converted from a magistrates' courtroom many years before and now contained an assortment of tattered, brown wooden desks. Each desk had assigned to it a detective of varying age, sex and description, and, of course, a telephone.

Taylor dragged fingers through the thick dark hair on his temples and massaged the knot of muscle in the nape of his neck, an old rugby injury that would never completely go away. The double-sided form on the desk in front of him bore a title: *West Midlands Forensic Science Laboratory.*

His eyes scrolled down the text. 'Wonderful,' he murmured as he stood to his full six feet four inches and took the two steps down into the main office.

WDC Jayne Morrison inhaled her Player's Number Six down to the filter. She pressed the remnants into an overflowing ashtray and calculated from Taylor's trajectory that he was heading her way.

He put the form down in front of Morrison. 'Bit of good news Mo, the lab's come up trumps on your expensive little smash and grab at Gracefield's Jewellers.' He drew up a chair against the side of the desk. 'They've matched the glass in that toe rag, Jimmy Broad's trainers to the window glass and his blood group to the blood inside the window.'

Morrison glanced down at the form and managed a half-pleased response.

'Well, it's good, Boss, at least I know now I nicked the right man, but he might still get away with it. You know how a fancy barrister can twist things.' She looked up. 'Have you heard about this thing the scientists are working on? Something called DNA. They say they'll be able to prove a person's identity against anyone else in the world from a speck of blood, rather than just say… it could be him.'

Taylor smiled. 'Yes Mo, I have heard of it. It's a way off yet though. Anyway, I was holding back on you… They also matched his prints on the inside of the broken window, so what say we go and nick the bastard again and you can have the pleasure of charging him?'

A cheer went around the office; there would be no shortage of volunteers.

DC Geoff Deakin sat at the desk opposite Morrison, a telephone pushed against his ear. He'd listened to the conversation, whilst trying to sound sincere to the caller that he really was on the verge of a breakthrough over his house burglary.

Taylor grinned over at his long-term colleague. His grin turned to a frown as he leaned over and started to thumb through the pile of crumpled paperwork distorting the shape of Deakin's in-tray.

A mumbled 'hmm' from Taylor was enough for Deakin to mount a defence.

'Sorry, Boss, I was in court all last week. I never got my days off and then that stabbing the other night.'

Taylor raised his eyebrows and tried to keep his smirk in check as Deakin continued to justify. 'The stick I'm getting off my missus... The lawn's three foot high and the garage fell down the other day.'

Laughter spread around the room.

'My lawn's four foot high, Boss,' chimed the overweight, ruddy faced DC Daniel Cheeseman. Cheeseman pressed a hand over the mouthpiece of his own telephone. 'So maybe I could get some time off before Geoff.'

The laughter increased as Deakin finished his phone call and waved a backhanded gesture at the voice from behind. 'Mind your own business, Cheddar.'

The arrival of the elderly control room sergeant interrupted the banter. He held one finger aloft in demand of silence; his wrinkled face wore a concerned expression.

'Inspector Taylor, you'd better take a look at this.' The sergeant thrust forwards the form held in his other hand. 'A heath fire up on Cannock Chase sometime last night, an isolated spot. Seems to have gone out on its own and the chase warden has just come across it. He's found a body there burnt to a crisp.'

THREE

THE TWENTY-SIX square miles of Staffordshire, which make up Cannock Chase, were strangely apportioned to the jurisdiction of Little Stoneleigh Police; the journey alone would take almost half an hour.

Back in the fifties Cannock Chase had officially been labelled as an *Area of Outstanding Natural Beauty*. The countryside was made up of woodlands and heathlands and was criss-crossed with footpaths, dusty gravel roadways and small remote car parks. Some places were marked out especially as picnic spots with wooden tables and benches. Others were unmarked trails. Over the years the vast expanse saw its moments of notoriety. Bodies of murder victims were discovered, including the three young girls slain by sex offender Raymond Morris in the sixties.

People often made use of the remoteness to commit suicide. Hanging was a popular method. A length of washing line tossed over a tree branch, perhaps car exhaust fumes, a vacuum cleaner pipe pushed onto the tail pipe and in through the window.

Taylor tormented the engine of his old Vauxhall Cavalier. His bulky electronic pager shot from one side of the dashboard to the other as he yanked the steering wheel hard to the left. The car's front wheels spun as they attempted traction with the dry, stony surface.

Geoff Deakin sat in the passenger seat keeping a firm grip on the overhead handle. 'You heard anything more about Sweeney?'

Taylor selected first gear for a particularly bad piece of track. 'Exeter CID phoned me yesterday. They wanted to know if we'd still got any contacts for him. It's over fifteen years since he lived in Little Stoneleigh and our file on him is less than useless.'

'Up to the top,' Deakin directed. 'Then swing a left… if the suspension holds out that is.'

Taylor coaxed more power from the engine. 'Good job you know your way around here, Geoff. There's no way I'd have found it.'

Deakin kept his eyes fixed in front. 'I was up at this car park last Christmas when that bloke strung himself up. Awful… those kids finding him.'

The car swept up the narrow track pursued by a cloud of dust as it bounced over the uneven surface. The fire hazards were made clear by the frequent presence along the route of large metal tubs containing rowing oar-shaped fire beaters.

The car park was an extensive and well potholed space with the same orange, stony covering which made up the track-ways. On the far side a Land Rover, a yellow police Incident Response car and a white, Scenes of Crime van were already parked in haphazard fashion.

Several figures stood in a huddle near the vehicles. Behind them the ground rose away steeply and was densely covered with bracken, gorse bushes and tall thin silver birch trees. A blackened area was clearly evident in the centre of this thicket. It extended some twenty or more yards back from the car park and about the same distance either side.

Three uniformed police officers, together with a plump red-faced man and a plain-clothes Scenes of Crime Officer (SOCO), formed the gathering.

Taylor and Deakin climbed out from the Cavalier amid a haze of dust as one of the police officers, a middle-aged uniformed sergeant, approached them.

'Afternoon Inspector. This is Andy Warburton, the Chase Warden.' The sergeant indicated towards the plump man. 'He found the body.'

Taylor extended his open right hand to Warburton and introduced himself and Deakin.

Warburton, a forty something, balding heavyweight, closely resembled an overgrown Boy Scout, complete with beige coloured shorts and light green shirt. He took Taylor's hand, shaking it vigorously.

'Bit of a shock I can tell you. I thought I'd have a look and make sure nothing was still smouldering, what with the dry weather, and then… sodding hell.'

Taylor tried to look sympathetic and finally retrieved his hand. He glanced over at the sergeant. 'Dave, can you take a statement from Mr Warburton, while we have a look?

The sergeant nodded agreement as Taylor and Deakin ambled away across the rough surface. A narrow corridor of fluttering blue and white incident tape strung between poles dictated their route to the corpse. This safe pathway, the work of the SOCO, would prevent damage to evidence and stretched some ten or more yards towards the centre of the burnt patch.

The glint of metal caught Deakin's eye. 'Oil can, Boss,' he pointed out. 'And I can smell petrol.'

They had been to enough arson cases to know that the smell of petrol lingered on long after the fire was out no matter how intense the blaze. The can, on the edge of the burnt area, seemed undamaged with its yellow *Duckhams Q20/50* logo clearly obvious.

Tinder dry grass and bracken had been reduced to a thick carpet of grey and black ash. Two sets of well-defined footprints belonging to Warburton and the police sergeant led towards the centre.

The body lay stretched out on its back. The head appeared to have imploded. A hole existed where the jaw should have been. Fragments of teeth and shards of blackened skull were on show. The rest, in contrast, was recognisable as a male and in spite of its roasted appearance most of the flesh remained on the bones. Some clothing was still apparent between the back, buttocks and arms where they made contact with the ground.

The crime scene investigation went on for several hours, taking in a meticulous in situ examination of the body and a thorough combing of the surrounding area. When this painstaking work was completed, the corpse was carefully lifted, amidst a welter of camera flashes, and installed into a black body bag.

The sound of the heavy duty zipper being drawn along its length finally signalled the end of a long day for Taylor and Deakin.

The Gardener's Arms Little Stoneleigh was a CID watering hole of many years. Two major factors dictated this: One being the forty-five second door to door brisk walk. The other, the fact that landlord, Tony was happy to serve the lads after hours.

'It helps to keep the pillocks out,' was Tony's philosophy on the subject. 'If they know The Old Bill come in late, they'll go elsewhere.'

Taylor and Deakin possessed shared history. They'd joined Staffordshire Police as young recruits on the very same day and endured the rigours of the police training centre at Ryton on Dunsmore, near Coventry, side by side. All that was over fifteen years ago.

Little and Large, they'd been nicknamed a few years later, probably before the two comedians even thought up the title for themselves. A chief inspector christened them as they worked the relentless fourteen-hour, seven days a week shifts on some murder inquiry or other. Deakin was supposedly: "Little", although his five feet ten inch, thirteen stones wouldn't normally have fitted this description. Taylor at six feet four and an athletic fifteen stone supplied the "Large".

Deakin knew it had to be "Sir" or "Boss" when there was anyone else around, but it was "Doug" in other circumstances. They'd even taken two family holidays abroad together and hadn't managed to fall out. Sadly that finished when Taylor's wife, Angie, left with their young son, Ben. Deakin's support and friendship helped Taylor through this difficult time.

The pair worked together many times on different squads and at different police stations. Deakin, never one for promotion, was happy to be a detective constable and was good at his job.

Taylor, the studious and deep thinking one did not enjoy fast-track promotion to his rank of detective inspector. The self-inflicted millstone he'd put around his own neck saw to that. Doug Taylor was not noted for following orders; he preferred to do things his own way.

It had been eighteen months since Taylor took on the job of DI in charge of Little Stoneleigh's CID. His team were a mixed bunch, all good detectives, psychologists, jokers and comedians.

As far as Taylor was concerned there was one fly in the ointment about working at Little Stoneleigh. The fly came in the form of Superintendent Malcolm Farmer, the sub-divisional commander and one of the force's longest serving officers.

Farmer spent most of his police service at Little Stoneleigh and during those thirty-four years as a copper a few unsavoury rumours rippled about. Nothing, though, ever completely floated to the surface. His rise through the ranks to superintendent had been a slow but gradual affair. Why ever he hadn't retired at the normal thirty years on the maximum pension puzzled everyone. The plain fact was that he must go this year. The Chief Constable told him: "No more extensions, Mr Farmer."

It was ten minutes after eleven when Taylor and Deakin made it into the Gardener's. Tony removed the towel draped over the beer pump handles and gave a knowing look. 'Evening gents. Two Bass is it?'

'Please, Tony… I'll get these Geoff,' Taylor conceded as he glanced around the room at the few remaining punters.

They settled at a table intent on relaxing as they mulled over the events of the day. Taylor took a sip at his pint with the thought of his conversation with the Force's CID boss going through his mind.

Detective Chief Superintendent Ray Burrington's flying visit to the scene came during the late afternoon, a bit of hands-on supervision and a chance to get away from his HQ based office for an hour. "Doug," he'd said. "I want you to run this investigation your way. Keep it small, keep it tight. It's a strange one, but we can't be certain yet that it's a murder. Let me know as soon as you have a post mortem result."

Deakin broke Taylor from his thoughts. 'Okay, Doug, what do you think?'

Taylor shuffled for more comfort on the hard, bench seat and stifled a yawn. 'Well, like we said earlier… that certainly looks like a shotgun wound to the face. I know we'll get to find out for sure at the post mortem tomorrow, but the intentional damage to the face and the burning must have been done to prevent identification.'

'Yes, strange,' Deakin agreed. He was already back on his feet, emptied glass in hand and heading for the bar. 'He was a tall bloke, but did you see those legs? Painfully thin, nothing to him, like a skeleton.'

Tony subtly draped the towels back over the pump handles after pushing the two fresh pints across towards Deakin. It was a tactful indication that these were the last beers he was pulling. The room had quickly emptied, the only other customers being the two old regulars in the corner with their dominoes.

Taylor lapsed back into deep thought as the glass was placed down onto his beer mat. The wasted state of the body was still going around in his mind. He broke into a response to Deakin's comment of two minutes ago as though it had been made that second.

'Yes, I'll give you that, not thin, more like emaciated. Drugs maybe? That could answer a lot of questions.'

FOUR

THE NEXT MORNING, Deakin was a solitary figure in the CID office. The wall clock showed half past seven. He allowed himself a weary smile. The smile grew a little as he dumped an inches thick wad of paperwork from his own desk into Cheddar's in-tray.

'There you go Cheddar, me old mate,' he said patting his hand down onto the pile. A picture formed in his mind of Cheddar's expression which he knew would be accompanied with some cursing.

Deakin collected a bundle of statement forms and a notepad from the office cupboard. He then took the stairs down to the backyard of the police station where Taylor was waiting.

Their destination, the Stafford cemetery complex, was a vast expanse of grave plots and also home to the ominously named Blackheath Mortuary.

The cockney twang of Ernie, the mortuary assistant greeted them in the foyer. 'Mornin' fellas, fancy a brew first?'

'Please Ernie,' they harmonised.

Ernie, a stocky, middle aged man, sported close cropped silver hair, green surgical overalls and white wellingtons. He bore the hallmarks of a former army physical training instructor. His perpetual smile was hard to comprehend for a man who witnessed the evidence of human depravity on such a grand and regular scale.

The strong and pungent smell of a particular brand of disinfectant permeated the entire building. It was the same smell Taylor and Deakin knew to expect in any mortuary and must have been a product insisted upon by the authorities.

Ernie gestured them through into his office, a clean, but well used space, with eggshell painted walls, modern flat-pack desk, calendar, notice board and sink.

Tea bags were dropped into mugs and boiling water poured. 'No sugar for Mister Taylor, and one for you, Geoff,' Ernie said with the confidence of previous experience. 'The SOCO's here and Mr Jenkinson is poised with his scalpel. Looks a bit of a strange one.'

In that same second the door from the office into the corridor opened with the sound of a spring being stretched under tension.

The gaunt imposing figure of Home Office pathologist, John Frobisher-Jenkinson entered. He wore the same green surgical overalls and white wellingtons as his assistant, but there the resemblance ended. An aura of wisdom and shrewdness radiated from this tall slightly stooped figure. A pair of deep-set questioning blue eyes sat behind dark framed spectacles, together with the wrinkles of a near permanent frown.

Jenkinson's stoop was probably related to bending over countless dissected corpses during his long career. Had it been possible for him to have performed his own post mortem, he would have swiftly sliced into the flesh identifying the particular misaligned and degenerate vertebrae as the cause of the problem. This humorous aphorism was frequently recounted by Jenkinson when called upon as an after dinner speaker.

'Good morning, gentlemen.' Jenkinson's voice flowed with the slow, thick, richness of double cream. 'Well, this is an odd one, chaps. Perhaps you'd like to acquaint me with the background whilst you enjoy your tea.'

Taylor outlined the circumstances during the ten minute tea break. The trio then followed the pathologist through into the examination room.

A bank of fluorescent light tubes hummed softly overhead; their stark bright light reflected sharply against white floor to ceiling tiles.

Stainless steel bowls, knives, saws and scalpels lay neatly placed on a metal table, spotless and gleaming.

On the wall above, there hung a large plastic, wipe-clean wall chart. At the top in blue marker pen the fictitious name *JOHN DOE* had been written.

Bold printed words stretched down one side:

BRAIN
HEART
LUNGS
LIVER
KIDNEYS

There were columns for weights and other details. The smell of the disinfectant hung heavily, but could not completely mask the smell of burning and the distinctive scent of petrol.

An echoing resonance was created by the airy space and the lack of any soft surfaces. A huge porcelain examination slab took up the centre of the room. Its gleaming whiteness was a startling contrast to the blackened, human-shaped mass that lay assembled on top.

Scenes of crime officer, Detective Constable Pat Gerrard, already present, stood, clipboard in hand and camera slung around neck. He made a tight-lipped smile. 'Morning, Boss, morning Geoff.'

'Hi Pat, thanks for coming,' Taylor replied out of politeness, aware of the fact that Gerrard had no option.

Jenkinson began, meticulously cutting, slicing and probing. In a matter of moments the ribcage and surrounding seared flesh was sawn through and spread open to reveal glistening, variously-coloured innards.

Ernie assisted, handing over differing stainless steel implements without instruction or request. In return he received an assortment of blood soaked appendages which he carefully distributed into individual metal bowls.

'Right, gentlemen,' started the pathologist. 'Shotgun wound to the chin and mouth area. Close range and plenty of shot recovered from the remains of the lower jaw. Almost certainly a twelve bore. I note that the majority of the shot has penetrated right through the head. I believe the body was shot from above whilst lying on the ground in its place of finding. Mr Gerrard tells me that shotgun pellets have been recovered deeply from the earth beneath the head and this fits with my theory. Burning extensively over most of the corpse. The face and both hands are the worst affected. There is strong evidence of an accelerant, the odour being reminiscent of petrol, as no doubt later tests will reveal.'

Taylor had dozens of questions in mind, but knew Jenkinson disliked being interrupted in full flow and was so thorough that he would more than likely cover all of Taylor's puzzles anyway.

The pathologist contemplated his audience. 'You may have noted, gentlemen, the emaciation of the body. I calculate that the subject was some six feet to six feet two inches in height, but in life weighed around seven stones.' Jenkinson's eyebrows reached high above his spectacles. 'Little more than a skeleton.'

The three detectives looked at each other in astonishment.

'Also clothing is of interest. The underside of the body is hardly affected by the burning and so a lot of the clothing has remained intact. Enough to be able to say that the chap was wearing a full suit… jacket, trousers, waistcoat, shirt, tie, underpants, socks, leather shoes… oh, and a vest.'

'Vest, waistcoat, that's a bit strange these days,' Taylor finally decided to comment. 'Any clues as to age yet, sir?'

Jenkinson paused with scalpel in hand and exhaled as though waiting to drop his bombshell. 'Oh yes, Mr Taylor, this gentleman was elderly, probably in his mid-seventies.'

'Christ,' said Deakin. 'Seventy odd, for God's sake who would do such a thing… blow an old chap's head off?'

Jenkinson looked up from his work, clearly timing his second bombshell to perfection. 'The shot is not what killed him Mr Deakin. This poor chap died from cancer… lung cancer. He must have been bedridden for many weeks before he died.'

Taylor frowned. 'So when do you think he did die?'

'That, Mr Taylor, will take me longer to determine. My best guess at the moment would be that he has been dead for at least one week, perhaps more.'

Deakin now held a handkerchief against his mouth and nose, the stench had become stomach-turning. 'Anything else sir… to give us an identification?' he mumbled.

'Not at this stage, apart from signs of a tattoo on the left forearm. It is, however, badly damaged.'

Jenkinson lifted the blackened left arm and turned it outwards to reveal the inner forearm. There, camouflaged by the crisply blackened surrounding flesh, could be seen the definite remnants of a tattoo, possibly lettering, maybe a picture.

Taylor moved in and took a closer look before glancing back at Gerrard. 'Difficult, but do your best with it Pat.'

Gerrard adjusted his camera lens as Jenkinson continued. 'Nothing recovered from the clothing. The teeth, of course, are smashed to pieces by the gunshot. It may be possible to do some reconstructive work, but don't hold any hope for a dental ID.'

'Hmm,' Jenkinson mused as he turned his attentions to the right arm. 'This arm is much more burnt than the other.' He carefully picked at some of the burnt skin with the point of a scalpel. 'Badly burnt here,' he added. 'I was wondering if there were any signs of more tattooing. I could slice this remaining section of flesh off, there are some new procedures available that might still be able to show any tattoo despite the damage.'

The pathologist was about to make an incision and start to cut the flesh away when he stopped and peered over the top of his glasses. His latex gloved finger now probed the right shoulder of the corpse.

'This is interesting.' He pressed more deeply. 'Site of an old injury… fairly ancient surgical techniques.'

The group were not given time to close in and examine the object of Jenkinson's interest before he had skilfully cut through the shoulder muscle revealing bright red and pink coloured flesh.

'Aha,' he declared jubilantly, as he carefully probed a pair of forceps into the deep cut and pulled from it a one-inch long, half-inch wide piece of twisted blackened metal.

Deakin screwed up his face. 'What the devil?'

Jenkinson opened the forceps, dropping the item down into a stainless steel bowl with a dull sounding *ting*.

'It appears gentlemen that our John Doe has been in the wars. Best example of a shrapnel wound I've seen in a while.'

Despite the continuing gory examination nothing more of any significance came to light. Another half hour passed before Taylor delivered his thanks to the pathologist and stepped back outside into the bright June sunshine and sweet fresh air, away from the nauseating smells.

The drive back to Little Stoneleigh took fifteen minutes and was filled with discussed possibilities, theories and facts. Taylor continued to summarise as he slowed and pulled off the road into the roughly tarmacked car park at the rear of the police station. 'So, it's not murder, and the Detective Chief Super will be pleased about that, but...' He broke off from the sentence craning his neck to peer over the car's bonnet as it crept forwards. A red and white traffic cone stood blocking the only available space. Attached to the cone was a wooden placard. Black lettering spelled a directive:

RESERVED SUPT FARMER.

A dragging sound accompanied the Cavalier's progress as the front bumper gradually pushed the cone forwards, crushing it against the wall of the police station.

Taylor resumed his conversation where he'd left off. 'We must play it low-key and not let too much of the detail out to the press or we'll be hounded twenty-four hours a day with these circumstances.' He turned off the engine and made to climb from the driver's seat. 'It's pretty obvious that there's a lot more to this.'

Deakin exited the car, straightening his back and shot a glance over at the distorted traffic cone. It was barely visible, pinched between bumper and wall. His shoulders shuddered as he stifled a laugh.

FIVE

Friday 13th June

TAYLOR set his stare upon the wall hanging calendar opposite his desk. The date of Friday 13th loomed as an omen, a feature pointed out earlier in the day by Superintendent Farmer. Those words repeated inside his head: "I want this bloody nonsense winding up and you and Deakin back doing some real work, so think of this as your unlucky day."

Eight days had passed since the discovery of the body, with little or no progress. Countless hours on the telephone, reams of missing persons' reports sifted through: "Mispers" being the official police jargon.

Some of the Misper reports came from as far afield as the Highlands of Scotland and others down into deepest Cornwall.

Sightings of vehicles took up a lot of time along with enquiries at garages concerning sales of petrol in cans. Video recordings from CCTV systems were trawled and press appeals made. A few cranks offered opinions, including the one regular with a crazy notion: "It came to me in a dream!"

Taylor rubbed his eyes before consulting his watch, quarter to ten, another long day. Deakin, on the opposite side of the desk, ticked off another Misper form.

They were working from a small ground floor room which, in reality, was the Janitor's store. The two vacuum cleaners, the brushes and a selection of mops and buckets evidenced this. It had been another battle with Superintendent Farmer to even acquire these frugal surroundings.

Deakin joined in the watch consultation before giving his colleague an expectant look. 'Pint?' he enquired.

Taylor nodded acceptance to the offer without objection. He felt, not much further forward with the case. It had been a twelve bore shotgun which was used on the man's face. Cancer had been the cause of death and he had died around the time Mr Jenkinson suggested, plus a bit more, possibly as much as nine days ago. His age couldn't be determined any closer than between seventy and seventy-five. There were no fingerprints on the can and the accelerant used was petrol. This was all information determined within the first two days.

Taylor pulled his jacket from the back of his chair and followed Deakin down the stairs, his mind still churning.

The tattoo remained intriguing. Much of it had been destroyed by the flames. A letter "H" began the sequence, but burning obliterated the next letter. An "S" followed this and then more damage before what was deciphered as "ORM". A jumble of lines and curves were evident above the lettering, without doubt a picture, but too spoiled to make out. They played about with it for hour after hour, both confessing to waking up at night with possibilities.

Enquiries all drew a blank on a missing elderly male or a man who'd been ill around the date of assumed death. There was nothing that would fit from doctors or hospitals about a missing patient or even a missing body. It was as if the old chap never existed.

A chatter of conversation, some low background music and a fug of smoke met the two detectives as they entered the bar of the Gardener's Arms. Landlord, Tony, quickly served up two pints and the men took up seats at a small iron-legged table. Taylor slid Deakin's frothing pint mug towards him and pocketed his change. 'You know, Geoff, if we don't get to the bottom of this pretty soon, we're going to have the plug pulled on us. Farmer has been moaning to headquarters to get us both back at the office. He's not interested, keeps saying: "The CID overtime is going through the roof and all we're doing is messing about with nothing more than an unidentified body." Why doesn't he retire and leave us all in peace?'

Deakin took a gulp. 'I know, Doug,' he raised his voice above the clatter being made by the two elderly domino players on the next table. 'It's bad enough trying to do the job with him obstructing every move, but with something juicy like this it makes you want to scream. You know as well as I do that this enquiry stinks. There's more to it. Someone had a mighty big reason to do what they did to the old man.'

Taylor wasn't listening; his gaze was firmly fixed on the next table. He reached out and patted the old domino player next to him on the forearm.

The man jerked his head around at the sudden unexpected intrusion. 'What?'

'Sorry.' Taylor apologised realising his involuntary action was out of order. 'It's your tattoo,' he nodded down at the faded blue wording on the man's brown and hairy arm. 'HMS Coventry, you were in the Navy, Second World War?'

The old man pulled his arm away from Taylor and shuffled along the seat, increasing the distance. Taylor's eyes continued to stare at the tattoo as the shirt sleeve was self-consciously rolled down.

'It's Arthur, isn't it?'

'It is Arthur, yes, and you two are police. Don't tell me it's now a crime to have a tattoo!'

It took less than five minutes and two gratis pints to get Arthur and domino partner, Les, on side. Arthur gave a proud account of his service aboard HMS Coventry. He also explained about the tattoo: 'It was a tradition, not everybody did it. It was a way of showing pride in the ship you served on. If you're sure on the "H" and the "S" then I'll guess the missing bit between is an "M". As for the name of the ship… you should be able to get hold of a list of possibilities that might fit.'

Midnight arrived before landlord, Tony, decided to politely remind the party, who now had three games of dominoes behind them, of the time.

Perhaps Friday 13th hadn't been such an unlucky day after all.

SIX

Saturday 14th June

AN OFFICE on the second floor of Exeter police station had been home to Pete Lacey and Reg Timson for almost eighteen months. The small space was probably designed with one single pen pusher in mind, but was now crammed with a double sided desk, overfilled filing cabinets, a coat stand and two chairs. It also contained all the other paraphernalia accumulated since the operation to target David Sweeney started.

Bright morning sunlight glared in between the slats of a pale green Venetian window blind. Lacey squeezed from his desk and spread a thumb and forefinger between the slats to take a peek at the outside world. Buses, cars and lorries buzzed along the busy Heavitree Road down below as everyone started their daily routine.

The office had been put to various uses over the years when a major inquiry came along, or a temporary squad set up to target a particular crime problem.

The Sweeney operation had been code named *Upstart*. No meaning lay behind the word. Operations were given a code name taken randomly from the dictionary, a word that started with the next letter in the alphabet from the initial letter of previous operation.

A cardboard sign, attached to the office door with sellotape, spelled out in black marker pen that this was where Operation Upstart was to be found. It gave notice to visitors that they had arrived at the place where Lacey and Timson spent the greatest part of their waking hours, sometimes as long as eighteen hours in one day.

The office had evolved during their occupancy; small additions providing touches of comfort. Photos of wives and kids, a transistor radio tuned to the cricket, an out of date calendar with large photographs of scantily clad women.

A metal tray lay on the floor which supported an assortment of grubby-looking cracked mugs along with the necessary brew making equipment. An electric kettle completed the collection and was so positioned that its dodgy looking cable could hardly reach the wall socket.

As the accepted experts on all things Sweeney, Lacey and Timson continued to enjoy the privileges of their own office. To a large degree they also still enjoyed their own agenda, but the court escape had turned Operation Upstart completely on its head. It was no longer just a campaign to convict a serious drugs dealer. It was now many times more serious. A fifteen strong team of detectives had been put together, tasked with arresting Sweeney and rescuing the kidnapped barrister at all costs.

Lacey remained unimpressed, preferring to continue at his own pace and using his own tried and trusted methods to bring closure to the whole proceedings.

'I still can't get my head around Jacob Bunn doing that,' Lacey said, his gaze still fixed on the street below. 'I mean he actually saved my life. I think it's almost restored my faith in humanity. How long's it been now, two weeks?'

'Pete…' Timson's tone showed his exasperation. 'It's been twelve days since Sweeney bust out of court. The papers have been full of it. It's been on the TV every night and you mention Bunn's out of character heroism several times a day. It's not getting us any nearer to finding either of them. You've got a meeting with the Chief Super in half an hour. He's being hounded by both the press and the Chief Constable and we've still nothing new to tell him.'

Lacey sat back down. 'Right… a meeting in half an hour you say? Let's go through it again. The Jag, what's the situation with the Jag?'

Timson looked back across the desk, relieved at a chance to change the subject.

'Well… ' he paused as he laid out a number of sheets of foolscap paper. 'It's a ringer. The number plates on it are identical to another black Jag from Stratford-on-Avon. That car was in Stratford, parked at the owner's business premises when Sweeney broke out of court; I've a car park video tape to back that up. Sweeney's mob have no doubt earmarked the car they used well in advance, and then kept an eye open for a similar Jag… age, model, colour and spec. This one from Stratford is up and down the country all the time. They've clearly spotted it on its travels, noted the number and got some plates made up.'

Lacey pulled his reading glasses from the bridge of his nose. 'Yes, so if a police officer for whatever reason, carries out a PNC check, the description fits the registration number and it's not on the stolen or interest list.'

Timson nodded agreement with the theory. 'All I've been able to do,' he said. 'Is draw up a list of stolen Jags which are similar to the one used at court… again, colour, age, model and so on.' He slid one of the sheets of paper in front of Lacey. 'There are only seven in the country which could fit.' He tapped his biro onto the document.

'Hmm,' Lacey murmured, not bothering to look down. 'But if it's not yet been reported stolen, then that could be a wild goose chase.'

Timson massaged his temples and then gave a frustrated sigh. 'True,' he conceded.

'Okay then, the gun,' Lacey said. 'Tell me again, how did he get that gun into court?'

Timson sighed. He'd been through this with Lacey so many times. 'Right,' he started. 'The interview room in the court cell block has a hopper style window, heavy duty security glass, iron frame… the works. It opens at the top by just eight inches. After Sweeney escaped, a long length of string was found on the floor of the interview room, with a ripped plastic bag on one end. The string is long enough to reach down from the roof to the window.'

'And SOCO checked the roof area for fingerprints and what not?' Lacey asked.

'Of course, but there are no decent surfaces for prints… just pigeon shit everywhere. There's a bit of a flat roof around the edges. It would have made it easy for Sweeney's accomplice to lower the gun down. But it's not for the faint hearted. It's nearly eighty feet. The court building adjoins part of the Castle walls. It's a security problem that hadn't been identified before.'

Lacey turned in his seat, reached for his coffee cup from the window ledge, one inch of cold, brown liquid. He gulped it down. 'What about witnesses in the court?'

'There was a police firearms expert in court, who recognised the gun as a 9mm Walther PPK semi-automatic. The bullet was recovered from the ceiling in good condition. The report from ballistics agrees with 9mm, but there's no record of bullets fired by that gun being used in any earlier crime.'

'What about unidentified bodies? Is there anything else, anywhere in the country?'

'Plenty of unidentified bodies from different areas, yes,' Timson explained. 'But not one that's even close to being Bunn.'

'And Sweeney's old home town, Little Stoneleigh in the Midlands, you said they had an unidentified body.'

Timson shook his head, but answered in the affirmative. 'Yes, they've got one, but there's no way it's Bunn. It's an old bloke who's died of cancer, then been set on fire.'

Lacey pressed his palms together. 'Things people do.' He looked up to see a uniformed sergeant, bulging briefcase in hand, was standing at the open door.

'Sergeant Lacey, DC Timson, good morning. I'm Sergeant Tim Brownfield from headquarters. You ordered a computer M log search on the black Jaguar used in the Jacob Bunn abduction. I have the result for you.' He hauled his briefcase up onto the desk and selected from it a sheaf of papers. 'I have an appointment with your control room today, so I've brought the details along with me to explain.'

Lacey eyed Timson with surprise. 'Do you know about this, Reg? What is this M log thing?'

'Yes,' Timson confessed. 'I ordered it. They run a check on the registered number on the car. It finds all the details of any PNC checks that were done on that number over the last six months. It might be helpful.'

Lacey turned to face the sergeant. 'I'm still learning with this computer thing, er… Tim, so did it throw anything up?'

'It did indeed.' Sergeant Brownfield's look became gleeful as an opening to illustrate his technical knowledge presented itself. 'Obviously,' he continued. 'It's traced the check you did after the abduction.' His pink well-manicured fingers flicked through the papers locating the relevant page. 'Which was Monday 2nd June, but someone in our force area also requested a check on that number during the early hours of the 29th May… four days before the Bunn abduction. I knew you'd want the details of this one, so I've taken the liberty of checking for you. It was done by WPC 2009, who turns out to be a young lady named Kimberly Harding down at Tedham nick.'

'I've met Kim,' Timson interrupted. 'She used to be on traffic department. She was up for commendation a few months ago. Did a super job catching a team of ram-raiders after a big heist. Stuck to them like glue. They couldn't shake her off and ended up wrapping their car around a lamp post.'

'That'll be the same lady,' Sergeant Brownfield agreed. 'She was on foot patrol in Tedham. It was a Thursday morning… about half past two when she saw the Jag. She spotted it twice and thought it suspicious, so she ran a PNC check. It came back clean, and as you know, registered to a chap in Stratford-on-Avon.'

Brownfield looked up from the paperwork. 'I think you'll find that the real Jag was safely tucked up in its garage in Stratford at that time.'

Lacey clasped his hands together and rubbed them briskly. 'This is more like it. Thanks Tim, but what were Sweeney's cronies doing in

Tedham at half two of a morning? We know he wasn't in the car, he was half way through his trial and safely banged up in a cell.'

'Up to no good that's for sure,' Timson responded. 'They may have been involved in crime or even plotting the court escape somewhere in Tedham. There could be a lead back to them, fingerprints, forensic, description. Tedham's only a small place, a bit of a country backwater.'

'Hmm,' Lacey mused as Sergeant Brownfield handed him the paperwork. 'Thanks for your help, Tim.'

Brownfield carefully fastened his briefcase before heading from the office, satisfied that his technical expertise might have helped in a serious crime investigation.

'Computers,' Lacey muttered with a shake of the head. 'Okay, Reg, I'm going up to see the boss. Give Tedham a ring and get this WPC over here. We also need to check through the incident reports covering Tedham for the night of the 28th to 29th May. Perhaps we can find out what Sweeney's cronies were up to.'

SEVEN

LITTLE STONELEIGH police station did not have air conditioning; the Victorians who built the place would probably have laughed at such an idea. Initiative had to be used during those rare periods of hot weather.

Taylor placed an ice cold can of coke down on the desk in front of Geoff Deakin. 'There you go, only a few left at the shop.' He loosened his tie, flicked his shirt top button undone and sat down with a sigh.

Deakin pulled up the wooden sash window as far as he dared, any further and it would jam. This he knew from experience. A welcome momentary breeze wafted in as he looked up, sweat shining on his forehead. He nodded a thank you for the coke. 'This has to be it, Doug.' He pulled a biro from behind his right ear and drew a bold blue oval shape around a word typed on the document in front of him.

Taylor rose from his seat and walked around behind Deakin. The document was headed with a crowned insignia and the words: *Ministry of Defence.* The circled word was: *STORM*

Deakin pushed the biro back behind his ear and read the text aloud. 'HMS Storm, a Royal Navy submarine, commissioned in 1943 and set sail in August. She saw action many times mostly in Japanese waters and survived the war but was scrapped in 1949.'

He turned his head, making eye contact with Taylor before continuing. 'She did have some crew changes. Casualties, transfers, promotions and that kind of thing. I've ended up with a list of names of men who made it through the war with the boat… apparently they call it a boat if it's a submarine.'

'So,' Deakin concluded. 'I've narrowed it down to possibly seven men who would fit in with the age parameters for our man. As to how many of them survived until the date our man died or where in the country they come from I've no way of knowing as yet.'

'Well done, Geoff.' Taylor's fist gave Deakin's shoulder a friendly thump. 'I feel as though we're getting somewhere now. Old Arthur from the pub has dropped me a phone number in for the Royal Navy Association. He says they should be able to give us a clue on the whereabouts of an individual serviceman as long as he has kept in touch over the years.'

Deakin reached for the can of coke. 'What a nice old guy.' There was a hiss as he pulled the can's metal tab upwards and eagerly gulped at it. 'We owe him a few pints.'

Exeter police station was a familiar building to Police Constable Kim Harding. She'd started her police service there as a rookie six years before, but had never visited this particular office. The telephone call she'd received at home just after lunchtime puzzled her until Timson fully explained the possible importance.

Pete Lacey's concentration was broken by a slight, but refreshing hint of perfume. Kim was standing in front of his desk. A crisp white uniform blouse and black and white chequered neck ruff enhanced her faultless complexion. The large brown eyes were crowned with dark, crescent-shaped eyebrows, which were raised in expectation. Her almost black hair was stylishly fashioned into an impish fringe and young girl's short ponytail.

A glimmer of a smile dimpled her cheeks. 'WPC Harding, Sarge.'

The hot weather allowed for the forfeiting of the uniform jackets. Her tight waist and shapely hips were an unexpected diversion from the paperwork on Lacey's desk.

'Oh, oh, right,' spluttered the off guard Lacey as he stood to greet the newcomer and succeeded in knocking his pot of biros from the desk.

He blushed at his clumsiness and bent forward to recover the biros as the realisation dawned that he was probably nearly old enough to be the young lady's father.

'It's about this PNC check I did then Sarge… turns out to be the car that broke that drug dealer out of court and kidnapped the barrister?'

'Looks that way, can't be a hundred per cent, but it does look like it. Pull up a chair. Tell me about that night, everything you can remember.'

Kim seated herself opposite Lacey and took her pocket book from her bag. She leafed through stopping at a page, where, in neat black biro had been written *Wednesday 28th May 1986.*

'I was on nights Sarge. I started at ten on the Wednesday and was due to finish my eight-hour shift on the Thursday morning at six. Nothing was happening. It's a quiet place at the best of times and midweek is really dead. The sergeant let me stay in to get some reports done first half and then after my meal at one o'clock I went out to do foot patrol on the town. It was bang on ten minutes before two when I set off from the nick.'

Lacey looked concerned. 'Patrolling on your own on night shift, do you do that then nowadays?'

She shrugged. 'Tedham's a pretty quiet place, Sarge, especially on night shift, and I'd rather be on my own anyway. I do a bit of martial arts stuff, I can handle myself.'

'Right then.' Lacey pushed himself backwards in his chair and feigned mock fear with his hands. 'Don't mess with WPC Harding.' He pretended to make a note of his words on his pad.

She smirked at Lacey's humour. 'Anyway Sarge, it was about two o'clock when I first saw the car. I'd been checking property along High Street… absolutely nothing about and then I heard this motor driving away from me down by the church. I saw it in the distance as it turned out of Moss Street… definitely a Jag. I watched it disappear up the road; heard it too, a powerful engine… probably the 5.3 model. It looked and sounded pretty new, so I'm guessing a Series Three, XJ12 Sovereign. It was a dark colour. Either black or maybe dark blue… must have been the same one I saw later. Not many of that model about, certainly not in Tedham and at two in the morning.'

Lacey's scribbling onto his notepad was now genuine. 'And you clocked the model, engine size and all that. You're clued up then… how so?' he asked, admitting to himself that he wouldn't know a Ford from a Vauxhall.

'Four years on Traffic Department Sarge… advanced driver, motorway, big bikes, done all that.'

Lacey's face showed his puzzlement. 'So, why this, pounding the beat at little ole Tedham. It looks more like a job for rookies and pensioners.'

'The usual copper's personal stuff, Sarge… love the job but no room for anybody or anything else. My husband couldn't take it anymore. I'd already asked for a transfer to little ole Tedham.' A grin flickered across her face as she mischievously returned Lacey's comment. 'I guess I was trying to patch things up but he'd gone anyway. So there I was and I'm still there now. To be honest I like it. I'm Tedham born and bred. I know most of the locals and my dad lives nearby. I've got a nice apartment near the town centre. I feel as though I get more time to make a better job of what I get involved in… the pace is a bit slower. Anyway that's my life story.'

Lacey blushed for a second time. 'I'm such a nosey sod, you should have told me to mind my own business.'

Kim faltered for a second, her body language showing a failed attempt at *couldn't care less.* 'No probs, Sarge,' she lied. 'None of it's a secret anyway.' She gazed at the ceiling as she tried to recall the rest of the story. 'I checked a few of the back doors to the shops and businesses and then took a look around the car park of the Castle Hotel. It was two thirty-five when I saw it again. It came out from the alley that gives access to the back of the shops. I was about twenty yards away as it pulled out and facing the driver's side window. He looked up at me. He'd angled his wheels so he was obviously intending to turn in my direction. But when he saw me he cranked the wheel hard over the other way and floorboarded it back down towards the main A30. I realised then that it was an automatic… you know… how the engine note drops up and down.'

Lacey blinked. *No, he didn't know,* but added the word "automatic" to his jottings.

'It was all very suspicious, Sarge. I did a PNC check on the car straightaway. I'd managed a look at the registration plate this time around. It came back to some chap living in Stratford… nothing on it, clean as a whistle. I still wasn't happy and if I'd been mobile I'd definitely have gone after it and pulled it over. I radioed in and put out obs to get it checked. I had another nosey around but there were no signs of a break-in or anything like that. No other patrols spotted the car to pull it over and check it out. In the end I figured it was someone who'd been drinking and was avoiding a breathalyser.'

'You got a look at the driver then?'

'Yes I did, and a bit of a look at the passenger.'

'Passenger eh? Was he in the car first time around?'

'Yes definitely, Sarge,' she tilted her head to one side as she put more thought to the memory. 'I got a pretty reasonable look at the driver, a nasty weasel face. I'd probably recognise him again.'

Lacey looked up from his notepad. 'You've done a good job to remember so much. Put me a statement together… as much detail as possible. I'm particularly interested in those descriptions and your knowledge of the vehicle.'

The detective sergeant got to his feet. 'I'll leave you to it. I've a briefing to attend downstairs. The team are kicking in a few doors later, upsetting some more of Sweeney's friends.' He made for the door.

'Okay Sarge, I'll get straight onto it now.' She pulled her chair in closer to the desk and took a biro from Lacey's tub.

Lacey paused halfway through the office doorway. He turned back. 'What do you prefer, Kimberly or Kim? '

'Kim Sarge, if that's ok.'

He was thoughtful for a second. 'Well Kim, how would you fancy working on this inquiry with us? DC Timson and I are getting a bit snowed under with stuff coming in and there's already been a half-hearted agreement to another detective from the boss. You could do the driving for a start. Reg nearly kills us every time we get through the back gates.'

Kim's eyes widened, her eyebrows now touching her fringe. 'Me, CID? Sarge, I'd love it if you could swing it.'

Lacey arrived back in the office at six o'clock and found the statement on his desk. He pushed on his reading glasses and settled into a chair. It took him fifteen minutes to digest Kim's neat handwritten account. Timson's yellow post-it note stuck to a corner of his in-tray prompted his next action. It simply said: CONTROL ROOM. He picked up the telephone and dialled.

A busy rattle of sound came ahead of the answering voice, a buzzing burglar alarm, a police radio, the chatter of a teleprinter machine.

'Control room, PC Downes speaking.'

'DS Lacey here, is DC Timson with you?'

'Reg, phone.'

The background noise persisted for a few seconds before Timson reached the phone.

'Any luck with incidents in Tedham?' Lacey enquired.

'A total blank. The only thing that went on an incident report that night was Kim's actual sighting of the Jag. It was a quiet night and nothing came in on the day report; no burglaries, no fights, no drunks, no damage, no nothing.'

'Bit of a disappointment,' Lacey replied. 'Carry on checking for a few days after, in case something got reported late. It's such a quiet place; if there was anything it should stand out like a sore thumb.'

'Thought you'd say that,' Timson replied. 'I've covered the entire week after the policewoman's sighting of the Jag. The only thing that came in was some minor damage… a brick thrown through a window at one of the properties.'

'Hmm,' Lacey made a disgruntled face. 'While you're on Reg…' A tenor of confidence had returned to his voice. 'I want you to check your list of possible Jags.'

'Do I detect a certain, *I've found out something interesting,* tone in your voice?' Timson said.

'I think so,' Lacey crowed. 'If you've got a Jaguar XJ12 Sovereign Series Three with a 5.3 engine, maybe black or dark blue on your list, then that's our car…' He paused. 'Oh, and it'll be an automatic.'

Timson started to flick through his paperwork. 'Bloody hell, can't I have a bit more detail?' There was a short delay before he delivered the bad news. 'Sorry Pete there's nothing on the list that fits accurately. The closest I can get is an XJ6 automatic. I'll have another look at that one though.'

'I'd have put money on that,' Lacey mumbled as he gave the portion of Kim's statement a second look. 'Reg, I've a feeling something is starting to come together with this. Tomorrow's Sunday, we'll take a day off. It might be the last we get for a while.'

EIGHT

Sunday 15th June, Belgium

A MEADOW of waist-high softly swaying grass surrounded a lone figure. The pasture pitched gently down towards a stream. The man hadn't seen that stream for forty-two years. The trees lining its banks disclosed its meandering route away toward the horizon.

Everything seemed so still and peaceful, so quiet, bathed in the hot June sunshine of what promised to be one of the best summers in years. The tower of the old church could be seen above the brow of a hill. It was all very different from how it had been the last time he was here, but that was September, September of 1944.

He lifted a hand to wipe the beads of sweat from his forehead, a strong but well-worn hand, veins and sinews showing through now greying hairs, liver spots of age dotting the skin.

His mind flashed back, the sound of gunfire, the smell of cordite, a scream, the rumble of a tank. He held the hand out in front of his face and watched it tremble as the memories swamped him. The sunlight seemed to flicker as though being switched off and on, the back of the hand changing intermittently from old to young, from sinews, veins and grey hairs to the bronzed flesh and muscle of a young man.

He flinched as his recollections tumbled him backwards forty-two years and his fingers closed to seize the memory.

He staggered backwards as two stretcher bearers ran out from the past, heads down against the pouring rain, a limp shape slung on the stretcher between them… arms dragging in the mud, head lolling lifelessly.

A bullet zinged as it smashed into the grey stones of the wall surrounding a ruined villa. He sprawled to his left as another bullet slammed into the side of the building. He was down on his backside, clutching his left knee with both hands, blood sticky against his palms.

A huge blast lifted him, hurled him, spinning through the air, over and over, facedown, ears ringing, eyes and mouth full of dirt, chest heaving, desperately trying to take in air.

The will to live took hold of him forcing him in a wide-eyed scramble along the ground and through the shattered villa's doorway.

He blinked and shook his head attempting to regain his senses. He was inside what was left of a kitchen. Fragmented confusion everywhere. Glass and pottery crunching under his boots. Shredded blackened curtains fluttering at a hole where a window had been.

The remnants of a flight of wooden stairs hung from the ceiling, the bottom four feet had been blasted into the matchwood that lay strewn around. The insecure structure nodded slightly from the effects of the last shell burst.

The roar of a German tank filled the air, blotting out every other noise.

Momentarily invigorated with adrenaline he took his chance. He threw his rifle up the shattered staircase to the floor above and started to clamber after it. His added weight changed the nodding to a slow, but definite, downwards motion. The old wooden joints, which had held the stairs in place for maybe two hundred years, started to part from the ceiling. He scrambled up the last few steps into the bedroom above as the force of gravity finally separated the entire assembly and sent it crashing down.

He lay panting on the bare floorboards and rolled over onto his back, eyelids blinking as he focussed on the low sagging bedroom ceiling above. A square loft hatch door was positioned directly above him.

Dust, plaster, glass and pottery covered the chest of drawers, which helped him to climb against all odds up into the loft. He pushed the hatch door back into place and gazed around in the darkness. Weak shafts of dawn sunlight pierced the slate roof where bullets had smashed into the tiles.

A precarious balancing act took him across the joists of the ceiling below to where he placed his face against one of the larger holes and stared out. His grip on the injured knee tightened as the pain seared with each pounding heartbeat, blood stickily oozing between his fingers.

His squinted stare at the outside world showed a murky rain-sodden scene. The sun of a new day was struggling to climb from beneath the horizon and break through black nimbus clouds.

A dark landscape spread out before him. Splintered and leafless trees, burning vehicles, bodies of both comrades and enemy.

A group of four German soldiers ran towards the villa and took cover behind its wall. There was hushed discussion and finger pointing before they cautiously started forward, rifles held out in front.

He could hear the crunching of heavy boots and voices as they shouted out warnings to anyone who might be inside.

Every beat of his heart crashed with increasing volume inside his head. He unclipped a hand grenade from his belt, holding it with his thumb through the pull ring. He squeezed his right arm to his body, gripping his rifle against his side. He stared unblinking at the loft hatch, listening and waiting completely motionless.

It would be fifteen minutes before the Germans left and he was able to breathe again. He pressed his rifle butt down onto the wooden laths between the joists. They buckled and started to crack. They would not hold his weight.

Feeling around in the darkness his fingers ran over the edges of a rectangular wooden board wrapped in thick paper. It was securely parcelled and bound around with strong twine, it was ideal. He laid it down on top of the joists then settled his trembling body onto it.

His left knee was so swollen he could now feel his battledress trousers pulled tightly around it. The pain dulled as consciousness drifted away.

Two hours passed before his eyes slowly opened. The sun had risen and won its battle with the clouds, thrusting shafts of brightness in through the punctured roof, giving perspective to the surroundings. Familiar objects took shape. A tattered leather suitcase, a dusty bowler hat, a tennis racket, piles of piano music, a child's shoe, boxes and books, evidence of the family who had lived there.

The sounds of battle were now distant, the occasional faraway explosion and rat-tat-tat of machine gun fire echoing through occasionally. It was a comfort, but every attempt to bend his throbbing knee dragged him back towards the realms of unconsciousness. Keeping his eyes fixed on the drooping roof close to his head he shuffled into a sitting position, murmuring against the pain. He one-handedly snapped a length of wooden lath away from beneath the tiles, a squinting stare demonstrating his awareness that he was weakening the structure even more. He repeated the process. The roof held.

The pieces of inch square wood were each almost two feet long. They were old and brittle, but strong enough for his idea. He slid to one side and using his pocket knife carefully cut the heavy-duty twine from the board beneath him. It was then that he saw the gummed-on label attached to the parcelling, a foreign sounding name and title.

He positioned the wooden laths back and front of his injured knee and bound them around tightly with the twine to form a makeshift splint. He had all but finished when he heard the familiar sound of English voices. An attempt to struggle to his feet was a disaster. The pain almost threw him back into unconsciousness. He contemplated the buckled roof above his head and then forced his rifle barrel upwards. The tiles shifted easily and clattered down to the ground outside.

The sunlight flickered again and dumped him back into the reality of 1986. Not one second had passed… the shaking hand was still held in front of his face. He dropped it to his side and moved off through the long grass down towards the stream. It had been such a long time ago.

NINE

Monday Morning

DEAKIN was back at his desk by eight o'clock on the Monday and quickly started work on another batch of Second World War sailors' names. A shadow spread across his paperwork as Superintendent Farmer stepped inside the open doorway.

Deakin half-rose from his chair in a reluctant display of respect for his commanding officer. He nodded at the jowly, sweating features. 'Morning Superintendent.'

Farmer, in his full superintendent's uniform, complete with gold braided peaked cap glowered at Deakin. 'Are you still fuckin' about with this unidentified body, Deakin?' His voice had a rasping quality to it.

Deakin stood properly to his feet and faced Farmer, but was wordless.

'Have you lost your voice Deakin?'

'No, sir,' Deakin eventually replied. 'We're making progress.'

'PROGRESS… bloody progress.' Farmer turned on his heel and walked back down the corridor. His voice diminished with each step. 'I want this simple job winding up and you and Taylor back doing some proper work. Tell him that if he parks his car in my space again I'll have it towed away.'

Two minutes passed and Deakin was still at his desk when Taylor came in with another armful of manila folders. He sniffed the air and made an attempt at a French accent. 'Do I detect a certain Eau de Farmer?' As he dumped the pile down on the free corner of the desk he recognised the hint of a smile on Deakin's lips. 'And what are you so cheerful about?'

'Farmer wants us both back doing some real work, but I think I have a name Doug. I think this is our man.' Deakin's biro tip rested against a scrawled name:

ALBERT DONALD LARKIN.

Taylor's eyes fixed on the name. 'O-Kaaay,' he said, stretching the word out to an inordinate length. 'Explain?'

'Right,' Deakin began. 'Date of birth would put him at seventy-one when the body was found. He served on HMS Storm, which fits the tattoo well enough. He was with the boat from when she was commissioned in 1943 until well after the war finished and didn't get discharged from the Navy until March 1946. He was wounded in the right shoulder… a shrapnel wound.'

Deakin looked up at Taylor, raising his eyebrows. 'He made the rank of petty officer and originated from the village of Tedham, near Exeter. He kept in touch with the Royal Navy Association up until about five years ago. So he's either died too soon and we have the wrong man or he's lost touch as he's got older. I've found an address in the village for him, which is about six years ago.'

Taylor made a mental calculation. 'Close to Exeter. I'll have to make a couple of phone calls. But we should be there for about half past two, traffic permitting and hoping my old Cavalier holds out. It looks like this is going to be a long day.'

The journey down to Exeter took three hours. Taylor's earlier phone chat with the Detective Inspector in charge of Heavitree Road Police Station was a courtesy call. A bit of police etiquette to let him know they would be on his patch and visiting a few addresses.

"Come on over here first," DI Ken Granger had said. "I know we've asked before, but if you have anything at all still in your files on David Sweeney bring it with you. We're getting nowhere with the case. You can have a bite to eat in our canteen and I'll fix someone to go along with you to the old chap's house. It's always better when there's someone who knows their way around."

Taylor took his Exeter counterpart up on the invite and as they neared the motorway turn-off they were looking forward to a meal.

Exeter police station canteen exceeded Taylor and Deakin's expectations. They carried their trays of steaming food over to a table and settled down to tuck in. A long queue of uniformed police men and women, detectives, traffic wardens and civilian staff continued to grow at the serving hatch. The most popular order being cups of afternoon tea.

Deakin adjusted the position of his chair and started with knife and fork. 'Looks good, Doug, can't believe they're still serving food at this time.'

Taylor agreed and enthusiastically set about his first meal of the day.

Lacey and Timson shook hands across the table as they introduced themselves and pulled out chairs.

'Don't like disturbing you while you're eating.' Lacey said. 'Tuck in and I'll tell you what's been happening. We'll be more than happy to give you a hand with what you have to do and we can compare notes along the way.'

Deakin wiped gravy from his chin with a thumb and licked it clean. 'Well, obviously we've heard about your job, but Sweeney hasn't been seen or heard of for many years in Staffordshire. It was actually a surprise to most of the bobbies at our nick that he actually originated from Little Stoneleigh.'

Taylor looked up from his meal. 'Thing is, there's little we can actually give you. No one ever knew who Sweeney's father was except presumably, his mother, Sadie. He had a stepfather, and word of mouth suggests he worked at a brewery in Little Stoneleigh. As far as we can gather the stepfather and Sadie split up several years ago.'

Taylor shook his head in apology as he continued to explain. 'I feel bad about this. You see our file on him, to be frank, is a disgrace. It's just a couple of sheets of paper. It doesn't even tell us if he still has relatives in Little Stoneleigh. Sadie, his mother, as you know, was set up by Sweeney with a pad in Tenerife. There are only a few people in the town who knew him or who will admit to it.' Taylor's frown deepened. 'Couple of schoolmates, well not even mates, they absolutely detested him, thought of him as a bullying, thieving thug, and that was as a twelve year old.'

Taylor paused from his lunch to open the briefcase propped against the table leg. He handed Lacey a slim-looking orange folder. 'That's it, I'm afraid,' his expression apologetic again. 'But if we come up with any more we'll get it down to you straightaway.'

'Okay,' Lacey conceded. 'We could do with finding this stepfather and we're hoping to get an authorisation for a trip over to Tenerife to see Sadie. But you know what it's like, budgets and all that. Anyway is there anything we can arrange for you while you finish off your lunch?'

Taylor grew thoughtful. 'There is one thing. We might need the help of a policewoman. I think we could be dealing with a wife and there could be a few tears involved.'

Lacey's eyes widened. 'I know just the lady.' He stood from his chair. 'Might take me half an hour though, so don't rush your grub.'

After the late lunch Timson listened to the strange story of the Cannock Chase body. The conversation continued as the three descended the staircase and arrived outside in the rear compound that adjoined the police garage. Timson led the way over to where Lacey was talking with a uniformed police woman.

A mechanic's air wrench whined loudly, in concert with a continual hammering as Lacey attempted to introduce the two Staffordshire detectives. He raised his voice to overcome the noise. 'This is WPC Kim Harding, she's working with us.'

Timson made a puzzled face. 'Since when?'

'Since fifteen minutes ago,' Lacey bawled back, but the noise stopped in that same instant and his voice echoed around the yard.

Kim surveyed the party standing before her and gave a smile of acknowledgement.

'Civvie clothes tomorrow then Kim,' said Lacey. 'Kim is ex-traffic and should be able to help out with some of the driving. That way I may have a longer life expectancy.'

Timson screwed up his eyes in mock annoyance. 'Are you on about my driving again?'

Lacey guided the way over to a corner of the police compound, commentating as he went. 'I have another meeting this afternoon and I'm going to take the chance to get through some paperwork, so Reg is going down to Tedham with you.' He turned to face the group, catching Kim's eye. 'Kim, we've been using this motor; it's on loan. The force is supposedly evaluating it as a traffic car, but it was the only thing spare, so I think we hit the jackpot.'

Lacey's hand extended towards a flame red saloon. The front wheels of its low profile tyres were turned out on full lock giving the car a snarling menacing look.

Kim regarded the car admiringly, 'Vauxhall Carlton Gsi 3000, twenty-four valve, some power, nice car.'

Timson raised his eyebrows, astonished at Kim's knowledge.

'Keys, Reg,' said Lacey, pointing towards Kim as he started to back off across the compound.

Timson duly handed over as Lacey turned and stuck one arm in the air as a sign of his leave taking; the hammering had started again and a verbal exchange was futile.

Kim tweaked the rear-view mirror and driver's seat. She then pulled down a small lever at the side of the steering column and adjusted the steering wheel to just above her knees.

Timson glared over from the back seat. 'I never knew about that.'

A ripple of laughter broke out. Kim looked over at Taylor sitting next to her and grinned. She threaded the steering wheel through her hands as she drove out of the compound. A sustained engine note and smooth clutch-work disguised all hint of gear changes as the car pulled effortlessly and powerfully forward. Timson sat quietly in the back.

TEN

IT WAS half past four when Kim steered the car into Chapel Close, Tedham. She hadn't needed directions.

'I was brought up in the town,' she explained. 'I work here now. Can't say I've heard of the Larkin family though. I guess they must have kept themselves to themselves.'

She drew the car to a halt outside number sixteen.

The house was a fairly anonymous semi-detached, with a cream painted garage at the side. The newly fitted, double glazed windows, the fresh paintwork and neatly trimmed lawns seemed to correspond with the SOLD sign in the front garden.

Timson strolled the few yards from gate to front door and peered through the opaque glass into a hallway before pressing the doorbell. 'Looks empty.'

Kim stood at the gate adjusting her black and white chequered police hat as Taylor wandered down the narrow path at the side. He arrived in a small tidy back garden surrounded by larch lap fencing.

'Are you after Alan and Janet?' questioned an elderly female voice.

'Sorry,' replied Taylor, puzzling as to the source of the voice.

A hand appeared over the top of the fence which separated the rear gardens of numbers sixteen and eighteen.

'Over here,' said a voice from beneath. 'Alan and Janet, they moved out six weeks or more ago.'

Taylor met the lady by her back door. She was now standing on the step but would still require another twelve inches in height to look Taylor in the eye. Kim followed up the path leaving Deakin and Timson still peering through letterbox and windows at number sixteen.

The neighbour was a pear-shaped and grey-haired soul complete with pinafore and flour-coated hands. Her eyes focussed on Kim. 'Oh, is there some trouble?'

'Nothing to worry about, love,' Taylor reassured, realising that an introduction was unnecessary. 'We're looking for someone who can tell us about Mr Larkin from next door.'

The lady dusted her hands together to remove the excess flour. 'Albert,' she said with a perplexed expression. 'Albert died last month. He hadn't lived here for five, maybe six years, he went into a home.'

Taylor successfully dodged the cloud of flour and listened as the lady explained.

'He wasn't able to cope after his wife died. The house was sold soon after. I thought you must be after Alan and Janet. They bought the place, but they only stayed a few years, they sold up and moved to Exeter.'

Timson and Deakin now arrived on the neighbour's path. The lady stared. 'Goodness, how many more of you are there?'

'Would you know which home Mr Larkin went to, my dear?' Timson asked, having overheard the conversation.

'Oh yes, it was Hollacombe House not far from Crediton. I always intended going up to see him, but couldn't get anyone to take me, then he died and no one bothered to let me know.'

Taylor nodded sympathetically. 'So how did you find out about Albert passing away?'

'From the local paper… the death notices. I was upset about it. I'd gone over to stay with my son in Bristol for five days and when I came back I read through the newspapers to catch up. Well, there it was and I'd missed the funeral. What really upset me was that he was cremated… that was awful.'

Taylor caught Deakin's corner of the eye glance, as a hint of black humour went between them with the mention of cremation. Taylor quickly recaptured his sympathetic face and tilted his head in puzzlement. 'You don't agree with cremation then?'

'Oh no, my dear, it's not that.' She wiped a little more of the flour from her hands onto her apron. 'It's just that I knew for a fact that he expressly asked for burial along with his wife. He'd told me that, but I don't know which cemetery she was buried at.'

The drive to Hollacombe House Nursing Home would take fifteen minutes along winding country lanes. Again it was a task which Kim accepted without need of a map.

Taylor swivelled in his front passenger seat to look at Timson and Deakin. 'So, whoever or whatever was in that coffin no longer exists.'

'Yes,' said Deakin. 'It certainly looks that way.'

The entrance to the property was neatly located between two towering beech trees. The building itself gave away clues to its history as a former stately home, with sandstone columns either side of a huge black painted door.

Kim parked the Carlton in front, alongside three other saloon cars and a white Transit minibus. The production of warrant cards quickly gained them entrance into the matron's office.

Taylor's summary drew a wide eyed look of astonishment. 'Mr Larkin...' the matron said. 'Mr Larkin died over three weeks ago Inspector, what on earth is this about?'

Clad in a smart, dark green overall, the lady was short and rotund with close cut curly grey hair and round silver-framed spectacles. She breathed in as she squeezed around the back of Timson's chair to pull the office door closed. 'Nosey staff,' she confided with a finger pressed against lips and eyes still wide.

With the four police officers and the matron crammed inside, the tiny office bordered on claustrophobic.

After rummaging in a filing cabinet a thick dog-eared folder was produced and flattened down onto the desk. Across the front was printed:

Hollacombe House Residential Home.

Written underneath in blue marker pen:

Albert Donald Larkin.

The matron opened the file and skimmed through some of the pages.

'Yes, everything is in here… well, photocopies at least. Birth certificate, marriage certificate, death certificate. All his medical history since he came to us. Nothing about his service in the Navy, although I do recall him talking about it. I think he had an exciting time.'

'Any children? Any next of kin?' asked Timson.

'No, I'm fairly certain about that. His wife died about six years ago. He did once say that there was a child who died at birth and his wife couldn't have any more. I think it was something he always regretted. He smoked a lot and of course. That finished him in the end, lung cancer, although…' She paused for a second and thumbed back through the file. 'He was seventy-one.' Her eyes were now examining the hands on the opposite side of the desk for any sign of nicotine, a medical lecture at the ready. 'He would have managed a few more years if he hadn't smoked.'

'And did he die here or in hospital?' Taylor asked.

The matron turned her full attention to Taylor. 'He died here. We looked after him until the end. I think you must have your facts wrong, Inspector. I was on duty when he died. I checked him over myself and was present when the doctor certified death. I even went to the funeral with one of the nurses.'

'It's a puzzle,' Deakin commented. 'Where was the funeral held?'

'At the crem. A short service with there being no next of kin. Our local undertakers always arrange everything for us.'

'The undertakers?' said Kim. 'I guess that would be Pedley's in Tedham then?'

'That's right, family run business in the town centre, been there donkey's years. Old Mr Pedley's a nice man. I'm sure he'll help you out, but I think you must have your facts wrong.'

'One more thing, Matron,' Taylor asked. 'Do you recall the tattoo on his arm?'

'Oh, clearly, I took his blood pressure enough times. It read "HMS Storm". There was a picture of the ship, or should I say boat?

He always called it a boat.'

Thanking the matron for her help they left her looking bemused at the entrance door and assembled again alongside the Carlton. Taylor chaired the car park meeting. 'It's getting on now, we've yet to see the undertaker and the coroner, and we'll need full statements from the staff here at Hollacombe House. We're not going to be able to do any of this until the morning.' He tilted his head in apology towards Deakin. 'Look, Geoff, we need to stay over tonight and get this side of things cleared up tomorrow.'

'I'll give the missus a bell,' Deakin replied, with an air of resignation. 'It's pointless going all the way back home now.'

Taylor turned to Timson. 'Will you be able to fix us somewhere to stay, Reg?'

'No problem, Inspector. I'll get a couple of rooms arranged for you up at our HQ at Middlemore. I'm starving now, so how about a curry and a couple of pints? We can call it a debrief. That is if Kim doesn't mind driving.'

Kim shook her head. 'Men.'

The Tedham Tandoori was on good form, the debrief went well. Deakin turned to Timson as Kim pulled the Carlton to a halt at Police HQ. 'Great curry, Reg,' he praised as he started to exit the car. 'Yes, really good,' Taylor agreed, pushing his door open. 'Thanks for your help today both of you. I feel a bit guilty about keeping you away from your own inquiry.'

'Our pleasure, Boss,' Timson said. 'In fact,' he added as an afterthought. 'It'll help you out no end tomorrow if you have someone who knows their way around.' He looked at Kim. 'So, Kim, if you could take this car home with you and get back up here to collect the Inspector and Geoff for … say nine?' He shot a glance at Taylor to confirm that the idea would work.

Kim gave a nod. 'No problem, I think I could get accustomed to this CID job… flash cars and exotic meals.' She traded a smile with

Taylor. 'I'd better watch the waistline though.'

Timson turned to Kim. 'I'd better have your home phone number, just in case.'

'I've heard some good chat-up lines, Reg,' she teased, and then added her phone number as Timson jotted it down.

ELEVEN

THE TELEPHONE rang for some time; a click and a soft rustling, followed by a heavy sigh.

'Kim, Kim, are you there?'

'Yes, yes,' she answered softly, a little cough as she tried to get some tone to her voice. She blinked at the glowing digital clock and rubbed her eyes: 02.20. 'Who is this?'

'It's Inspector Taylor, Kim. Sorry to wake you, but something serious has happened. Can you get up here to me straightaway? I must get back to Staffordshire.'

'Thirty minutes should do it, sir.' She reached over, switched on the light and motivated by the urgency in Taylor's voice, swung her legs out of bed. 'I'll see you on the car park.'

Taylor stood waiting at the entrance to the police HQ car park, briefcase in left hand and light grey suit jacket over an arm. He squinted, dazzled by the Carlton's headlights as Kim pulled up alongside. Yesterday's shirt and a dark shadow of stubble did not detract from his rugged good looks, but his face showed concern. He threw the briefcase over into the back and fastened his seat belt.

'What about Geoff?' Kim asked.

'I've briefed him,' Taylor replied. 'He's going to have to carry on down here. There are still enquiries to be made at the undertakers and the crematorium. I've given him my car keys and he'll be making his way back later on in the day.'

Taylor settled back into his seat as he explained. 'What has happened has pulled these two cases together. A car has been torched in the night on Cannock Chase… a Jaguar. It's the same car park where Mr Larkin was found. There's a badly burnt corpse on the back seat and all bets are on it being Jacob Bunn.'

Kim accelerated out of the police headquarters complex onto the main road and covered the one mile down to the M5's junction 30 in a little under a minute. They joined the carriageway from the slip road at 120mph.

Taylor grabbed a corner of the eye glance at Kim, her profile illuminated by the glow from the dashboard instruments. She bore a look of determined concentration as she expertly overtook the few other vehicles, selected the auto-cruise mode and settled back into her seat.

She listened intently as Taylor explained what he had learned from his 2 am phone call from Staffordshire's Police Control Room and what arrangements he'd made with Deakin.

Taylor watched the odometer as it steadily moved around with the passing of each mile. 'You certainly know how to handle this car.'

Kim went through her traffic background, recent domestic upheaval and her transfer to Little Ole Tedham, as she'd now taken to calling it.

Taylor shared his similar restructured circumstances.

Another hour and a half passed before a glimmer of dawn started to show on the horizon and allowed Taylor to see Kim's features more clearly. She looked fresh and alert, her hair neat, despite the record time taken to pick him up.

She'd remembered Lacey's instruction: "Dress in civvies".

'I hope I don't look too casual, especially in view of what we have in front of us. It was such a rush. I just threw some things on.'

Taylor had already noticed Kim's informal, but smart, cheesecloth blouse and light blue denim jeans. 'Don't worry about that, I'm not complaining,' he said.

Kim pushed down the left-hand indicator as they swept past the 300 yard marker for the M6 motorway's junction 11. She motored on through Cannock and along the A34 out towards Stafford. It was getting lighter by the minute, but the thickly wooded areas either side of the road, which formed part of Cannock Chase, seemed to soak up the light.

She nudged the powerful car smoothly up to 85 and 95mph along the road, effortlessly overtaking the few commuter cars starting to appear.

Taylor's brief directions were all that were needed. Kim stepped on the brakes, changed into second gear and turned the car off the road in one seamless action. Twinkling blue lights filtered through the blackness of the forest as she drove on up the stony track. Half a mile later she pulled onto the car park and steered into a space between a patrol car and a fire engine.

A uniformed constable, clipboard in hand, stumbled across the uneven surface gesturing for them to go no further, clearly his job for the day. Taylor offered his warrant card through the driver's window. 'Detective Inspector Taylor, Little Stoneleigh CID and WPC Harding, Exeter CID.'

Progress was delayed a little longer as the officer insisted upon a meticulous record of time, identity and vehicle details.

'Wow, I do feel important now.' Kim made the light-hearted comment as they walked over towards an array of portable floodlights.

'You okay with this kind of stuff?' Taylor asked thoughtfully.

'Seen too much of it already, sir, with being on traffic, used to deal with a fatal accident every couple of weeks. A good many of them were burnouts like this. As you know, you get hardened to it, but it still strikes home occasionally.'

The eye watering, white glare of the 1000 watt flood lights illuminated the scene like an unending lightning strike. The vehicle could only be described as a shell, clearly a large car and barely discernible as a Jaguar with its square boot lid sticking upright. Brown, oxidised, buckled panels now replaced gleaming black paintwork. The chunky fat tyres were completely burnt away, leaving dozens of steel cords hanging loosely from wheel rims. A smooth, black mound sat above the air intakes – melted down remains of the windscreen glass.

The inside of the car was similar, metal alone surviving. A jumble of twisted black wiring showed where a polished walnut dashboard used to be and the hitherto lush leather seats were now nothing more than distorted spring frames.

Collapsed down on the rear spring frame sat a blackened charcoal mass, a heavy-looking smouldering lump. A human skull crowned the mass, black bone and teeth. Tiny wisps of smoke still curled up through each eye socket. Four jagged stumps protruded from the body, the remnants of arms and legs.

An unbroken line of fine grey ash completely encircled the car, appearing almost ritualistic and indicating the intense heat generated.

SOCO man, Pat Gerrard nodded a thank-you at Kim Harding as she probed a tangled mass of charred cable loom near the car's bulkhead to one side to point out the tiny metal vehicle identification plate. This VIN plate would reveal the true identity of the Jaguar. Its discovery allowed Gerrard to get to work with a wire brush and expose the complex series of digits.

Taylor looked over at Kim. 'Why this car park?' He rubbed his unshaven chin. 'This must be your Jaguar and the chances are pretty high that it's Jacob Bunn sitting in the back seat. But why here on the same car park as Mr Larkin. Both miles away from Tedham and Exeter?'

Kim frowned. 'The obvious connection to this part of the world is Sweeney, but whatever could the old man have to do with any of this?'

The next two hours were taken up with exhaustive scenes of crime work and photography. Taylor commandeered the passenger seat of a patrol car as a makeshift office whilst he organised an incident room back at Little Stoneleigh.

Pat Gerrard ambled over and waited by the car's window as the detective inspector finished off a call using the force's latest piece of high tech equipment, a mobile telephone. A thick black cable connected the everyday style handset to a shoebox sized metal casing which stood between Taylor's feet.

'You'd better come and have a look at this Boss,' Gerrard said as Taylor closed the call.

The pair made their way to some scrubland on the edge of the car park.

CID boss, Detective Chief Superintendent Ray Burrington, now at the scene, stood arms folded. He nodded an acknowledgement to Taylor as Gerrard pointed a finger into the bushes and went on to explain.

'Obviously we couldn't see it until the sun came up.'

Taylor's eyes were already fixed on the target of Gerrard's finger, a black barrister's gown draped around a five feet high sapling. A thickly blood-stained barrister's wig hung from the uppermost twigs.

Burrington led Taylor over to a quiet corner. The Detective Chief Superintendent's face showed his concern. 'Doug, we can't keep this inquiry small any longer, we're going to have to link up properly now with Exeter. The body's on our patch, so we've won the murder inquiry. I'm saying murder, and I know the old man turned out to be otherwise, but this certainly seems to be the missing barrister.'

Taylor grimaced. 'The press have got hold of it already,' he said. 'We've just stopped two of them creeping through the woods with cameras.'

He dragged the palms of his hands down from his eyelids to his chin in an effort to shake off the tiredness. 'I've organised an incident room at Little Stoneleigh Police Club. It was the only building available. It'll be up and running from tomorrow.'

Burrington nodded, 'Deakin's still down south?'

'Yes sir, he's got quite a job on with statements and other enquiries. DS Lacey and DC Timson are eager to get up here and compare notes.'

'Yes, understandable.' Burrington said. 'I've spoken with their boss. They'll have to hold on for a while. We're going to want them to bring all their information and statements up with them. I'm also thinking dental records as well. At least this body has its jaws and teeth intact.'

The police chief wore a sympathetic face. It was a face he rarely used. 'You'd better get some shut eye Doug. I guess you've been up most of the night. There's nothing more you can do today. Get a room arranged for Constable Harding at headquarters, she'll have to get some rest before she starts back.'

TWELVE

GEOFF DEAKIN found Pedley's Funeral Directors on Tedham High Street. A large sign above the central door of the double fronted property proclaimed in ornate gold lettering on a black background that: F. Pedley and Sons, had been undertakers since 1912.

Mr Pedley greeted the unfamiliar figure in the foyer of the building. 'Good morning, sir, how can I help you?'

His hands were clasped together against his chest and he wore that concerned, sympathetic look that undertakers keep as stock-in-trade. He was a short, overweight man attired in white shirt, black jacket and grey pin striped trousers. He accepted Deakin's warrant card for examination.

He brushed the few remaining strands of grey hair over the top of his head with a white podgy hand as he listened to the detective's summary of the finding of the old man's body. His eyes grew wider with each word.

'Fuck me!' he finally exclaimed, his undertaker's facade now completely removed. He pulled a packet of cigarettes from his trouser pocket and poked a Benson and Hedges into his mouth. 'Do you use these?'

He presented the open packet towards Deakin.

'No thanks, Mr Pedley, gave up six years since.'

'Good for you, only leads to an early grave,' Pedley smirked at his own joke as he lit up with a bright orange disposable lighter. He gestured with his cigarette-clutching hand towards a collection of chairs which were positioned around a polished mahogany table in the centre of the foyer. 'Anyway, it's Frank, Frank Pedley. Our family has had this business over seventy years and I must confess I've never heard of anything like this before. It simply cannot be Mr Larkin… I was there at the crem.'

Deakin seated himself across the table from Pedley. His view of the undertaker's face was obscured by a spray of imitation lily of the valley sprouting from a black glass vase.

'I'll have to go up to the crematorium to make some enquiries... statements and the like. Tell me Frank, what happens to the coffin? When would the lid be screwed down for the last time?'

Pedley inhaled deeply on his cigarette. 'Well, it varies according to the circumstances. It could be two days or more prior to the funeral. The body would be kept in our cold storage before that. It all depends on the wishes of the relatives. They might want a last look at the deceased. In the case of Mr Larkin, there were no next of kin, so the lid would have been screwed down at least two days before the funeral.'

'What about coffins, Frank; are they all made to measure... I mean for each person?' Deakin jotted on his notepad without looking up as he threw questions at Pedley.

Pedley shook his head. 'I know it's a technical point, but it wasn't a coffin. It was a casket which Mr Larkin had. Most people have caskets nowadays.'

Deakin paused from his note writing and looked across at Pedley.

'A coffin has six sides, you see.' Pedley held his hands pointing inwards at an angle, making an inverted V, as he explained. 'The shape chamfers off where the head lies. Caskets are more common nowadays, just four sides, cheaper to make. Back to your question. No, in the main they're done according to height and are ready-made... standard sizes if you like. We keep a few of the most popular ones in stock and get pretty well what we need from the suppliers fairly swiftly.'

'What about weight?' Deakin nibbled at his biro. 'Our body was emaciated when he died and is estimated to have been not much more than seven stones.'

The undertaker exhaled a cloud of smoke through his nostrils. 'Yes, now you say it, I do recall that there wasn't much to Mr Larkin.

I collected the body from Hollacombe with our Tom, my eldest son and it was him who later helped me put the body into the casket. An easy job with Mr Larkin being so light… not many like that; it can be a bugger of a job when you get a hefty one.'

'I'll tell you what, Dad,' a voice filtered in from an open office doorway. 'I lifted the casket from the hearse at the funeral.'

The man walked into the foyer. Forty something, smartly dressed, taller than his dad, but facially obviously a Pedley. The new arrival introduced himself.

'Andrew Pedley, Officer. Number Two Son as Dad likes to call me. Pleased to meet you.'

A hand was outstretched, which Deakin shook as Pedley Junior carried on.

'I heard most of your conversation… Jimmy, our work experience lad helped me at the funeral. I remember that the casket was an average weight and probably contained a twelve or thirteen stone body… definitely not a lightweight. It's the lightweights and the super heavyweights you remember.'

Deakin made a note of Andrew's remarks before throwing in his next question. 'So, if the coffin… casket,' he corrected himself… 'that went up to the crematorium that morning did not contain Albert Larkin's body, then who or what did it contain, and how could it have been swapped over?'

Frank Pedley shook his head again. 'It's a bloody mystery, and I can't see how anyone could have been in here without us knowing, let alone taking bodies away.'

His nervous attempt to flick ash from his cigarette into the ashtray fell short and spread across the table.

Andrew Pedley's worried expression matched that of his father. 'You know, Dad, I hate to make more of this, but there was that incident when someone chucked a brick through the reposing room window. It would be around the time when Mr Larkin's body was here.'

Pedley Senior's head shaking became incessant. 'No, no. It was vandalism, some local yob I presume.' He looked over at Deakin as he continued. 'I came in one morning, the window was smashed and there was a house brick lying in the middle of the floor. There are bars on the window, the window was still closed, just a great hole in the glass.'

'Show me, Frank, show me the window,' Deakin said, rising to his feet.

Frank Pedley led Deakin down a short corridor to the rear of the building whilst Andrew disappeared back into the office.

A sturdy door delayed progress as Frank fumbled with a hefty bunch of keys. It eventually opened up onto to a generously sized airy room. Against one wall, eight ceiling-high, cream painted refrigeration units hummed softly. Opposite this was the room's only window, a large single pane of opaque glass fitted into an old style wooden frame, probably an original fitting from when the building was erected.

Frank gave a nod of the head. 'That's it… big hole, glass everywhere and the brick was down there.' Another nod was directed down towards Deakin's feet.

Deakin stood with his back against the fridge units and studied the window. His innumerable burglary investigations over the years had unwittingly advanced his knowledge of the trappings and accessories of the building trade, particularly where doors and windows were concerned. The frame, according to Deakin's knowledge was an "Awning Window", as it was hinged at the top and opened outwards from the bottom. Regular maintenance and painting had no doubt extended its life beyond the norm. He stepped closer to examine the series of half-inch wide iron bars which were screwed on the inside of the frame.

Pedley Senior folded his arms and blinked a few times before adding to his explanation. 'The bars were intact, they were only fitted a couple of years ago and the window was still closed. I phoned the police and they said they would make a note of it, but as it was only damage they weren't much interested.'

Deakin produced a retractable tape measure from his pocket and began examining the window frame more closely. 'The police never came around you say, Frank, so do you still have the brick?'

Andrew now re-joined the group. He was leafing through the pages of a small blue diary, but heard Deakin's question. 'I put it in the garage,' he said. 'I'm pretty sure it's still there.'

He made his way over to a pair of sturdy-looking white painted double doors and pushed down on the security bar. The doors opened up to reveal the gloom of a vast garage which housed a gleaming black Daimler hearse, parked with precision, inches from another sleek and lustrous funeral car.

Frank Pedley applied his thumb to a wall switch causing a series of fluorescent strip lights to buzz and flicker into life. Following Andrew's lead, the three men squeezed along through a gap between a wooden work bench and the hearse. They came to a halt against the garage's triple sized folding timber doors.

Andrew bent and picked up a standard sized house brick which was standing on end near to the doors. He handed this to Deakin.

Deakin's head gave a little shake as he turned the brick over in his hands. 'Can we get outside from here into the yard where the window is?'

'Of course,' Andrew said putting a shoulder to a small door fitted within the main doors. Deakin followed Andrew outside into the streaming bright sunshine.

The backs of the High Street shops curved around in a horseshoe shape onto the cobbled courtyard. The space served as rear access and parking for the undertakers and other High Street shops. A single, narrow arched entrance led out to a side street.

Alongside the garage and adjacent to the barred window of the reposing room a square of concrete formed a parking space for a black Mercedes estate. Clearly this was another funeral car. 'Does this park here overnight?' Deakin asked.

'No, I take that one home with me,' Pedley senior responded with a shake of the head. 'In case I get called out in the night.'

Deakin squeezed in between the car and the wall, and looked closely at the window. The blurred image of the bars could be seen through the opaque glass and fresh putty evidenced its recent installation.

'This brick is too big to end up in the reposing room,' Deakin said. 'If it had been thrown, the window bars on the inside would have stopped it. I've measured it; it'll just fit between the bars if you carefully push it through. You can also see from the inside that four of the bars have been removed and replaced recently.'

'How can you be sure?' Frank Pedley asked as a rippling frown accompanied his head-shaking.

'The paint on the screws is chipped,' Deakin explained, '… and that wasn't done by the glazier who installed this new pane of glass. It's glazed from the outside and the window opens outwards.'

'This is amazing,' said Andrew. 'But how could someone undo the screws from the outside?'

Deakin was sketching a rough diagram of the window onto his pad and delivered his opinion without looking up. 'It wouldn't be difficult. Once the glass was broken, they would have reached through and opened the window, then probably used a small cordless screwdriver. The screws on the bars, as you say, were fitted two years ago, they're in good condition. I'll bet the whole procedure took about ten minutes and maybe a similar time to put it all back afterwards.'

Mr Pedley positioned himself a few yards back from the window listening attentively to the now plausible theory. 'So, the brick was a cover then, a decoy to make us believe it was vandalism. It never entered my head that anyone would well…'

Deakin folded his notepad and stuffed it into his jacket pocket.

'I'm going to have to get back to Exeter. I know it's been a good while since this happened, but the scenes of crime people must look at all this. I'll make arrangements for statements to be taken from you. I'm sorry I can't tell you anymore, but something else has happened in the night, connected to this. Something even more serious.'

Mr Pedley pulled his cigarettes out from his pocket again and looked over at his son, his increasingly corrugated forehead amplifying his bewilderment. 'More serious, more serious,' he repeated.

'One other thing,' Deakin said as he followed the Pedleys back through to the foyer and gathered his papers together. 'I could do with the date when you discovered the damage.'

Andrew held up the diary in his right hand. 'Yes, I thought you'd need that. We found it on the morning of Wednesday 4th June, which I'm afraid to say, was the date of Mr Larkin's funeral.'

Deakin widened his eyes. 'That would fit, that would certainly fit. Mr Larkin's body was discovered on the morning of Thursday 5th June and it looks like it was dumped the evening before that… Wednesday 4th June.'

Deakin thanked the Pedleys and was about to leave when old Mr Pedley inhaled deeply on his cigarette and gave Deakin an expectant look. 'Exhumation then?'

Deakin frowned. 'I wish that were possible, but you've already told me that Albert Larkin was cremated.'

The two Pedleys exchanged equally mystified glances with each other. 'No, no, no,' Pedley senior exclaimed. 'He was buried according to his wishes, along with his wife.'

Deakin screwed up his eyes. It was his turn for bewilderment. 'But you said the service was at the crematorium, and for that matter so did the matron at Hollacombe. She actually went to the funeral. In fact, Mr Larkin's next door neighbour was annoyed that he'd been cremated rather than buried.'

The expression on the faces of the two Pedley's changed in unison from puzzlement to understanding. Frank went straight into an explanation. 'I see what's happened here officer. The crematorium in question also has an extensive cemetery. We frequently arrange funerals there using the facilities of the crematorium's chapel for the actual service. The body is either disposed of by cremation or burial, dependent on the original wishes of the deceased.'

Deakin placed his papers onto the table and pulled out a chair again as Mr Pedley got back into his stride. 'You see, Mr Larkin's wife also had her funeral service in the crematorium chapel and was then buried, as was Albert himself. It's a mistake often made when people read the death notice. As soon as they see the phrase "Funeral at Tedham Crematorium," they immediately think the person is to be cremated rather than buried.'

'So… Deakin speculated, 'Albert's next door neighbour read the paper and also concluded that he'd been cremated?'

Frank Pedley's head shaking transformed into a series of emphasised nods.

Andrew interjected. 'I'm no detective, Mr Deakin, but there is little doubt that the person who substituted whoever or whatever went into Albert Larkin's casket must also have been under the same misapprehension that it would be cremated.'

THIRTEEN

SEVERAL GAMES of crown green bowls were taking place in bright sunshine on the pristine turf square at the rear of Staffordshire Police HQ. Taylor pulled the Vauxhall Carlton to a halt on the nearby car park as Kim Harding looked over from the passenger seat, her eyes red with tiredness. 'I'm glad you got me a room.'

Taylor stifled a yawn. 'Yes, I'm all in too, but this has really disrupted your day. You could have had anything planned, but here you are... up half the night, hundreds of miles from home, nothing to eat all day…'

Kim pursed her lips and gave her head a little shake. 'No, I hadn't anything planned and it's been an exciting day. Anyway I managed a bacon butty from the mobile canteen.'

It was now her turn to stifle a yawn.

'Sure,' Taylor said dismissively. 'That's hours ago, its half past four now. I'll tell you what… get a few hours rest and I'll take you out for a steak. We'll sort out about you getting back tomorrow.'

Her smile overwhelmed her tiredness. 'Sounds great,' she pushed the car door open and climbed out. 'Good job I found thirty seconds this morning to stuff some clothes and things into a bag.' She opened the boot lid and hauled out a small, brown suede holdall.

She paused by the driver's door, holding the bag in front with both hands and bent towards the window, toes pointing inwards.

'Tell me,' she tilted her head to one side and mischievously narrowed her eyes. 'How did you get my phone number this morning? It was Reg who wrote it down and then you got straight out of the car.'

'Well,' Taylor felt himself blushing. 'I thought I'd better commit it to memory as you read it out. I thought it might come in handy… you know save a bit of time in case something happened, and well… it did.'

She gave Taylor a sideways grin and curled her bottom lip between her teeth.

'Okay, see you about eight?'

At Exeter Police Station Lacey sat slumped in his office chair, both feet resting on the edge of the opened bottom drawer of his desk. He'd found this to be the optimum position for perfect and instantaneous sleep on occasions when fighting it was not an option.

Timson bowled in, a piece of paper in his hand. 'A sleeping policeman,' he commented.

There was no response from Lacey.

Timson increased his volume. 'That Jag, Pete, you were right. All that stuff you said, Jaguar XJ12 Series Three, 5.3 thingamabob Sovereign automatic, all spot on. Staffordshire have just been on the blower.'

Lacey twitched back to life and gave a shake of the head. 'So Kim was right after all… where was it pinched from?'

Timson screwed up his eyes. A knowing grin creased his face. 'Oh, I get it, so it was Kim who came up with that bit then?'

'Okay, okay,' Lacey held up his hands. 'Found me out; now for God's sake tell me where it was stolen from.'

'That's just it,' Timson revealed. 'It wasn't pinched, or at least it's not reported stolen anyway. It's owned by a chap named Lewis out at a place called Middleway, other side of Taunton.'

Lacey scrambled to his feet and grabbed his jacket. 'Well, come on then, what are we waiting for?'

The two detectives made it quickly down to the police station's ground floor and out into the rear yard where they made a bee-line for a tatty red van.

'Bloody hell,' Timson said, digging into his pocket for keys. 'Here's a fine thing. We get given this super-duper car to flirt about the country in and as soon as a young lady appears on the scene you give her the keys! She shoots off hundreds of miles away and we're left with this nail.'

An urgent voice shouted across the yard. 'Hold on a second.'

The pair spun around to see Geoff Deakin peering through the driver's window of Doug Taylor's Vauxhall Cavalier. 'Geoff…' Timpson said, wide-eyed. 'Could be a breakthrough on that Jag. We're off to a place called Middleway. It's about forty-five miles, just off the M5, other side of Taunton.'

'Right then,' Deakin shouted back. 'I'm all done now, so I was planning on getting back anyway. If I follow you up there we can find out what's been going on.'

Lacey turned on his heel and headed over to the Cavalier. 'I'll jump in with you Geoff. We can follow Reg and update each other on the way.'

Timson watched his colleague's retreat. 'Is this another excuse to avoid my driving?'

Deakin was quickly into an explanation over the burial and cremation mix-up as the journey got underway.

'That's good news, but exhumation is a pretty unusual thing,' Lacey debated. 'I've only been involved in one before this in all my service. The paperwork is a nightmare but these circumstances certainly warrant it. I'll make a start at it as soon as I get back. Heaven knows how long it will take to organise.'

The Cavalier's right-hand indicator ticked as Deakin took the slip road and accelerated onto the M5 behind Timson. He glanced over at Lacey.

'They went to a lot of trouble removing Mr Larkin's body from the undertakers. Whatever or, indeed, whoever they put in its place was clearly intended for cremation, but you can see how they made the mistake. I got hold of a copy of the local newspaper that published the death notice.'

He leant over from his driving position and patted the briefcase, propped by Lacey's feet.

Lacey recognised the offer, unclipped the briefcase and pulled out a copy of the *Exeter Express and Echo.* He turned its pages as Deakin continued.

'It was Wednesday 28th May. A week before the funeral and therefore, a week before they stole Mr Larkin's body. It looks like Kim's sighting of the Jag in Tedham in the early hours of 29th May was nothing more than a recce on Pedley's Undertakers. They were preparing to do the swap… planning it.'

Lacey ran a finger along the text of the death notice and nodded agreement with the theories as Deakin continued. 'One of our constables has visited Bunn's dentist. He's photocopied his dental chart and faxed it up to Little Stoneleigh. We'll get it followed up with a full statement and the original documents. Your pathologist could have preliminary confirmation on it being Bunn sometime later this evening and maybe even a suggestion at a cause of death.'

Lacey sat back in his seat, deep in thought before giving his opinion. 'That report of a broken window that came in a week after Kim spotted the Jag… it was Pedley's Undertakers. That was when they did the swap.'

Deakin followed Timson's van off the motorway and tailed along behind as the outing took in a few country lanes. Eventually a black and white name sign for Middleway came into view.

'There could be anything waiting for us at this place', Lacey said. 'The Jag must have been nicked, so why hasn't it been reported? It was first spotted in suspicious circumstances by Kim in the early hours of the 29th May.' He took a few seconds to make a mental calculation. 'That's twenty days ago. Then it was used to break Sweeney out of court. Now it turns up burnt out one hundred and fifty miles away on your patch at Cannock Chase with Bunn's body in it. But still no report from the owner.'

Middleway, a quiet hamlet included several upmarket homes, a pub and a small grocery store. The journey took all of an hour, but there was plenty of sunlight left.

Deakin slowed in behind the CID van and drove at a crawl whilst Timson dawdled, elbow through open window searching for the right house.

The two vehicles eventually came to a halt either side of an impressively large gateway flanked by tall rhododendron bushes. An intricate wrought iron name sign proclaimed the correct location: "The Elms".

Deakin pulled the Cavalier's handbrake up. 'Lovely looking pad.'

Timson was already out from the van and pushing open one side of the wooden double gates.

The three detectives crunched up the curving gravel driveway towards the front door of what was a substantial black and white Tudor-style thatched cottage. A bell tinkled somewhere inside as Lacey tugged on the brass handle fitted to the brickwork. He gave it a few more tries before resorting to some hefty door knocking. This proved fruitless and so the three casually split and wandered off in different directions to see if anyone could be found.

Timson followed Deakin through the side gate and entered into a neatly tended back garden. An old wisteria grew up the side of the building; it was clear that over the years it had been lovingly pruned around a ground floor window frame. The window hung ajar, a small pane of glass near the handle was smashed.

Deakin peered in catching sight of sparkling fragments of glass on the floor beneath. Timson pushed at the back door. It swung open to reveal a tasteful antique-style kitchen: pine furniture and cupboards, ancient black and red quarry floor tiles.

Lacey remained at the front of the house, nose pressed against window and view barred by net curtains. He took a step back, eyes turning to surgical incisions as they locked onto a golf ball sized yellow globule sticking to the brickwork. His furrowed brow increased as he carefully pressed a finger end against the firm, pliable lump. Instinct drifted his expert vision upwards to where a red burglar alarm box nestled in an overgrowth of ivy. The same yellow fungus-type mass could be seen oozing from the grilles of the box and all around its edges.

'Of course,' he muttered and made his way around to the back of the house.

'The place has been screwed,' Deakin said as Lacey stepped into the kitchen.

'Yes, I guessed it. They've squirted that expanding foam into the alarm box to clog up the bell… must have brought a ladder. They've come prepared alright.'

Timson was concerned. 'So, where's the owner? Whoever's done this has already murdered one person. We'd better get the team in… forensics and the works.'

Lacey carefully set off along the hallway. He wanted to know what had happened to the house owner.

The burglar alarm control panel fitted near the front door was smashed, wires and components hung from its plastic case, the battery-powered siren long since dead. Drawers and cupboards hung open, contents tipped onto the carpet. Each time he entered a different room he expected the worst, but no, there was no sign of anyone and no signs of a struggle, just a search for something.

Piles of paperwork littered the lounge carpet. Lacey's eyes homed in on a green Vehicle Registration Document. He skimmed through the content; every detail of Kim's complex description of the Jaguar was accurate. The name of the car's owner was printed in block capitals: SIMON ERIC LEWIS.

Lacey made his way back into the kitchen and was surprised by a visitor standing in the open doorway.

'I'm not frightened of you.' The elderly lady's voice was marginally raised as she stared sternly in at the three detectives. A gigantic Alsatian dog was at her side. The thick leather strap between lady and dog hung loosely. The animal turned its massive head looking at the three detectives as though deciding which one to eat first.

'I've called the police and if you try to escape I'll set Gandalf on you.'

The dog, without putting strain on its lead, curled up its nose and showed a set of sharp yellow teeth as it let out a low rumbling growl.

'We *are* the police,' Timson said in ventriloquist fashion, hardly daring to move his mouth, let alone any other part of his body.

The dog slowly tightened the slack in its strap and increased the volume of its growl as Lacey carefully moved his hand towards his jacket pocket. 'Can I show you my ID card?'

'Sit, Gandalf,' the lady ordered.

The dog obeyed, but a drool of saliva hung from its mouth as it secured its gaze intently upon Timson.

After a few moments of explanation, the tension was relieved.

'Simon and Maureen have gone away to Sorrento; they've wanted to do Pompeii for years. They went almost three weeks ago and should be back within the next few days. This will be an upset for them. I can't see that anyone could have taken his car though, he always locks it in the garage.'

'Yes, my dear,' Timson said. 'I've looked through the garage window and it's empty. They've obviously broken in for the keys… must have known they were off on their hols.'

FOURTEEN

IN STAFFORDSHIRE Taylor drove the Carlton into the Police HQ car park and nudged the gearstick into neutral.

He'd managed a shower, a shave and a change of clothes, but as for sleep, – No. His telephone had made sure of that with calls from the office and headquarters. Various experts, different departments, and a lengthy update from Geoff Deakin, who was still busy down South, made even a doze impossible.

Kim strode confidently over to the car, short black pencil skirt, black and white short sleeved top, small red clutch bag and red high heels. Her dark hair was tidily arranged in an impish fringe and combed slightly above the shoulders.

Taylor's jaw dropped a fraction. Temporary paralysis delayed his planned show of chivalry. He was left scrabbling to remove his seat belt as Kim popped the door herself and eased down next to him.

She slung her holdall over into the back, shuffled for comfort and fastened her safety belt before turning to face him. Her smile showed perfect white teeth and dimpled her cheeks.

Taylor took on a deep breath and shook his head, intentionally exaggerating his embarrassment. His stare locked onto Kim's eyes. 'You look fantastic; how the hell… where did you get…?'

'I told you,' she said. 'I threw a few things into a bag. Now come on, I'm starving.'

'Yes, Milady… anyway what's with the bag, you're not thinking of starting back tonight surely?'

'Well, I thought I should. Pete and Reg have a lot to do back there and I am part of the team now.'

Taylor took the opportunity to update Kim on the news during the fifteen minute drive down to Little Stoneleigh.

'Pete Lacey has faxed the dental records through. The pathologist knows enough to tell us for certain that it's Bunn all right. It'll have to be followed up with the original records and done by a dental expert.'

Kim shuddered. 'How callous, taking him hostage and then just executing him. Do you have a cause of death yet?'

He steered the car around a roundabout from the main road and down towards the town centre. 'There's a gunshot wound to the heart, but there are other injuries that have yet to be properly examined. It'll be a while before we know everything.'

They drove out to the other side of the town. A number of restaurants and pubs were scattered amongst the usual assortment of shops and banks. Taylor pulled into a small car park adjacent to a quaint whitewashed building which fronted onto the road. A green neon window sign read: *Granville's Brasserie, Restaurant and Music Bar.*

'You'll like it here,' he promised. 'Great atmosphere; food's excellent and usually live music.'

It was a warm evening and so the doorman's knee length, black overcoat was unwarranted. Clearly the dome-headed giant saw it as some kind of bouncer's fashion accessory. The beads of sweat rolling down his pugilistic features evidenced the theory. His folded arms and a feet-apart stance supplemented an intimidating glare which he practiced on all arrivals.

Taylor's cheery expression morphed into one of sternness as he caught sight of the man.

Equally the bouncer's hard look was diverted from the other customers to concentrate directly on Taylor. The folded arms were retained as one slow nod was delivered along with two slowly and mockingly phrased words. 'M i s t e r T a y l o r'.

Kim picked up on the mutual dislike. She looked up at Taylor as he led the way towards the end of the room. 'I gather he's not on your Christmas card list?'

'Billy Daniels, no, he's the one downside about the club. He's a jerk, a complete arsehole, if you'll excuse my French.'

Kim covered her mouth with the palm of her hand and stifled her laughter as a waitress joined them.

Taylor's serious face quickly became history as he acknowledged the girl with a raised eyebrow smile. 'Hi, I booked a table for two… half-eight, name of Taylor. Is that one free?' he gestured towards the back of the room.

'That'll be fine, sir.'

Menus and wine lists were handed over as the couple took their seats.

The club was busy, a couple of office parties. Excited chatter and the clatter of cutlery were peppered with the occasional gust of laughter as a story was told or an embarrassing tale related. Kim's smile broadened along with the cheery atmosphere. She gazed around soaking up the ambience created by background music, reduced lighting and polished oak wood floors. Sepia photographs of the old town centre hung from the walls along with antique, metal advertising signs: *Lifebuoy Soap, Fry's Milk Chocolate, Cherry Blossom Boot Polish.*

Three musicians stood hemmed-in by their instruments and equipment on the tiny stage by the front window. A guitar was being tuned, volume checks made and microphones tested as they prepared to perform.

Kim smiled. 'This is great.'

A pact to keep the conversation away from the investigation would never work. It was an unusual and serious case. Their mutual love of music did at least allow them to unwind as the young pianist set the scene with some bluesy soulful chords.

Their food arrived as the group started. It was curious how the din created by so much chatter and laughter could be silenced in seconds with the masterful use of the keyboard. Lilting soulful strains of Ray Charles' melodies drifted across.

Kim caught Taylor's eye and made a mischievous face. 'Wonderful steak, Doug, oh, sorry, I mean, *sir*.'

Taylor grinned. 'Doug will do nicely,' He sliced into the succulent fillet steak of his Tournedos Rossini. 'After all, I asked you out, so we must call it a date.'

'Fine by me,' she commented as she concentrated on her plate. 'To think, I should have been on nights at Little Ole Tedham tonight.'

'Yes, why do you call it Little Ole Tedham?'

She looked up from her meal. 'Oh, just a joke someone started.' Her eyes drifted towards the door and fleetingly landed on the bouncer who was standing in conversation with another man. She puzzled for a second, her expression giving away her interest.

Taylor spied the reaction. 'What is it?'

'Oh, nothing, nothing,' she replied, shrugging and got back to her meal.

Delicious desserts followed the steaks. Taylor with tiramisu and Kim, crème brûlée. It was ten thirty when the coffee arrived and Taylor's pager began to buzz. He reached into his jacket pocket and peered at the message. 'From Geoff, he's made it back home in my old banger. I'll have to give him a ring when we leave, there's a phone box outside.' He gave his coffee a stir. 'I need to swap stories with him. He's drawn the short straw… stuck down there all day.'

Taylor took a sip and then got to his feet. 'Must go to the boy's room.' He carefully weaved his way through the mass of people as Kim sat relaxed, sipping her coffee and reflecting on the day's events.

The relaxation was short lived. There was an audible *clink* as she hastily returned the drink to the saucer. The cup rolled on its side, a pool of hot coffee spreading outward. Kim half stood, knees bent, both hands pressing down on the table as she stared towards the door. It was the same figure that caught her attention earlier. The man instantly turned away and started to push through a cluster of people who were coming into the club.

Kim was now out from behind the table and making towards the door. 'Excuse me… let me through, EXCUSE ME.' She pushed on someone's back. 'Let me through.'

'Hey.' one man shouted as the lager splashed from his glass.

'How rude,' shouted another voice.

It seemed to take an age to reach the exit.

'POLICE,' she shouted with an urgency that made the bouncer blink and jerk his head up.

'Which way did that man go?'

'Who are you on about?' the doorman sneered aggressively and positioned himself fully into the doorway, hands on hips to block Kim's way out.

Someone moved forward from a group of bystanders on the pavement behind the bouncer, his arm outstretched, his finger pointing up the road. 'He went off towards Garrett Street. He was in a rush to get out. Has he pinched something?'

Kim forced her way past the bouncer.

FIFTEEN

THE COFFEE STAIN was still steaming and spreading out into the table cloth as Taylor returned. The empty cup lay on its side in the saucer. Kim's red clutch bag was perched on the corner of the table. *She wouldn't have gone to the ladies without her bag.* He snatched it up and scanned the crowded room, trying to gather any hint to why or where she'd gone.

Through the front window he picked up on an animated conversation in the street between the doorman and the bystanders. It took Taylor seconds to push his way through the crowd. He was a towering athletic man who preferred good manners and pleasant behaviour, but he was worried.

He cornered the bouncer outside the door. 'What's happened, Daniels?'

'Beats me, Mr Taylor,' the bouncer said, thrusting his open palms upwards and pushing his fat neck down into his collar. 'I can't believe that anyone can run like that in high heels, what legs though, right up to her ar… '

'Cut the crap, Billy, where's she gone?' Taylor's stare was menacing.

'Well, like I said, she was gone in a second, up the road and out of sight. Perhaps she got fed up with you. I do like your bag, Mr Taylor.' Daniels was playing to the crowd.

'She was chasing after a bloke,' shouted one of the bystanders.

Taylor eyed the man and then turned his attention back to Daniels. 'Who was she chasing, do you know him?' He pushed Kim's bag into his inside pocket.

Daniels' answer came slowly, '… No'

Taylor closed right up to the doorman's face, causing him to take a step backwards. 'Billy,' Taylor hissed through clenched teeth.

It was Daniels only warning as Taylor's right hand shot forwards and gripped his throat. The bystanders parted and spilled out onto the road.

Daniels' bulky overcoat-clad body trembled as Taylor squeezed the flabby flesh of his throat pushing him with one arm into the recessed entrance of the hardware shop next door. 'Now, why would you be lying to me, Billy?'

He forced the doorman's head against the door frame and downwards towards the pavement.

'Sorry, sorry, Mr Taylor.' Daniels' voice trembled, vibrato fashion. 'He's been in a few times. He started to come in over the last two or three weeks. Always on the pull. Goes for the flashy birds and spends money like he owns the mint. Absolutely loaded… wads of cash.'

Daniels started to choke. His eyelids flickered in anticipation of a punch as Taylor increased the pressure.

'He was asking about you, Mr Taylor,' Daniels gasped.

Taylor was baffled. 'Asking about ME?' He slackened the throat grip to allow the doorman's words more resonance. Daniels was now at floor level and Taylor's broad white-knuckled fist hovered ominously from eighteen inches.

Daniels needed no more prompting. 'Okay, okay,' he jabbered. 'He knew you were CID, slipped me twenty quid for nothing. I saw him driving a Jaguar Mr Taylor… a new black Jag.'

Taylor fell silent, released his grip from the quivering lump and took a step back. The bystanders were watching safely and silently from the centre of the road.

'When did you see him in this Jag?' Taylor demanded.

'A few times over the last week or so,' Daniels blabbered as he struggled to his feet. 'But maybe yesterday or the day before was the last time. He went off up Garrett Street, Mr Taylor, up Garrett Street.'

He repeated himself several times, pointing with a shaking hand in hopeful expectation that Taylor would also take that course. Taylor did exactly that, sprinting to the top of the road, leaving Daniels coughing and clutching at his red finger-marked neck. The bystanders started a hearty round of applause.

Taylor quickly put two hundred yards between himself and the club. He could now barely hear the distant animated voices. He slowed his pace to conserve energy. The road was deserted, street lamps sporadic, no houses, more like the countryside with each step.

He stopped to lean against a shabby concrete bus shelter, catching both his breath and his thoughts. Was he panicking? No, and there was no other route that Kim could have taken if Daniels' version was correct. She must have gone this way. Then he spotted the red high-heeled shoes lying in the grass at the edge of the road.

'Kim, Kim,' he shouted as he jammed a shoe down into each jacket pocket.

He ran on for another five minutes. No buildings here, no street lights at all. The road had become a narrow single track flanked by tall dark hedges. He breathlessly rounded another bend in the lane.

Looming above the hedge and silhouetted in the moonlight stood a factory chimney. A faded white painted name ran down its length, just legible in the gloom: *JOHNSON'S*,

Taylor knew the place. Johnson's Brewery had been derelict for over twelve years. He'd visited a few times – break-ins and a couple of small fires. High security fencing now encircled the grounds.

He slowed to a walking pace as he imagined he heard the remote cry of a female voice. With his head cocked to one side he picked up the pace again trying to home in on any further noises. A sudden screech of tyres and the sound of a big car up ahead propelled Taylor back into a sprint. He knew that the brewery entrance was just around the next bend.

He could hear the sound of the car fading as he rounded the corner. He caught a distant glimpse of it – no sidelights, but bright red brake lights as the panicking driver stamped on the pedal. The car disappeared around a bend two hundred yards away. It was enough to confirm the image before it vanished into the night.

A pair of massive stone gateposts stood menacingly in the shadows shrouded in foliage and set back from the road. The Victorian wrought iron gates, long since stolen, had been replaced by a pair of heavy, steel mesh barriers. A scarred red metal sign was bolted to one side:

DANGER KEEP OUT

An eighteen inch gap separated the makeshift gates. A brass padlock with a bunch of keys still attached lay on the concrete.

A scream penetrated the blackness. Taylor's eyes locked onto the outline of a collection of derelict buildings, the source of the scream.

He squeezed through the gap and sprinted across the darkened forecourt towards the buildings. His eyes fixed on two dimly lit windows in a small outbuilding. There were two, maybe three, vehicles parked nearby. He slowed to a tip toe sneak, heart racing. Figures moved inside and raised male voices could be heard.

A sensation of urgency swamped Taylor as the muffled sounds of a scuffle were perceived.

Anger and determination drove away caution as the tip-toeing was exchanged for a crazy, blind charge forwards in the gloom. The area was littered with rubbish and building materials. His foot caught on something. He sprawled heavily, face down, arms outstretched. He noiselessly scrambled back to his feet and found that he was tightly gripping a four-foot length of hefty, cast iron drainpipe – ideal! He assaulted the rickety wooden door head down and shoulder first with the power of a bull, crashing through as though it were made of cardboard. The entire lock and part of the frame splintered away.

His mind took the scene in like a camera, in that instant when the flash goes off. It froze time. The room was a small office and probably a security lodge when the brewery was operational. A tall thin man crouched against the far wall, his face ashen, eyes fixed wide open. He was smartly dressed with expensive jeans and a cream Versace top. Blood streamed from his broken nose and spouted from a gaping cut to his lip. His left hand gripped the back of Kim's blouse collar. She was face down on the floor, her left arm forced up her back by the man's right hand. The needle of a hypodermic syringe was embedded up to the hilt into her left wrist. Her blouse and upper arm were covered with splashes of the man's dripping blood.

Another man, short, muscular, close cropped fair hair, wearing dark clothing was kneeling on Kim's legs, pinning her down. The fingers of his right hand were wrapped around the barrel of the syringe. His thumb, white from pressure, still remained in contact with the fully depressed plunger even though the contents had been emptied into Kim's motionless body.

Taylor's momentum joined forces with adrenalin and anger propelling him forwards into the room. The freeze-frame picture jolted back to life as the sole of his right foot landed a bone crunching stamp in the fair-haired man's back. The drainpipe was unleashed in a vicious sweeping blow at the other man, glancing off his shoulder and up into his face. A shower of blood spattered against the wall as the man crashed unconscious into a corner.

The syringe was plucked from Kim's wrist by the impact and hit the ceiling before rolling across the floor. Her head thumped back against the wall as the fair haired man sprawled face down. Taylor leapt on him, straddling his back and drove the iron piping down onto his neck with both hands. A pitiful gurgling scream came as his face pressed hard into the stone floor and his neck came close to breaking point.

'GET UP AND MOVE AWAY,' commanded a calm sounding voice from behind.

Taylor jerked his head around ready for more violence, but was stopped in his tracks. The outstretched right arm of the figure which owned the voice now pointed the barrel of a ·38 revolver directly at his head. The man's left hand adjusted the last inch of a dark blue woollen balaclava over a prominent chin. A pair of piercing determined eyes blinked once. The fabric of the balaclava around the mouth, contorted as a lecture was given:

'I will shoot you through the head if you don't do exactly as I say.'

The voice accompanied a gesture with the gun, a flicking of the wrist. It indicated to Taylor in no uncertain terms that he must do as he was told.

Taylor started slowly to get to his feet. He was still holding the drainpipe in one hand. 'What have you done to her, you bastards?'

The gunman nodded towards the corner of the room where his unconscious partner was slumped, his face a swollen red pulp.

'That idiot and your interfering lady friend have caused me a lot of trouble. She…' his eyes flicked over to Kim's lifeless body. 'She… whoever she is… is without doubt a case for the mental asylum. I do, however, know who you are Mr Taylor, and I must tell you that you will do exactly as you are told or face the consequences.'

Taylor viewed the end of the gun barrel respectfully and weighed up his options. He dropped the drainpipe and stepped towards Kim, leaving the prostrate man gasping and vomiting.

'You'll pay for this,' the man choked as he hauled himself to his feet.

'What was in that syringe?' Taylor demanded. He was kneeling next to Kim, gently pulling her away from the wall and turning her onto one side.

She let out a whimper. Her eyelids fluttered.

The gunman kept his revolver trained on Taylor's every move. 'She'll be okay, but you need to teach her some manners.' Piercing blue eyes glared from the balaclava as he turned towards the fair haired man, now slouched against the wall, and issued more orders. 'The cuffs.' The eyes flashed adding urgency to the instruction.

The man edged slowly around the table, blindly fumbling his hand inside the central drawer whilst keeping his stare fixed on Taylor.

Taylor's huge right fist was clenched into a white knuckled bunch, as he sought any glimmer of opportunity to smash the man's jaw into a dozen shards of shattered bone. His stare swapped from one man to the other and then rested upon the gun.

'Don't be silly, Mr Taylor,' the gunman said with a disdainful lilt.

There was a dull metallic rattle as the other man pulled two pairs of shiny, new looking ratchet-type handcuffs from the drawer. He tossed a pair down onto the vomit and blood-stained floor at Taylor's feet and slid the others across the table to the gunman, who pocketed them.

'Put them on, Taylor,' was the fair-haired man's attempt at an order. There was a tremor to his voice.

Taylor folded his arms and rose to his full height. He cleared his throat and exchanged glares with the gunman. He was wearing a definite, *and what if I don't,* expression. The gunman drew his thumb onto the hammer of the revolver and slowly pulled it back. There was a sharp metallic *click* as the hammer settled into the cocked position. He then purposefully, but unhurriedly, swung the gun around and downwards finding his new target – Kim.

SIXTEEN

TAYLOR was familiar with the weapon now pointing at Kim, a model 60, snub-nosed, five shot Smith & Wesson ·38 calibre. He'd used one many times on the police practice range. It was a type of shoulder holster revolver, which Staffordshire Police favoured for detective work.

Taylor also knew just how dangerous the gun had become with the hammer cocked. The slightest of movements by the trigger finger would fire it.

The man flicked his wrist again, clearly a mannerism he was comfortable with. Under these circumstances, a mannerism that made Taylor's blood run cold.

'The cuffs Taylor,' he snapped.

Taylor obliged, fastening the cuffs on loosely. 'Okay, okay. Be careful with that gun.'

The aim was returned back in Taylor's direction. 'A little tighter thank you Mr Taylor. We don't want them slipping off, do we?' He repeated the wrist action as he spoke.

Taylor's eyes locked onto the man's gun grip, finger pressed against trigger, thumb flexed onto the hammer's spur. One tiny movement of that trigger finger would be enough. He had no option. He pressed the handcuffs tighter feeling them bite into his wrists.

A scornful sneer of victory wrinkled the fabric of the balaclava. The thumb eased the gun's hammer spur back a further fraction. A second metallic *click* this time signalled the pressing of the trigger and the subsequent release of the hammer to the control of the thumb. Taylor's eyes widened. One slip now and that powerful trigger spring would snap the hammer forward from beneath the thumb and fire the gun.

A blink of relief came as the hammer was slowly slotted down to its resting place.

He was quickly down again at Kim's side easing her over and arranging her into the recovery position. It was a difficult task with his hands cuffed. He brushed some of the dirt away from her face and gave a sigh of relief on hearing her steady breaths.

'Very touching,' was the gunman's sarcastic remark.

Mumbled groans now entered the equation as the bloodied individual, the subject of Taylor's drainpipe attack, started to stir in his corner. He rolled over revealing his jaggedly cut and swollen face.

'Oh, my God,' he moaned, his voice distorted by the swelling. 'What's the bastard done to me?'

The gunman showed no compassion. 'Get in the washroom and sort yourself out. Get the padlock and keys and lock that bloody gate… I don't want anyone else wandering in.'

The man staggered to his feet and dragged himself out through a doorway into a corridor.

'Right Taylor.' The gunman's words were emphasised with a jab of the pistol. 'Do exactly as I say or you know what happens. Get that bitch out of here.' He turned to the fair haired man. 'Put them in the store and chain them up, we haven't got time for this.'

Taylor needed no more persuasion. 'Okay, okay.' He bent and cradled Kim's shoulders, gripping her under the arms as best he could with the restrictions of the handcuffs.

The fair-haired man grabbed Kim's ankles, lifted up and barked an order at Taylor. 'Through that door.'

Taylor's faltering backwards steps took him along a passageway lit by a low wattage bulb. His face hardened with concentration as his senses soaked up the detail: voices, descriptions, groans of the injured accomplice, the geography of the building, running water – the washroom.

Further along the corridor the gunman snapped out an instruction and signalled to a second doorway. 'In there.'

Taylor kicked open the door behind him with the heel of his shoe and backed into the darkness. The gunman followed, free hand groping on the wall in search of a light switch. One dim bulb up in the rafters came to life, its weak yellow light giving away few secrets. The room was unusually high-ceilinged, at least twenty feet and appeared to be a dumping ground. Shapes of rotten wooden beer kegs, rusty iron tools and an assortment of other unwanted junk and equipment loomed in the shadows as Taylor's squinting gaze pingponged about.

Some items were propped against the walls, others hung on iron brackets. Pieces of steel mesh barrier fencing leaned against one wall, together with a pile of concrete paving slabs. High up, below the rafters a rusting girder sat between the walls with a thick linked chain dangling to just above the floor.

The fair-haired man stopped by the chain and deliberately dropped Kim's legs to the ground with a thump. Her bare feet lolled over to one side, soles covered in a patchwork of tiny bloodstained cuts. Taylor grimaced, still awkwardly cradling her head and shoulders, and hoping no real damage had been done.

'Right,' the gunman directed. 'Handcuffs on her.' He pulled the other handcuffs from his pocket and tossed them to his accomplice.

Taylor's face showed his horror. 'Is that necessary, I mean… she's out of it. What in God's name have you done to her?'

'Don't push me, Taylor.' He jabbed the revolver's barrel aggressively as though pointing a finger. 'I've seen what she's capable of, and it's necessary alright.'

'Okay, tough guy,' the other man said with attempted mockery. 'Dump her down.'

With difficulty Taylor lowered Kim's head onto the stone floor and pushed an old hessian sack beneath her as a makeshift pillow.

'How sweet,' the fair-haired man ridiculed in a further failed attempt to regain credibility. The tremble in his voice gave away his fear as he fumbled to handcuff Kim's right wrist.

Taylor wanted to punch the man's lights out and his face showed it. He made do with backing away as more stabbing gestures from the revolver dictated proceedings. He watched helplessly as the other part of Kim's handcuffs was fixed to a link of the dangling chain.

'Right, copper.' Came yet another failed macho attempt by the fair-haired man. 'Fasten yourself to one of those.' He threw down the handcuff key and pointed to a row of ornate cast iron shelf brackets that were bolted to the brickwork.

The gunman saw hesitation in Taylor's body language. He intervened by pointing the gun barrel purposefully. 'Get on with it.'

Taylor reluctantly obeyed. Clearly attempts to plot for a future escape were being watched. He picked the lowest of the brackets working out that this would allow him to squat on the floor with his left arm raised. He locked the handcuff onto it and gave a derisory head shake as he threw back the key.

With the safety catch back in place the gunman slid the pistol into his pocket and turned towards the door. 'That'll do for the time being… we've got work to do.'

The room plunged back into gloom as the gunman casually brushed his fingers over the light switch and slammed the heavy wooden door shut. The steps of the two men made gritty contact with the stone block floor of the corridor as they retreated back to the office. The minimal glow beneath the door lasted only seconds before the audible *click* of another switch took away even the vaguest of outlines.

Taylor sat back against the wall, legs stretched out in front and hard, cold brick floor beneath. In this low down position his shackled left wrist was at head height and soon suffering from pins and needles. He flexed his fingers to stave off the condition and then also widened his eyes, blinking rapidly in an attempt to quickly accustom his sight to the darkness. He needed to make sense of the surroundings.

With his head turned to where he knew Kim lay motionless he visualised the heavy chain leading from her wrist up towards the roof. He now even fancied he could actually make part of it out.

The weak source of light enabling these sketchy outlines came from above. His distorted observations and logic drew a picture of a loading bay door high up the wall where the iron girder stretched from one side of the room to the other. A tiny glint of starlight was visible through the cracks around the edge of this door.

Taylor brooded in the shadows as he worked out that the girder was the jib of an old crane system. It must have been designed to continue to the outside through the loading bay door and Kim was handcuffed to the hauling chain.

Heavy rusting machinery lay about the floor and propped against the walls. The strong sickly smell of old gear oil hung in the air. Taylor stretched out his arm towards Kim, but it was pointless. She was several yards away. He pulled at the iron wall bracket and tried a cumbersome sideways stamping motion with the sole of his shoe. It refused to budge at all.

Sitting back down, he thought for a while. *Who were these men? They certainly knew who he was.* He went over the words of the nightclub doorman… "He'd got a Jaguar, Mr Taylor… a new black Jag". *Could they really be involved in Bunn's murder?*

He angled his head, straining to listen to the distant conversation. It was futile; he couldn't distinguish a word. He could though, make out the sound of a television and the occasional musical jingle of adverts. He slumped back against the wall and sighed heavily in the blackness as he concentrated his mind onto the layout of the building and its contents.

He felt with his free hand into his inside pocket and pulled out his pager. Deakin would be puzzled why he hadn't phoned. He held the broken remnants and loose battery for a second before tossing them across the room. The device had been smashed in the struggle.

'Damn,' he muttered and sank back down into a frustrated heap.

SEVENTEEN

A DULL RATTLE broke the silence. Taylor's squinted gaze drilled through the darkness searching out the cause. An almost imperceptible movement high up in the rafters narrowed his squint into a pinprick and locked on. The grainy outline of the chain which led down to the invisible Kim Harding had developed a slight sway.

'Kim, Kim. Are you okay?'

A shuffling sound preceded a soft gasp.

'Kim, can you hear me, it's Doug?'

A full fifteen minutes passed before Kim managed to sit upright and comprehend Taylor's explanation of the events. She rubbed vigorously at her left wrist as his voice came from the corner: 'See if you've enough spare chain to get over here.'

She rose shakily to her feet and stumbled the few steps in Taylor's direction that the chain would allow. It wasn't enough.

Taylor gestured unobserved. 'The light… you might be able to reach it.'

Kim's left arm stretched out as she tottered over to where she suspected the switch might be. The chain pulled tightly on her other wrist. Seconds ticked by before her quivering, searching finger eventually achieved success. The poor light was barely enough to illuminate her, half-crouched and chin down against her chest. Oil and dirt were ground into her knees and the trendy black and white blouse was a torn and bloodied rag.

Taylor tugged pointlessly at the iron wall bracket.

Kim seemed dazed as she stared at him chained in his corner. She dropped her head down to her chest and sobbed quietly.

'Hey, don't do that,' Taylor's voice bore a low concerned tone. 'You must have given them a rough time.'

She lifted her head and gave a little nod of agreement. 'Not rough enough. They're going to kill us, aren't they?'

'Hmm,' Taylor muttered not wanting to openly agree. 'Tell me what went on at the club. Was it the driver of the Jag you saw in Tedham? Is that what happened… you saw him?'

'That's right, as soon as I caught sight of him I thought he looked familiar and then when he turned to face me I recognised him. That same weasel face I'd seen looking out of the Jag window.'

She rubbed her sore wrist as the memory of the struggle and the injection came back. 'He realised I'd spotted him and he was out of the door and away. It took me ages to get through the crowd and the bouncer didn't want to help. I ran up the street in those bloody silly shoes, but he'd got a head start.'

She sat back down on the sacking doing more wrist rubbing. 'There wasn't anywhere else he could have gone, so I carried on. I dumped my shoes; they were slowing me down and making too much noise. I came around a corner and there he was opening the gate. You should have seen his weasel face. He thought he'd lost me.' Her lips now bore the hint of a smile. 'I didn't say anything, he was obviously going to have a go, so I flatfooted him straight in the mouth, put him down on his arse. I turned him over to get his arms up his back when someone grabbed me from behind, took me unawares, a classic arm lock, nearly broke my shoulder blade.'

Taylor's frown went unnoticed in the gloom. 'Which one of them was this?'

'Someone else,' Kim said. 'None of the three in that room… a big man, unfit and out of breath straightaway. Weasel Face came in front and punched me in the stomach as the big man pushed me across the courtyard. Every time I struggled the big man jammed my arm further up my back. The other two were waiting by the door, the taller one had half pulled a balaclava on his head, I could see a bit of his chin. He was waving his gun about and shouting out orders. I got a look at the shorter fair haired one.'

Taylor gritted his teeth with anger as Kim continued.

'I heard a car drive off… wheels spinning like hell. I guess that must have been the big guy getting the hell out of it. Weasel Face took over and pushed my head against the floor with my arms up my back. I felt the syringe go into my wrist… it must have been the fair-haired man who injected me. The next thing is… I wake up in here.'

There was a sound of ripping material and loose change spilling onto the floor as Taylor tugged clumsily with his free hand at his jacket pocket. 'I've got your shoes… if you'll be any more comfortable.' The shoes clattered down close enough for Kim's reach. She squirmed one-handed to fit them on. 'Stupid bloody things.'

It was Taylor's turn to force a smile.

Kim checked her handcuffed wrist and tugged hopefully at the chain snaking away up above her. She went silent for a few moments, deep in thought. 'Damn,' she finally said. 'I left my bag on the table in the club.'

Taylor shook his head as he produced the bag from his inside pocket. He gave a magician's musical introduction. 'Da-dah.'

Her eyes lit up with determination.

He added his upbeat comment as he tossed the bag over to her. 'So, here we are chained up in a dungeon with a bunch of thugs waiting for us with a gun and you're going to start doing your face!'

She made a good one handed catch and then squatted back down unclipping the slender red bag and fumbling inside. A triumphant grin creased her tear-stained cheeks as she peered over at Taylor. A tiny flash of chrome merged with a metallic jangle as she held up a small set of keys.

Taylor pulled a bewildered face. He knew he should be in on the joke by now, but found himself frowning. All he could see was a car key, a house key and a police station locker key.

Actually there was something else attached to the split-ring, but it was so commonplace that Taylor almost overlooked it. An inconsequential every day piece of baggage that uniformed police officers keep on their keyring without a second thought. That stubby two inch metal cylinder – handcuff key!

'You don't think…?' he said.

'I don't *think,* I *know*. These are Hyatt cuffs, standard police issue in most countries and on sale by mail order anywhere. One key fits them all.'

As she slotted the little key into the handcuffs the distant low mumble of voices became louder.

Taylor's voice was serious. 'They've opened the door, someone's coming. Hide your bag and the keys. Can you reach the light?'

Kim quickly hid the keys and bag under the sacking. She stretched over to the light switch almost pulling her arm from its socket as she flicked it off. She was back, sprawled on the floor, as the door opened with a dim glimmer of light from the corridor.

Weasel Face's stick figure was silhouetted in the doorway holding a gun. He fumbled for the light switch. The resulting feeble glow showed several pieces of sticking plaster criss-crossing his pallid features.

'What's going on, no escape plans then?'

Kim hauled herself up into a slouched sitting position, successfully exaggerating her true condition ten-fold. 'I need the loo,' she whimpered.

'Oh, we're back in the land of the living are we?' he taunted. 'Not so ferocious now then.' He stood back and pointed the gun directly at her head. 'No tricks.'

He tossed the key to the floor in front of her, signalling for her to undo her handcuffs.

Kim did exactly as instructed and threw the key back.

'Good girl', he said condescendingly.

Taylor, propped with his back against the wall, watched Weasel Face with contempt as he ordered Kim out into the corridor. 'Turn right and then in there. No tricks or I shoot you now.' He followed her in, gun still pointing.

Kim obeyed, washing her hands and face in the grubby basin with cold water. She took handful after cupped handful of water and drank and drank. She then indicated towards the toilet, the man nodded his approval.

'Leave the door open,' he ordered with a sickly grin.

She suffered the indignation as though he wasn't even there. 'You nasty little bastard,' she mouthed at him as she walked out into the corridor.

She sat back down on the floor and replaced her handcuffs without any instructions.

'Very good girl, you're learning to behave. Perhaps I can get you to do a few more tricks when the others have gone and I've got you all to myself.'

His tattered face became even more hideous from behind his lecherous gape. He turned to Taylor. 'Okay copper, your turn for a leak, take it if you want, but don't try anything or you're dead. All I want is an excuse.'

He dropped the key down onto the ground and moved backwards.

Taylor unlocked the handcuffs and cast a corner of the eye squint, first at the man, then at the gun.

'Just give me a fucking reason, copper.'

Taylor attended to his needs in the grubby little washroom. A small, crazed, brown stained basin was attached to the wall. The place was filthy, cracked plaster, tiles and spiders' webs. He attempted to wash his hands with the trickle of cold water and a thin sliver of dried-up soap.

He played for time, drinking from his hands and catching a look at the man's blurred reflection through a shard of broken mirror which hung tenuously above the basin. The slice of glass had a jagged, dagger-like point; he took a few more sips as he judged the situation. Could he snap it off the wall and then jam it into the man's throat before he could fire the gun?

The man raised his voice impatiently. 'Get a fuckin' move on, Taylor.'

Taylor turned, anger flaring behind his eyes. It was too risky. He flicked his hands dry. 'So what happens now then?'

'Mind your own business. If I'd had my way you two would be history by now, so get on with it and get back in there.'

Taylor resentfully obeyed, fastened the handcuff back on and chucked the key over. He settled down in his corner without a word, leaving the man standing in the doorway baffled by his sudden obedience. The light was extinguished and the door slammed shut.

They waited until they heard the voices and the TV fade as the office door was closed. Taylor watched Kim's outline as she eased up onto her haunches in the dark. A sharp metallic *click* preceded a satisfied: 'Yes.'

EIGHTEEN

FREE FROM her shackles Kim stood to her feet and felt her way over to the switch. The light barely illuminated Taylor's outline, crouched and fastened to the iron bracket. She took hold of his handcuffed left hand as she knelt down. Her hair was a mess and her clothes ragged, but the big brown eyes had regained that air of determination.

Taylor's recent growth of dark stubble accentuated his rugged and handsome, but worried, features. He hadn't noticed the small cuts to his forehead or the brown rust stain across his shirt and jacket from the iron drainpipe.

She leaned over and kissed him on the cheek. 'Thanks for looking after me.'

She undid his handcuffs.

He blinked a few times and inhaled, feeling invigorated by the attention. 'There's no way out of here,' he said. 'Other than through the room where they are.' He lifted his eyes towards the loading bay door set into the wall. 'That's far too high up.'

They set to work examining the contents of the room.

It was some time later when Taylor switched the light off and eased the door open. He inched into the darkened corridor with Kim close behind. They hardly dared breathe as they crept forwards in the direction of the muffled voices.

A small crescent of light filtered from under the door. The occasional snippet of conversation was discernible as they drew closer.

Taylor deftly bent and peered through the keyhole of the old mortise lock. He silently shifted position a few times as he attempted a half decent look into the room. His sudden rigid stance suggested that he had seen something.

He turned back to Kim and whispered. 'Money, piles of

banknotes, thousands and thousands of pounds, probably millions.'

The sound of the musical introduction for a news bulletin came sharply over the television. The reporter's voice was clear:

"Police in Staffordshire, have teamed up with Devon and Cornwall Police in the search for the missing barrister, Jacob Bunn. A body was found early yesterday morning in the burnt out wreck of a Jaguar car in an isolated area of Cannock Chase, Staffordshire. The vehicle is believed to be the one used as a getaway car two weeks ago when violent criminal, David Sweeney took Mr Bunn hostage at gunpoint during his escape from Exeter Crown Court where he stood accused of serious drugs charges."

"Unconfirmed reports," the presenter continued. *"Have suggested that Mr Bunn's barrister's robe and wig were found draped around bushes at the scene. A Staffordshire Police spokesman would not verify that dental records had already proved that the body is that of Mr Bunn, but added that fears were growing for his safety."*

Laughter broke out in the room.

Taylor and Harding analysed the humorous party-like response to the TV report. Silent, independent verdicts were made as to what lay in store for themselves at the hands of these men.

The joviality in the room petered out as the voice of the gunman, clearly the leader, started to talk.

'Okay Price, you've done your bit and made a few stupid mistakes into the bargain.'

Taylor thought the sentence through. The gunman appeared to be talking to Weasel Face, so now they had a name. Weasel Face was Price.

The voice gave more orders, which again seemed to be directed at Weasel Face. 'It's time for a pay-out. Time to say our goodbyes and go our separate ways. You're going to get a visitor at exactly ten minutes to six, so don't mess up. Have the gate open ready for him. Give him his cash and get the gate shut as soon as he's gone. It shouldn't take any longer than a minute. He's paranoid about being seen, so you'll be able to get rid of him quickly.'

Price's voice grew louder now. 'I'd rather shoot the bastard. You know how I feel about him.'

Taylor looked at Kim. The poor light allowed her the faintest glimpse of his baffled expression.

The gunman now countered Price's remarks. 'His pay-out is two hundred and fifty grand, which is small beer compared with yours. The balloon will go up when someone realises those two are missing. We don't want that trail leading back to this place. He's still useful to us. Get rid of those two, follow the plan and it will still work out.'

Price remained silent.

Taylor was back down to the keyhole as the leader started again.

'I want this place cleaned out completely before you leave.'

Taylor adjusted his position. He could make out the back of the gunman's head, no balaclava and a fleeting squint of short dark hair.

'Clear everything out,' he ordered. 'I want all the papers and notes burned. Wipe everything down, just in case the police do end up here.'

The distinctive sound of paper being torn accompanied the sentence. Another modification to Taylor's crouched position proved it to be the gunman himself who was ripping up the papers.

'You've got your share of the cash, so let's stick to the plan. Now, go and check the cars over, I don't want any breakdowns.'

They heard Price close the outer door as he went outside.

'The less that fool knows the better,' the gunman said. 'He's already caused us a mountain of problems.'

Taylor closed his eyes as he concentrated his hearing on the first chance of a decent sentence from the third man.

'Yeh,' came the muttered agreement. 'As far as he's concerned, it's a split of the money and then goodbye. He mustn't get any inkling about Belgium or the big picture.' The sound of a wooden chair being dragged across the floor alerted Taylor and Harding to their dangerous situation, someone had stood up from the table. They both turned and tiptoed back down the corridor. Taylor silently closed the door and they settled back in the darkness awaiting their fate.

Fifteen minutes passed before car doors and the hum of engines was made out. The dragging of the metal barrier gates across the concrete preceded the sounds of two vehicles driving off into the distance.

NINETEEN

THREE FEEBLE slits of weak sunlight crept in around the loading bay door as dawn began to win its battle against the night sky, but the gloomy room benefitted little from the effect.

The sound of the TV increased as the office door opened. A light switch clicked on and Price's evil intent was broadcast by the self-assured swagger of his corridor footsteps. The weak, yellow glow tried vainly to penetrate into the room as the door opened.

Price stood framed in the doorway: a black, stick outline in the shape of a Lowry style figure. He raised his gun in classic pistol stance, both hands together and legs apart, aim levelled down at Doug Taylor. 'Time to go.' He gave an emphasised mocking laugh.

Two six inch tongues of orange flame, spat from the gun barrel as the shots were fired in quick succession. The blasts made the brickwork of the old building ring like a bell.

Taylor's shoulders collapsed forwards as the bullets pierced through and embedded themselves into the wall behind. Price swung his aim down at Kim, the red high heels just visible in the dim light where she huddled beneath the sacking.

'Right, we'll have a bit of fun now while I decide what to do with you. Up on your feet BITCH. Let's see you naked.'

His eyes widened as the realisation that something was not right dawned. 'What the…?'

The chain was missing.

His frantic kick at the sacking revealed only the shoes and a bundle of rags.

The rusty chain roared as it raced over its metal pulley wheels. Price had no time to react, save for a feeble upwards movement of his weasel features. The entire building pulsated as the half a ton of metal tools, wooden beer barrels and paving slabs supported upon a square of metal barrier fencing hurtled downwards under the pull of gravity.

The product of their back-breaking labour struck him and flattened him into the brick floor.

The vibration of the impact filled every part of the building and seemed to carry on like a tuning fork for an age. A vortex of dust motes swirled upwards, caught in the thin beams of sunlight burning their way in around the loading hatch.

Kim emerged from behind the brick pillar that supported the gearing and pulley wheels of the crane and padded across the dirty floor, shoeless. Taylor followed her out into the centre of the room and then silently collected his bullet-perforated jacket from the ground. He undid the buttons and pulled out the sacking stuffing. The vibration stopped, but the chain still swayed.

They viewed their handiwork. A trickle of blood oozed from beneath the steel mesh, forming small rivulets, criss-crossing and separating between the tight lines of the floor bricks. These merged to form an ever growing bright red puddle.

Price's lifeless right hand, still clutching the gun, and one foot were all that could be seen poking from the jumble. A silence descended on the old building, broken only by a dull metallic clatter as death released the villain's grip on the weapon.

Taylor fixed his stare onto Kim's worried eyes. Neither needed to say a word. What had happened, what they had done had saved their lives. Taylor bent to pick up the gun, but then stopped short.

'No, best leave it as it is,' he instructed himself.

'Got no shoes at all now,' Kim commented.

She followed Taylor through to the office. The TV still chattered in the corner until Taylor silenced it.

She pointed down at the five blue plastic boxes that were positioned by the door. 'My God, look at this lot.' Each box was piled high with cash. Square cling-film wrapped blocks of twenty pound notes.

A handwritten label was stuck to each of the blocks. Thick black marker pen: *£50,000.*

Taylor surveyed the boxes. 'Jesus Christ, there must be millions. Thing is I couldn't see too well through that keyhole, but there was much more than this. I think they've taken a lot with them.'

On the table stood a cardboard box. The coloured printing on the side showed that it originally contained thirty-two cans of Heinz baked beans. The slight distortion to its once rectangular shape was created by five more of the cling-filmed £50,000 blocks. Alongside was a mound of loose foreign banknotes, American dollars, French francs and other European cash.

Taylor's eyes locked onto the box. 'Two hundred and fifty grand,' he observed. 'This little lot must be for the visitor that Price disliked so much.'

He pulled back his tattered jacket sleeve and checked his watch. 'It's after half-five now. This person is going to arrive in less than fifteen minutes.' He pondered as he calculated the best strategy. 'I think we should make it look like the place is deserted... like they've done the dirty on him and gone off with his money. We'll see if we can get a look at him.'

He peered out through the window. A grubby white Ford Escort van was the only vehicle still on the courtyard. A set of Ford vehicle keys attached to a larger bunch lay on the table. 'You can probably see that van from the road. Let's hide all the cash in it and shift it out of sight.'

Time was getting short now and out of necessity Kim's tattered feet would have to endure a little more pain yet. The boxes of cash needed to be loaded into the van, and quickly!

Within one minute a single box remained in the centre of the table – the £250,000 intended for the mystery visitor. Kim picked it up intent on stowing it with the others.

Taylor held his hand up. 'No, hang on with that one. Maybe we should hide it somewhere else, in case anything goes wrong, something to barter with.'

He scooped up the remaining wads of foreign currency from the table and stuffed them into the box.

Kim paused, holding the box in both hands against her tummy as Taylor checked the rest of the room. He picked up a tattered, waste-paper basket and emptied its contents onto the table. A confetti of torn paper fragments fluttered out along with other waste oddments.

He sifted through some the fragments. 'This is what he was tearing up. We'll hide it out of the way as well; maybe we can do a bit of jigsaw later on.'

He carefully swept the paper fragments to the edge of the table with the palm of his hand and collected them into a plastic supermarket bag. Using a wooden ruler from the table he gingerly delved into the main pile of rubbish for any stray scraps of torn paper. The ruler tapped against something solid. A hypodermic syringe rolled into view. Kim's mouth set in a tight line of disgust as she watched.

Taylor used his handkerchief to carefully extract the syringe from the other rubbish. The needle, still attached, retained a faint red trace of Kim's blood smeared along its length. He held it up to the light.

Kim grimaced, finding herself rubbing feverishly at her left wrist as the incident was recalled.

Taylor tilted the syringe back and forth, noting a tiny residue of yellowish liquid still discernible inside the barrel. Carefully wrapping the syringe in his handkerchief he stored it together with the bag of shredded paper into the expected visitor's now overstuffed box.

Another wristwatch check showed that time was getting short. Taylor snatched the keys from the table and dashed out to the van.

'Hide that box outside in the bushes,' he shouted back.

The van started up without a problem and a cloud of diesel smoke drifted across the courtyard.

The site, an immense complex was littered with crumbling outbuildings, dilapidated offices and garages. Taylor drove around to the back, well out of sight from the road and selected an old vehicle service shed. He nudged the van in through the open doors and used the bumper to push beer barrels, boxes and other rubbish out of the way. After dragging the rotted doors together he ran the fifty yards back to the office.

They stood inside using the last few moments to take stock of the situation. *Had they covered everything?*

'Let's find somewhere to hide near the entrance. We need to get a look at this person.'

The foliage was dense on one side of the gateway, a jumbled mixture of laurel, privet and holly. Taylor eyed the makeshift gates and thought out the best possible viewpoint. Comfort was not a consideration. He took hold of Kim's hand, pulling her to him, and then turned his back to the dense entanglement. A snapping of twigs and small branches followed as he drove his broad shoulders backwards into the interior. Kim held her face against his chest and moved with him in a shuffling embrace, wincing as she trod shoeless onto prickly holly leaves.

Taylor bulldozed on, stopping when he could go no further. They were well hidden and probably three yards into the bushes. He adjusted some more of the branches and leaves and checked the view. It was perfect.

Kim looked up at him amazed at his strength.

With difficulty they turned through 180 degrees until Kim could peer out through the thicket with Taylor's hands clasped loosely around her waist. He nudged his chin into the back of her head as they settled to wait for the visitor. Within two minutes an approaching car was heard.

TWENTY

THEY CAUGHT a glimpse of the car's white paintwork as it pulled up. It parked against the steel mesh gate, front bumper almost touching, as though the driver expected it to be open.

Taylor's eyes searched through the leaves and branches for a better view quickly distinguishing the shape of a Ford Granada. He pulled Kim closer as the driver went to open the door and felt her heart rate increase along with the tension.

She slowly twisted and looked up at him, mouthing her words. 'That car was here last night. This is the man who grabbed me from behind.'

The car door opened. The suspension raised up. An overweight figure clambered out and shambled around to the front of the car, both hands gripping the mesh gate and rattling it.

Taylor tightened his hold around Kim even more. He breathed in deeply as he gawped through the foliage.

The man shook the gate violently, his face red with rage. 'Price… Charlie, Charlie,' he half-shouted. 'Get this gate open… PRICE.'

Kim dug Taylor in the ribs with her elbow. 'Can't breathe,' she gasped from the corner of her mouth.

Taylor slackened his grip, but his stare was rigidly set upon the figure.

'What is it?' she whispered as she read his alarmed expression.

Taylor gulped hard before managing his hushed words. 'It's Farmer, Superintendent Farmer… my boss, the commander in charge of Little Stoneleigh Police. He's the visitor… my God he's part of this!'

Farmer trotted back to his car and pulled the keys from the ignition, his eyes were wide; his florid cheeks rippled as his head darted from side to side. The gate should have been open. Price should have been there ready with his money. Farmer couldn't afford to be seen by anyone.

His hands were trembling as he selected a particular key from the bunch and guided it into the padlock.

Taylor's eyes were glued onto Farmer as the padlock was removed. 'Yes, he's well involved,' he muttered.

Farmer dragged the gates apart and scrambled back into the driving seat. A cloud of exhaust smoke erupted as he gunned the engine back into life and jarred the clutch out. The wheels spun into a blur, flinging loose pebbles across the road as the car slewed into the compound and out of sight around the back of the buildings.

Farmer quickly reappeared on foot. A panic stricken, shuffling run, sweat dripping from his chin as he forced his waddling body to drag the gates shut.

'The cheating bastards, after all I've done,' he panted.

The pair remained completely motionless, silently absorbing the implications of the police chief's involvement.

'He's going to be pretty mad when he can't find his money,' was Taylor's hushed observation.

Kim detected a hint of humour in his voice, surprising, in view of the tension of the moment.

They adjusted their position as Farmer ran across the yard to the office, yanked the door open and disappeared inside. The sounds of a wild search for his cash were clearly heard as doors were thrown open and furniture tipped over.

A sudden silence announced that Farmer had found something unexpected – like Price's body!

Farmer staggered from the office pressing a hand to his mouth and slumped against the wall collecting his thoughts for a full minute before disappearing back inside.

He was soon out again, gulping for air and loping over to the gate, panting and pressing his sagging jowls hard against the square metal mesh. Taylor and Harding, just yards away, watched open-mouthed as his ball-bearing eyes darted left and right, looking up and down the lane. A nervous wrist watch check was made before he heaved the gates open, sucked in more air and ran back across the yard and out of sight.

A full minute passed before mystified glances were exchanged. Farmer's panic level had been off the scale, so why the delay?

Two minutes ticked by and their eyes were glued on the gap between the buildings. Kim's stomach churned 'Oh, God, do you think he's had a heart attack?'

The words hardly left her lips as the Granada shot into view in a cloud of dust. It jolted to a halt on the small patch of tarmac between the road and the entrance.

'No such luck,' Taylor observed, still intently watching the display. 'But it's on the cards if he keeps this up.' The hint of humour was even more apparent.

Farmer struggled out of the driving seat holding one of the car's rubber floor mats in his right hand. After another panic stricken glance up and down the lane he began a shuffling backwards trot towards the gates, dragging the mat in the dirt to obliterate his car and foot tracks.

Taylor's stare locked onto the display. 'The crafty old sod.'

In less than a minute Farmer closed and padlocked the gate. He jumped back into the car and floored the accelerator, leaving the brewery behind in a cloud of blue exhaust smoke.

Kim knelt and massaged her toes.

Taylor looked down sympathetically at the blood smeared feet. He was confident that a couple of sticking plasters would solve the problem, but lifted Kim up by the waist and forced his way backwards out from the bushes.

She gingerly picked the best spots to put down her feet as they made their way across the compound.

'Who else is involved in this? Taylor puzzled as he opened the office door. 'And what the hell is going on?'

Kim limped inside and took up a precarious one legged stance to examine a cut to the sole of her foot. 'God knows,' she replied. 'But we should be safe here for a while. There's no way Farmer is going to report what he's found, so let's decide what to do next.'

Taylor pursed his lips, deep in thought. 'We should be preserving this place as a crime scene really, but I guess it's pretty well contaminated by us already.'

Kim pulled out a chair and started to examine her other foot. She looked up at Taylor. 'That was strange… the time Farmer had arranged to arrive at. We heard them say he would be here at exactly ten minutes to six. Why so precise?'

Taylor deliberated the question. 'I think I can answer that. You see, here in Staffordshire the police shifts start and end at 6 am, 2 pm and 10 pm… in the main anyway. The new shift coming on duty has to be in the station for the duty parade fifteen minutes before the start of the shift. During those fifteen minutes you can be almost certain that everyone finishing a shift and everyone starting a new one will be nicely out of the way inside the police station. Ten minutes to six is a good time not to see any off duty or on duty policemen in this part of the world.'

Kim gave an understanding nod. 'So, what's going to be the connection here to Little Stoneleigh with Sweeney? I know he originated from here, but that was years ago. It sounds like he's not been near the place since he made it big time.'

Taylor nodded. 'That's another puzzle. The file I handed to Pete Lacey yesterday should have given all the background needed to make some sense out of this, but it was little more than useless.'

'There was a suggestion,' he added. 'That Sweeney's stepfather used to work here at this brewery as a drayman. It's been derelict for years though, and all the records have been lost. It was a busy place back then… employed dozens of folk. What happened to him or even what his name is, God only knows.'

Kim listened carefully to Taylor's comments. 'Farmer was the man who grabbed me last night. I could smell the same tobacco on him even from the gate. Thinking about it, the hold he put me in was an old police restraint hold.'

'Yes,' Taylor agreed. 'But what keeps going around in my mind is: *who, or what was in that coffin?* Breaking into an undertaker's with a dead body, if it was a body, is an awful lot of trouble to go to. Geoff must be wondering what's going on. He would have expected me to ring him last night. Right now I feel like there's only him I can trust.'

Kim folded her arms. 'Well, thank you very much for that.'

He turned back to face her. 'Listen, after what we've been through together, I know I can trust you.'

He cupped her face with the palms of his hands and kissed her full on the lips.

She pulled him towards her in a long tight embrace, both hands pressing into his back. She leaned back, just enough to separate their lips. 'And I know I can trust you.' She rested her head sideways against his chest.

Taylor realised the romantic interlude was ill-timed. 'I'd better get Farmer's box. We can have a quick look at those papers that were torn up.' He turned towards the door and hurried across the yard.

He was back within a minute, grimacing at his own enforced unprofessionalism and dumped the box down onto the table. 'Classic example of how to mess up a crime scene.'

Within seconds he spread a handful of the torn paper fragments from the supermarket bag across the table. None were much bigger than a thumb nail. Portions of bold handwriting written in crisp, neat, blue fountain pen made up a complex jigsaw puzzle. He turned over some blank ones and rearranged them until a jumble of letters and some part words were revealed. He selected a few with a fingertip, dragging them into a separate piece of clear table space. The words "Ghent" and "Ferry" stood out, but others seemed mostly part words: Bel, Har, over, stend.

'Make anything from it?' Kim asked.

Taylor was motionless for a few seconds as he stared down at the scraps and got his thought processes into gear. Then he was talking: 'Well, we heard them mention Belgium and Ghent is a city in Belgium. We also have the word ferry.' He moved the relevant fragments to another space. 'So the torn fragment that reads as "over" is probably Dover,' he paused. 'And if that's right then "stend" has to be Ostend… it's the main port for Belgium from Dover.'

He became silent again, and then: 'We've already discovered that Farmer is up to his neck in this and that must include Jacob Bunn's murder. The two men who were here are going to be on that ferry and away before we can get anywhere near the port.' He paused for a second, massaging his neck with his right hand. 'In an ideal world I'd nick them first before dealing with Farmer.'

Kim raised an eyebrow. 'Well, my passport's in my bag in the Carlton. It's still in my maiden name. I never managed to change it over.'

Taylor stared at the wall unblinking as he entered into more deep thought. He turned slowly. 'I need to speak to Geoff, before we make any rash decisions. We'll take Farmer's box of cash here and we need to look more closely at those ripped papers.'

TWENTY ONE

TAYLOR'S JOG down to Granville's car park was completed without witnesses. He was back at the brewery within fifteen minutes. Kim's idea to wait hidden with Farmer's box on the outside of the compound saved a few precious seconds.

The Carlton jolted to a stop on the tarmac strip between the gateposts. Taylor shot Kim an eager glance as she scrambled barefoot out from the bushes and into the passenger seat. She dumped the box of money and the other items over into the back and pulled the door shut, aware that Taylor already had the car in motion.

Kim grabbed her holdall from the back as Taylor quickly put distance between them and the brewery. She rummaged through yesterday's neatly folded clothes and pulled out her trainers. 'Heaven,' she sighed as she pushed them onto her feet.

Taylor gave the rear-view mirror a worried glance, but there were no other cars. 'You alright?'

She nodded as she laced up the trainers. 'What now?'

After taking a couple of back lanes they came out onto the dual carriageway of the main A34. Taylor's eyes were as much on the rear-view as they were on the road ahead. He took a quick glance at Kim. 'We'll go back to my place. Hopefully we can freshen up a bit and I'll ring Geoff.'

Kim flicked down the sun visor and inspected her face in the vanity mirror. 'God.' She rubbed at an oily grime smear that was staying put on her forehead despite her persistence. 'I need a shower.'

'That's okay,' Taylor said. 'But I'll have to squeeze this car into my little garage. I don't want anyone knowing where we are until we've decided what to do… ' His voice tailed off as his attention fixed onto a car approaching on the other carriageway.

The old white Ford Granada contained both a driver and a passenger. 'There he is,' Taylor said with a good deal of urgency in his voice. He was nodding at the other car. '…It's Farmer!' He shuffled down in his seat as he said the words and managed a sly stare. The two cars came alongside each other with just two lanes and the central reservation separating them.

Kim looked back through the centre of the headrest, watching the car disappear away from them. 'Did he see us?'

'Not a chance. Not in this car. He won't know about it, but he's here for a reason. We're only half a mile from my place. He must somehow know I'm involved. He's looking for my car, to find out where I am. I'll put money on it, but who was that in the car with him and how has he found out about me so quickly?'

Taylor eased off the accelerator and checked the rear-view mirror yet again as he questioned his memory about the indistinct features of Farmer's passenger. 'Billy No Mates.'

Kim half-laughed. 'What?'

'William Keith Daniels,' Taylor said. 'Better known as Billy No Mates. More form than all the Grand National runners put together, and a snout of Farmer's. He's the doorman at Granville's, the one who didn't want to help the police with their enquiries. So that's how he's found out, and he's just been snooping up at my place.'

Taylor turned off the main road and carried on for another half mile to the small hamlet of Yarnstall.

A solitary oak tree, a red telephone box and a typically English village green indicated their arrival. Taylor swung the car into Pear Lane, a narrow tree lined avenue populated with a handful of fairly upmarket cottages. It was clear that at this still early hour, none of the residents had yet begun their day.

He drove for a few yards at a crawl and then manoeuvred into the driveway of a decent-sized cottage. A hand painted black and white name sign fastened to the aged red bricks of the building spelled its name: *Old Mill Cottage.*

Considering there had been no rehearsal, the feat of quickly and covertly installing the Carlton into Taylor's small garage was an achievement in itself. They slipped into the cottage through the door leading directly from the garage into the kitchen.

Kim offered no objection to Taylor's suggestion that she showered whilst he fixed some breakfast and made his telephone call to Geoff Deakin.

'Take your time,' he said. 'It'll be quite a conversation.'

At this same moment Farmer silently coasted his car past a line of semi-detached houses half a mile from Little Stoneleigh. Most of the residences were reasonably tidy and one or two had a garage and a small patch of lawn. He looked through the driver's window, paying particular attention to the house with a partially demolished garage and an overgrown lawn. The driveway was occupied by Doug Taylor's Vauxhall Cavalier. Farmer gave his passenger a conspiratorial wink before driving off.

Geoff Deakin frowned as he watched the car glide quietly past his house. The half inch of pinched back curtain had been sufficient, he knew Farmer's car well enough. Worry over Taylor's failure to ring had caused a poor night's sleep and now this peculiar event added to the mystery. 'What the Devil is going on?' he muttered to himself.

The ringing telephone interrupted his puzzlement.

Twenty minutes later Deakin replaced the handset and sat down on the sofa shaking his head.

Kim was naked, the stinging hot water of Taylor's shower almost penetrating the pores of her skin as she worked and worked at cleansing her body and mind of the recent events. Sweat, grime, vomit and blood were physically and mentally washed out of existence. She indulged herself as if showering for the first time in her life.

The stress, the mental torture, the fear, the exhilaration and the adrenalin had all played their part. She soaked and soaped; she massaged her sore wrist. She shampooed and stood with her forehead against the tiles as the hot water flowed over her, tingling her scalp and gushing off her chin and breasts. She cried a little.

After drip-drying inside the shower for a while, she finished the job with a towel before shuffling into the vast white bathrobe left on the bed.

Her entrance into the kitchen briefly relieved the stress of the past hours, fingertips just visible from rolled sleeves, hem brushing floor tiles, pink towel, turban-style around her head.

Taylor turned from the cooker with sleeves rolled. He grinned and then gestured down to the frugal breakfast of toast and cereal. 'Tea or coffee?'

Kim pulled up a chair. 'Tea please,' she managed a smile.

He seated himself opposite and poured the drinks.

'Geoff's been up most of the night,' Taylor explained. 'He was anxious when I didn't ring back after he'd paged me. He knew something was wrong. He's finding all this very hard to believe.'

Taylor described Deakin's sighting of the Superintendent's car passing his house. 'Farmer is already implicated in Jacob Bunn's murder and God knows what other crimes. I guess he thinks I'm at Geoff's house with my car being outside. It looks like he has no way of contacting the others who were at the brewery. Daniels must have told him what happened at the club, so he'll be wondering who you are.'

Kim shrugged. 'I'm beginning to wonder myself, but it's not going to take him long to find out.'

Taylor quickly showered and shaved. His mind raced as he went over the events of the last hours and tried to put things into context and maybe even work out what might happen next.

He went back down. Kim had fathomed out his antique washing machine and tumble-dryer and was ironing yesterday's cheesecloth blouse. He came up behind her and put his arms around her waist.

'Careful, you'll make me singe this.'

She put the iron down and turned into his arms pulling him tightly to herself.

The phone rang. Taylor counted the rings before it went silent again.

'Seven times, that's Geoff.'

The phone rang again.

'Hi, Geoff.'

'You must get out of there,' Deakin's voice commanded. 'That bastard Farmer's trying to stitch you up. I'm at the nick now. I came straight in after you phoned, but Farmer was already here. He's barred me from using the telephone, so I've sneaked into the Chief Inspector's office while there was no one watching.'

'What do you mean *stitch me up*?' Taylor's voice emphasised his astonishment.

'That nark of his, Daniels, the doorman, he's been into the nick and reported that he saw you in Granville's last night with a woman. He's said you were pissed and that the woman went off with another bloke. Daniels has said he knows the man and that he's something to do with the old brewery. He says that you chased after them shouting that you were going to kill the guy.'

Deakin's voice now took on a hushed tone. 'Farmer's taken charge of the inquiry. He says he knows you stayed at my house last night and he's threatened me with suspension. He's sent a patrol up to the brewery to make sure that the man is okay. He's getting a team together to go and search my house for you. He's talking about having you charged with threats to murder.'

Taylor glared at the phone in disbelief. 'For Christ's sake, he's manipulating the whole damn circumstances. He's sending the uniforms up there knowing they're going to find that man's body. He's going to get us arrested for murder. The place is smothered in our prints, including the crane and all the stuff that killed Price.'

'Exactly,' Deakin whispered. 'I've given you a bit of breathing space. I've told him you did stay at my house last night and he thinks you're still there, but you must get ou… '

'What the hell are you doing Deakin?' It was another voice in the background. The phone went dead.

Taylor snatched his passport from the table. 'Have you ever been to Belgium?'

TWENTY TWO

LITTLE STONELEIGH CID office was a busier bustle than was usual for a week day morning. Several strangers were present, including a sharply-suited, hatchet-faced chief inspector from headquarters. He stood, arms folded, gazing distrustfully from the doorway leading into Doug Taylor's office. Behind him two suited minions bagged up the contents of Taylor's drawers and desk.

Cheddar gave the Chief Inspector a wary gaze as he picked up the ringing telephone from his desk. 'CID, DC Cheeseman speaking.'

'Hello, mate,' came the reply, 'DC Timson, Exeter, here. I've been trying all morning to get hold of DI Taylor, Geoff Deakin or our WPC, but I'm getting nowhere at all. I've tried the murder incident room and your headquarters, but they bat me off. Won't tell me sod all. Can you tell me what's going on, or get one of them to ring me, or DS Lacey?'

Cheddar held the receiver tightly against his ear and made a point of poking a finger against the wall-hanging calendar beside him. He felt the Chief Inspector's eyes boring into him, saw them narrow, watched the head tilt as the hearing strained to listen to the conversation.

'No, Sarge,' Cheddar said loudly into the telephone as he studied the calendar. 'No dates to avoid in July or August, I'm not going on holiday, so any date will be okay for that court case.'

The Chief Inspector relaxed his stance and chose a different target.

There was a puzzled silence from Timson.

Cheddar discreetly cupped his hand over his mouth and set his eyes on the Chief Inspector.

'Right,' he said, his tone now a low whisper. 'I haven't told you this… Something went on last night involving your policewoman and DI Taylor. They were in a local nightclub. The doorman's been into the nick early this morning. He's made an official complaint… a statement, all sorts of allegations. He's said that DI Taylor and the policewoman were both pissed and that she ran out of the club after another bloke she'd taken a shine to.'

Cheddar paused mid-sentence to check the status of the Chief Inspector. 'It gets worse. The doorman has said that the DI came out of the club after her like a madman, pushing his way through. He says he tried to calm Mr Taylor down, but ended up on his back in a shop doorway with Doug Taylor trying to strangle him in front of a load of witnesses.'

'Christ,' was all that Timson could manage as Cheddar's hushed voice went on to complete the story.

'The doorman says that Inspector Taylor ran up the road after the man, threatening to kill him. We've searched the old brewery on the outskirts of the town and found a body, crushed to death by a great pile of scrap iron. The dead man, or what's left of him, seems to be the same one that the policewoman went off with.'

After a long pause Timson reacted… 'Christ Almighty.'

Cheddar's voice became a little more relaxed as the Chief Inspector retreated into Taylor's office. 'Geoff Deakin has been suspended from duty and Superintendent Farmer has forbidden him from speaking to anyone. Thing is mate, I've known Doug Taylor a long time and I don't get this story. The Super really has it in for him.'

'So what's happened to WPC Harding and the Inspector, where are they now?'

'No one knows… they've vanished. We've found a pair of red high heels near to the body. If they belong to your policewoman then there have to be worries for her safety. Farmer ordered a search of Geoff Deakin's house because DI Taylor's car was found parked there. Now there's a team going through the DI's house as well.'

Down on the south-east coast, as the time approached twenty

minutes past ten the 6,700 ton Prins Albert ferry readied to leave the Port of Dover. Loading was well underway and the destination, Ostend, would involve a six hour passage across the North Sea.

An old model, blue Mercedes saloon rumbled across the metal linkspan from the dockside and through the bow doors to join the other 300 vehicles on the car deck. Following the instructions of an arm waving, overalled crew member the driver trundled the car into an inch perfect position. He clicked the handbrake up against its ratchet to the highest position and silenced the motor.

With a small holdall gripped in his left hand he confidently made his way with the other passengers up the metal steps to the decks above. He'd booked a cabin. A busy time lay ahead and he needed a shower, a rest and a meal.

The smell of diesel hung heavily in the air as the colossal engines churned out a boiling wash from the stern and got the vessel under way.

On the northbound carriageway of the M5 traffic was light. But with 87,000 miles on the clock, Lacey and Timson's Bedford van, the runt of the Exeter CID vehicle pool, was out of its depth. The engine screamed for mercy as Timson kept his foot jammed to the boards in an effort to make progress.

Lacey's white knuckled left hand kept a tight grip on the overhead handle. 'The shit's flying so thick Reg,' he shouted above the rattling. 'We're going to need a golfing umbrella if it's get any worse'.

Timson's eyes were fixed on the road ahead. 'I'm worried. What could have happened to that pair? Kim's dad's been on to the Chief Constable, the poor chap's worried sick. It's as if they've been beamed up like on Star Trek.' He turned to Lacey. 'Our flash Vauxhall has disappeared and so that's now on PNC as stolen. It was only on loan to us, the dealership is going spare.'

The blast of a car horn riveted Timson back into concentration.

Further north and on the M1 the traffic situation was the opposite. The southbound carriageway was busy with both London bound traffic and holidaymakers en route to the coast. The Vauxhall Carlton ate up yet another mile of the outside lane as Kim pushed the car to its limit whenever possible.

She shot Taylor a weary glance. 'I'm tired. It's going to get dangerous carrying on much longer.'

'Yes, I don't know how you've carried on so long. We'll need the time of the next ferry to Ostend and I don't feel safe in this car; it's probably already listed as stolen.'

Kim stared straight ahead, eyes unnaturally wide, fighting off tiredness. 'If Farmer's been on to Pete Lacey or Reg Timson, or even read the log kept at the Cannock Chase murder scene, he'll know the colour, model and registration number by now.'

'You're in front of me,' Taylor agreed. 'I'd overlooked the murder scene log. We'll have to lose this car and get another. I need to hide it where it won't be easily found.' He frowned. 'God, I'm even thinking like a criminal now.' A shake of the head preceded more desperado thoughts. 'The first thing I'd do as a copper, if I found it, would be to check all the nearby car hire firms.' He gave Kim a hard stare. 'Do you want to go on with this? I'm getting you deeper and deeper involved and…'

'Enough,' she cut him off. 'I'm up for it if you are, but right now I'm shattered and we need to ditch this car... ' The sentence tailed off as a blue, half-mile notice board came up on the left:

JUNCTION 11 – LUTON CENTRAL – DUNSTABLE.

It was the smaller sign: *Travel Lodge,* which attracted Kim's attention. She pressed down on the indicator, drifted into the nearside lane and took the exit. The slip road met a roundabout where she branched off onto Dunstable Road. After two hundred yards she pulled into Halfway Avenue at the side of the Travel Lodge building.

Taylor looked over at the street nameplate spotting the irony. 'I wish we were halfway to solving this. Thing is I don't think we've even started.' He rubbed his tired eyes. 'Fix a room here and see if you can find out the ferry times. Try and get some rest. I'll off-load this car and see if I can find us another from somewhere. You said your passport's in your maiden name?'

'Yes, Kimberly Fry.'

'That could be handy, book the room in that name so I'll know how to find you… okay?'

Kim unfastened her seat belt and her weary smile gave approval to the plan. 'Hopefully see you later.'

She stretched over to the rear seat and took hold of the handles of her bag, making to haul it through. She felt Taylor's breath, warm against her cheek.

Half-turning her head she loosed her grip on the bag as he pulled her tightly to him in a long passionate kiss.

TWENTY THREE

IN LITTLE STONELEIGH Police Station a meeting was taking place. Detective Chief Superintendent Ray Burrington had made the ten mile trip from his own office at Police Headquarters on the other side of Stafford. He needed to find out exactly what had taken place, but found himself slowly shaking his head at Farmer's summary.

Farmer instantly decoded Burrington's disbelief. 'I must admit to being taken aback myself,' he said from across the other side of his desk. 'But Taylor's always been a wild card and he has a reputation for violence… remember that incident in the cells, the prisoner with the broken nose?'

'I can't agree with that, Malcolm,' Burrington interrupted. 'That prisoner attacked Taylor with a knife because your men hadn't searched him properly. I'd have broken his nose.'

Farmer puffed out his cheeks and gave a slow head shake. 'I always knew he was a bad lot Raymond, and now this dreadful business has finally proved me right. If Taylor had done nothing wrong he would have been in here this morning with an explanation. He wouldn't be on the run with a dozen witnesses having seen him beating up Granville's doorman and then chasing after a man who is now dead.'

Farmer leaned across the desk offering his open pack of cheroots. Burrington declined the offer and moved his chair a little further back from the desk in readiness for the stinking aroma that he knew would follow.

Farmer's neck temporarily separated from his double chins as he threw his head backwards and blew a dense column of smoke towards the ceiling.

'The evidence is all coming together on this. Taylor's prints are all over the place at the brewery, even on the machinery that killed Charlie Price.' He wafted with a hand as he continued. 'And that young tart of a policewoman. Her dabs are everywhere as well. Looks like she's been wandering about as though she owns the place.'

Burrington kept a poker face. He gave no clues to Farmer of his thoughts on the matter. He had always trusted Doug Taylor. Saw something of himself in the young detective from when he first joined the department. But as much as he despised Farmer he could not deny the evidence, or the facts.

He got to his feet; he'd had enough of Farmer for one day. He felt sick at the thought that he could have been so wrong about Taylor. The stinking cheroot smoke had also now become too much to bear. He turned on his heel and slammed Farmer's office door shut.

Farmer squashed the cheroot down into the ashtray, pleased that it had encouraged Burrington's departure. He needed to make a phone call, one that required privacy, secrecy even! He waited by his office window until he saw the Chief Superintendent's four by four leave the police station car park.

'Right,' he smugly purred, pulling off his uniform jacket and slinging it over the chair back. He then took an old cream raincoat from his coat stand. It was not raincoat weather, but the coat would serve its purpose to cover the remainder of his uniform.

He was soon behind the wheel of the Granada on a two mile drive. His chosen destination was nowhere special, just an ordinary red telephone kiosk. The location though, in a remote layby, shielded by a high hedgerow to hide his car, made it worth the extra drive. It was from here that he made most of his clandestine calls and arranged his dodgy deals. He didn't need prying eyes.

He allowed himself a smile at the sight of the empty phone box and pulled the Granada to a halt.

The Tupperware box on the passenger seat brimmed over with ten pence pieces. Farmer always kept a ready supply of coins to fund these calls. He'd been pilfering from the one-armed bandit in the police social club for years. It was another of his little perks. No one knew about his duplicate key for the machine and if anyone were to consider that the takings were suspiciously below par he'd be the first to be informed!

He climbed from the car, squeezed into the kiosk and then carefully arranged coins, notepad and biro onto the tiny shelf before starting to dial.

Eighteen hundred miles south west of the United Kingdom, in San Andres on the island of Santa Cruz de Tenerife two people waited in the 34 degree heat next to a Spanish telephone kiosk.

Sadie Sweeney stared up at the cloudless blue sky through Ray-Ban sunglasses. Her face still determinedly clung to the last vestiges of those stunning, pouting features that used to be.

Her forty-five years, the brandy, the cigarettes and too much sun had steadily eaten into that natural beauty.

She had passed those dark gypsy features on to her son. People often used to stop her as she pushed the pram through Little Stoneleigh town centre. They would smile down and poke a wagging finger at the chuckling little mite with the gorgeous round brown eyes. Such well-meaning behaviour stopped after a few years and no one would dare to poke a wagging finger at David Sweeney now.

She went over the events, not just the recent happenings, but everything that had so irreversibly turned her life around. Who was she kidding? *Turned it upside down*, that would be closer. She checked her watch and looked up at the man beside her.

Steven Gorton's shadow successfully provided shade from the sun for Sadie. His six feet, six inch frame was planted firmly on the pavement, arms folded and with a natural look of aggression permanently welded to his face.

She sighed yet another exaggerated sigh of impatience and followed up with a hacking smoker's cough. The anger in her eyes easily seen even through the sunglasses.

'The fat bastard's late. Is this the right phone box, Steve?'

'Yes, Mrs Sweeney, he always rings me on this one. It usually works out unless the phone's out of order, but I've checked the dialling tone and it…'

The payphone's shrill ringing interrupted Gorton. Sadie made a grab for the handset, but Gorton's hand stopped her. He gently but firmly pressed down onto hers, his voice calm.

'He'll hang up if anyone else answers, Mrs Sweeney, even you.'

She gritted her teeth with exasperation as she accepted the advice.

Gorton picked up the receiver: 'Yes,' his abrupt comment.

He listened to Farmer giving some unnecessary introduction in an exaggerated attempt at friendliness. Then he cut in – venomous contempt in his voice: 'Shuttt…uppp, Farmer.' He lengthened the two words, delivering them in a slow, intimidating tone. He'd never met Farmer in person, but the numerous clandestine telephone calls between the two gave him an insight into this twisted, pathetic character. Other discussions and overheard talk helped Gorton form a mind's eye picture of the corrupt conniving police officer. It was, however, a fact that Gorton was also a twisted character, very twisted.

'Give me the facts, Farmer. No police bullshit. No lies. No excuses. You know what will happen if you try to fuck with me.'

Farmer pumped more coins into the phone box, his hand trembling at the sound of the thug's voice. He knew all about Steven Jeremy Gorton, and had good reason to be apprehensive. The surreptitious and illegal application Farmer made to New Scotland Yard for the man's criminal record resulted in the return of a thick and detailed file. The reading of this satisfied his interest in the foul mouthed thug who was quick to give out orders. It also struck the fear of God into him.

Farmer covered his tracks well by making the application for Gorton's file in someone else's name. PC Jack Duffield had been employed as the Local Intelligence Officer at Little Stoneleigh nick for several years. His job included keeping tabs on local villains and building files for visiting crooks. Criminal record applications to Scotland Yard were done by Duffield on a regular basis and would never arouse suspicion. Farmer's timing of the deception was particularly fortuitous as it aligned perfectly with the elderly constable's retirement. No one would ever know.

The mugshot and description of the giant ex-boxer from the Moss Side estate of Manchester were disturbing on their own. The violent crimes listed inside the file raised Farmer's heartrate even more. The two murders he had been acquitted of because of the excellent defence afforded through the offices of one Jacob Bunn added even more foreboding.

Any initial smugness Farmer held dissolved into horror after he read of the torture Gorton was known to have inflicted on his victims. The sickening mutilation done with an electric carving knife and the fingers chopped off with a wood chisel.

Farmer took a nervous swallow before continuing the conversation. 'I'm just a small cog in this Steve,' he eventually managed. 'You know I wouldn't try to pull any dirty tricks on Sadie. All this has me as confused as you.'

keywords written on his notepad were scanned by Farmer as he bluffed his way onwards. The story must sound convincing. There could be no mistakes.

'I was stunned… ' he spluttered. 'When I heard David had broken out and taken Bunn hostage. And then dumping his body on my patch as well. He must have been keeping him up at the brewery. I never even thought about that and you know I wouldn't have tried to get in touch with him. I mean… you know how he feels about me. I figured he'd gone straight out of the country. I even wondered if Jacob arranged it all, but when Jacob's body was identified… well I didn't know what to think.'

A bead of sweat dripped from Farmer's forehead and splashed down onto the notepad.

'Okay, Farmer,' Gorton eased the handset away from his ear to allow Sadie a chance at hearing the conversation. 'So, what happened to Charlie, what the hell happened there?'

Farmer shuddered as he recalled the reality of the story: *shouting out for Price at the brewery entrance, and then finding his body*. It was not a version he would tell Gorton.

He gave his concocted account: 'I came on duty at the nick early… about eight. A report had come in from the doorman at the jazz club in the town. He'd called in at the police station on his way home. They'd had a late night and he has to lock up.'

Sadie leaned forwards, screeching at the phone 'You're bullshitting now, Farmer.'

'No, no, Sadie, he was still in the nick when I came in. The sergeant had made a big thing about it… statements and everything because the doorman had made an allegation against my Detective Inspector… Doug Taylor. He'd said Taylor assaulted him and then threatened to kill Price. It was over a policewoman the Inspector was with. Price muscled in and she'd gone off with him.'

'I knew that pervert would let us down,' Sadie hissed.

Farmer's eyes widened. He felt a little more comfortable. He felt as though his story was being believed.

'Just a minute, Farmer,' Gorton interrupted. 'Who's this bouncer and how much does he know about our operation?'

'Nothing, absolutely nothing. He's a doorman at Granville's Club, but he seemed to know Price. He said he'd met him a few times and knew about his connection to the old brewery development. So I realised it was Charlie.'

Sadie heard Farmer's explanation. 'The bloody fool.'

Farmer pumped more coins into the phone and carried on with his story. 'The sergeant sent a patrol up to the brewery, and there was Price crushed to a pulp under a mountain of scrap iron and paving slabs.'

Gorton fixed Sadie with a corner of the eye frown as he fired questions at Farmer. He was emphasising his mistrust of the man.

'Any sign of anyone else? Did you go up there yourself?'

'Oh, yes, eventually,' Farmer replied, his confidence growing. 'I took charge of the operation… you know, senior officer.'

'Cut the bullshit, Farmer, and stick to the facts,' Gorton interrupted.

There was a slight tremor to Farmer's voice. He coughed in an attempt to cover it. 'I got the fingerprint men on the job. There were dabs everywhere, which I can tell you now in the main belong to Taylor and the woman he was with. She's a policewoman from Exeter, name of Harding; she's working on the case down there.'

Gorton went silent as he took in the new information. 'No sign of David then, Farmer?'

'No, nothing, nothing at all.'

'Ask about the money,' Sadie mouthed to Gorton.

'Any money lying about, Farmer? David ordered Price to get all remaining cash together to pay for the latest transaction.'

'Nothing!' Farmer's eyebrows were now at their highest. 'Not a penny!'

'Farmer… ' Gorton's voice sounded dangerous. 'Six and a half million quid has gone missing somewhere. There's another hundred grand in foreign currency that David kept at the brewery for trips abroad, so who the fuck's got it all?'

'I-I-I don't know Steve, honest.' Farmer's voice trembled with fear. 'No sign of any money there at all.'

'What about motors and paperwork, anything to trace back to the operation?' Gorton quizzed.

'No paperwork at all. Just an Escort van in a garage at the back, but no problems with that. It was nicked from down south… on false plates. I guess Price pinched it to move the cash about. His prints were all over it… oh, and Taylor's.'

'Taylor's!' Gorton's elongated pronunciation augmented his bewilderment. 'Okay, Farmer, I'll tell you once. If there turns out to be one small thing that makes me think you've anything to do with this, I will start with your balls.' He ended the call.

Farmer's hand trembled as he replaced the receiver and exited the phone box. Rivulets of sweat streamed down his crimson cheeks.

Fumbling for keys he made for the car door but then, with a change of heart, lifted the boot lid and surveyed the five blue plastic boxes.

TWENTY FOUR

LUTON AIRPORT was a ten minute drive from the Travel Lodge and Taylor needed to get rid of the Carlton. It now seemed certain that every police force in the country would be on the lookout for it.

He pulled into the long-term parking zone and nosed the car into a bay in the middle of a row of other cars. He was quickly out from behind the wheel and rummaging in the boot. They were going to need cash and some quick decisions had to be made. He separated one of the cling-film wrapped blocks containing a £50,000 lump of Farmer's £250,000 pay-out and ripped it open. Taylor's head shaking accompanied a despairing sigh. He knew he shouldn't be doing any of this as there could be incriminating finger prints inside the plastic wrapper, but now his were all over it too. The head shaking gave way to a shrug of the shoulders as he separated the cash into two equal looking lumps. He stuffed one into his hastily packed suitcase along with his belongings and the other into a plastic Tesco bag.

The indicator lights flashed as he pressed the remote key and headed towards the taxi rank, shopping bag in one hand and suitcase in tow with the other. His appearance and body-language exhibited nothing more remarkable than a standard holiday-maker.

The taxi driver was a pleasant talkative sort whose eyes frequently settled on the rear-view mirror to make contact with his passenger.

Taylor placed the Tesco bag on his lap to keep its cash contents hidden. A sighting of this could make the driver more than a little suspicious.

Luton town centre was just two miles from the airport and Taylor held some hope that the Carlton might remain undiscovered for many days. His thinking being: *even if the police did find it they would conclude that a flight abroad had been taken.*

He leaned forward to speak to the driver when it became apparent that they were in the heart of Luton. 'Anywhere around here will be fine… oh, where's the post office?'

'Post Office mate, is second street on the left, can't miss it,' chirped the driver as he pulled into the side of the road and calculated the fare.

Taylor's business at the Post Office took less than ten minutes.

His next task, the purchase of a replacement car, would normally have demanded a great deal of thought, time, research and financial consideration. The pressing urgency of the situation, the large wad of banknotes and the enthusiasm of the car dealer to acquire some of that tax free, ready cash negated the usual restraints.

Just one and a half hours had passed when Taylor steered the BMW 325i Sport off the motorway and parked in a space near the Travel Lodge entrance.

'Any problems?' Kim asked as she opened the hotel room door.

'No.' He kicked off his shoes and dropped down into a chair. 'I'm all in.'

She waved a piece of paper with some handwriting on it. 'The next sailing from Dover to Ostend is half past four. We have to be there a minimum of half an hour before.'

He offered a sleepy face as Kim gave more instructions.

'So, you've time to get a shower and freshen up.'

'Okay, ma'am, all understood,' Taylor playfully threw up a salute as he made for the bathroom.

The sound of shower water striking tiles and a haze of steam soon filtered into the bedroom through the half-open door.

Kim eyed the set of keys Taylor left on the window ledge. She raised her voice above the shower noise. 'You managed to get another car then?'

'A pretty punchy BMW,' he shouted back as he soaped his hair. 'Almost new and low mileage… should be okay.'

She leaned with her back against the outside of the bathroom wall, arms folded. 'I don't want to ask, but how have we paid for it?'

The shower stopped abruptly. Taylor reappeared, white towel around waist, dark wet hair flattened against head. Droplets of water glistened on his face and streamed down his hair-matted chest. The worried look he wore matched one from several hours earlier when he'd pointed out the deeper trouble they were getting into. 'I couldn't hire one… too much paperwork required. Proof of identity and all that. They'd be on to us in no time. I've bought one… paid cash, used Farmer's money.'

He stared straight into her eyes, half-expecting her to hit him.

'Well, needs must' she said. 'I knew you'd have to anyway and if we ever get to the bottom of this and survive, what's a few thousand quid? We don't know who we can trust, we must keep anonymous. Oh, and I'm in need of some clothes, I'm sick of this little outfit.'

Taylor shrugged. 'I guess promotion's on hold for a while.'

She looked up at him, her smile broadening, but still hardened with a hint of worry. She put her arms around his shoulders and pulled him towards her, his wet chest soaking through the now familiar cheesecloth blouse. They fell back onto the bed and made love.

TWENTY FIVE

GEOFF DEAKIN'S garden looked a mess. This was probably the first time he'd stood at the window and not felt guilty about that overgrown lawn and tatty garage. The fact was, he never even noticed on this occasion. He sank back onto the sofa surveying the ceiling, going over the events in his mind.

Not so long ago he'd been involved in a fascinating and serious investigation, which was finally showing some promise. Things had changed swiftly though, and now he found himself suspended from duty on suspicion of assisting his boss, a fugitive, wanted for questioning in a murder case!

He jerked from his thoughts as the telephone started to ring. His hand hovered and he stared vacantly for a few seconds unsure whether to answer or not. He snatched it up.

'Yes'.

'Geoff… Pete Lacey here, can you talk?'

'I can, Pete,' Deakin replied. There was a guarded tone to his voice. 'There's no one here now. They've all gone, but I'm not supposed to, I've been warned by Superintendent Farmer to speak to no one.'

'How do you feel about that Geoff?' Lacey's voice was caring, but he gave Deakin no time to answer. 'We're worried about Kim. Her dad's fretting and the whole thing stinks. It sounds like Farmer has it in for your DI. We need your help, Geoff, and maybe it's a bit of a nerve, but we're already in town.'

It took Timson ten minutes to find Deakin's suggested rendezvous point. He pulled the van over against the kerb. 'Do you think this is it?' He leaned forward in the driving seat checking out the surroundings.

'Must be,' Lacey said. 'Whitgreave Road, an alleyway by a post box… that's what he said. I'll get in the back.' He squeezed himself into the tiny rear seat as a trotting figure appeared.

Deakin's furtive over-the-shoulder glance came as he clocked the van. He slowed to a walking pace, still panting and with an expression which exposed his anxiety.

Timson stretched across to spring the passenger door open. The wheels were turning even before Deakin's fumbling fingers secured his seat belt. Lacey's raised voice was barely audible from the rear of the rattling van. 'Okay Geoff?'

'Think so, Pete, think so. I'm not too sure if they've managed to set a tail up on me yet, and if they have I think I've lost them. We need to get away from here. Somewhere we can have a quiet chat.'

Deakin gave directions over the next fifteen minutes along country roads and through a couple of small hamlets until they came to the village of Woolseaves. 'Pull over here,' he said, pointing to the Black Dog pub. 'Should be okay, looks pretty empty.'

Lacey groaned as he extracted himself from the back of the van onto the pub car park. He straightened up, pushing his fist into the small of his back.

'Wonder where that Carlton is right now,' he muttered as they entered the pub by a side door.

An array of polished beer pumps adorned the bar. A tiny TV mumbled on low volume from its perch on a wall bracket. An elderly couple sat chatting with travel brochures spread before them.

Lacey took a look at the blackboard which listed: *Specials of the day*.

'Will we still get any food in here, Geoff? We're both starving.'

Deakin gave a shrug. 'Bit late now Pete, but not for me. This whole damned thing has me worried sick. I could manage a pint though.'

The drinks soon arrived. Lacey winked at Deakin and slid a pint of bitter over to him. Timson managed nothing more than a disapproving grimace at his own glass of lemonade.

'The one benefit to come out of Reg doing the driving,' Lacey said as he held his beer up to the light and examined the clarity.

The humour did not encourage the pensive Deakin.

'Cheer up, Geoff,' Timson said. 'The way to find out what this is all about is for the three of us to put all our cards on the table. We need to pit our wits against the two real villains in this: Sweeney and Farmer.'

Deakin made a mournful face at the comment. 'Yes, Farmer, what a bastard.'

Lacey unfolded the dossier of papers from his briefcase. 'What I can't get out of my head is why you have such a flimsy file on such a big time crook. I know he hasn't lived on your patch for years, but it's where all his roots and original contacts are.' He was holding the same orange folder that he'd been given by Taylor the day before. 'As for this… well, it's bloody useless.'

'My feelings too,' Deakin agreed. 'The more I think about it the more suspicious I get. Up until about twelve months ago our intelligence officer was PC Jack Duffield. He'd been a copper in and around Little Stoneleigh all his thirty-one years in the job. He did that job for the last seven years of his service and he knew everybody. His records were immaculate. He had a file on pretty well everything and everybody.'

The landlord arrived at the table with a generous sized plate of sandwiches and, as a bonus, a plate of chips.

Timson sprinkled salt and vinegar onto the chips. 'So, what happened to PC Duffield?'

'He retired,' Deakin explained. 'I often see him at the police social club. He lives in Whynerston, nice little village not far away.'

Lacey selected a couple of the sandwiches and a handful of chips from the plate. 'So, what's Jack Duffield like, is he likely to help us?'

'Oh, yes,' Deakin now managed to grin. 'Jack's a smashing guy and like most of us absolutely detests Farmer.'

Lacey nodded as Deakin delivered his opinion. He pulled a notepad from his jacket pocket. 'What do you know about a doorman at a nightclub in Little Stoneleigh?'

Deakin stopped Lacey before he could go any further. 'It was Billy Daniels. He's a bouncer at Granville's; Doug phoned me. I tipped him off about what Farmer was up to. When I arrived at the nick I found out Daniels had been in and made a statement… a complete pack of lies.'

Lacey penned the name *Billy Daniels* onto his notepad as Deakin continued.

'I can't believe this is happening. Granville's is a great club, but for some reason they employ Daniels. He's a nark for Farmer.'

Deakin then went on to describe his early morning sighting of Farmer and Daniels outside his house. He followed up with Taylor's explanation about the incident at the club and what took place at the brewery.

Lacey shook his head, incredulous at the speed such an intricate web of deceit had been crafted. 'Daniels must have been paid by Farmer to make that statement. What you've told us about him being with Farmer this morning confirms it. How about we look Jack Duffield up, if you think he'll help us out?'

Deakin picked at a few chips, now feeling a little more at ease in friendly company. 'Nothing to lose, absolutely nothing.'

TWENTY SIX

WHYNERSTON, five miles west of Little Stoneleigh, another of Staffordshire's tiny villages – a pub, general store, school, church and post office. It seemed a nice place to live with one small housing estate of pleasant bungalows nestling against a cricket pitch.

Following Deakin's directions Timson slowed the van to a halt outside the driveway of 36 Sherbert Close, a smart detached bungalow with a well-tended garden. A Ford Escort stood in front of a garage on a driveway of recently brushed paving slabs.

Lacey twisted in his seat to face Deakin as Timson manoeuvred up to the Escort. 'Are you sure he won't mind us parking in his drive, Geoff?'

'No, not when he sees it's me.'

Deakin had hardly finished the sentence when the glass panelled front door opened. A tall heavily-built man stepped out onto the drive. A good head of neatly groomed silver grey hair sat atop a creased, but still handsome, face. The eyes gave away the age as late fifties and sat beneath unusually thick black eyebrows which were at odds with the silver hair.

The man frowned. 'Can I help you?' A commanding tone to his voice implied: *What the hell do you think you're doing parking on my drive?*

Timson immediately decoded the man's identity from age, build and demeanour, and handed over his Police ID card. He gestured to the back of the van. 'Mr Duffield, we have a friend of yours with us, thought you might be able to help us out with something.'

Duffield gave a cautious half-smile as he read the card. 'Long way from home, Devon and Cornwall Police.' His face changed to a broad grin as Deakin awkwardly extricated himself from the van. 'Geoff, what the devil…? Right, you'd better all come on in.'

Duffield led the trio through into his lounge and seated them low down on sofa and armchairs around a coffee table.

With the introductions out of the way, the next half an hour was spent on filling Duffield in with all that had taken place.

Mrs Duffield produced tea and biscuits, and disappeared back into the kitchen as her husband sat back in his chair, arms folded, listening without interruption.

Fifteen minutes passed before Duffield exhaled loudly and blew his cheeks out into the shape of two small balloons. 'What a story. I'd heard bits about it and seen things in the press, but my God.' He leaned forwards in his chair, made a gleeful face and clapped his hands together with a loud smack. He then rubbed them briskly for several seconds. 'Right, where shall I begin?'

Lacey grinned at Duffield's eager response. 'Well this doorman… what can you add about him?'

'Our good friend William Keith Daniels,' Duffield said. 'Billy No Mates, AKA the Human Punch bag.'

Timson made a puzzled face at the nickname. 'How so?'

'Because,' he explained, 'he'd had so many thrashings from other crooks he'd dropped in the cart. He was constantly getting beaten up.'

Duffield was clearly enjoying tapping into those memory banks that had lain dormant for over twelve months. He leaned back in his chair and patted a finger against the side of his nose. 'He was Farmer's snout and continually grassing on people. He's a nasty piece of work; he'd sell his mother for a fiver. He's got form for everything from assault to burglary. He'll do anything for money. His other nickname on the town as you'll know Geoff, is "Billy No Mates". No one would have anything to do with him… he'd grassed them all up to Farmer over the years.'

Duffield clapped his hands again with another loud smack, more brisk rubbing followed. 'Next question?'

The audience laughed. Lacey took charge. 'Okay, Jack,' he held back his grin 'We wondered if you could tell us any more about Sweeney?'

Duffield tilted his head over to one side. 'I can tell you everything you want to know about Sweeney and I can tell you why that file is so bloody useless. It's because Farmer made it that way.'

Deakin looked mystified. 'What on earth do you mean?'

'I came on duty one morning and found him in my office rooting through everything. He told me that a directive from headquarters had ordered that: "All files over three years old, without any movement on them must be weeded." That's what he called it, "weeded… weeded and destroyed". I had a right barney with him. I told him it was downright ridiculous. Anyway, he ordered me and said that he'd check-up that I'd done it. The only file he'd pulled out was Sweeney's.'

'So, did you weed it, Jack?' Deakin said.

'Oh, yes, of course, well, after all he is the superintendent.'

Timson screwed up his eyes in disgust. 'So, it was destroyed then?'

Duffield winked at Timson. 'Don't be daft, young man, it's in my garage. I always knew these things would be wanted someday. Half a mo, I'll go and fetch it.'

Duffield eased himself from his armchair and left the room. He returned within a few minutes holding a bulky dog-eared blue folder. He placed the file in the centre of the coffee table.

'I knew there was something going on. I mean, why did he pick on Sweeney's file as an example to me? You'd have thought he'd have gone straight in at the files beginning with "A" not "S". If I hadn't caught him in my office I'm pretty damn sure that Sweeney's file would have vanished and no one would have known any different.'

Deakin produced the first genuine smile he'd managed all day. 'How long ago was this, Jack?'

'About eighteen months ago, a matter of a few months or so before I retired.'

Lacey leafed through the file as he spoke. 'So, Jack,' he said, without looking up. 'If you hadn't caught Farmer in the act and this hadn't all gone pear-shaped, no one would have known any different. You'd have retired and it would have been as if all this amazing detail and background never existed.'

'Correct,' Duffield agreed. 'It's a fact that Sweeney wasn't much involved with Little Stoneleigh for many years. But if you read that file you'll see that the occasional snippet of info still filtered through. He was definitely in touch with his stepfather.'

Lacey raised his eyebrows to the maximum level. 'You know who his stepfather is, Jack?'

Duffield nodded. 'I don't need to check the file for that, but it's all in there. He's named Edward Steele. He runs the off-licence on the corner of Mill Street… lives in the flat over the top.'

Lacey took a handful from the folder and spread it out. Dozens of ancient looking lined card forms spilled out covering the table's mahogany top. Capital letters in red typeset, spelled out the subject's name at the top of each card:

DAVID PAUL SWEENEY

Line after meticulously filled-in line of detailed information followed the name. Bold two-fingered typing listed crimes committed by the young Sweeney. Others suggested ones he was suspected of. More text itemised his acquaintances and people who he'd been seen with. New addresses he'd moved to with his mother over the years were recorded along with occasions he'd spent in children's homes and approved schools. Court appearances took up two whole pages.

Mugshot photographs were stapled to some of the cards. Each one showed a slightly older Sweeney, from a young boy, to a youth and then to a young man as the years went by. A column at the side showed the name of the police officer forwarding the information, or dealing with the case. The detail was endless.

Lacey selected one particular card. Smoothed the turned-up corners and started to read out aloud.

'On Saturday, 9th May 1970, Sweeney's mother, Sadie, married at Little Stoneleigh Registry Office to Edward Raymond Steele, a drayman at Johnson's Brewery. There are no convictions recorded against Steele. It is believed the couple intend to set up home together with David at Steele's address: 17 Williams Way, Little Stoneleigh.' Lacey looked up from the card at Duffield. 'The detail in these files is amazing, Jack. A bit different from the first one we saw.'

'Yes, that's how we used to do it. Now take a look at the end column. Look who put the info in.'

Lacey stared at the card and then up at his colleagues before reading out the name. 'SERGEANT FARMER.'

'Correct,' Duffield said. 'Later to become Superintendent Farmer.'

'You'll note,' Duffield added. 'That Farmer's name crops up many times throughout the file. He was forever putting in info on Sweeney and he dealt with him as case officer on the majority of his offences. If you look through any other files for anything Farmer did, you'll be hard pressed to find much. He was, to use a phrase of the wife's: "An idle bastard".'

There was an outbreak of laughter. Mrs Duffield peered around the door wearing a *behave yourself Jack,* expression.

Lacey chuckled as he surveyed the mound of papers which were spread across the table. 'Can we take this lot Jack? It'll give us chance to go through it properly.'

'Be my guest, I shouldn't even have it anyway.' Duffield sat back in his chair. 'I guess you'll be going to see Edward Steele?'

Lacey gave a closed-eyes slow nod indicating the urgency of the impending visit.

'Well, be careful, he's a decent enough bloke; pretty genuine and honest, but he's always been protective of David even when it started to come out that his stepson was a lost cause. He thought the world of Sadie even after they split up, so tread carefully. I would add that he probably hated Farmer more than anyone I know.'

Lacey tidied the papers back into the bulging folder and engaged in an earnest parting handshake with Duffield.

After settling into the van's passenger seat Lacey twisted around.

Deakin was contorted into an inelegant jumble of knees and shoulders, but was now wearing a definite smile. The humorous encounter with Duffield seemed to have lightened his mood.

Lacey still held the folder in his right hand. 'I'm not surprised that Farmer wanted this destroyed. He's played a big part in Sweeney's life all the way through and seems to have had a fixation with him… a vendetta even. Now let's go and find Edward Steele.'

TWENTY SEVEN

KIM QUICKLY approved of the BMW. She'd used the 325i model a lot during her time as a traffic officer and made short work of the journey down to Dover.

Taylor took the chance to doze for most of the time. He'd filled the immaculate silver grey saloon up with petrol before they'd started out. 'What am I doing?' was his whispered comment as he'd settled the bill with yet another loan from Farmer's illicit cash.

Dover Castle presented a dramatic silhouette to the east against a cloudless sky as Kim found a space on a pay and display car park and killed the motor. 'Okay, sleepyhead, we're here.'

She pulled the keys from the ignition and looked at the notepad on Taylor's lap. 'That's quite a shopping list. We'd better get on with it before we run short of time. We're supposed to board a minimum of thirty minutes before sailing remember.'

The shopping trip took almost an hour and a half and resulted in most of the items on Taylor's list being ticked off.

'It's not a holiday, Doug,' Kim said as Taylor crammed some of their purchases into the car's boot. There were several changes of clothes, suitcases, hand luggage, binoculars Polaroid camera, food snacks, a set of cheap two way radios from the Tandy shop, road maps, torches, language guides.

Taylor went quiet. Kim's words reminded him of how far he was stepping out of line.

'This might come in useful,' he eventually said, handing Kim a small glossy booklet.

She read the title: *Berlitz Pocket Guide Bruges and Ghent.*

Taylor took the wheel for the short drive to the ferry terminal's giant concrete car park and pulled in behind one of several lines of waiting vehicles. They left the car and wandered over to the booking office to get the paperwork sorted out. After a thorough double check Taylor slid the wad of paperwork and passports under the glass partition and followed it up with yet more of Farmer's cash.

'Well, Miss Fry,' he said, as he handed Kim's passport back to her. 'Farmer's going to have nothing left at this rate.'

He was not comfortable with his joke which produced nothing more than rolled eyes from Kim. He grabbed a copy of the local evening newspaper from the kiosk next to the booking office. They walked back to the car, eyes drifting up to take in the towering outline of the Reine Astrid ferry which stood moored and waiting. The ship's uniformed staff waved and shouted orders to herd the snaking line of vehicles in through the giant vessel's bow doors from the ever emptying car park.

Taylor stood with his back resting against the BMW turning the pages of the newspaper. There seemed no immediate rush. Kim linked her arm in alongside his. 'Anything in there?' she asked.

Taylor stiffened as he spotted the article. He gave Kim a sideways glance before starting to read out aloud. 'Fears are growing for the safety of Police Constable Kimberly Harding from the Devon and Cornwall Constabulary. WPC Harding has not been seen since Tuesday, 17th June, after the discovery of a man's body in suspicious circumstances at Little Stoneleigh in Staffordshire... ' He stopped short of completing the story.

'What… what is it? What else?' She pulled the newspaper from his grasp, stared open mouthed and then read out the remainder. 'WPC Harding's father, Mr Geoffrey Fry, has been said by a family friend to be beside himself with worry. He has made a plea for his daughter to get in touch with him or for her captors to let him know she is safe.' Kim held a hand to her forehead covering her eyes in an attempt to compose herself. 'Doug, I can't go on with this, I must let him know.'

Taylor pulled her to himself. 'We'll have to do something. Should we go to the police now and try to explain?'

Tears welled up in her eyes. 'No, nobody's going to believe us.

We have to see it through. I just wish I could let him know.'

Taylor became thoughtful for a moment. 'There is a way. I've been thinking for some time now. I know that I can trust Geoff, but it all depends on how well he's being tailed and how much homework has been done. Farmer's bound to have crime squad involved by now. He has a couple of his lackeys who work on the squad, but we might still be in time, come on.'

He took hold of Kim's hand and started quickly towards the row of telephone boxes alongside the car park.

In Little Stoneleigh Timson steered the van from the main thoroughfare into Mill Street, a narrow cobbled route leading to a cluster of small shops and business premises. He bumped the nearside wheels up onto the pavement and switched off the engine.

Deakin provided the directions. He knew the spot well enough, and for that matter the off-licence that stood a few paces from their parking spot. He'd never visited the place though, either as a detective or, for that matter, to buy beer. It always looked such a grubby little hole.

Lacey climbed from the van, looking at the shop and analysing the situation. *Cellarbrations* read the sign, a well thought out gimmicky name. The peeling paint and grimy windows smacked of years of neglect, though. A lack of enthusiasm from those eager early days when the little business first opened seemed apparent. The place certainly lacked a woman's touch.

Deakin was thankful for the discreet parking spot, away from the main road, but remained apprehensive as he clambered out from the back seat. Lacey recognised the signs of angst. 'Okay, Geoff?'

'Yes, should be alright,' Deakin responded with a furtive look in both directions. 'We should be able to get in without being seen.' The group turned to head for the shop door, but the chiming tone of Deakin's pager stopped them in their tracks.

Lacey was familiar with the sound and gave Deakin a worried

look. 'Hope they're not on to us.'

Deakin dug into his pocket, retrieved the pager and squinted at its screen. 'Well, it's definitely Doug,' he said. 'And he's using a code. We used to do it when we went on holiday together with the kids... anagrams and key words, things back to front.'

'So, what's it say?'

Timson craned his neck over Deakin's shoulder to look, as Deakin read aloud.

'FLY BACK TO PEACE 890162.'

Lacey's forehead corrugated into a frown. 'What the hell does that mean?'

In a Dover telephone kiosk on the edge of the ferry terminal car park Kim watched the last few vehicles crossing the ramp into the car decks of the Reine Astrid. The huge concrete space had been crammed just fifteen minutes before, but was now almost empty. She instinctively checked her wristwatch. 'It's not going to work, Doug, it's too late.'

The sudden ringing of the telephone attached itself to Kim's lingering words. Taylor snatched the receiver up. 'Yes.'

'Hi, Doug,' came Deakin's voice. 'It took me a while to unravel it, but we managed. I'm with friends, Pete Lacey and Reg.'

'No time now, Geoff,' Taylor cut in. He turned back to Kim. 'Get the car started, we can't miss this ferry. Tag onto the very end of the queue. I just need a few minutes.'

It was a close call but Taylor caught up with Kim just in time.

'Sorry, sorry,' he shouted an apology towards one of the crew men as he arrived breathless at the BMW's passenger door, his passport in his hand.

Kim followed the arm waving instructions that were given to her and delivered the car into its allotted space. She pulled on the handbrake and turned off the engine. 'Are you sure that phone call is going to be safe?'

Taylor's voice was calm. 'Hope so, anyway it's done now'.

Kim climbed from the car, her expression tearful, her lips set in a tight line. 'What about Dad?'

'Pete's going to go and see him, tell him you're okay and that you'll make contact somehow as soon as things are safe. He'll have to impress on him the importance of saying absolutely nothing.'

Taking just hand luggage, they trudged up the metal companionways from the car deck along with the crowds of other people.

Taylor explained the coded message. 'Fly back to peace,' he said. 'As in the bird of peace… "Dove". It was the closest I could think of to Dover. That gave the STD code and the number was the phone box number backwards. Geoff is on the same wavelength.'

She nodded her understanding. 'Well it certainly worked.'

Taylor's suggestion that they book a cabin seemed sensible. 'Maybe we can get a bit of rest and a decent meal. I'd like another look at the torn papers too.'

TWENTY EIGHT

DEAKIN, LACEY and Timson arrived back at the Mill Street off-licence. Their short diversion to a High Street telephone kiosk only set them back fifteen minutes but put Deakin's blood pressure up into the danger zone. He could not risk being connected to these clandestine investigations Timson bumped the van back up onto the kerb and turned off the engine. 'Right, we'll try again.'

The trio waited outside until the lone, middle-aged customer loaded his carrier bag, handed over his cash and stepped out onto the pavement. A bell pinged as the man closed the door behind him and moseyed off up the street delving inside his bag.

The bell sounded for a second time as Lacey pushed on the door and led the way inside. Cardboard boxes of bottled beers and plastic-coated slabs of drinks cans were piled shoulder high leaving a narrow passageway through to a small wooden counter. Labels, adverts and posters were pasted onto any available wall space giving details of offers and competitions; some were weeks out of date. A dank smell hung in the air.

The three detectives exchanged apprehensive looks as the door behind the counter opened.

Edward Steele shuffled in, a fairly tall man, perhaps a little over six feet, but painfully thin. The off-white, nylon shirt he wore was open at the neck, with sleeves rolled to the elbows. It bore evidence of a faded, vertical blue stripe pattern beneath a multitude of stains, indicating days, if not weeks, of wear.

The few strands of grey hair, which still clung to his scalp, grew from above his left ear and were plastered over the top of his head. The gaunt facial features suggested an age of almost seventy, although the truth lay closer to mid-fifties.

He glared at the three men framed between the towers of boxes, placed both hands on the counter, leant forwards and locked his elbows. 'Coppers,' was his blunt comment.

Lacey returned the stare and nodded. 'Correct, Mr Steele.'

'I wondered how long it would take you. Surprised it's taken so long. I'd have thought Mr Bloody High and Mighty would have had his boys around before now.'

'Who do you mean, Mr Steele?' Lacey quizzed, expectant of the answer.

'You know who I mean… Farmer, or has he finally retired, is that why it's taken so long to get the knife in again and twist it?'

Deakin intervened. 'Listen, Mr Steele, we're off to a poor start here. If you'll give us time to explain, I've a feeling that we may share some common interests.'

Steele stood his ground. 'I've no time for this. I have a business to run. I've nothing to say to you lot, you're all the damn same.'

A feeling of stalemate took over. It was now Timson's turn to attempt to usher Steele into cooperation. 'Mr Steele,' he said firmly. 'Have you heard anything from David since he escaped from court?'

Steele looked visibly shaken, his worn out frame jerked forwards as his elbows unlocked. He raised his eyebrows.

'What kind of shit is this? David's not going to come here. He's looking at spending the rest of his entire life behind bars after the latest stunt he's pulled.'

Lacey agreed with Steele's words. 'Well, I can't say I'm surprised at your thinking, or your attitude to the police, but we need to talk. You'll have heard that the body of the barrister has been found on Cannock Chase.'

Steele fixed his stare on Lacey. 'Look, I'm sorry about Jacob Bunn. I've seen the news and even a shit like him doesn't deserve that. But if you're here on behalf of that corrupt conniving bastard, Farmer, then there's not much for us to talk about.'

Deakin took his turn. 'Mr Steele, if you'll cooperate with us you'll see that we're far from being here on behalf of Superintendent Farmer.'

Steele said nothing, but came from behind the counter, squeezing between the detectives to the door. He flipped over the open/closed sign and thrust the heavy bolt into place. Still wordless, he returned to the counter pointing a finger for the three to follow him through into the back room.

The room was much the same as the shop itself, piled high with boxes and other disorder. A square, dark oak dining table took up the centre of the room, its surface covered in various piles of paperwork. They settled into chairs around the table as Steele opened a cupboard and produced four tumbler type glasses and a half consumed bottle of Jameson's Irish whiskey.

Without consultation he glugged a two-inch measure into each glass and slid three of them through the paperwork across the table. A single grubby-looking coffee mug sat on one corner of the table. It was surrounded by a multitude of heat ring marks built up over many years.

It didn't take him long to get into his stride. He'd been prompted into cooperation by Deakin's remarks: *'We're far from being here on behalf of Superintendent Farmer'*.

'David was always a bad un,' he began. 'Make no mistake, but when Sadie and me got together, I tried with him, I tried, I worked at it. I used to go camping with him; he loved it, just me and him. He was a good footballer, really promising, Stoke City were interested in him at one time.'

Steel ignored the persistent knocking on the shop's door. Clearly one customer was refusing to believe that the sign saying closed really meant what it said.

He looked down at the table and took a sip from his glass. 'Every time I seemed to be making progress with David that bastard, Farmer, popped up, stirring the shit, searching the house and arresting David. He'd turn up in the middle of the night, taking stuff from his bedroom, accusing him of things, causing trouble between Sadie and me.'

Steele pulled a pack of Capstan Full Strength from his shirt pocket and drew out a cigarette. He concentrated his watering eyes down upon his fingers as he repeatedly tapped the end of the cigarette onto the pack.

His audience regarded him in silence. They were all experienced enough to know when to keep quiet. Steele was pouring his heart out. It was vital that those gaps in between were to be left silent as he built the courage to tell more. No questions were needed.

Steele gave the cigarette between his fingers a contemptuous five second stare before reopening the packet and pushing it back inside. He sighed and got on with the tale. 'I even sorted the lad a weekend job down at the brewery where I worked. There was a fire one night and Farmer pinned it on David. He made the evidence up. It wasn't David, I know it wasn't. The lad cried, he never used to cry, he was a hard little bugger, but he cried. He said to me, "I didn't do it, Dad". He used to call me Dad.' Steele covered his face with his hands and rested his elbows on the table. He sniffed. 'It was a real steep slide down for David after that. He went completely wild, fighting, shoplifting, breaking into people's houses, smoking, bullying, you name it and he did it, he was a crime wave on his own.'

Steele lifted his head and sat cupping his chin in his hands. A single tear trickled down his left cheek. He sniffed again and drew in a deep breath. 'He did approved school, children's homes and stuff like that. We didn't see much of him then, apart from the countless times he ran away. He'd always make his way back here… usually in the middle of the night. That gave Farmer even more opportunities to come around, kicking doors in and throwing his weight about… causing trouble between me and Sadie.'

A feeling of guilt for Farmer's behaviour all those years ago prolonged the lack of comment from the detectives until Deakin broke their silence.

'What was it with Farmer? Why did he have this obsession with David?'

'That's the point,' Steele said. 'The real obsession was with Sadie. Farmer used David as a means to an end… blackmail, threats, lies, fabricated evidence. Sadie thought the world of David. Farmer was showing her he could ruin David's life and hers along with it unless she did what he wanted, but she wouldn't.'

Lacey held his yet untouched glass. He looked across the table at Steele. 'What did he want from her?'

Steele cocked his head to one side and made a perplexed face. 'Sex, of course.'

The three detectives met each other's gaze. Timson took his cue. 'So, you're saying that Farmer hounded David and ruined his life so that he could use Sadie as he wished?'

'That's about it,' Steele's voice diminished to a murmur.

Lacey got to his feet and walked over to the window, he took his first sip of the drink. 'That would be rape in any law book,' he said. 'And did she, did she give in to this?'

'No,' Steele shook his head. 'No, not while we were married. She would never give in to him despite all the trouble he caused, all the heartache.'

Lacey turned to face him. 'You say she never gave in to him while you and Sadie were married, does that mean…?'

Steele's shaking head accompanied a long sigh. 'Yes, yes, he raped her many times before we married. It was threats and violence then as well, but different threats.'

He cupped his glass with both hands and studied its contents. 'Sadie was sixteen, her father was an idiot, always drunk and involved in petty crimes. Then he moved in with the big boys… an armed robbery at Woodall's factory, they took all the wages.'

Steele's hands trembled as he found the courage to continue. 'I always promised Sadie I would never tell anyone this.' He hesitated, took a swig of his drink and then…. 'Farmer told Sadie that unless she gave in to him he would see to it that her father would get fourteen years. She would probably have been better off without her father. Her mother died a couple of years before and she was looking after her younger sister and brother.'

Lacey sat back down at the table. 'So why didn't you report all this? Even after you and Sadie married it should have been investigated. Farmer would have gone to prison for years.'

'No.' Steele shook his head and turned to Lacey. 'No, it doesn't work like that. Farmer held all the cards, he always did. Who would believe such a story… allegations like that against a policeman, a detective? Farmer was a rising star in the police then. He was on his way to the top, remember. He was a detective within three years, and look where he ended up, as one of the top brass.'

The three were mute. They knew that there was some hard truth in Steele's words.

'He even took four thousand pounds of the robbery money… Sadie's dad's share. Her dad got eighteen months in prison. The others were all given long stretches.'

Deakin stared at his two colleagues. 'I always knew Farmer was corrupt, but this… my God, I can't take it all in.'

Steele interrupted. 'There's more, something else you should know, something else I vowed I would never tell.' He picked up the cigarette packet again and looked straight across the table. 'Farmer is David's father.'

TWENTY NINE

A STUNNED SILENCE filled the tiny room as the magnitude of Steele's last sentence sunk in. Lacey broke that silence. 'Christ Almighty, are you saying that David was the product of Farmer raping Sadie?'

'Yes.' Steele's head nodded uncontrollably. 'No question about it.' He was sobbing now. 'She was a young girl then. She told me everything… it was difficult for her. It took a long time for all the truth to come out. He repeatedly raped her, both whilst her father awaited trial and then afterwards while he was in prison. It was always by threats and violence.'

Steele drew in another deep breath and lifted his gaze from the table. The worry, the anguish and heartache of years had been released from him for the first time. 'David is a criminal of the highest order. He controls an enormous drugs empire. He's made millions of pounds from crime and is without doubt responsible for the ending of many people's lives. He's a gangster in the truest sense of the word.'

Steele pulled the cigarette from the packet again. He tapped the end down onto the table a dozen or more times before sticking it into a corner of his mouth. He fumbled in the pocket of a creased jacket hanging on the back of his chair and pulled out a box of Swan Vesta matches. His hand trembled as he inhaled, drawing the match flame towards the end of the cigarette, illuminating his gaunt features and amplifying the pain of so many years.

'He'd phone me every once in a while, he was always offering me money, he said he'd buy me a house abroad or anywhere I wanted. He wouldn't have turned into the monster that he is if it hadn't been for Farmer.'

Steele sat back in his chair. 'He offered to get this place refurbished, and as he put it: "Make it into a little gold mine for me".

I always turned him down. I didn't want anything to do with drugs or crime. As soon as I saw the TV giving the news about him breaking out of court, I knew that would be the last I'd hear of him.'

Deakin leaned forwards across the table. 'So, he did visit you here then?'

Steele made a matter of fact face. 'Occasionally, but he was always careful about it. He said he didn't want anyone knowing that I was connected to him. He even made his mum revert back to her maiden name so that it wouldn't be so easy for anyone to put two and two together.'

Steele blew a column of smoke up towards the ceiling before continuing. 'And then he told me that he'd bought the old brewery. He said he intended developing the site... flats and whatnot. Said he wanted to pack the illegal stuff in and become an upstanding member of the community.'

Timson leaned forwards on his chair. 'So, the brewery is David's then?'

'Yes, but you won't find it traceable to him, all that stuff was always done through third parties, all manipulated through his fancy barrister.'

'You mean Bunn?' Lacey said.

Steele shrugged his shoulders and gave a nod. 'Yes, Bunn did all the fixing for him… "His brief" as he called him.'

The tapping on the shop door started again. Steele got to his feet. 'Let me serve these customers or I'm not going to make any money today.'

Deakin watched Steele close the door behind him. 'He's answering a lot of questions here. I don't think we've much to lose by putting our cards on the table. He has every reason in the world to hate Farmer's guts.'

The idea made sense and when Steele reappeared and took his seat, it was his turn to listen. His expression was impassive throughout Lacey's recounting of the story.

'I know some of what you've said from the papers and TV.' A slow head-shake accompanied his words. 'Farmer's up to his fat neck in this just like he was years ago. The only reason he's still alive is because David is using him with him being a copper… inside information, computer checks and that sort of stuff.' He reached over to flick a drooping pencil of ash from his cigarette into the coffee mug. 'But Farmer's no fool, he knows David detests him. He knows he'll have him killed when his usefulness expires.'

'Anytime soon then,' Deakin said. 'And this explains why Farmer didn't retire at the first opportunity. It's why he's been hanging on for the past four years.'

Steele twisted the corners of his mouth downwards. It was as good as a "Yes". 'David doesn't know everything, he doesn't know about Farmer being his father.'

Steele poured himself another whiskey and pushed the bottle across the table. 'Help yourselves. As for this Charlie Price, David did time in Walton prison near Liverpool with Price. They were mates and Price became a major player in the organisation. David didn't tell me that much really, but enough for me to work out that he trusted him. He didn't tell me too much because he knew that I still have principles and disagreed with what he was doing.'

'You never met Price then?' Deakin asked.

'No, and I don't think David would ever have told him about me. The only way that Price could have known about me would be through Farmer. David told me about buying the brewery. He wanted me to go up and have a look around. I turned him down. I didn't want to be associated with anything to do with it. I thought his story about becoming a so-called, upstanding member of the community, was a load of crap. It was a good little cover for some part of the operation.'

A few scribbled words took up a dozen lines of Lacey's notepad. He looked up from his jottings. 'So, what about the two men with Price, who could they be?'

'Not a clue,' Steele said. 'And as for this Belgium business, I don't know what that could be about. I mean David had things going on everywhere, but all that money, it must be to do with drugs.'

'When did you last speak to Sadie?' Deakin enquired.

'She phoned me yesterday. It's the first time she's made contact in years. She's worried sick and wanted to know if David had been in touch. She's changed so much, she sounded hard. She knows how I feel about what David's been doing and that's why we split up.'

Steele inhaled deeply, burning through a quarter inch of cigarette, fashioning concave cheeks and exposing the outline of facial bones. He exhaled, speaking at the same time. 'Farmer's always played his part, always stirred up trouble. I guess the real split between us came when David became so wealthy and offered us a property in Tenerife. I wanted no part, it was dirty money.'

'So, Sadie went then?' Lacey asked.

'Oh, she tried to persuade me, but that life, that easy money, it changes people. Soon you're involved yourself, playing a part in ruining other people's lives. It was all the trouble caused by Farmer, it got to her, eating away at her. She yearned for the high life, the sun, the money… so she went.' He clicked his fingers in the air. 'Just like that.'

THIRTY

TAYLOR AND HARDING slept. It didn't last long, but it was the first proper chance at real rest that their minds and bodies had been allowed since this all began.

It was a mere two hours later when Kim's long black eyelashes fluttered back into the real world. She gently unwrapped Taylor's arms from around herself and slid off the bunk, trying not to wake him. It didn't work.

'We haven't had long,' he said. 'But I feel so much better.'

'Me too,' she agreed. 'Let's freshen up and get a meal, then we'll see if we can make some sense out of this?'

The ferry crossing was smooth, save for the minor rolling sensation that catches travellers unawares in the below deck corridors. The meal could be described as edible, but nothing more than that.

Eyeing the waiter approaching, Kim casually piled their dishes onto the end of the table and nodded a thank-you before resuming her study of the Ghent pocket guide.

Taylor hastily opened his newspaper to shield the jigsaw of paper fragments he was working on. He resumed the pastime as the young man retreated laden with a precarious tower of dirty plates.

'Do you know anything about Ghent?' Taylor asked as he glided a couple of the fragments back and forth with a fingertip looking for a fit.

Kim put the book to one side, dragged her chair closer to his and stared down at what he had achieved so far. 'No, I can't say that I do. A school trip to Brussels was my closest. How about you?'

'Bits and pieces, it's supposed to be an interesting, beautiful place, history, architecture, churches and that.'

Kim joined in, turning and checking the other sides of the paper scraps. This added a few more part letters and words to the puzzle, further examples of that stylish, blue fountain-penned script.

She tapped a fingernail down onto one of the half-inch square pieces and read out a meaningless term: 'Belf'. Her puzzled frown persisted as she mouthed another foreign sounding portion of a word also written on the same fragment: 'Hoog'.

'Hmm,' Taylor lolled his head from side to side. 'I guess these must be names or places, they both begin with capital letters.' He added the words to a notebook list already started.

They spread the tatters of paper more widely across the table, moving pieces about, trying to fit the jagged edges to find a physical fit. Occasionally it worked and parts of a small incomplete jigsaw started to take shape.

'Some of it is Flemish sounding,' Taylor observed. 'Perhaps addresses… so many *O's*, here's another example.' His biro pointed at one of the fragments where the peculiar word "poort" was written.

'Yes,' Kim murmured. 'But no capital letter.' She placed her index finger onto the fragment and guided it around the rest of the puzzle until it came alongside the piece that read, *Hoog*. It fitted perfectly. 'Hoogpoort!' she exclaimed.

'Yes, definitely,' Taylor agreed.

'Here's something else.' She lined two fragments together. The torn edges matched up. Kim read the word aloud. 'Belfort.'

'Yes,' said Taylor. 'And again a capital letter.' He gave a shrug. 'But Belfort is a city in France, so let's hope this is not a red herring.'

Kim picked up the pocket guide and flicked through to the index page. 'Yes, it's listed… Belfort, Ghent, page sixty-one.' She turned the pages and then read aloud. 'Opposite the cathedral, the Belfort, completed in 1380.' She looked up at Taylor. 'It's a building, it says here in brackets it's a belfry, Belfort means belfry.'

Taylor's look of enthusiasm matched Kim's. 'So, if we head for the cathedral we may be a little closer to our friends.'

They sipped their coffee and continued with the task, hoping for more revelations.

One more seemingly meaningless word was assembled from the paper scraps: "Bavo". The couple's intended analysis of this was thwarted when the ship's public address system gave warning that they would soon be docking. The voice also added the advice that passengers should move their watches on one hour and collect all their belongings.

In Little Stoneleigh, Superintendent Farmer stood alone in his kitchen. His shirt flap hung out over the backside of shiny, over ironed police uniform trousers. A folded-arms stare was locked onto the pile of banknotes on the table, just one of the £50,000 cling-film blocks which he had torn open. A single block from one of his five boxes full.

He spread the cash with the palm of his hand and then glanced up tensely at the window. He needn't have been so nervous, the curtains were tightly closed.

Smiling with self-satisfaction he clasped his hands together. 'Thought they could rip me off,' he purred through yellowing teeth. 'But they're not smart enough to outwit Malcolm Farmer.'

The ringing telephone put a stop to his jubilation. 'Farmer,' he rasped into the mouthpiece.

'DS Corfield, Crime Squad, sir… er… Superintendent. I'm afraid we've lost Deakin.'

'WHAT?' Farmer shouted. 'WHAT?'

'Yes, sorry Boss, it looks like he'd actually gone out somewhere before we even set up on plot. His car was still there, so we've been sitting watching an empty house.'

'Right,' Farmer said, containing his anger. 'Well, you'd better find him then. Let me know as soon as you locate him…' There was a slight pause before Farmer's question: 'How come you're so sure he's not in?'

'Well Sir, after his kids turned up from school and let themselves in, we were a bit sus about it. Then his missus arrived back from work and still no sign of him. So I got one of the lads to do a Mickey Mouse enquiry at the door after him… you know double glazing. She said he was out.'

Farmer quivered a little as he temporarily kept the lid on his anger. 'Right,' he said and carefully replaced the handset into its cradle.

His fist slammed into the kitchen door. 'Useless fucking idiots.' He swept the money back into its box and gave his throbbing knuckles a feverish rub.

'Time for a supervisory visit.' He dragged his uniform jacket from the chair and pulled it on.

It took Farmer ten minutes to drive from his home down to North Street on the outskirts of the town centre. The avenue of majestic old dwellings was a couple of streets away from Little Stoneleigh Police Station.

Farmer's intended destination, a large Victorian house, blended in perfectly with the neighbouring homes.

It took a closer inspection to reveal that it was no longer a family residence and hadn't been so for many years. The major clue to the building's current use being a small sign: *POLICE*, above the entrance door. The well-lit upstairs rooms and office-like Venetian blinds were also a giveaway.

Farmer pushed open the unlocked front door and was met by the smell of beer and cigarette smoke. The open doorway on his right gave access to the neatly set out bar of Little Stoneleigh Police Social Club.

Half a dozen faces turned to see who had arrived and then equally as quickly turned their backs. Jack Duffield was the only drinker who kept his stare fixed onto Farmer.

'Evening,' Farmer said as he went by the door and started on down the hallway.

Duffield belched in reply before also turning his back. 'Bastard,' he muttered.

Farmer gripped the polished wooden handrail as he manoeuvred his bulk up the creaking stairway.

The upper floor of the club now served as a hastily arranged major incident room, hence the makeshift sign on the wedged-open door:

JACOB BUNN. MURDER ROOM

The name *CHARLES PRICE* appeared to be an afterthought, but showed that this death was also being investigated as murder.

Bright fluorescent strip lights lit the large rectangular room, which originally served as a palatial Victorian bedroom. Four beige-coloured computer monitors rested on desks each with a WPC tapping at a keyboard.

'How are we doing?' Farmer asked in a phoney, pleasant voice.

The young uniformed sergeant was surprised by the unexpected visit. 'Fine, sir, fine, one puzzling thing though.'

'WHAT?' Farmer's raised voice gave away his annoyance at the possibility of another snag.

'Well,' the sergeant replied. 'A call came in from Exeter Police HQ. They wanted to speak with DS Lacey or DC Timson, the officers dealing with the Sweeney case.'

'Yes, yes,' Farmer butted in. 'I know who they are. No one told me they were up here?'

'That's just it, Superintendent; I didn't know they were coming either. Apparently they set off before lunchtime. They should have been here hours ago.'

THIRTY ONE

IN THE STREET outside the incident room Timson parked the van against the kerb and silenced the engine. Jack Duffield's directions and description of the unlikely police owned building were accurate.

Fortunately, after their visit to the off licence Lacey had telephoned his Headquarters back at Exeter, a routine call, in case anyone had been trying to get in touch.

The Control Room constable was keen to speak with him. 'Yes Sarge, we've had a Mr Lewis from Middleway ringing for you. He's just back from his holiday and is hoping that you've got some information on his stolen Jaguar. I thought you'd best ring him yourself and be the one to impart the bad news. I've even telephoned Little Stoneleigh's murder incident room to track you down.'

Heavy parking forced Timson to leave the van some way down the street. This actually suited their next piece of subterfuge quite well.

After locking the driver's door Timson joined his colleague on the pavement. A tall privet hedge overhung the path almost touching the van.

Crouching in the shadows down by the van's rear wheel the two men took turns at rubbing their hands onto the tyre and into the dirt on the underside of the wheel arch. Timson added a streak of the grime to his face and a little to one of the knees of his trousers. Not until this strange ritual had been completed did they make their way over to the building.

Stepping into the hallway, the open door on their right gave a view into the Police social club. The half dozen, mostly elderly men, occupying the room, were chatting and supping from pint mugs. A lone barman expertly pulled down on a wooden handled beer pump.

One customer stood casually slotted coins into an electric fruit machine. The poor fellow little realised he may as well have handed the money over directly to Superintendent Farmer.

Apart from the fruit machinist, who was too engrossed, each one of the rather grizzled looking occupants turned to see the new arrivals.

Jack Duffield's years of experience at not giving the game away produced a false but authentic looking puzzled face. 'Can I help you, gents?'

Equally nonplussed by the unexpected second meeting of the day, Lacey answered accordingly. 'Exeter CID, mate, we're looking for the police incident room. We were told it was here.'

'Have you any ID?' Duffield questioned with a mischievous frown.

Lacey produced his warrant card from his shirt pocket and flipped it open for inspection. He covertly winked at Duffield.

'Upstairs, my friend,' Duffield directed.

They made their way up and into the incident room, Lacey still holding his ID.

An overweight, white-shirted, senior officer looked up from a desk as they entered and set them with an uncompromising stare.

Lacey's eyes homed in onto the chromium plated crowns on the man's shoulder epaulettes and the gold braided peak of a police cap which lay on the desk. The rank of superintendent, and consequently the man's identity, were both quickly deduced.

Flipping open his ID again Lacey started to make an introduction.

Farmer got to his feet holding up the wide palm of his hand cutting Lacey short before the introductions could be concluded.

'I'm running this inquiry. No one told me you were coming up here.' His voice rose in volume with each word. 'I'm told you started off hours ago, so what the hell have you been doing? I don't take kindly to you snooping around on my patch without informing me first.'

'We've come straight here, sir,' Lacey insisted. 'We've had a puncture, out on some country road in the middle of nowhere. It's taken us ages to get help… we'd got no wheel brace.' He held up his filthy hands. 'Could do with getting cleaned up, sir, if that's okay.'

'Yes, me too,' added Timson, brushing his hands together and examining the dirt on his trousers.

Farmer rested his double chin down onto his chest. His eyes were filled with suspicion.

'Okay,' he finally said. 'But when you're done…' He paused and wagged a finger at Lacey. 'You'd better sit down and tell me what you know about all this. I'm particularly interested in your contact with my errant Detective Inspector, who you will know, is a major suspect in a murder enquiry. I also want to know what this policewoman of yours was doing up here with Taylor.'

Lacey mentally summed up the situation. *First contact now confirmed expectations. Little Stoneleigh's Superintendent was a nasty piece of work.*

Farmer gestured with the back of his hand over towards the young sergeant. 'Show them to the gents.'

Lacey and Timson followed the sergeant's directions along a corridor and were soon standing side by side over washbasins removing their self-inflicted grime. Lacey exchanged a glance in the mirror with Timson's reflection. 'Wagging his finger at me… For two pins I'd break it off and push it up his arse.'

Timson's mouth broke into a grin, but he knew his colleague and he wasn't joking.

After cleaning themselves up they returned to the office and took seats opposite Farmer. Their well-rehearsed version of events had undergone considerable planning. It was important to only supply Farmer with the factual detail already available through normal police channels. He must not learn of any of their clandestine enquiries or meetings.

They were part-way through when the sergeant interrupted. 'Sorry, Superintendent… a phone call for you. It's DS Corfield, crime squad.'

'Right,' Farmer said keenly, 'I'll take it in there.' He indicated to the typist's empty office. 'Don't go anywhere yet, gentlemen.' His finger wagged again in Lacey's direction. 'I haven't finished with you yet.'

Lacey's eyes were set upon the offending digit. He stroked his chin with his left hand to hide the annoyance spreading across his face.

Timson looked from Farmer to Lacey and back, relieved as Farmer withdrew into the office.

Corfield's voice was triumphant. 'We've found Deakin, sir. He must have been in the pub all day. We eyeballed him ten minutes ago walking… well, staggering.' Corfield added a nervous laugh before continuing. 'He came from the direction of the Lamb Inn. He was that pissed he nearly fell through the hedge.' Another edgy snigger was thrown in. 'Drowning his sorrows I'll bet. He couldn't get his key in the door. His missus didn't look too pleased with him.'

'Has he seen you?' Farmer quizzed.

'Not a chance, sir, only things he could see were his feet, and they must have been blurred. Oh, and another thing Superintendent, we've intercepted a cryptic message on Deakin's personal pager. It could be from your DI, but we can't make head or tail of it. I'll send you the details through.'

Lacey and Timson didn't bother to take Farmer up on his offer of a half-pint in the bar downstairs. He was clearly putting on a show of forced pleasantness to establish if they knew anything he didn't want them to know.

'Smarmy bastard,' Timson said as he unlocked the van.

Their next stop, The Brooks Hotel, lay a quarter of a mile from Little Stoneleigh. Taylor threw the suggestion in as an afterthought during the last few seconds of the frantic Dover phone call: "Don't take Farmer up on an offer of a room at HQ. He's got you where he wants you if you do. Book in at a local hotel... The Brooks on the main A34. I'll ring you there in the morning… half seven UK time."

There was no chance for a discussion over the matter. Taylor had put the phone down and sprinted away to catch the ferry.

Lacey cringed at the price of the rooms. A picture formed in his mind of the reaction of the Chief Inspector in the accounts department back at Exeter.

THIRTY TWO

TAYLOR TOOK the wheel for the drive to Ghent and they quickly joined a bumper-to-bumper queue making its way out from the ferry.

'Good job you bought those things to stick on the headlights, I'd never have thought of it. This driving on the right is going to take a bit of getting back into.'

The traffic thinned out quickly and it wasn't long before the BMW was out onto the main A10. The forty-mile ride was going to take them about thirty-five minutes.

The Belgian landscape rolled away from either side of the road. Endless rows of tall slender poplar trees stretched towards a darkening horizon. The occasional church spire or farmhouse were the only manmade structures to punctuate otherwise flat fields. Conversation drifted between the events of the past two days and occasionally back to their own personal circumstances.

Kim turned on the interior light and smoothed out the road map on her lap. She touched a pencil down onto the map, gauging their position as the car swept past a road sign on the right: A10 Ghent 20k. Other smaller signs came in quick succession indicating the towns of Nevelle and Saint Martins-Leeme.

Taylor checked the mirror and switched the right hand indicator on as they approached the turning for Ghent. He glanced at Kim. 'If this gamble is proved right we must be careful from now on. Remember, there's one of this pair who could walk right up to us and we wouldn't know him from Adam.'

She gave him a sideways glance, 'I'd know him as soon as he opened his mouth.'

The buildings were now larger and more tightly packed as they ventured deeper into the city. Ancient industrial buildings and old factories were giving way to twinkling shopfronts, cafés, restaurants and department stores. A police car overtook them, klaxon blaring. It was another advertisement that this was a bustling metropolis.

Taylor eyeballed a series of road signs marked: Centrum. He followed the route carefully for fifteen minutes as it took them directly into the heart of the city. Several more pointers with the word: Kathedraal dictated the last part of their trip.

Kim reached down for the department store carrier bag propped between her feet. The green and gold trade mark printed on its side read: Fullaway's Ladies Outfitters, Dover. She delved inside 'Time for my disguise,' she said, unwrapping folds of white tissue paper from the shoulder-length auburn wig now in her lap.

She pulled down the car's vanity mirror in the sun visor and in the dim light provided by the mirror's low wattage bulb manipulated her own glossy black hair into the right shape. She then skilfully caressed the wig into place until it took on a completely authentic look.

Taylor looked over at her as he slowly drove along the narrowing streets into the heart of the city. He gave a shake of the head. 'Brilliant, how much did this cost Farmer?'

'Do not ask, Monsieur.'

'Yes, that's going to be the next problem… the language.'

Kim mounted a pair of tinted dark rimmed glasses on the bridge of her nose and turned towards him. 'What do you think, Monsieur?' she tilted her head to one side.

He nodded approvingly. 'Wouldn't have recognised you.'

She pouted her lips at him. 'I did A-level French you know, and brushed up with a course not long ago, so I can manage pretty well.'

'Wow, I am impressed. We'll need some language expertise. According to the guide book the locals are split between Flemish, English, French and German.'

He pulled the car off the cobbled street into a car park, selected a space and switched off the motor. He lowered his head looking upwards through the top of the windscreen at the rooflines of the surrounding buildings.

'We're right in the centre. I figure that must be the cathedral.' His finger pointed up to a majestic floodlit Gothic structure looming high above the other buildings. 'So, that puts us right on the doorstep of the Belfort. Fancy a stroll? We'll see if we can find somewhere to stay.'

Taylor reached over to the back seat and took hold of a wide brimmed straw hat. It was another purchase from Dover. He placed it onto his head, tilting it at a jaunty angle as he viewed himself in the car's mirror. A grin creased his cheeks as he gave Kim a wide-eyed expectant stare.

She left her opinion until they both climbed from the car. 'What do you look like?'

The BMW's indicator lights flashed twice as Taylor aimed the remote ay it.

A multitude of slender cobbled streets and broad cobbled roads radiated away in all directions. Tall narrow buildings with steeply pitched roofs and ornate, stepped gabled fronts formed a fairy-story skyline from every aspect. The city centre was still busy, twinkling lights, throngs of people, couples strolling, quaint little cafés, bars and restaurants.

Steel tram lines sunk into the roadways supported giant, rumbling brightly lit trams which took their power from a sparking web of overhead cables. The street level was taken up with all manner of different shop fronts. Only the cafés and bars still remained open, many with small outside tables, where people sat enjoying an evening meal or a beer. The rolling strains of a barrel organ floated across from an unknown source.

Kim took in the atmosphere at every step. 'What an amazing place.'

The brim of Taylor's hat nodded as he silently agreed with the comments. He halted momentarily looking for a street name. 'We don't want to lose our bearings,' he said as his eyes searched.

The brown and white street name plates were fixed high up on the brickwork at every crossroads. Reading them involved a neck-craning, upward glance. The couple quickly adopted a routine to keep a check on their whereabouts as each new street, road or alley was reached.

After a short while they arrived at the end of a wide, well-lit street which opened out onto the city square. Two enormous religious buildings towered upwards into the night sky, both dramatically illuminated by floodlights. It was a spectacle warranting closer inspection tomorrow, but clearly they had found both the cathedral and the belfry.

They eyed a few possible hotels as their stroll took them to a branch in the road. Taylor checked out the street name: Hoogpoort. He stopped and nodded up at the sign. 'One of the names on the pieces of paper.'

'Yes,' Kim agreed. 'Yes, so it was a street name.'

They walked a little way along Hoogpoort until a large brightly lit hotel came into view. It was the grandest one seen so far and sat in a prominent, imposing position on the city square directly across from the cathedral.

They turned to face each other upon reading the illuminated sign:

BELFORT HOTEL

Kim raised her eyebrows in surprise. 'So it's also the name of a hotel.'

Taylor stared at the building. 'The chances are,' he speculated. 'That the reference in the torn up notes was to this place rather than the old belfry. I'll bet this is where they're staying.'

He turned through one hundred and eighty degrees studying the buildings on the other side of the square. His gaze fastened onto the Hotel Harmony.

'So we stay there.'

The Harmony was a sixteenth century red brick building which oozed history from within its very foundations. Maybe it didn't have the extra staff that the Belfort had, but it looked tidy and comfortable. The pair also considered that it was reasonably priced, even though it wasn't their money with which to be economical. A room with a view out across the square was important enough to merit the payment of a small extra fee.

After parking the BMW on the hotel car park they took the lift up to their third floor room and dumped their bags onto the bed. The room was clean, high-ceilinged and spacious. Taylor gazed through the window across the square before pulling the heavy red velvet curtains closed.

'Now would be a good time to take a quick look at the Belfort Hotel,' he suggested. 'It's getting quieter now. Most people are off the streets and in the bars or heading for bed, but we must be careful. You look so different with that wig but my straw hat is not going to fool anyone.'

'Okay,' she said and with a theatrically nonchalant look tipped the tinted glasses down onto the bridge of her nose. She continued the jokey display by flicking the ends of the long auburn wig out over her cardigan with the backs of her fingers. 'What do you want me to do?' An absurd *'Allo 'Allo!* accent added to the humour.

A more serious tone took over when the lift delivered them to the Harmony's ground floor. The doors slid open to reveal a well-proportioned lobby. The reception desk took up one corner and was surrounded by a curving highly polished, wooden counter. A young lady sat behind. 'Thank you Monsieur,' she said, as Taylor handed over the room key. She attached the key to its numbered hook on the board behind the desk as the couple made their way outside.

The heat of the day had finally given way to a late evening breeze. Kim pulled the top of her cardigan together.

A few figures, mostly couples, could be seen strolling along pavements or chatting in the bars. Taylor and Harding joined in, using the pretence of a hand-in-hand tourist pair as they made their way across the square towards the Belfort Hotel.

Instead of taking the front entrance they made a bee-line for a passageway down the side of the building and out into a poorly lit rear car park. A line of metal rubbish bins stood alongside the entrance to the hotel's kitchens. A couple of dozen cars were parked in designated bays. Keeping back in the shadows, they stood quietly for a few seconds and looked.

'Over there,' Taylor said. 'In the corner, by the wall, British number plates.'

'Yes, clocked it,' Kim said, nodding over at a blue Mercedes.

Taylor jotted down the registration number in his notebook and included a Ford Escort also bearing British plates.

After a brief discussion they walked back towards the front. 'You okay with this?' Taylor asked.

Kim pursed her lips and blinked. 'Yes,' was all she said as she turned on her heel and started towards the hotel's brightly lit entrance.

THIRTY THREE

THE OAK and brass revolving door of the Belfort Hotel required a steady push from Kim's flattened palm. The luxurious lobby area was lit by three huge, multi-bulb, twinkling chandeliers. Her pretence of relaxed confidence was impressive.

A number of cream painted doors and affluently carpeted passageways led away on each side. A smartly uniformed receptionist looked up from his desk, his thought being... *did the lady need assistance?*

Kim started her self-assured expedition, ostensibly knowing exactly where she was heading. Behind the tinted glasses, though, her eyes were wildly searching left and right as she took in the geography of the building. She was seeking any clue that might steer her confidently past the reception desk and hopefully not into a broom cupboard.

A murmur of laughter and the clinking of glasses drifted over to her from somewhere. She homed in on the noise and without hesitation started on down a capacious, lavishly decorated staircase. The receptionist went back to his work.

At a half-landing where the stairs turned a corner the noise grew in volume and with this came the aroma of tobacco and alcohol. At the foot of the stairs she came to a double glass door through which she could see a busy lounge bar. Several couples sat at small tables and others relaxed in sumptuous, two-seater sofas which were positioned in what was a considerably sized rectangular room. She took a deep breath and entered.

Two men were standing together by the marble fireplace, their tall glasses of Belgian beer located on the mantle shelf. They were engrossed in conversation. Kim's eyes landed on them, searching for any similarity to the men at the brewery. These men were both older and plumper than the profiles in her mind. One glance from her, however, was sufficient to halt their conversation. They gawped in unison. Kim raised her eyebrows and smiled at them. She registered the encounter for future use as a possible cover plan. The men turned back to each other, one made a comment, laughter followed.

She made a casual heading in the direction of the ladies room, a journey which enabled her to briefly study some of the clientele.

Three or four groups of varyingly aged men were lined along the bar engaged in conversation and sipping at their drinks. She carefully eyed them as she made her way through.

It was as she pulled the door to the ladies room open that her attention centred onto a figure sitting at a table. The back of the man was the only available view, but something struck her about his build and stature, the shape of his head. There seemed to be an air of arrogance as he gestured over to a waiter with a flick of his fingers. A chair on the opposite side of his table stood empty.

The door to the ladies closed behind her. She shuddered as the memory of the violence at the brewery came back. Could this be the same man? She took a few seconds to collect her thoughts, regain her composure and plan a strategy.

The one deep breath she took did nothing to calm her bounding pulse. She pulled the door open and stepped back out. Her attention immediately targeted the faceless head and shoulders, consuming every scrap of scant detail available.

The man seemed to be pondering over a collection of documents arranged on the table. The shiny reflection of photographic paper caught a glint of light from the chandelier. He was scrutinising a small snapshot, carefully holding it up to the light for closer inspection.

With a plan now forming, Kim knew where to head. Her steps took her confidently forwards, whilst her mind was bombarded with thoughts and vague recollections. The flick of the gun wrist came to her mind. The arrogant gestures, the height, weight, the build. She tried to visualise the scene at the brewery, the leader with his balaclava.

This man was sitting at a table, but seemed about the right height. Those fluttering butterflies inside her tummy were telling her to be careful, but she needed to know more.

She arrived in front of the two men who had been ogling her as she came in. 'Bonsoir,' she said, smiling.

Such was their surprise as they turned to face her that one almost choked on a mouthful of beer as he attempted to beat his friend in returning the greeting.

They were German businessmen who did not speak much French and so within seconds the agreed language turned to English, which they could manage quite successfully. The scenario gave Kim's impersonation of an English-speaking Frenchwoman some credibility and her French expertise added an authentic accent.

The Germans could hardly believe their luck, this vivacious looking young woman wanted to make small talk with them! They happily swallowed her loosely knitted story: She was a photographer, attracted to Belgium by the religious architecture.

Kim manipulated the conversation into her own comfort zone and gave a polite nod of acceptance to the offer of a glass of wine. Maybe the drink would calm her tattered nerves. The discussion droned on for some time as several sly glances attempted to snatch facial features and add them to the target's head and shoulders.

Several minutes went by before this paid off. The entrance door pushed open and a white haired gent entered the bar. In that same instant the man seated at the table swivelled and looked towards the door.

The voices of Kim's new friends became an unintelligible distant murmur as an imaginary balaclava was pulled onto that head and judgement was made of those haughty characteristics. The prominent chin and pretentious body language were collated inside Kim's mind along with other hints. Now she was sure. This was indeed the man who wanted her dead.

Her focus was broken as the white haired man, who had just entered the bar, made his way through the bustle of people. An overweight German tourist was leaning with his back against the bar. His distended stomach clearly blocked the man's way through.

'Excuse me,' the man said in a southern English accent.

The polite request was ignored as the German gave a disdainful look. The older man contemplated the obstruction and without hesitation shoved his way through. The German recoiled from a sharp elbow in the stomach.

Kim watched as the older man's irritated glare persisted. 'Oh,' she heard him lie. 'I'm so sorry.' Free from obstructions he then moved casually through and headed for the vacant chair opposite Kim's target man. The two men pulled in closer to the table and began an intense conversation.

Fifteen minutes went by before the men finished their drinks and stood from the table. Their discussion persisted as they moved slowly through the bustle towards the door. The younger man's height and physique fitted Kim's recollection of the gunman to perfection.

A problem now lay in store though, as she calculated that their route to the exit would take them within a yard of her, and that might be a little too close for comfort. A distinct possibility existed that the man might recognise her.

She continued to endure the necessary charade with her drinking partners, but took one last stare at the man. Her woman's eye for certain detail drank in the short, expensively groomed hair, the moustache and the classy-looking dark framed spectacles. His clothes were tasteful and stylish: a tweed jacket with brown cord elbow patches, a waistcoat to match the patches and matching cord slacks. He was affluently dressed.

The stare lingered just a tad too long, their eyes momentarily met. She instantly turned away but felt the man's gaze boring in. Had he recognised her? She sipped at her wine, eyes wide and head turned away as the inane dialogue of the two German's continued to drone.

He was right behind her now, close enough to touch, close enough to slam a hand onto her shoulder and swing her around. The fluttering butterflies in her tummy became wildly flapping pigeons as he spoke: 'Bonsoir, Madame.'

His French greeting confirmed two things to Kim: It WAS the gunman from the brewery and he had not recognised her.

'Monsieur,' Kim responded, keeping her face half-turned.

She resumed her conversation, unsure about the subject. *Something about jazz?* she thought.

She breathed a sigh of relief as she followed the men's progress through the doorway and up the stairs towards the lobby. It was only now that she detected the older man's limp. A mental picture formed in Kim's mind of the progress of the two men up the stairs before she turned on her temporary hosts. 'I must be going now,' she said with her French lilt. 'It has been nice to meet you.' She was hardly conscious of the protests from one of the men or of his offer of another drink. Her quarries were already at the half landing.

Her jog up the stairs enabled her to catch a glimpse of the men disappearing out of sight into the lobby. She quickly covered the last few steps and stopped with a hand flat against the wall to peer around the corner.

'Tomorrow it is then,' she overheard the older man say as he headed for the revolving exit door. The younger man offered nothing more than a conceited nod of agreement and turned towards the reception desk.

Kim moved back out of view, listening and waiting to hear the man's voice. The short sentence, when it came, was delivered with arrogant pomposity: 'Mr Swann, room 302.'

She heard the clunk of his key with its thick, plastic room number fob being placed down onto the reception desk. The usual pleasantries from the female staff member followed: 'Thank you, sir. Ring zero for room service if you require anything. Goodnight.'

Kim took another covert glance, guessing she would see "Mr

Swann", as she now knew him to be named, waiting for the lift. But no, he had slipped inside one of the two telephone kiosks in the foyer. A blurred outline of his back, handset to ear, was visible through the opaque wired glass panel.

Thoughts entered Kim's mind: *Why was Swann using this telephone when he had one in his room? Could she get into the vacant telephone kiosk next to Swann and possibly overhear some of the conversation?* She needed to be careful, he must not see her.

The plan was immediately put on hold, her two German drinking partners were heading up the stairway towards her.

'Damn,' she cursed under her breath, worried that her behaviour may be starting to look suspicious. She fumbled in her bag pretending to look for something, but found herself forced into more mindless chit-chat. A full minute went by before the men wished her goodnight and set off towards the exit.

She hurried across the lobby but quickly realised that the idea was finished, someone else was now using the phone next to Swann.

She quickened her pace out onto the street hoping for a chance to follow the other man, but he had vanished.

She found Taylor sitting at a table inside the Tête à Tête Restaurant.

He held his hand aloft to attract her attention. 'I was getting a bit worried,' he confided. 'I'm on my third beer, this Belgian stuff's strong. Any luck?'

'Oh, yes,' her eyes were at their widest. 'I got chatted up by a couple of Germans.' She feigned thoughtfulness, looking upwards and pressing her finger against her lips. 'Or perhaps, I chatted them up. Anyway his name's Swann and he's in room 302.' She threw the comment in unceremoniously before ordering a Martini and lemonade from the hovering waiter.

'God,' Taylor emphasised the word as Kim explained the detail. 'You're sure he didn't recognise you?'

'No, definitely not, given half a chance he'd have been joining the Germans trying to chat me up. It must be this wig; I think I'll keep it.'

Swann's phone call from the downstairs kiosk was a mystery. 'He'll have a phone in his room, so why use the kiosk?' Kim said.

'Because he doesn't want the call to be traceable,' Taylor said. 'We need to get this info through to Pete Lacey tomorrow, along with the car numbers and see what he can find out. I don't know how you've pulled it off.'

He cupped his hand under her chin, leant forward and planted a kiss on her lips. 'Come on, it's late. It's been a long day, we could be busy tomorrow.'

THIRTY FOUR

THE BEDSIDE clock showed eight forty-seven. Kim watched it tick around minute by minute. She'd been woken by Taylor's eight-fifteen attempt not to wake her. He'd slipped out of bed, dressed and gone out.

She lay on her side, comfortable and warm, eyelashes fluttering as a jumble of thoughts went through her mind. The preceding forty-eight hours had been exhausting and sleep scarce. The loss of another hour with the time zone change did not help. The sound of the key slotting into the bedroom door brought her back to reality.

Taylor immediately caught sight of her wide open eyes. 'Hi, you just woken up?'

'Hmm, a few minutes.' *He'd been so careful not to wake her it was a shame to tell him.*

Taylor dumped the armful of glossy magazines and English newspapers he was carrying down onto the bed.

'Could only get yesterday's at the moment.' He separated the newspapers and pushed them closer to her. 'I got these though,' he patted the pile of magazines. 'They're travel guides, leaflets and booklets about Ghent… all in English. I thought we could swot up and maybe find out what's so important to Mr Swann and his friends.'

Kim propped herself up in the bed with a couple of pillows. 'Did you get through to Pete?' She unfolded the Daily Mail and started leafing through.

'Yes, they booked in at The Brooks Hotel as I suggested, I think I've gone through everything.'

She looked worried. 'What about Dad?'

'Pete can't risk ringing him at home,' Taylor replied. 'It's bound to be tapped, but he's pretty sure he'll be able to get in touch later today when they get back to Exeter. I've given him all the details, car numbers, names, everything I could think of.'

The Brooks Hotel in Little Stoneleigh was without doubt the best hotel the two Exeter detectives had ever stayed at on police business.

Lacey's phone call from Taylor was taken whilst relaxing in the comfort of a luxurious king-sized bed and followed by a long soak in his giant en suite bath.

He joined his colleague down in the hotel's restaurant for a sumptuous full English. 'Best get our money's worth,' he advised. As the thought of that expenses bill landing on a desk at Exeter HQ went through his mind.

Timson offered little return conversation save for the odd grunt as he cleared his plate and began mopping up operations with a slice of toast.

'Phew.' he finally exclaimed as he caught Lacey's eye and pointed a finger at a one of the hotel direction boards: *Hotel Swimming Pool.* 'Should have brought my trunks.'

The pair came down to earth at half past nine as they arrived back at Little Stoneleigh's murder incident room. The single flight of stairs was an effort after that breakfast. The boxes of copy files and statements from Sweeney's trial and the paperwork concerning his courtroom escape did not help. It took them two trips from the van.

The murder room had been set up in record time. The boffins from Headquarters were keen to get their new computerised system into action. Many of the wall shelves were beginning to fill up with files and folders. The teams of detectives had burned some midnight oil to achieve all this.

A baby-faced uniformed inspector sat at a desk, a stencilled, cardboard placard proclaimed his status: *Office Manager.*

Timson's attempt at a friendly introduction broke no ice. The Inspector did not look up from his desk, 'I've been told to expect you, leave the boxes over there.' He waved his pen towards a corner of the room.

A bead of sweat dripped from Timson's brow as he struggled towards the corner and deposited two of the boxes down onto the floor. 'Farmer's been putting the poison down by the look of it,' he mumbled.

Lacey gave a nod. 'No doubt another one of his hand-picked men.'

They were keen to get back on the road, but the prospect of a little nose around during Farmer's absence was a chance not to be missed.

When the Inspector unhooked a jacket from the coat-stand and started down the stairs it was as though Lacey had been given the green light. He caught the eye of a young policewoman who was busily typing details onto a computer keyboard.

'Mind if I have a look through some of the statements? There may be something that rings a bell from our end of the inquiry.'

'No, carry on, Sarge, copy statements are up there,' she pointed to a wall mounted shelf.

Lacey lifted down two cardboard lever arch files marked: *Witness Statements.* He quickly thumbed through the *A to L* volume until he came to a four page account titled with the name: *Daniels, William Keith.* Like all the others in the folder it was a computer printed copy. A furtive glance over at the office staff preceded a mischievous wink at Timson. Lacey unfastened the central chrome plate holding the documents in place and noiselessly tore out Daniels' statement.

Timson moved to one side of Lacey, shielding him from view and allowing him to deftly fold the statement and slip it into his jacket. Lacey then inspected the second file for any mention of a statement from Edward Steele. He was not surprised when the search drew a blank.

A little more time was spent browsing through the other statements before they thanked the office staff and indicated their intention to head off back down South.

Lacey climbed into the van. 'They won't miss that. It's only a copy.'

Timson smiled. 'Bloody thief,' he muttered, before twisting the ignition key and bringing the rattling engine into life again.

They joined the southbound carriageway of the M6 motorway at quarter past ten and began the voyage home to Exeter.

Back in the third floor room of the Hotel Harmony, Taylor had found it difficult not to climb back into bed. He'd arranged for breakfast in the room. A shower and more coffee followed before they settled at the table in the bay window.

They flicked through the pages of the brochures and travel guides trying to select interesting detail about the area. After half an hour Taylor summarised some of his own discoveries. It wasn't much. 'Most of the attraction to Ghent seems to be the architecture, the churches and the cathedral. There's a lot of history to the place.' He read from the text: 'Probably the most beautiful city in Belgium.'

Kim smoothed out the glossy pages in front of her and read out her own brief résumé. 'There are two rivers, the Scheldt and the Leie. Ghent is Belgium's third largest city. Cloth making seems to be something it was famous for. Most of the tourist attractions, as you say, are based on architecture... buildings, churches and the cathedral.

She read out the cathedral's name: 'Saint Bavo's.' Her eyebrows rose as she looked up from the brochure at Taylor. 'Bavo... one of the words on the torn papers.'

The link to what had taken place back at the Brewery quickly encouraged them to take a walk from the Harmony across the Sint-Baafsplein Square. Within fifteen minutes they were standing gazing at the vast arched doorway of Saint Bavo's Cathedral.

A slowly moving river of cars, trucks, trams and cycles encircled the towering structure and an ever building throng of shoppers and tourists continued to fill the broad reaches of the cobblestoned square.

The magnificence which met them as they stepped inside took their breath away. Their vision was uncontrollably drawn upwards to the vaulted ceiling eighty feet above and to the enormous proportions of the place.

Taylor's eyes were everywhere as soon as he necessarily removed his hat. 'It's down to you Kim. I've no idea what this man looks like remember.'

'Okay,' she reassured. 'I'll keep my eyes open for him.'

A well-stocked gift shop inside the cathedral provided Taylor with another large collection of leaflets and information handouts. They then tagged along with a crowd of American sightseers and listened to the guide's commentary about how the cathedral came to be built.

Tragic tales from the building's history were recounted including the effects of the two World Wars. Details of the stunning works of art which were displayed formed a large part of the tour.

An hour and a half later they emerged, blinking into the bright sunlight. Kim replaced her sunglasses. 'That was interesting.'

'Yes,' Taylor agreed. 'But I can't see how it's helped.'

They explored a few of the narrow side streets leading off the square until they came across a tiny restaurant.

Taylor gave a nod over at the place. 'Let's grab a bite to eat. I think we'll be okay in here.'

THIRTY FIVE

THE TWO-HUNDRED mile trek from Little Stoneleigh had taken Lacey and Timson three hours. Tedham village church stood directly opposite Kim Harding's father's home. Its bell tower clock showed the time as twenty minutes past one as Timson steered in against the kerb and switched off.

'This motor smells a bit hot,' Timson commented as he looked through the van window taking in the sight of the well-tended garden surrounding Geoffrey Fry's bungalow. A fairly new-looking small saloon was parked on the sloping driveway.

The net curtains in the bungalow's front room twitched even before Timson pushed his door open. Mr Fry was quickly on the step, hands clasped tightly and wearing a worried face. He nodded as the detectives made their way up the path. No introductions were necessary. The visit lasted thirty-five minutes.

When they arrived back at Heavitree Road police station they were confident that they had done their best to assure Mr Fry that his daughter was safe. Whether they believed this themselves was a different matter.

The twelve feet high, motorised gates at the rear of the Police Station closed silently together as Timson pulled the van alongside the petrol pump and climbed out. A sudden lack of engine racket woke Lacey from his passenger seat slumbers.

Timson shouted to a greasy overalled figure. The mechanic was peering into the engine compartment of a nearby patrol car. 'Just the man… do us a favour Ken, check this bag of nails over and fill it up. It's had the thrashing of its life and there may be more to come.'

He tossed the keys over and received a nonchalant thumbs-up in return.

Back in the office Lacey leant against a grey metal filing cabinet and leafed through the pages of Daniels' statement. 'Jack Duffield was right about Daniels. This statement's such a pack of lies. Farmer must have paid him well. It makes Kim and Doug Taylor out to be a right pair. I feel awful getting her involved in all this.'

Lacey turned his attention to his in-tray. A six-inch square jiffy bag parcel sat on top. The parcel bore a Special Delivery sticker. He turned it over in his hands and studied the postmark: *LUTON*.

'Right, I know what this is.'

He slit the top of the parcel open with a deadly-looking, ivory handled stiletto letter knife. This trophy from a previous murder trial had its very own, but not particularly unique nickname: Exhibit A.

He tipped the contents of the bag onto the table and watched the expected hypodermic syringe roll out. He looked around at Timson.

'Better get this off to the lab right away.'

Timson wore a resigned look; he knew the route well enough. The police forensic science laboratory was in Chepstow, almost ninety miles from Exeter. It would take him an hour and three quarters to get there, or maybe an hour and a half if he gave the little van its second thrashing of the day.

'I'll get straight on the road. Can you ring through and tell them to expect me? It must be a priority job.'

Lacey picked up the telephone. 'Sure thing and then I'll get on with those vehicle checks Doug's given me. He's ringing here at seven o'clock our time. It'd be good if we could have all the answers for him. It's going to be another long day.'

The interview room at Little Stoneleigh Police Station was a familiar place to Geoff Deakin; he'd conducted many interrogations from here, but never from this side of the table before. He stared down at the tape recorder watching its tiny wheels revolve as more questions were delivered.

The two senior detectives sitting opposite were known to him. He'd been involved on several major inquiries with them in the past, but the atmosphere was different now.

'Listen, Geoff,' one of the officers said patronisingly. 'We know your part in this is minor. In fact, it's probably nothing more than a bit of misguided loyalty to your boss, but the longer you keep quiet the more the suspicion piles up against you.'

The other officer leaned across the table. 'We can get your suspension lifted, if you come clean and tell us all about it.'

Deakin knew there was much more at stake than having his suspension from duty lifted.

'I'm not trying to be awkward gents,' he said. 'I know my position. If you've got the evidence to charge me with something then you must do it. I've said all I wish to say.'

Out in the corridor Farmer stood with an ear pressed hard against the door. He quickly pulled away as the Interview in Progress light was switched off.

The door opened and a man stepped out shaking his head. 'No, he's said nothing more. We've no evidence to charge him with anything at this stage. Has anything come in about the whereabouts of Taylor or WPC Harding?'

Farmer's cheeks wobbled. 'Nothing.'

THIRTY SIX

IN GHENT Taylor settled the café bill and got to his feet. 'That was good, fancy a wander around?'

Kim eased herself out from between the table and chair as Taylor reluctantly replaced his hat and added a pair of sunglasses to the disguise. They made their way outside and across the cobbled Sint Baafsplein square in front of the cathedral. A tram rumbled by on its metal rails, the criss-cross of overhead cables fizzing and sparking.

They started down one of the side streets, but within a few yards Kim took hold of Taylor's arm. 'Look, over there… walking towards the cathedral.'

Taylor matched Kim's line of sight and pinpointed the two men. 'So the guy with the briefcase is Swann?' He held his sunglasses up for a better look. 'The limping man with the blazer… he was the one in the bar?'

'Correct. Limper and Swann, sounds like a musical duo.'

Taylor turned to her. 'How do you feel about following them?'

Her decision was made. 'I'm on to it.' She turned and headed towards the men.

Taylor used the pretence of window shopping and watched as Kim kept forty yards and numerous tourists between herself and the targets. Her suspicious gaze followed them as they entered through the cathedral's main door.

She necessarily loitered for a few seconds before following them inside. Her first step into the cool, echoing interior brought with it realisation that the two men had been swallowed up by hundreds of tourists who were now dotted around the vast space. She made a bee-line for a group of sightseers and mingled. Her hope being to use the crowd as cover until she regained the eyeball.

It was several minutes later before Kim breathed a sigh of relief and focussed on the pair. They were thirty yards from her near to the central altar and in conversation with a cathedral tour guide. She closed in, planning to keep out of open sight behind the giant stone piers and wooden lattice carvings.

The guide's animated arm movements suggested some kind of detailed explanation to the men.

Kim used the opportunity to gain a few more yards. Last night's hotel bar encounter raced through her mind. If Swann saw her full-face in the brighter lighting of the cathedral he may just recognise her. She did not want to take that chance.

The conversation lasted a few more seconds before the guide nodded good day to the men and then walked over towards another group of tourists.

The older man took a piece of paper from his jacket pocket and showed it to Swann. Kim quickly dug into her bag and pulled out the small opera-style binoculars purchased in Dover. She put them to her eyes and looked upwards at the ceiling high above. After a few seconds of this tourist-charade she swung the glasses down and levelled them over at the men. A little clumsy thumbing of the central focusing wheel followed before she homed in.

Out on the pavement, Taylor took up a position a few yards back from the cathedral's entrance and contemplated the possibilities. The towering Gothic door was held wide open with an iron chain fixed to the wall. He could see a glass partition just beyond the door and through this a view existed inside the building. It was less than perfect, but did afford a glimpse into the interior. It also allowed him to see the outline of people making their way back outside.

The doorway exited straight onto the street's age-weathered flagstones. Rows of black painted, cast iron bicycle stands stood either side of the doorway to cater for the Belgian cycling obsession. A mix of varyingly coloured makes and sizes of bicycle filled every possible slot.

Rubbing the fingers of his left hand across his chin Taylor weighed-up the situation and then selected a particular bicycle in a stand to the left of the doorway. He looked up and down the square, hoping that no one would come for this machine during the next few minutes.

He took the Polaroid camera from around his neck, set it onto the cycle's saddle and crouched to squint through the viewfinder. After tilting and turning it for some time he eventually satisfied himself that the doorway was clearly in shot.

He stood to his feet with the flat of his hand pressing down onto the camera and resigned himself to a long and uncomfortable wait. He could only hope that his odd behaviour would not, in the eyes of locals, be considered too peculiar even for an English tourist.

Back inside the cathedral Kim relocated a few times as she tried for a better view of what Limper had taken from his pocket. Both men examined the object and now concentrated their attention on one of the many side chapels within the cathedral.

A sudden unannounced roar filled the building as the 6000 pipe, Klais organ, burst inspiringly into life. The ever-flashing cameras of Japanese tourists momentarily ceased and wandering sightseers stopped in their tracks as the powerful tones rolled through the cathedral.

Kim lowered her binoculars. The interruption seemed to have ended the men's mission. The older man pushed the item into his pocket and the pair started a stroll back down the aisle as the musician got into his practice for the evening's recital. The overture from Bach's Cantata Number twenty-nine charged the senses as the pair approached the exit.

Outside, as Taylor's wait entered its fifteenth minute, the baking sun was making him decidedly uncomfortable. The sketchy outline of the two men now heading for the door signalled a risky, but to Taylor's mind necessary, end to this particular juncture. After one last check through the camera's viewfinder he bent towards the handlebars, mimicking an attempt at unlocking the chain. He waited until the glass partition opened and the mighty organ's harmonics flooded out into the square.

The pair blinked at the bright sunlight as they took their first outside steps. Taylor squeezed his thumb down onto the shutter button and almost in the same action snatched the camera out of eyeshot.

With nothing more than his bent-over back now on show Taylor resumed his clumsy bicycle fumbling.

The older man glanced towards Taylor, but saw nothing more than a bungling cyclist. The two men walked off across the square.

Kim Harding found Taylor sitting on a bench hiding behind a newspaper. Her explanation of the events raised more questions.

'So, could you see what it was?'

'It was a photograph, definitely a black and white photograph, but of what I have absolutely no idea.'

He pulled his own photograph from his shirt pocket and placed it on Kim's knee.

She carefully picked it up by a corner and examined it. The two men were both in camera shot if not a little out of focus.

THIRTY SEVEN

IT WAS quarter to seven when Timson made it back to Exeter, jacket slung over shoulder, index finger crooked through collar tab and face a glistened deep pink.

'Bloody lift's out again,' he gasped.

Lacey looked up. 'Tell me about it. I thought you weren't going to make it in time, Doug should be ringing soon.'

Timson draped his jacket over a chair back. 'It's taken the lab man ages. It's a complicated procedure and I've probably broken every speed limit between here and Chepstow.'

Lacey made an expectant face. 'You have a result then?'

Timson slid his notepad across the desk. 'Indeed I have. The scientist has moaned about queue jumping. This would have taken two weeks normally; he's going to send the full report to us later.'

Lacey slowly read the wording written on the pad, struggling to get his tongue around the phrasing. 'Methohexitone Sodium,' he recited. 'Never heard of it, what is it?'

'A powerful anaesthetic, anything around 150 milligrams would knock a person out for ten or fifteen minutes. No dangerous after effects though, as long as you don't get too much.'

Lacey pursed his lips. 'Where did they get it? It's sure to be something covered by the Dangerous Drugs Act; not something you can buy over the counter or even get from a doctor.'

He theorised for a moment. 'A hospital most likely and not the kind of drug Sweeney would normally deal in.'

Timson's mystified expression matched Lacey's. 'The scientist was out of time but promised me priority on it. He's going to research it and get back to me with the particular uses and how it could be acquired.'

'What about prints… any fingerprints on the syringe?' Lacey asked as he jotted onto his pad.

'Yes, he's lifted a good print from the syringe barrel. He's sending it direct to Scotland Yard tomorrow.'

The telephone interrupted them. It was Taylor. There were stories to exchange from both sides. Lacey took the lead with his findings on the two British vehicles parked at the Belfort Hotel. 'The Escort is down to a man from Winchester. It checks out. Along with his wife he's on a holiday across Belgium. They booked it ages ago and so I'm sure it's legit.'

Lacey turned over a page. 'The Merc is a different story. It was sold at a car auction in Taunton four weeks ago to a Mr Timothy Smith. The address given, 95 Tipping Street, Taunton is duff, so the Merc almost certainly has to be the car this Mr Swann is using.' He made a hopeful face. 'I hate to ask, but what happened to our Carlton?'

There was a silence from the other end followed by Taylor's attempt at an apology. 'Ah, sorry Pete, your lovely red Carlton; I think it's best if we let it get found on its own. If I tip you off where it is, someone's going to start asking you difficult questions like: Who told you?'

It wasn't what Lacey wanted to hear but the rationale was sound. An agreement was also reached that Taylor would ring Lacey each evening at six o'clock Belgian time.

Kim had organised a snack out on their balcony, a Caesar Salad. Taylor relaxed back into his chair and poured two glasses of chilled white wine as he explained his telephone conversation. 'Your dad's relieved. He's not going to say a word and he's only going to talk to Pete and Reg. He was just happy to know you are okay.'

Taylor's notepad lay next to his wineglass. His occasional scribblings brought a smile to Kim's cheeks. He'd jokingly called this his accounts. It was supposed to be a list of the money that they'd spent from Farmer's cash along with the necessary justification.

Kim looked down at the pad. 'Do you think anyone will believe that?'

'God knows, but it makes me feel a bit better.'

She sipped the wine and lifted her head to look through the window. Something caught her attention. 'Look who's coming this way… it's Limper.'

It was Taylor's best view yet of the mystery man. He made a mental estimate, placing him as mid-sixties. He was slim with a shock of silver hair combed neatly across his forehead. He wore an open-necked, short-sleeved light grey shirt and black slacks. Despite his age and a slight limp to his left leg he appeared to be a muscular and fit man.

They watched as he drew closer.

'Looks like he's coming in here.' Taylor hardly finished his sentence before he was heading for the door. 'My turn at a bit of surveillance. This one hasn't seen me.'

He bounded down the hotel stairs, slowing his pace before rounding the corner into the hotel lobby. He arrived in time to see the man ping the brass bell on the reception counter. Taylor nonchalantly strolled across to the display shelves that were packed with tourist brochures, and began browsing.

A male receptionist appeared from the office doorway behind the counter. 'Monsieur Travers, room 214… Yes?' The young man turned and unhooked the room key.

'Yes, 214 it is,' the man agreed.

To Taylor's surprise the limping man made off briskly up the stairs rather than taking the lift, which by chance stood waiting with its doors open.

With his detective mode now firmly switched on, he went out onto the steps and stood, hands in pockets, studying the hotel's car park. It didn't take long for him to single out the yellow Triumph Dolomite with British registration plates.

He memorised the number and returned to the room with a smug smile. 'I didn't have to chat anybody up to get the info,' his name's Travers and he's in room 214.'

Kim's eyes narrowed. 'I'd like a look in there.'

Midnight arrived as Taylor took one last look out through the bedroom window. The square below was all but deserted and another intriguing and eventful day seemed at an end. He could not have known just then, that bed would still be hours away.

He went to tug the curtain closed, but stopped as he saw a figure making towards the hotel car park.

'It's Travers… he's going for his car.'

They were outside within two minutes. They could have been quicker, but necessarily slowed to a leisurely stroll as they passed through the foyer.

THIRTY EIGHT

THE TRIUMPH DOLOMITE, earmarked for Travers, had been replaced by an empty car park space. Kim fired up the BMW and set off in the direction of a distant set of tail lights, adjusting the seat and mirror on the move.

She needed to keep a fix on those lights, but there were still other vehicles about and Travers had a head start. It was not going to be easy.

Taylor pointed a hand towards the main route out of the city, 'I think he took a left.'

Tight-lipped and eyes unblinking, Kim raced the powerful car up through the gears. They were nearing the outskirts of the city, shops and cafés flashing by. She slotted the gearstick back down into second as a major junction came up ahead. The engine note whined and the rev counter flickered into the red. With a sharp downwards tug on the steering wheel the car was around a left-hand bend and away under full power. They were now on an almost deserted main road and heading away from the city. 'Damn,' she hissed, increasing the speed and dismissing one set of tail lights after another.

Keeping the possibility of an unwanted police car firmly in mind her vision darted between rear-view mirror and road ahead as she wound the BMW up to 90mph. She abruptly took her foot off the throttle and relaxed back into her seat as a distant set of lights came into view. 'That's him,' she exhaled with satisfaction.

It took another thirty seconds to assure themselves that the tail lights were indeed the Triumph's. Kim turned to Taylor and gave a confident nod, then instead of accelerating to catch the car she slowed and steered into the first side road on the right. Taylor smiled, he knew her trick. If Travers was watching his mirror for any following cars the tactic would hopefully allay his suspicions.

Kim turned the car's lights off and in the same instant pulled the steering wheel sharply around using the intersection to make a U-turn.

She settled the car to a halt with its nose nudging out on to the main road and kept her eyes firmly on the disappearing Triumph. She let it gain some ground before moving back out onto the main road, still without lights.

They were now well outside the city limits. An eerie stillness commanded the landscape as a cloud shrouded moon struggled to offer nothing more than the occasional hint of silvery detail. A couple of trucks were all that they encountered and these were both heading in the opposite direction, back towards the city.

With the passing of a few miles and the growing confidence that Travers did not suspect anything Kim switched the lights back on. She curbed her cravings to close the gap, keeping just the Dolomite's tail-lights in sight.

Ten more minutes went by and eight miles were covered before a roadside name board flashed past:

NAZARETH.

Kim pulled into the kerbside and watched the Triumph turn right from the main road. It then journeyed on down toward the place which shared its name with the childhood home of Jesus.

She allowed the separation to grow a little more before getting back to work, lights-off again and heading down a winding, high hedged lane.

Occasional sketchy moonlit glimpses of the village of Nazareth were caught through gaps, a distant black cluster of buildings and a single street lamp. Harding kept the bobbing tail lights of the other car just in view. It was important not to lose touch, but equally important not to raise suspicion.

The landscape flattened at the foot of the hill and a few more signs of civilisation emerged with a small street of darkened shops and some parked cars.

Up ahead the Triumph slowed to a walking pace and falteringly came to a halt a couple of times. It seemed an indication that the driver was searching for somewhere or something. Kim pulled the BMW in behind one of the parked cars, using it as cover. They watched and listened, engine off and windows down.

Unlike its namesake, Nazareth was just a collection of small businesses and a couple of cafés. The pitched roofs of a few houses and the remnants of disused farm buildings could be picked out standing behind those on the roadside.

The Triumph's lights showed a sudden, confident turn from the main road into a lane on the right. The manoeuvre suggested that the driver had found where he needed to go. An immediate bright red glow of the car's high-wattage brake lights filtered through from the turning and then quickly went out. The abrupt turn, the brake lights and now the complete silence declared that the driver had pulled up and switched off.

The drive from Ghent through to this hitherto unknown destination allowed for a rushed contingency plan and now was the time to put it into action.

Taylor hopped out of the car and started a brisk but stealthy walk towards the junction. Keeping in the shadows against the shop doorways he gave the lone street lamp a wide berth.

It was apparent that the population of Nazareth were all tucked up in bed. Not a single light showed. A distant barking dog's attempts to break the silence were futile.

Taylor reached the turning where he'd last seen the Triumph. A high-walled brick built barn towered up from the pavement forming the corner of this narrow junction. He flattened his back against the brickwork, pressed his right cheek hard against the gritty masonry and slowly edged forward for a view around the corner.

A vast weeping willow partially obscured a large church. A lone figure now crept through the graveyard, nothing more than a smudged outline. A furtive over-the-shoulder glance, a small bag in his left hand, a limp! Travers melted into the blackness.

The Triumph stood parked in deep shadow at the side of the church gateway and was only revealed when a glint of moonlight flickered onto its window glass.

Taylor edged his way around the side of the barn and silently clambered over the low wall into the graveyard. He picked his way carefully between memorials, crosses and slabs of weathered granite.

He moved closer towards the rear of the church and positioned himself behind the trunk of a gnarled Yew tree.

Travers seemed to have evaporated into thin air. Taylor took a slow and silent breath. Maybe he was the one now being observed!

He crept from behind the tree, moved forwards a little and then came to a stop. He was stooping, knees bent, and with both hands gripping the rusting bars surrounding a large crumbling stone monument. He stared into the black void that his brain told him was the back of the church. Gradually as his sight adjusted, some distinguishing features materialised: Buttresses, windows, a steeply pitched tiled roof above a porch – a rear doorway.

His wide unblinking eyes settled onto the Gothic outlines and slowly narrowed down into a suspicious squint as he detected movement. The oily outline of a figure crouching against the door began to separate from the grainy black backcloth.

Taylor watched, mesmerised as the tiny yellow glow of a low-powered pen torch lit a portion of the church door. Travers fumbled, trying to shield the light with his body as he inserted a huge iron key into the lock.

Taylor's squint became more intense as Travers struggled with the lock. Finally a dull mechanical *clunk* broke the silence as the old mechanism shifted around. Travers pushed a shoulder against the door and a predictable creaking groan was the only other sound as the door submitted and opened up. Travers vanished inside and carefully closed the door behind him.

Back in the car Kim felt frustrated and more than a little helpless.

The two-way radio lay on the passenger seat issuing its unrelenting hiss. The original plan to keep both radios switched on revealed there was no way to stop the constant hissing. Consequently, Taylor's set would remain switched off in his pocket for emergency use.

Kim recalled what he'd said. *'Well, I suppose we couldn't expect much more for a tenner of Farmer's money.'*

She made a little frown as she started to wonder what might be happening.

Taylor had carefully crept to within twenty yards of the porch. He was about to edge a little closer but jolted to a halt as a bright beam of powerful light inside the building lit the stained glass windows. This was nothing like the pen torch that Travers used on the door lock. Taylor could clearly see the strong beam arcing around as Travers concentrated it high up on the ceiling.

Almost as quickly as he'd entered, Travers was out of the church and back into the porch. Taylor was caught off guard. He dodged back behind a gravestone. His right foot slithered outwards, scrunching into the dry pebble-laden earth making an almost imperceptible sound.

Travers dropped down on all fours, his outline quickly fading into the shadows.

Taylor froze. The shrubbery at the side of the gravestone still gave him a well-hidden view. Minutes ticked by, but he dared not move. The figure was almost indiscernible, dissolving before his eyes. He strained unblinking trying to watch for any movement.

Kim checked her watch, ten minutes to two, she gave a sigh. Taylor had been missing almost thirty minutes. She hated the not knowing and toyed with the idea of sneaking to the end of the street, maybe she could find Travers' car. She sat back into her seat. She had no real idea which way Taylor or Travers had gone and Taylor's parting words were pretty precise. 'Stay put. Any problems and I'll turn the radio on and let you know.'

She leaned forwards in her seat, cocking her head towards the open window as the still night air was broken by the distant sound of an engine starting up.

The hissing radio supplied Taylor's fragmented sentence. 'Okay, c-ming back n-w, keep your h… down.'

Less than a minute later the Triumph drove past and up towards the main road. Kim craned around, to watch the rear red lights disappear from sight into the darkness of the twisting high hedged lane.

Another ten minutes went by before Taylor appeared silently jogging back along the pavement.

They sat out a full half hour in the car before starting back. An unscheduled meeting with Travers in the hotel lobby at this time of night would look suspicious.

THIRTY NINE

THE NEXT MORNING a sand-filled, red fire bucket held the front door of the Hotel Harmony ajar. It was hardly half past nine but the light breeze drifting in across the square was welcome. Another baking hot day looked likely and the foyer and restaurant were already warm enough to warrant that extra ventilation.

Taylor arrived downstairs ahead of Kim intent on arranging a breakfast table with a view across the square. He was surprised to see Travers already seated. The man showed not the slightest hint of last night's clandestine visit to Nazareth Church. His cleared breakfast plate lay in front and he'd made a start on the toast and marmalade.

Outside, shoppers and sightseers already filled the city square. A group of camera toting Japanese meandered, arms pointing and necks craning. Pedal cyclists darted fearlessly in and out of impossible traffic gaps whilst sparking trams rumbled effortlessly by on their iron rails.

Kim chanced a glance at Travers as she entered. She took her seat and met Taylor's eyes with an exaggeratedly astonished expression. 'Can't believe he's down here and acting so normal after last night's antics,' she whispered.

Taylor's shake of the head implied full agreement. 'Me neither… we'd better take a buffet breakfast this morning… he could be on the move any time soon and we need to find out what he's up to.'

Just fifteen minutes went by before Travers folded his napkin, and stood from the table. A few stray crumbs were flicked from his jacket before he casually headed outside.

Kim dropped a half-eaten slice of toast back to her plate and eased up from her chair. 'Okay, I'll follow. I'm not going to get close. He could suspect something if he sees me too often. You'd better keep your head down in case he's meeting Swann.'

Taylor gave a frustrated nod. 'So who is the Inspector here

anyway?'

She turned back and winked. 'Rank doesn't count today.' She was quickly through the lobby and out onto the hotel steps. She gave Travers a full thirty seconds of limping progress across the square before starting after him.

The crowds of sightseers gave good cover and Kim covertly watched her quarry make a definite bee-line for the Belfort Hotel. His arrival outside the entrance came as the enormous bell tower clock began to chime ten.

On cue, the hotel's revolving door spun slowly around and Swann stepped out onto the pavement. He nodded at Travers.

Taylor busied himself with another tour of the cathedral, but was soon back in the room and going through tourist brochures. He gave some more thought to the tattered pieces of paper recovered from the brewery. He checked and rechecked names and words with maps and guide books.

The last thirty minutes of his wait for Kim's return turned into a pensive, balcony vigil. A full three hours passed before he eventually sighted her distant figure strolling back.

His tunnel vision was so intense that he almost missed another figure down on the car park. He moved back away from the rail and watched Travers load an oversized and heavy looking holdall into the back of his car.

Taylor met Kim in the corridor outside the room. 'You've been ages, I was getting worried.' He pushed the door open for her.

'That's nice of you. It's been quite a trek.' She plonked herself down in the armchair by the window and kicked off her shoes.

Taylor made some coffee as Kim gave her résumé.

'They went into a sports shop and a camping shop… you know… outdoor activities gear. Not one, but three... I guess they couldn't get all the stuff they needed from one place. Oh, and tool shops… DIY stores.'

She cupped the mug of coffee with both hands holding it against her chin. 'I had to be careful, I couldn't get close enough to see what they were after, apart from one shop where I could see from outside. It was rope and string, a holdall, maybe a rucksack as well, you know, like you have on your back when you're hiking. They must have put what they bought in the holdall.'

'Weird.' Taylor shook his head, 'I watched Travers put the holdall in the boot of his car. It looked full of gear.'

'They went into a sports shop,' Kim said, nodding at Taylor's description. 'They were there for ages. I even chanced a glass of coke in a café over the road. When they came out, Swann had a long, black zip-up type bag. It must have been about six feet long. Lord knows what it was.'

Taylor shook his head again as Kim continued. 'And then the tool shop. I don't know what for, but the holdall was pretty well full when they came out.'

Taylor raised his eyebrows. 'Is that it?'

'Yes, they went into a restaurant for some lunch. That was awkward. The only place I could go to watch was a bookshop probably fifty yards away, a hopeless view.'

Taylor leaned over, taking hold of Kim's hands and gently pulling her to her feet. 'You've done a great job, but what the hell are they planning to do?'

He pulled her close sliding his hand under her blouse and stroking the smooth downy flesh on the small of her back, they fell back onto the bed.

Taylor awoke with a start at twenty past six, cursing himself as he fought with his boxer shorts. 'I should have phoned Pete at six.'

Lacey was quick to answer Taylor's breathless call. 'Almost given you up Doug,' he said.

The story of the night time visit to Nazareth Church intrigued Lacey. He promised some research on the place as well as a check on

Travers and his car. The peculiar shopping trip interested him. It seemed likely that it might be connected to some future visit to the Church.

Taylor checked the cars before returning to the room. The Mercedes remained in place on the Belfort car park and the Triumph Dolomite hadn't shifted since its return to the hotel in the early hours. There appeared to be no likelihood of movement from either suspect.

Taylor's suggestion of an evening meal received approval. 'The Amadeus Restaurant looks ideal.' He attempted to justify the idea. 'It's right in the square. We can watch both hotels if we get a window seat.'

Kim narrowed her eyes in mock suspicion. She had, after all, watched him read through the extensive menu displayed in the window during yesterday's outing to the cathedral.

The candlelit interior, high ceilings and elaborate décor with heavy velvet drapes and huge art nouveau mirrors stepped them back into a pre-war era. More than a hint of France was added with a rolling romantic melody from the piano accordionist.

It seemed rude not to sample the speciality dish, an enormous rack of ribs!

FORTY

THE NEXT MORNING a British Airways Boeing 737 jet taxied over to the terminal building after landing at Manchester Airport. At five minutes past nine it was a mere twenty minutes late in its flight from Tenerife. The hostess bid the queue of suntanned holidaymakers a safe journey home as they bustled to make their way through the exit doors and onwards to the luggage carousel.

The man from seat 15C bent over more than the other passengers as he squeezed his six feet six inch frame out into the aisle. With only a small black bag and no hold luggage to collect he would be through customs and on his way in no time at all.

Steve Gorton had selected one of his many fake passports before setting off from Tenerife. He took a quick peek at the details inside to remind himself of his name before heading for passport control.

At that selfsame moment three hundred and twenty-five miles away in the restaurant of the Hotel Harmony Doug Taylor and Kim Harding pulled out chairs and settled down for breakfast. Travers had beaten them to it again. He sat calmly reading his newspaper, with only remnants left on his plate.

Their own meal would be anything but leisurely. The need to follow Travers again was a possibility and anyway, last night's feast left them easily satisfied with toast and coffee.

The first few bites had hardly been swallowed before Travers was on his way back up the stairs to his room.

A waiting game appeared to be compulsory. With another pot of coffee ordered the two made themselves comfortable in the lounge, uncertain as to whether or not Travers would reappear.

Taylor's concentration on his magazine was broken sooner than expected by Kim's kick to his shin. Travers, clad in grey tracksuit and with rolled towel beneath arm, bounded down the stairs and disappeared at a trot towards the hotel's indoor swimming pool.

Taylor rubbed his hand on the affected shin. 'I'd love a look in his room.'

They were on their feet and up the stairs without another word.

As they arrived on floor two it was apparent that the maid was at work. A wicker linen basket stood halfway along the corridor with its lid propped back against the wall. A bedroom door hung open and the sound of a vacuum cleaner droned noisily from inside.

'Bad timing,' Taylor commented as he focussed on the closed door of room 214, uncertain if it had been cleaned or was still on the list. He guided Kim with his eyes towards the linen basket.

She moved silently towards the open bedroom door, aware that her role was to keep watch.

With a partial line of sight into the room she settled into a spot where she could act out an interest in one of the corridor's wall hanging paintings.

Taylor acknowledged her cagey nod of the head and pressed a hand against Travers' door. He lightly felt at the security of the lock. There was not much give. He had his credit card ready for the operation and attempted to press it into the gap between the door-lock and frame. He cursed to himself. The door was a solid fit, and this old-fashioned burglar's trick wasn't going to work. Next he pulled out his own room key and slid it into the lock. It fitted to perfection, but would turn neither left nor right. He vibrated the key in and out of the lock at the same time as attempting to turn it.

Kim's cough interrupted his technique. Taylor turned on his heel and started back towards the lift before the maid emerged from the doorway.

'No, it's not going to work,' he said as Kim caught up. 'These room keys are all made from the same profile. They'll fit into every bedroom door perfectly, but should only work on one. If the lock is a bit worn you can sometimes jiggle the key enough to turn it, but that one feels pretty new. We'll have to come up with another plan.'

Steve Gorton's drive down the M6 to Junction 15 took him a leisurely fifty-five minutes. The hired Ford Sierra was no getaway car, but it served the purpose.

He followed the direction signs from the A34 down into Little Stoneleigh, memorising the layout. He gave Granville's Club a curious glance before he parked the car. He needed to make a little shopping trip and Woolworths would probably provide him with his needs.

By eleven he was back in the car and cruising towards the outskirts of the town. He slowed as the old brewery came into sight. He'd been before. The place had been a good safe house for the cash and drugs swaps. The vans and teams of men arriving at a building site did not create any suspicion. It was a good cover and Gorton supplied the necessary muscle in case of unwanted visitors.

Gorton looked from the driver's window digesting the available information. Fluttering blue and white tape across the gateway publicised the serious incident. Uniformed constables and plain clothes investigators, even after so long were still busy measuring, photographing, searching and dusting for fingerprints.

The white Ford Granada inside the gateway proved interesting to Gorton, or rather the uniformed figure slouched against it. He slowed almost to a stop to get a better look.

Farmer was loading his mouth with chips from a newspaper wrapper. Gorton recognised him from a photograph supplied by Sadie. The photograph must have been taken several years ago as Farmer, with age, had grown even more repulsive.

Gorton drove on with the thoughts of the last twelve months going through his mind. He recalled trying to convince both David Sweeney and Sadie that they put too much trust in Charlie Price.

He pursed his lips as he drove on down the lane towards the canal bridge. He was confused that he could have been so wrong about Price, who was now dead and had paid the ultimate price for his loyalty to Sweeney. In Gorton's mind Price had been the prime suspect as the grasser putting all the information through to the police. He did, after all, know everything about the organisation and was always involved in the planning for drugs and money exchanges.

A few hundred yards further along the road Gorton pulled the car to a halt on a small lay-by adjacent to the Trent and Mersey Canal. He switched off the engine, unclipped his seat belt and rested his elbow through the open window. He sat and reflected on the possibilities. Surely the two police officers hadn't killed Price? That was absurd. Or was it? There was a lot of money involved. More money than two coppers would see in several lifetimes, and the hue and cry now hitting the press since they went missing indicated strong evidence against them.

Sweeney's break from court didn't appear out of character to Gorton. There were a lot of questions though. Who planned it, where did the gun come from?

These things, Gorton knew only too well required a lot of planning. A getaway car, a driver and a safe house would be priorities. He hawked noisily and spat phlegm through the car window as he deliberated Farmer's involvement.

He relit a half-smoked roll-up. The thought went through his mind about how much Sweeney detested Farmer, the corrupt policeman who ruined his childhood and blighted his family. Farmer only remained alive because of his usefulness. That usefulness would be terminated upon his retirement from the police. 'Terminated along with Farmer himself,' to use Sweeney's own words.

Gorton tilted his head, making a matter-of-fact face as he thought about Jacob Bunn's death. *Yes, definitely par for the course, but why dump his body where it was waiting to be found?* Sweeney had disappeared without trace along with all the money intended for the last drugs transaction. All six and a half million pounds of it. Could Sweeney really have left the sinking ship? Could he really have murdered Jacob Bunn? Could he abandon his mother, the one who was always there for him?

Gorton sucked hard at his cigarette. *Yes*, he thought, *yes, to everything apart from abandoning his mother. That part didn't fit.* He flicked the cigarette end, watching it tumble to a smouldering stop in the centre of the road and then cast his thoughts back to Farmer. He was the key, he knew what had happened and he was the main reason for this visit to Little Stoneleigh.

A cardboard container lay on the passenger seat next to Gorton. It was poking out from a red and white Woolworths' plastic carrier bag. He allowed himself a smile at the wording on the box:

ELECTRIC CARVING KNIFE: Powerful 150 watt motor: Twin stainless steel blades: Slices through all meats with ease.

Maybe there was someone else who could help Gorton unravel some of the mystery before tackling Farmer.

FORTY ONE

GORTON DROVE back into town and manoeuvred into a space on the car park of the Queens Hotel.

In no time he stood facing the receptionist, bag in hand and deciding what name to book in under. Inside an hour and with a cheese roll and a can of lager behind him he was back out on the High Street. He had business to attend to and this was a good time.

Granville's Club was closed and deserted. No surprises there, it was after all a nightclub. A stroll past the building and a casual through-the-window stare gave Gorton all the information he needed. The guitar shaped clock on the back wall showed the time as half past three.

He'd not stooped to this end of the criminal spectrum for many years, but experience told him that this was the best time to screw a nightclub. The cleaners had been and gone, and the staff wouldn't be back until getting on for opening time. A glance at the upstairs windows gave him confidence that no one lived on the property, there were no curtains.

'Piece of piss,' he muttered as he studied the various notices and adverts.

One caught his eye. Bold, thick green marker pen:

TONIGHT – Saturday

Jazz Mattaz

Don't miss em!

Doors open at eight.

Without so much as an over-the-shoulder glance he strolled from the High Street into the side entry. A sturdy, six feet high wooden gate was fitted into a wall of similar height. It was clear that this gave access to the club's rear yard. He pressed a palm against it feeling the presence of a heavy bolt half-way down, too far to reach over. Effortlessly he hoisted himself up. The leather soles of his shoes made gritty contact with the yard's brick surface as he dropped down.

A pair of bright yellow kitchen gloves were produced from a pocket, the largest size available. The tightening rubber emitted a creaking rasp as he stretched them onto his giant hands and flexed his fingers. With a self-assured shrug he tested the iron bars protecting a ground floor window until he sensed some movement.

Within two minutes Gorton was inside the club's kitchen. Two of the bars, ripped from the brickwork by his powerful hands, now stood propped against an outside wall. No other force was necessary. The window had been left open due to the hot weather and it was always thought that the bars would stop any burglar! He nonchalantly sauntered from the kitchen into the club area, picking his way through the deserted room until he spied the door marked *Staff Only*.

The locked door yielded at the first nudge of his shoulder. He climbed the stairs, dismissing the *Staff Toilet* door, and tried the door marked *Office*. Two more shoulder nudges splintered the old wooden frame and the door flirted open.

The office was well-used and untidy. No doubt its keeper knew exactly where everything was. The green metal filing cabinet caught his eye. He tugged at the top drawer and gave a frustrated sigh. It was locked. He turned and scanned. The wooden writing desk was littered with the previous week's paraphernalia: posters, notes, biros, a microphone with its top hanging off, envelopes. Everything was piled up on top of a large plastic-edged blotter.

Gorton lifted the corner of the blotter with his yellow-sheathed index finger. His roll of the eyes accompanied a shake of the head as he picked up the small key hidden beneath. He slotted it into the filing cabinet's lock and turned. The top drawer slid out easily on its metal runners to reveal a line of manila card files.

Lying flat down on the edge of the files was a sealed brown envelope with wording in biro: *£200 – Group*.

He placed the envelope on top of the cabinet and then surveyed the yellow marker labels which stood up from the files:

GAS
ELECTRIC
WATER
PHONE
INSURANCE
STAFF
BARCLAYS.

He selected the *STAFF* file, pulling it from the drawer and setting it down on the only available space on the desk. Thumbing through its contents he stopped at the page marked: *DOORMAN/SECURITY.*

The details recorded in the file on *William Keith Daniels* were limited to his national insurance number, pay scale and some information on his sickness record. They also documented his current address: *27 Bath Street, Little Stoneleigh.*

Gorton returned the file to the drawer, replaced the £200 envelope, pushed the drawer in, locked it and put the key back under the blotter.

He looked around the room for a few seconds and then yanked out the central desk drawer. He shook the contents out. Biros, staples, drawing pins, batteries, scraps of paper and other office trappings rained down onto the floor. A rusty Old Holborn tobacco tin clunked at his feet. He rattled it, flicked off the lid and removed the three five pound notes and loose change.

Back downstairs his eyes landed on the fruit machine, dark and silent against the wall. Taking hold of it by the top edge he pulled it forwards and set it facedown onto the floor. The stainless steel blade of a flick knife flashed as it snapped out with a precision sounding *click*. He dug the knife into the black painted wooden back of the machine slicing into the ten-inch square panel, which he knew secured the cash container.

He left through the kitchen door, unbolted the gate, peeled off his gloves and coolly strode back into the main street.

FORTY TWO

HUMDRUM would describe Taylor and Harding's day so far with most of their time spent in the lounge of the Hotel Harmony. After his visit to the swimming pool Travers did not show his face again. The failed attempt to get into his room served as the only event to break the monotony. The occasional stroll across the square suggested that Swann was taking an equally lazy day – the Mercedes remained inch perfect in its parking spot.

As six o'clock approached Kim made her way back upstairs and Taylor set his sights on the hotel's telephone booth to call Pete Lacey.

He was back in the bedroom within twenty minutes, sitting on the edge of the bed and relating the conversation. Kim, seated at the dressing table, listened and gave the occasional nod.

'Pete says that Nazareth Church is a bit of a tourist attraction… something to do with the war. He's trying to find out more.' Taylor tapped a finger onto his notepad. 'As for Travers' car, the Triumph Dolomite, it was purchased from the same car auction as Swann's Mercedes in another fictitious name and address.'

Taylor widened his eyes. He had kept the most important news till the last. 'He's also managed to get some info through from Little Stoneleigh. He's spoken with Cheddar…' There was a pause. Taylor felt the need to clarify. 'That's DC Cheeseman… one of my team. Cheddar has told him the post mortem result has come through on the body in the Jag…'

Kim's expression was serious. 'Well, go on, tell me what it says.'

'Cheddar doesn't know anything about our situation,' Taylor explained. 'But he's a shrewd detective. He dislikes Farmer… knows what he's like.'

'Well,' Kim urged. 'The post mortem?'

'It says that dental records prove conclusively that the body is

Jacob Bunn. A gunshot to the heart killed him and after death another bullet was fired into the top of his left shoulder.'

Kim tilted her head to one side as she visualised the sickeningly violent scene. 'What, the second shot was … to make sure?'

'Maybe, maybe not,' he made a shrug of uncertainty. 'The kill shot,' he put emphasis to the phrase. 'Went right through the chest and out through the back, leaving a big exit wound. We couldn't see that hole with all the burning at the scene, but it must have been obvious to the murderer that he was already dead.'

Kim narrowed her eyes. She held her lips tightly together in a look of disgust.

'Evil bastards. Why shoot him again? Can the pathologist be sure the shoulder wound was done after death?'

Taylor pursed his lips. 'Yes, but the bullet from the heart wound went straight through and is lost. The shoulder wound bullet, however, penetrated down thorough his abdomen and was recovered from the top of his right femur bone. Ballistics have identified it as from the same 9mm gun that Sweeney used in court, which he shot into the ceiling. Cheddar has also said that no money was recovered from the brewery.' Taylor raised his eyebrows. 'So, where do we think that's gone then? I mean, we saw it… we put it in the van.'

Kim took a deep breath.

'Yes, one guess is enough… Farmer! We thought he took a long time getting his car. I bet he couldn't believe his luck.'

Taylor gave a firm nod. 'That's not all he took away with him. Pete told me that no gun was recovered from the brewery either. So Farmer's got Price's gun.'

In Little Stoneleigh the front door of Granville's nightclub was open. The manager, Kevin Owen stood on the step, arms folded and not looking pleased. Opening time approached and the arrival of the two CID officers had been a long time coming.

Cheddar stared over the roof of the Ford Escort CID car at his colleague as he closed the door. 'I was hoping to get off on time today, Mo.'

Jayne Morrison tucked her pad of statements under her arm and patted her jacket pocket, checking for cigarettes. 'Huh, that went out the window ages ago.'

Owen watched their progress across the car park, their identity obvious even without a police uniform. 'Kids again,' he said as the detectives drew closer.

'Yes?' Cheddar said questioningly, before turning the sentence into an apology. 'Sorry, it's taken a while to get to you; we were out on another job, miles away. Has the SOCO been?'

Owen led the way through the club, responding to Cheddar's question on the move. 'Yes, he's not long left. No fingerprints though, he said the burglar was wearing gloves. Apparently he can tell from the marks he's found.' Owen's tone gave away a hint of scepticism.

'What's been taken?' Morrison asked.

'A bit of petty cash, from the office drawer upstairs, about fifteen quid. They had a go at the bandit.' He gestured over to the prone fruit machine. 'But couldn't get it open.'

Cheddar took a diversion from Owen's guided tour and wandered over, looking down at the fruit machine. He pursed his lips as he examined the superficial scrape marks on the back.

'This can go back on its feet now.' He bent and lifted the heavy machine back into place with ease. 'Show us where they got in.'

Owen was unceasing with his narrative as he led the way through to the kitchen.

'Damned good job they didn't get into the office filing cabinet, there's two hundred quid in there for the band tonight. We'd have been in a right mess. They've caused a bit of damage, door frames and what not.'

Arriving in the kitchen Owen showed the detectives the open window with its missing iron bars. Cheddar listened gratefully to the manager's interpretation of what had taken place, but seemed more interested in the dusty footmark in the base of the Belfast sink beneath the window. He ran the fingers of his left hand over his long since shaven chin and stepped from the kitchen doorway into the yard. The rusty bars were still propped against the wall. He frowned as he inspected them.

Owen led the way up the stairs to the office. 'My doorman hasn't turned in for work yet either, and I need to open up now. We should be busy tonight, so we'll be in a right mess if he doesn't come.'

Bath Street, Little Stoneleigh lay a quarter of a mile from Granville's and made an easy walk to work for Billy Daniels. The several streets of two up two down terraces formed a run-down part of town.

Gorton pinched back two inches of yellowing lace curtain. The front window of the house looked out onto other similar homes A few cars were parked, mostly tatty old models; some showing evidence of DIY repairs and vandalism, snapped aerials, patches of rust, wheel trims missing.

Graffiti seemed a popular pastime: *Jodie's a slag, Fuk Of* and other misspelled words had been spray painted on some portions of brickwork.

Gorton shook his head slowly as the surroundings evoked childhood memories. He moved back from the window as a gaunt-looking young girl shuffled along, cigarette drooping from her mouth. The tiny occupant of the old-fashioned pram she pushed was probably not all that many years younger than herself.

Gorton decided to leave through the back door, it was after all, the way he'd entered and there would be less chance of witnesses.

He spared no second thought for the horrifying carnage as he walked through the small back room and into the kitchen. The bright yellow rubber kitchen gloves, which were still stretched onto his hands, contrasted with the dreary background. He swilled the blood from them into the sink, seeing it wash down onto the pile of filthy dishes, takeaway cartons and discarded tea bags.

He dried his gloved hands on the tattered curtain that hung over the sink, picked up his Woolworths' carrier bag and pulled the backdoor closed behind him. The yellow gloves were peeled off as he made his way from the rear yard. The other shopping bag he carried contained a meagre twenty thousand pounds, the first of the missing cash to be recovered.

In Ghent Taylor took Kim's hand as they descended the staircase from their hotel room. An evening meal in the Harmony's own restaurant had been planned. They would have loved to explore more of the city, but duty did still call, even if, in an unorthodox way.

Apparently Travers was taking his own meals here, and as a scheme was still being hatched to search his room they needed to pin down all his movements and time things to perfection.

Kim looked fabulous, a white silk blouse, dark blue cord trousers and black high heels. Their table, right alongside the window, afforded a good view across the square to the Belfort Hotel. It was distant but observable, especially as the crowds had now faded away back to their homes and hotels.

They both chose to try a local speciality dish; something called Whitloof. Taylor pulled a bewildered face as he turned the chicory and ham roll over in its cheese sauce and sliced off a piece.

'Mmm,' he mumbled approvingly, eagerly readying a second piece. 'This is good.'

The guess that Travers would be eating in the hotel restaurant proved correct and he took his place half an hour after they arrived.

Kim gave an appreciative nod as she finished off the last morsel from the back of her fork. She took a look over at Travers. He created a curious, distinguished figure, slowly and casually eating his meal. The usual newspaper lay folded in half on the edge of the table. He was absorbed in his reading, but occasionally peered over his glasses at the other guests.

The pair purposely dawdled with their desserts, synchronising the last few mouthfuls to perfection. Travers got to his feet, folded his napkin and returned it to the table. Out in the lobby the lift doors stood open but predictably the man bounded away up the stairs.

Taylor gave a frustrated sigh and ordered coffee in the lounge. He leaned back in his seat. 'Car keys?'

Kim patted her handbag. 'Yes, we can sit it out and see if anything's going to happen.'

FORTY THREE

ECCELSHALL ROAD, Little Stoneleigh, half a mile from town, was a pleasant residential spot and much more upmarket than the crumbling terraces around the Bath Street area. The roads radiating from either side were tree lined with mostly detached, privately owned homes built in the 1930s.

Gorton drove slowly and one-handed as his eyes moved from the road ahead to the torn slip of paper held in his left hand. The tall slanted lettering was Gorton's own writing and showed an address: *Bainbridge Crescent.* The number *15* had been written, but with a question mark against it. More of the same laborious tall lettering gave a description: *House on left, silver birch tree, green front door.* A dark smudge of dried blood showed on the corner of the paper.

The car's wheels were hardly turning as he came to a street on his left. He read the black and white road nameplate and took the turn into Bainbridge Crescent.

Privet hedges and larch lap fencing defined the boundaries of most of the homes. Trees sprouted from the tarmac pavement throughout its curving length. One house though, looked rather shabby by Bainbridge Crescent standards and that silver birch outside the gate clearly blocked the sunlight.

The loose stone chippings of the road surface crackled under the Sierra's tyres as Gorton coasted past the house and focussed onto the number fixed to its green front door: 15. The information given proved surprisingly accurate considering the circumstances under which it was obtained.

In the lounge of the Hotel Harmony, Taylor and Harding were still sitting it out. They held some concern that their sustained presence may start to attract attention as they occasionally sipped imaginary coffee from long since emptied cups.

Eleven o'clock came and went and still no sign of Travers, but also no reasons to suggest that he had left his room. Taylor's opinion that the delicious meal should really have been followed up with a large malt whisky received a smirk and a shake of the head from Kim. Their pledge to stay alcohol free on this night would be obeyed. A jointly held intuition suggested that something was going to happen.

The hunch became reality as Travers appeared from the stairway, not his normal impeccable self. No jacket and tie, but wearing jeans, training shoes and a tight-fitting dark coloured pullover. In his right hand he held a set of car keys. He was through the lobby and out onto the car park in an instant.

'We'll have to wait a while,' Taylor advised. 'If he sees us come straight out he'll suspect something.'

Kim agreed. It wasn't worth blowing their cover, but Travers was already behind the wheel of the Triumph.

By the time Kim managed to pull the BMW out onto the square Travers was gone. Their progress had been thwarted by an elderly Belgian gent in a battered Renault. Oddly, the last sighting of the Triumph's tail lights did not suggest a return to Nazareth. The car had taken a route, towards the industrialised part of the city.

Taylor cursed under his breath at the bad luck as Kim powered the car in the general direction of Travers' last known heading. 'I don't know what to do,' she said. 'We've lost him.'

Antiquated street lamps poorly illuminated their route through narrow alleys and side roads. Kim raced the car from one junction to the next hoping for a renewed sighting. It was late by Belgian standards and the roads were now quiet. The Dolomite would stand out like a sore thumb, but there was nothing.

The floodlit cathedral acted as a landmark to guide them back into the centre of the city. Twenty five minutes passed before Kim pulled to a halt alongside the monument to Ghent's favourite artist: Jan Van Eyke. She banged both hands down onto the steering wheel. 'Let's go to the church, we've nothing to lose.'

Quarter to one arrived before the journey across the city and the eight miles to Nazareth were covered. The village was embraced in the same darkened quietness as on their last visit. The steady winding gradient took them down to the High Street where Kim neatly parked against the kerb.

Taylor reached over and hauled the grip bag from the rear seat as Kim turned off the engine. He pulled out a pair of trainers, pushed backwards in his seat and slipped off his shoes. Kim wrestled her own trainers from the bag and then copied Taylor's routine to the letter.

Taylor's comment was expected. 'What are you doing?'

'I'm coming this time.'

There would be no debate. Taylor rolled his eyes, tugged two pullovers from the bag and handed one to Kim. He gave her a sideways look. 'This could be a waste of time.'

FORTY FOUR

GRANVILLE'S in Little Stoneleigh was busy, *packed out* would be a better description. Manager, Kevin Owen had closed the doors early as the place was at capacity by eleven and with no doorman he'd got enough to cope with. Fortunately it had been a great party atmosphere all night and so Daniels' absence hadn't made much difference.

Nevertheless, Owen was livid that his employee had not turned in for work.

'No phone call, nothing, he's a liability.' The comments were shouted above the din so that barmaid Emma, standing next to him could hear.

Taking his eyes momentarily from the glass of wine he was pouring he directed his voice for a second time. 'Thanks for coming in my hour of need. I'd rather pay you than that jerk anyway. I think he causes more trouble than he stops.'

'Yes,' Emma yelled back as she topped up a pint of lager. 'I certainly won't argue. I need the money, and anyway, look at this crowd, great bunch and not even a hint of any aggro.'

Owen didn't reply, his attention had been diverted by the uniformed police constable waving through the window to be let in.

The sight of a policeman could spell a visit to the Magistrates Court and the revoking of the club's drinks licence. Owen took a worried look at his wristwatch: quarter past one, still well within his permitted hours. His signal to the young glass collector resulted in the officer being admitted through the side kitchen door.

Some interested chatter quickly started up about the constable's attendance. A couple of customers standing at the bar went onto tiptoe for a better view through to the kitchen. Owen's conversation with the officer though, would have required a lip reader to interpret. It was nevertheless clear from his animated body language and facial expressions that serious news was being imparted.

'My God, I can't believe it,' Owen said. 'He was here last night. What makes you think he was MURDERED?'

The policeman shook his head. 'I'm sorry, sir, I'm afraid I'm not allowed to tell you anything more at the present time, but believe me it was murder all right.'

The drama unfolding in Little Stoneleigh was in stark contrast to the stillness of Nazareth village. One solitary bedroom light showed as the only sign of life. Taylor and Harding hurried across the cobbles and slunk into the shadows on the other side of the road.

A distant noise stopped them in their tracks. Several frozen seconds followed as they both tuned their hearing to the remote hum of an approaching vehicle. The engine note came from the main road and existed as the only vehicle to be encountered since leaving the city behind.

They watched unseen from a shop doorway as two pinpoints of light became visible descending the hill towards the village. A puzzled glance was traded when the headlights were abruptly extinguished and the sound of the engine died away.

Taylor pressed his left shoulder against the edge of the doorway and twisted his neck at an acute angle. He concentrated a one-eyed stare at where the headlights were last seen. Kim, down on her haunches and crouched in against his legs hoped for a similar covert view. 'What's it doing?' she said.

'Not sure, I thought it had stopped, but it's a narrow road there. No wait, it's still coming. The driver's freewheeling in with no lights on.'

They flattened themselves into the doorway as a tatty-looking Citroen van noiselessly cruised by losing speed. It eventually rounded the bend up ahead and disappeared out of sight.

'Two people in it,' Kim said. 'But I couldn't see any more.'

Taylor pulled at her hand. 'Very strange, come on.'

The phrase déjà vu came to Taylor's mind as they reached the old mill building at the end of the street. A full moon had arrived, but its light was stifled by a bank of stationary clouds. A cautious glance around the corner showed nothing more than the grainy black shape of the church surrounded by swaying, rustling trees.

With knees and backs bent forward they stealthily advanced until they came to the four-foot high boundary wall. Maintaining this low crouching stance they moved along its length until they reached the back of the cemetery. With fingers gripping the top of the wall and eyes now accustomed to the dark they slowly raised up just enough to scan the outlines of gravestones and bushes. The church itself presented nothing more than a black featureless mass, with only the silhouette of its towering roof and steeple on show against the night sky. Low whispers passed between them as they debated their next move.

A plan was hatched and a decision made. Kim hitched her left leg onto the top of the wall, intending to slide over into the church grounds. She was partway through the manoeuvre when Taylor's arm softly gripped her waist and in an unspoken warning urged her to drop back beside him.

'What is it?' she breathed.

'I've seen something in the doorway.'

In Little Stoneleigh Farmer was in bed, not asleep, not even dozing. He had too much on his mind to allow sleep to soothe his worries away.

The telephone rang and shook him from his thoughts.

Middle of the night call-outs were never to his liking, but the position of sub-divisional commander did occasionally demand his personal attendance to the scene of very serious crime. These infrequent disturbances to his off-duty time were even less palatable when they came during the early hours of a Sunday morning.

The name of the murder victim made his blood run cold.

'BILLY DANIELS.' Farmer repeated the victim's name as the station sergeant described the awful scene at the nightclub doorman's house in Bath Street. His eyes grew in size with each vile detail.

It took the superintendent a few minutes to hurry into his clothes. He forced his feet into his still laced shoes, tightened his belt and fixed his clip-on tie.

With the front door open as far as the security chain would allow, he peeked through the gap. His nervous swallow preceded the removal of the chain. He stepped out into the gloom and silently closed the door. The few yards to the Granada were taken with his right hand buried deep into his anorak pocket and a tight grip kept on Price's pistol. He skirted the car, surveying the moving shapes of bushes and shrubs and then stopped, back against driver's door, left hand fumbling clumsily with car keys, eyes darting.

Farmer need not have worried. Gorton did not intend paying a visit just now. The giant thug had determined that the little soirée planned with the police superintendent would require a full evening.

FORTY FIVE

BLUE AND WHITE police incident tape was becoming a popular sight in Little Stoneleigh. The latest length to indicate a no-go crime scene now sealed off the end of Bath Street to all but police personnel and residents. A young constable lifted the tape one-handedly to allow Farmer's car to enter. He then religiously noted on his clipboard the time of the sub divisional commander's arrival.

The small street was a blaze of strong floodlighting and blue flashing beacons. Figures dotting its length included uniformed officers, suited detectives and white overalled SOCO investigators. The entire population of the street peered from windows. Dogs barked and a drunken voice from somewhere shouted out. 'Fuckin' coppers.'

Farmer bumped the Granada's nearside wheels up onto the pavement and switched off. He headed directly for the detectives clustered outside the front door of number twenty-seven.

Cheddar greeted him. 'Morning, Superintendent.'

Farmer turned on him, his tone aggressive. 'Lot of staff here already. 'What time did this get reported? Why wasn't I informed earlier?'

Cheddar set his stare on Farmer. 'It's gone half-one now, sir. It came in around eleven as far as I know. Some kid from down the road said he was after his football, and saw Daniels through the window; frightened the shit out of him. He'll have nightmares for the rest of his life.'

'Football,' Farmer quizzed. 'At eleven o'clock at night?'

Cheddar nodded. 'Yes, I know... I think he was here to screw the place, but the end result was the same. We're not far behind on this. It's only a few hours old.'

Cheddar paused for a second as he observed Farmer. *The old bastard's shaking, and the colour of his face, white as a sheet.*

'You okay, sir?' Cheddar asked. 'You don't look so good.'

'Mind your own business Cheeseman, and show me the scene.'

Cheddar took a suspicious look at Farmer. He knew that the Superintendent used Daniels as an informant. The break-in at the club where Daniels worked, together with Farmer's relationship and now Daniels' murder all had a similar smell. He didn't know much about DI Taylor's current situation, but his own detective's intuition now sounded alarm bells.

He led the way through Daniels' front door, more thoughts passing through his mind: *Farmer was a very experienced police officer by his length of service alone. He'd seen it all before, murder, shotgun jobs, heads blown off, awful road accidents, limbs severed, people burnt to death. So why was he in such a state? Okay, so Daniels was a snout of his, but he cared nothing for him. He cared only for number one.*

The flash of the police photographer's camera guided the two men along the tiny passageway. Cheddar took a second look back at Farmer as another camera flash announced their entry into Billy Daniels' living room. It also revealed the horrifying spectacle in stark white detail and the fact that "Dying Room" may have been a more appropriate title for the small space.

Farmer gaped at the scene, his trembling hand gripping his mouth tightly as his cheeks billowed with vomit. The cheeks receded back to their normal shape as Farmer swallowed, coughed and straightened himself up.

Daniels' body lay face-up by the fireplace, arms twisted behind back and no doubt tied. He was shirtless and his feet were bound together with a thick plastic security tie. Trousers were below knees and a gaping bloody hole was all that remained of where his genitals had been. A great gush of now congealing and blackening blood covered his legs, trousers and stomach.

'Looks like that bit was done whilst his heart was still pumping,' Cheddar commented, watching Farmer's reaction.

Farmer stretched his neck upwards and pulled at his collar. He managed a stifled 'hmm' as though attempting an air of nonchalance. 'Any prints?'

'Gloves, sir, SOCO has been and dusted, just glove marks.' Cheddar studied Farmer as he spoke, his detective instinct analysing the reaction. 'You'll notice, Superintendent,' he went on. 'That the thick leather trouser belt has been cut clean though, a very, very sharp knife.'

Daniels' face was pummelled, both eyes swollen to the size of cricket balls and completely closed. His throat was cut right down to the spinal cord, which could be clearly seen through the gaping wound.

Farmer took a deep breath to relieve the nausea. Cheddar continued talking. 'It looks like he's probably been tortured before the fatal cuts, either the throat or the genitals, *MASSIVE* blood loss from both.'

'There's a puzzling thing,' Cheddar added, pointing to the power point fitted to the left of the fireplace. 'I know there's a lot of blood about, but that power point is covered in bloodied finger marks, well, glove marks.'

Farmer jolted at this comment. 'Right, I've seen enough, you seem to have everything in hand.'

'Yes, sir, there's a senior detective on his way over from headquarters now and I guess he'll be setting up a team.'

Farmer widened his eyes, took on a deep breath and stepped out through the front door into the street's artificial brightness. Without a backward glance he shambled back to his car, head down deep in thought.

Cheddar caught Jayne Morrison's eye. 'Looks like a worried man,' he commented as he followed Farmer's slow progress up the street.

Morrison delved in her shoulder bag, pulling out a pack of Players Number Six. She gave a closed-eyes nod back towards Daniels' front door as she pressed a cigarette into the corner of her mouth. 'It doesn't get much worse than in there, but Farmer's seen similar in the past and he's never reacted like that before.'

SOCO man, Pat Gerrard, stood by the open rear doors of his van. He winked over at Cheddar and Morrison as he lifted his suitcase sized equipment box up into the back.

Cheddar returned the wink as he shrewdly interpreted Gerrard's body language.

'Thought he was going to spew back in there Pat. Now that would have made a mess of your crime scene… you've found something then?'

'A few hairs and fibres, but they could be anybody's.' Gerrard gave Cheddar a *corner of the eye* look as Farmer's noisy engine signalled his departure. 'Gather you didn't want him knowing too much yet, so I kept the best till last.'

Cheddar and Morrison huddled around Gerrard, eager to hear his update.

'The burglary at Granville's earlier,' Gerrard started. 'Kitchen gloves… little pimple marks on the finger tips. The lab will probably even tell you what manufacturer, Marigold at a guess.'

Cheddar was all ears. 'Yes, go on,' he encouraged.

'There were two tiny cut marks showing on one of the fingers of the glove dabs that I lifted from Granville's. No doubt these were created during some past use of the gloves. Well, I've found the same cut marks showing on the glove dabs I've lifted from here… from around the power point in blood. It's as good as a fingerprint in matching the same gloves.'

Morrison offered her open pack of cigarettes towards Gerrard. 'So, whoever did Granville's also killed Daniels then.'

Gerrard smiled a thank-you as he fumbled two fingers into the pack. 'Looks like it unless someone's hiring out burglars' gloves.'

FORTY SIX

THE TINY YELLOWISH glow of a pen torch hovered in the rear porch of Nazareth Church. The old door issued a creak of protest as it swung open. For Taylor it all seemed to be a re-run of his last visit, just enough radiance to make out two hunched-over figures. The image vanished as the men stepped inside and closed the door.

Crawling on all fours and hidden by the wall, Taylor picked out the shape of the Citroen van close against the side of the church. They waited a few seconds before scrambling over the wall and creeping closer.

The church's stained glass windows were abruptly illuminated from inside as a powerful torch beam played back and forth. The door opened again, one man was out and walking stealthily on the grass, towards the van.

The vehicle's interior light came on giving a fleeting glimpse of Travers pulling something from the passenger side. The light went out as he silently closed the door. He disappeared back inside the church carrying a heavy-looking holdall and a very long narrow bag.

Kim whispered to Taylor as they risked a few more forwards steps. 'That's the stuff they bought from the shops.'

The porch was in almost complete blackness and the door pulled shut. Low imperceptible voices could be heard along with the odd muffled bump.

The torch beam flashed around the interior and intermittently lit the windows giving an indication of the whereabouts of the intruders. Taylor crept into the porch and pressed an ear to the door. He then knelt and attempted a view through the keyhole before giving the door crack a try.

Kim held her breath until he arrived back at her side.

'No,' he said. 'I can't see a thing or make out what they are saying.'

Her hushed voice suggested an alternative. 'Let's see if we can get up to a window.'

They crept alongside the building near to the van and considered the possibilities. The base of the windows stood some six feet from the surrounding turf, it was not going to be easy. Without a word they both looked around in the darkness for a solution.

Kim pointed towards a lean-to shed near the van. 'I can make out some bins over there.'

Taylor ventured over and gave the cluster of metal dustbins the once-over. He selected two that were empty and made his way stealthily back across the grass with one in each hand. He positioned them upside down and side by side beneath one of the windows. With the palm of his hand he pressed firmly against one of the bins to test its stability. 'Seems okay, up you go.'

Kim clambered up aided by Taylor's firm grip on her forearm and flattened her hands against the window's stone lintel. She slowly raised her head above the bottom edge of the window, just enough to see in. Taylor carried out a more stringent test upon his bin. It was expected to support a lot more weight. He shakily climbed on and eased upwards until his eyes were parallel with Kim's.

A clear glass border surrounded the stained glass pattern of the window, albeit opaque, thick and covered with a layer of grime.

At first they could barely make out the two men inside. Not until the powerful torch beam shone for any length of time in one particular spot could they obtain some perspective. They watched intently as another powerful lamp came to life and was positioned on the backrest of one of the pews. Its beam illuminated the central aisle where both men were busy unpacking equipment.

Another smaller light now added its radiance to the scene. This one bobbed back and forth in sync with Travers' every move. He was wearing a caver's helmet with a lamp fixed to it. The images were now more easily deciphered.

Travers put the long bag down in the aisle and pulled at the six-foot zipper. His helmet lamp flickered across the face of the other man.

It had never been in doubt that it was Swann, but what could never have been foreseen was what Travers pulled from the long bag.

Taylor turned to look at Kim, his voice hardly more than an astonished sigh. 'Did you see that?'

Her reply came from behind a cupped hand. 'Well, I think so, but to be honest it was so bizarre I wasn't sure that I could believe my eyes.'

'Yes,' Taylor replied 'A bow and arrow.'

Swann directed the light downwards as Travers kneeled, attending to something on the church floor. Arm-pointing and torch shining then focussed up at the ceiling as an animated discussion took place. One of the colossal wooden beams stretching the width of the church seemed to be the centre of the men's attention.

Travers aimed the bow upwards and pulled back slowly on the string. It was impossible to see clearly exactly what was happening, but the arrow was released. Perhaps three seconds went by before an audible clatter announced its return to the church's tiled floor.

The bulky holdall was unpacked by the light of a shifting torch beam, although the contents could not be made out. The two figures then became engrossed in hurried activity. Their outlines moved from shade into torch glare and back again as they got on with their tasks. Clearly a length of twine had been attached to the arrow and now a sturdy rope was hauled up over the beam via that twine.

Fifteen minutes of concentration and eye strain went by. Taylor forced the knuckles of his fist into the small of his back attempting to relieve the ache created by balancing himself for so long in the awkward position. He rubbed his eyes and focussed again as something began to rise from the church floor towards the ceiling.

'It's a rope ladder,' Kim breathed.

Mesmerised, Taylor made no reply as the incredible scene unfolded in front of them. The ladder swayed from side to side and continued upwards as the men pulled steadily down on the rope. Within a few minutes the top of the rope ladder was adjacent to the beam.

Travers now moved back and forth tying off securing ropes onto to heavy church pews and stone piers.

'It's like the SAS,' Taylor commented. The words hardly left his lips when a dark shape started to clamber skilfully and quickly upwards.

The bobbing helmet lamp gave away the identity of the climber. Incredibly it was the older man, Travers! Attached to his back was a small rucksack. The straps of a climbing harness hung loosely from his waist. In no time he reached the beam forty feet above and then sat, legs dangling, astride it.

Taylor shook his head as he climbed down from his bin. 'That guy's amazing,' he whispered up at Kim. 'He must be nearly sixty-five and yet look at him go.' He added another comment before disappearing into the shadows: 'I'm going to have a look in their van while they're busy.'

Kim's silence was acknowledgment enough. She kept her nose pressed to the glass.

Swann's torch beam remained fixed onto the rafters whilst Travers busied himself for several minutes with a jemmy from the rucksack. He was prising at some of the woodwork on the ceiling above his head.

A rumbling sound suddenly engulfed the church as some of the ceiling started to collapse, there had been no warning. Kim flinched as she watched a section of the woodwork rip away and tumble in a cascade, smashing down to the floor below. Clearly Swann expected this and was standing well back with the torchlight still directed upwards.

Taylor was back at Kim's side almost before the noise subsided. 'What the hell?'

Kim turned with a finger to her lips. 'Shh,' she warned. 'He's pulled a great load of woodwork away from the ceiling.'

Taylor steadied himself and peered in again. Even in the darkness a cloud of dust could be seen hovering in the centre of the church. Swann's beam cut through, picking out Travers standing precariously on the cross-beam and pulling at the ceiling with outstretched arms. More timber came loose and tumbled to the floor with another almighty crash.

Travers' body language now took on a different attitude. He waved down at Swann and shouted something as he pointed at a particular section of the roof.

Swann, head craned upwards, locked his torchlight firmly onto the spot as Travers started to delicately coax something away from the rafters. In a sudden heart-stopping moment Travers visibly jolted and swayed as the object came free and transferred its weight into his unprepared arms. He tottered for a second before regaining his balance and resting the item onto the beam.

Taylor and Harding watched unblinking as the blurred, poorly lit drama unfolded. They concluded that the sole purpose of the expedition was to retrieve that wooden ceiling panel. Their guess at the size of the mystery object put it about five feet by twenty inches.

Travers was now back astride the main beam, legs dangling either side and with the panel flat across his knees. He quickly tied on a rope and lowered it into the waiting arms of Swann, forty feet below. The rucksack and tools followed before Travers nimbly made his own descent.

He was quickly at work unfastening the securing ties before running the remaining rope through his fingers and allowing the ladder to drop steadily to his feet. With one final tug the end of this remaining rope snaked up and over the beam. Travers expertly rolled the ladder, coiled the ropes and stowed them into the rucksack as Swann packed up the tools.

'Okay,' said Taylor. 'Time to go,' he hopped down onto the turf. 'We'd better put these bins back and get hidden.'

They made it back over the graveyard wall, silently panting and took up a covert position to watch.

Less than five minutes elapsed before the two men emerged from the porch. A couple of journeys were made over to the van to replace the equipment. The gloom allowed enough perspective to pick out Swann carefully installing the mystery panel into the vehicle. Travers locked the church door and hurried over to join Swann.

The van completed a low-revving, lights-off U-turn and slowly drove back towards the main road.

Taylor took hold of Kim's hand as they walked silently through the deserted village. They sat in the car for half an hour picking over the events before starting back. Hopefully, they'd given Travers plenty of time to collect his car and return to the hotel.

Three o'clock chimed out from the Belfry's massive "Robert" bell as they pulled into the hotel car park. The Triumph had also made it back, but a look through the car's windows and a tug at the door handles did not provide any clues to the mystery.

FORTY SEVEN

TAYLOR WAS shamed out of bed at half eight by the hiss of shower water against tiles. Kim's entrance from the bathroom dressed in only a hotel dressing gown was the final catalyst. He closed his eyes tightly in a long yawn and then sprang from bed, grabbing her around the waist. She giggled and they fooled around for a few seconds. They fell back onto the bed. She tapped one finger onto the end of his nose. 'We should be downstairs by now in case he sticks to his normal routine.'

Kim was dressed and ready before Taylor padded out from the bathroom wearing just his black boxers and towelling his hair. She checked herself in the mirror, turning her head left and right as she adjusted the wig. 'I'll see you in the restaurant,' she said.

'Okay, order my breakfast, I'll be a few minutes.'

Travers was already sitting at his table and looking his usual immaculate self. Last night's commando outfit replaced by jacket, tie and sharply creased slacks. His half folded newspaper lay on the corner of the table. He sipped tea and nibbled buttered toast between paragraphs.

He looked up as Kim went by his table catching her eye and half-rising from his seat. 'Bonjour, Madame.'

'Bonjour.' She felt herself blush.

Taylor arrived less than ten minutes later shaking his head at the man's incredible punctuality. 'Can't believe he's already down here after last night.' He snatched the chance for an interested stare as Travers folded his napkin, got to his feet and made for the stairs. 'We need to get back to Nazareth as soon as it's safe to leave them. We've got to put some sense to all this.'

A leisurely, but exasperating couple of hours followed as the pair sat in the lounge sipping coffee and reading. Any conversation ultimately turned to last night's events and to the secret of Nazareth

Church. They were both impatient to return and unravel the mystery, but Taylor's caution was probably wise: 'No,' he said. 'We're going nowhere while they're both on the loose. They could disappear and we'd never track them down. We need to be able to tie at least one of them down.'

At quarter past eleven Travers appeared from the staircase. His tracksuit and rolled towel gave away his intentions.

'That'll do.' Taylor threw down his newspaper. 'Let's go.'

Twenty-five minutes later Kim pulled the BMW into the lane at the side of Nazareth Church and closed the sunroof. Taylor, sitting in the passenger seat, fanned himself with one of the travel brochures. The midday sun of another sweltering day blazed directly above them.

Kim pointed the remote back at the car as they headed towards the church gates. 'Hope we can get in,' she said.

A set of ladders leaned against a builder's pickup close to the side of the building. Taylor shook his head. 'They must have cancelled the Sunday service after last night's damage, it doesn't look good.'

They took the gravel pathway towards the front entrance, looking the building over. It was the first time they'd seen it in daylight. Taylor pointed out some of the detail, signs of wartime damage, obvious bullet holes in spite of the passing of the forty-two years since it happened.

'Look up there.' He pointed up at the sandstone tower. A foot wide circular crater scarred the stonework. 'Probably a shell from a tank or big gun. This place must have seen plenty of action.'

They walked around to the back of the church and stepped inside the porch. Taylor turned the iron ring and pushed a palm hard against the door, it didn't yield. 'This door looks as old as the church itself and that big lock must be the original one too, so how has he got hold of a key?'

The front entrance was a similar, but larger version of the rear. The huge Gothic style, blackened wooden door with its ornate metal strap hinges was closed. A makeshift cardboard notice taped on:

Kerk is voorlopig
gesloten voor renovatie.
Pastoor

Taylor faced Kim. 'I can guess it's telling us the church is closed because of the damage. So, how should I address the vicar, is this it?' he pointed to the sign, 'Pastoor, like Pastor?'

She shrugged. 'I don't know Flemish, but I guess he'd be happy with just Pastor.'

Taylor placed a hand on the iron ring and twisted. An echoing metallic click came as the door silently swung open.

The sudden drop in temperature and the lack of the sun's glare inside the church was refreshing. A wooden partition separated the entrance from the main building.

Four men in overalls stood halfway down the aisle. Broken lengths of woodwork, shattered panels and other evidence of last night's activity were strewn on the floor and surrounding pews. The men were deep in conversation. One pointed upwards whilst another made notes. They stopped and turned to look at the new arrivals.

Taylor shot a false, confused face at them, squeezed Kim's hand and strode forwards. 'In for a penny,' he muttered from the corner of his mouth.

The men stared vacantly for a moment before one of them put his notepad down onto a pew and started towards them. His baldness reflected the light from the stained glass windows and his expression implied a mix of both welcome and concern. His tightly buttoned grey overall looked to be at least a size too small and showed two inches of black sock separating between a pair of brown shoes. Unbuttoned around the neck the garment allowed sight of a white clergyman's dog collar. The Pastor smiled broadly, but held up the flat of his hand.

'Neen, neen, Meneer, Mevrouw.'

Intent on bluffing his way into a conversation Taylor carried on walking forwards in feigned ignorance of the fairly clear instructions to go no further.

'Sorry, English,' he stated. His fake confusion now at its peak.

Taylor's determined pretence at blankness was thwarted as his gaze uncontrollably lifted upwards to the ceiling. Kim too found herself captivated by the most extraordinary and unexpected sight.

FORTY EIGHT

THERE WERE no fabulous paintings on the church ceiling, no frescos, nothing that could be attributed to Michelangelo or Da Vinci. It was all breathtakingly the opposite. They had watched Travers' sketchy silhouette perform a precarious balancing act the night before from one of the huge timber cross-beams. Their attempts at perspective and detail then were thwarted by grimy stained glass, darkness and danger. Now they could see curious and abnormal if not highly skilled workmanship. Layer upon layer of the most un-churchlike items, an incredible patchwork of different materials fashioned into a huge roof supporting collage.

An old metal *Dubonnet* sign looked down at them, whilst another advertised, *Ricard.* There were more: *Pieters Bier*, *Luck's Coffee*, another was for a brand of tobacco. There were dozens of wooden panels of all manner of shapes sizes and colours; some were painted, some with lettering stamped onto them.

The churchman stopped in front of them and reverted to almost faultless English.

'You're British,' he said. 'Of course, you couldn't have known. I'm sorry, but I have closed the church for today. There's been a problem during the night. Some of our wonderful ceiling has fallen down. It's a blessing that it did not happen during a service.'

'What a dreadful thing,' Taylor said. 'We've come over from Ghent especially to see the church. We go back home tomorrow. This, and the cathedral, were to be the highlights of our tour.'

Kim couldn't quite believe her ears, but the act had the desired effect. The clergyman beamed.

'I shall not disappoint you,' he said. 'The structural engineer has already made a cursory examination and declared the building safe. He's as puzzled as I am about it. It seems to have been one area where the structure was weak. The rest of it is as good as when it went up in 1944. I can leave the builders to it for now; I don't expect much work from them on a Sunday anyway. You obviously know the story of the ceiling or you wouldn't be here.'

'Well, we do,' said Kim. 'But it would be nice if you were to explain. It's such a fantastic story… if you have the time.'

Taylor looked on, a smile creasing the corner of his mouth as Kim carried out her own deception.

'My pleasure,' said the clergyman, eager for an appreciative audience. 'This entire region,' he started, 'was, as you no doubt know, the scene of fierce fighting during the Second World War. The City of Ghent was actually liberated from here in Nazareth. Did I hear you say you have visited the cathedral?'

'Yes, we're staying not far from it,' Taylor confirmed.

The clergyman gave an approving nod as he got on with the history lesson.

'The German commander in charge of the forces fighting here accepted defeat and surrendered to the British commanding officer. This act, so unusual for the Germans, prevented the probable destruction of Ghent. The church was badly damaged in the fighting, though. The unusual repairs to the ceiling that you see were the work of British soldiers, who were ordered to stay behind for various reasons.'

Standing with heads tilted back they contemplated the ceiling. Kim fumbled in her bag for the binoculars. She put them to her eyes and targeted an area where thick, black lettering could be seen stamped onto some of the timber slats:

100 CRTG 0.50 CAL 1 – TRACER.

Taylor gave an understanding nod as Kim attempted to read out the wording. 'Old wartime ammo crates,' he explained. 'That's where some of the timber is from. It actually all looks very good, if not a little unorthodox. It's been really well done even though it's been made up from bits and pieces. So, why was it left like this? It's over forty years since the war.'

The pastor looked up as if to view the ceiling for the first time.

'It is a magnificent job, worthless, but priceless. It was done by skilled men, trained in carpentry and metalwork. They built bridges to get this far. About ten years ago it was suggested that it should be put right. The idea was turned down flat. It's just everyday pieces of wood and metal but very precious. A shrine within a shrine to those who lost their lives.'

Kim felt her neck beginning to ache, but couldn't stop gazing upwards. 'What a story, I'm glad you left it alone.'

'I am the fourth Pastor here since this took place in 1944. I understand that a group of British soldiers did most of the work. They suffered injuries and could not continue with the fighting. They formed a part of a small contingent who stayed on in the district to help the locals organise repairs and get the community back on its feet. I believe the repair of the church was their own project. The roof became an immediate priority due to the terrible weather at the time, hence the use of anything they could get their hands on.'

The workmen were now sitting on the pews drinking coffee from a flask. Taylor squatted down on his haunches, examining the pile of dusty woodwork and debris. 'As you say, lucky it happened when no one was in the church.'

A detailed tour followed with an enthusiastic discussion about the wartime roof repairs and the unusual materials used. As they arrived by the church's altar Taylor pointed over to a door. He'd worked out that this was the door he'd seen Travers and Swann use the night before.

'Some of the architecture is superb and very original. It's fortunate that the old doors appear to have escaped the wartime damage.'

The clergyman beamed at Taylor's sympathetic and knowledgeable remarks. 'You're well informed on the subject. Sadly, the church did lose a lot of its stained glass, but the doors and all the interior woodwork survived intact.' He gave a shake of the head as he pointed towards the door. 'That door, unfortunately, has no key and to my knowledge never has had one for many years. It must have been lost somewhere along the line, but rather than ruin the old lock, we don't use it.'

They thanked the Pastor for his help, shook his hand and turned to leave the church. They had gone only a few paces when he called them back.

'We do have a church photograph album, with a few wartime photos. Some show the damage, if you'd like to see.'

Kim smiled. 'That would be fascinating.'

The man collected the album, a large, leather bound book, from an adjoining office room and set it down on a table at the back of the church. He opened it to reveal stiff grey, card pages. Each one showed varyingly sized black and white snapshots, images of years gone by, snippets of people's lives. Dozens of happy events had been captured, multitudes of faces looked back as the pages were turned.

One picture showed a wedding group in front of the main church doorway, whilst another, obviously a christening, depicted a smaller party. A page was turned. Church staff and choir boys were the subjects, with clothing and haircuts indicating an early twentieth century date. A later, larger photograph, perhaps in the 1920s, showed a tree blown down across the church gateway, several men, sleeves rolled up, holding axes and saws, and all grinning. A steeplejack waved from the top of a ladder perched up against the tower in yet another photograph, his 1930s lorry parked by the church wall.

A tarpaulin was stretched across the roof in another photograph, with ropes tied to the guttering in a battle against the weather. The wind seemed to be threatening to tear the temporary cover away. A group of British soldiers, circa Second World War, were pictured in the foreground looking up and hunching their shoulders against the rain.

Taylor turned the page, revealing another view of the church, this time from the back. It was from the same time frame as the previous photo and showed part of the tower with a gaping hole in one corner. A window frame hung out and a pile of broken masonry lay on the grass beneath. Half a dozen soldiers grinned back from four decades ago. One figure was unmistakable in his British battledress. That shock of hair, not white as they had seen it a few hours before, but dark and youthful.

Ten minutes later Taylor and Harding were settled at a pavement table outside the little café on Nazareth's single through road. Kim caught Taylor's eye and gave a shake of the head. 'What do you think about that then?'

Taylor rested his arms down onto his knees and stared down at the uneven flagstones. He gave his opinion without looking up. 'Travers puts something up on the church ceiling during the war and then comes back forty-two years later to get it back.' He shook his head.

The snack and red wine they ordered had to be rushed, they were short on time. Kim checked her watch. 'Travers will be like a wrinkled prune if he's still in the swimming pool. Shouldn't we be getting back?'

Taylor sat back in his chair; folded his arms and looked across at her. 'I guess so,' he begrudging replied. 'I was enjoying the view, and this wine is superb.'

FORTY NINE

DETECTIVE SERGEANT Pete Lacey's office wall clock showed the time as exactly five o'clock. He was waiting, chin resting on palm of hand for Doug Taylor's phone call. They had a lot to discuss.

A note pad lay open on the desk and Lacey's jottings were on show. Capital letters: thick black biro, a verbatim record of the forensic scientist's words:

METHOHEXITONE SODIUM. DENTISTS.

There were other words on the pad and it seemed that capital letters were the order of the day:

WILLIAM KEITH DANIELS, ELECTRIC CARVING KNIFE, GORTON?

The phone rang.

Half an hour passed before Lacey and Taylor brought the conversation to an end. Taylor's throw-away line prior to his parting goodbye sparked something in Lacey's mind: "I guess we're both on record as Mispers now."

Lacey remained stationary at his desk with that police jargon word Mispers, revolving in his mind. He clasped his hands together in front of his face as if in prayer and rested his elbows on their points staring unblinking at the wall in front. *Had he overlooked something?*

'Penny for em,' Timson said, as he entered.

Lacey's response was instantaneous. 'Get the missing persons file, Reg.'

Timson left the room and returned a few minutes later with a bulging dossier which he set down on the desk.

Lacey turned the pages. 'If I remember rightly we have only one recent outstanding missing person which looks dodgy.'

'I think you're right,' Timson said, puzzled at the sudden diversion onto a seemingly unconnected sphere. 'A bloke named Alan Craine. He seems to have simply vanished one evening.'

Lacey made no comment as he thumbed papers back and forth to locate the first page of the pro-forma for the missing man.

A meticulous description, together with a list of personal details followed. All this had been written out longhand by the case officer. The requirements of the form had been fully addressed, including particulars of Craine's family and relevant points of medical history.

Witness statements from Mrs Craine and a few other close associates narrowed down the last known movements of the missing man. A photograph helpfully pinned to the top left hand corner of the paperwork provided the most recent image Rebecca Craine could find of her husband.

Lacey looked down at the snapshot. A fit and handsome looking thirty-five year old grinned back at him. The man held a pair of hedge trimmers in one hand and posed beside a privet bush, which had been roughly pruned into the shape of a bird. The photograph was a snippet of someone else's life. It was personal, but for a second Lacey couldn't stop himself from grinning back at the photo imagining the playful tomfoolery that must have surrounded the incident.

The grin quickly fell away. A red warning light glimmered weakly in Lacey's mind. Something was wrong.

Lacey knew everything about missing persons' forms. He had undertaken the review and the subsequent revamping of the Devon and Cornwall version of the form into its current shape. The job was dumped on him three years before following a terrible tragedy. The lack of detail and a poor investigation into a missing girl had resulted in her death at the hands of a known sex offender. She was wrongly presumed to have run away from home when in fact she had been kidnapped and kept for several days before being murdered. More detail and a better investigation may have found her in time.

Lacey was well chosen for the task. His bosses knew him to be the obsessive that he was. Detail and more detail being his passion.

Because the Misper form was his baby he couldn't leave it alone.

Operation Upstart had, for the past eighteen months, taken over his life, but he still found himself checking the Mispers on a daily basis.

The Craine Misper case came in on Lacey's rare Sunday off. He'd browsed through it before he'd even hung up his coat on the Monday morning. He didn't like it then and that was now a week ago. That red warning light was gathering in brightness.

At the Hotel Harmony Taylor bounded up the stairs to the third floor. He had no idea that his joke about Mispers had diverted Lacey into unknown territory. The telephone conversation had provided him with enough worrying new information as it was.

Kim was sitting at the dressing table as he pushed the door open. Their eyes met in the mirror. 'You've got that serious, worried look,' she said as she gently pulled a brush through her hair.

He skimmed his notepad over onto the bed and pulled a chair up alongside her. 'First things first,' he started. 'The drug that you were injected with, Methohexitone Sodium… it's safe, there can be no adverse effects. It's used by dentists apparently.'

Kim frowned. 'Well good, but where on earth did they get it?'

Taylor shook his head. He'd been relieved to hear that Kim was in no danger from the injection, but his next news was very serious and he needed to move on. 'That jerk from Granville's… Daniels, the doorman, he's been murdered. Tortured and brutally butchered. No doubt to get information from him.'

Kim put the brush down and turned to face Taylor as he recounted the harrowing news in detail.

'Pete's done a lot of work on Sweeney and his cronies,' Taylor added to his summary. 'He's confident that it's down to a minder who works for Sweeney, a man named Steven Gorton.'

'So, how's he worked that out?' Kim asked sceptically.

'Jacob Bunn defended Gorton on a murder charge a while back… a gangland killing. Gorton was obviously the murderer, but Bunn fixed it somehow and he was acquitted. Anyway, the victim was sliced up with an electric carving knife, and that's putting it nicely. The forensic boys are confident that an electric carving knife was also used on Daniels.'

Kim grimaced. 'How utterly vile, but yes a very unusual MO. So, Gorton's been sent to get the money back then?'

'You'd think so.' Taylor leaned back in his chair. 'Farmer's treading on dangerous ground now. It must be him who has the money and that should put him at the top of the list for Gorton.'

Kim stood to her feet. 'Yes Farmer's got the money,' she said. 'All the more reason to place the blame on us, especially if he thinks Gorton would suspect him...' She paused deep in thought as some of the additional bits of information slotted into place. 'Farmer's hoping to manipulate the facts, to make it look to Gorton as if we've taken the money.'

'That's how I see it', Taylor said. 'Gorton clearly will stop at nothing. Farmer is on thin ice.'

'He's not the only one,' Kim said.

Taylor looked at her, sensing her emotion and certain that she was fighting back tears. She wouldn't look at him but instead turned her back and busied herself with make-up.

Taylor took a shower.

Kim was sitting in the bay window looking out across the square when he settled into the chair next to her, hair still wet and with his unbuttoned shirt tucked into his jeans. He placed a hand upon the top of hers. He knew what she was thinking.

'Do you think we should go to the authorities now,' she asked. 'To explain what's happened? They'd have to investigate Farmer after they heard us out. Surely he can't make anything stick on us? It's my dad I'm worried about, especially now this psychopath Gorton is wandering about. He could do anything.' Tears glistened in her eyes. 'It was in the newspapers about my dad, remember? If Gorton thinks we have the money then…'

Taylor squeezed her hand. He was about to comment when Kim

sprang to her feet, eyes riveted onto the cobblestones down in the Square. 'He's on the move,' she said, finger pointing at the limping figure briskly walking away from the hotel.

Taylor quickly dragged a comb through his hair and finished buttoning his shirt 'Right, we know what to do.'

They were out through the bedroom door within two minutes. All thought of the last conversation temporarily side-lined.

Down in the lobby, hotel manager, Cédric Peeters sat behind the reception desk engrossed in paperwork. A pleasant mid-fifties man, Peeters was crowned with an extremely obvious toupee which showed as jet black against his own thinning grey sideburns.

He looked up from his work as the lift bell pinged to announce its arrival. The doors slid open to reveal a solitary figure.

Kim looked stunning in a tight-fitting midnight blue, sequinned evening dress. She stared over at Peeters. Her raised eyebrows accompanied a frown, fluttering eyelids augmented her *please help me* look.

Peeters immediately stood to attention as if under sergeant major's instructions.

'Madame looks wonderful tonight,' he said, eyes as wide as dinner plates and head tilted to one side. 'Simply wonderful, but is there something Madame needs? Some assistance?'

He stepped from behind his desk.

'You're very kind. Could you help me?' She said.

'But of course, Madame.' Peeters said almost tripping in his rush to cover the few yards to the lift door. 'Anything, anything at all. What is the problem?'

'It's the lift you see, I've had a little trouble,' she enticed him inside. 'I've been pressing this button.' She pointed to the row of lift operating buttons and pressed one as she continued with the charade. 'I wanted to come down from the third floor to the lobby and kept ending up on the second floor. How I eventually arrived here I don't know.'

'Oh, Madame, it is a simple mistake…'

The lift doors closed.

Taylor sloped into the foyer from the stairway and took a furtive glance around. The green display at the side of the lift showed it was heading upwards. There were no witnesses as he reached over the side of the counter and lifted key number 214 from its hook.

FIFTY

THE MANAGER gave a nervous laugh as the lift doors reopened back in the empty lobby.

'Yes, Madame,' he flustered after his impromptu outing. 'Many people make the same mistake. This floor, the lobby, is the ground floor, so you press *G*.' He pointed at the buttons. 'The floor above is floor one, your room is on floor three and you will see that your room number begins with a number three.'

Kim acted out the pretence as she continued to scrutinise the buttons.

'You're absolutely right; my room number does begin with three. How silly of me, I understand now.' She stepped from the lift, making one last request from the manager as he reinstalled himself behind the counter. 'Could I order a coffee in the lounge please?'

'Certainly, Madame. I'll see that it is brought in to you.'

Taylor let himself into room 214. He assessed the contents before touching anything. Everything must be left absolutely as he found it. He felt secure in the knowledge that Travers had left the building on foot, rather than in his car. He was clearly staying local and hopefully out for the evening.

The room was tidiness itself with absolutely nothing out of place, even the towels in the en suite were neatly folded.

He pulled the Polaroid camera from around his neck and slung it onto the bed as he checked inside cupboards and drawers.

Rows of neatly folded underpants, handkerchiefs, socks and T-shirts presented themselves for inspection, but no passport. Taylor concluded that Travers must either have it with him or had not yet collected it from reception after booking in.

'Damn,' he murmured, disappointed, but then raised his eyebrows with interest as he spotted the plain unaddressed white envelope. It lay in the drawer of a bedside cabinet beneath a complimentary tourist guide of Ghent.

In the Lounge Kim settled into a comfy chair to act out more magazine browsing. Her real interest lay through the window and across the square.

Only a few minutes passed before she threw the magazine to one side and got to her feet, eyes staring through the window and glued onto a distant figure. There could be no doubting the identity. Travers, complete with newspaper under his arm was heading back towards the hotel.

'Oh God, no.'

She made it through to the lobby and into the guests' telephone booth in seconds. Such a derailment of the scheme had been considered, planned for even. As she pulled the door closed and rummaged in her handbag for coins and a phone number the blasé countermeasure began to look rather shaky. Her usually confident fingers fumbled to press coins into slots and stab out numbers onto the key pad.

Seconds went by like minutes before she heard the number ringing out in the earpiece. The hotel's telephone switchboard came to life in that same moment, buzzing loudly. Kim clenched her teeth and glared through the small wired glass window of the booth at the manager, willing him to pick up the call.

'Come on, come on… ANSWER the bloody thing.'

More of those minute-long seconds ticked away before the manager threw his pen down onto the desk with frustrated annoyance. He swivelled in his chair to face the buzzing switchboard.

'Come on, come on,' Kim snarled through now grinding teeth.

The manager's hand reached over to the switchboard phone. A lady guest emerged from the lift. The manager half turned back.

'Oh no, don't talk to her.' Kim mouthed the words, wanting to shout them. She could now visualise how close Travers would be.

The switchboard's buzzing seemed incessant.

The manager looked up at the lady. 'One second, Madame, please allow me to deal with this call.' He flicked a switch and held the handset to his ear. 'Hotel Harmony.'

Kim heard the manager's words clearly over her handset watching him in the same instant that he spoke. She marshalled her voice into its clearest and most precise tone. She didn't want to have to repeat the instructions.

'Please put me through to room 214.'

The words were uttered as she calculated Travers' progress across the square. *Almost at the door,* she decided.

The manager swivelled to look at the row of key hooks. 'I fear, Madame, that the guest is not in at the… oh, my mistake, one moment, Madame.'

A *click* on the line substituted the manager's voice with the steady *bur, bur* of a ringing tone. Kim held a picture in her mind of Taylor in the room… startled by the telephone, but knowing what the signal meant. She put the still-ringing handset onto its side and stepped out from the booth in the same second that Travers entered the Foyer.

Kim's smile at Travers permitted her *ladies privilege.* He smiled back and gallantly allowed her to stand at the reception desk in front of himself behind the other lady.

The bedroom telephone startled Taylor. He had just pulled the document out from the un-gummed envelope and unfolded it. An embossed heading proclaimed the fancy name of a solicitors' firm. His eyes quickly scanned the text:

In the matter of the estate of the late Mrs Elenora Travers.

He was out of time. Kim's signal could mean that Travers was on his way up the stairs right now. Maybe he was arguing with the receptionist over his missing key.

Taylor folded the letter, quickly returned it to the envelope and positioned it back in the drawer. There had been no time to read it.

He yanked open the wardrobe door, the phone seemed even

louder, almost shouting at him to 'GET OUT'.

Neat rows of clothing hung crisp and regimental on the wooden hangers. There seemed to be nothing worth the risk of getting caught. He was about to close the door, when a navy-coloured blazer caught his eye. Taylor's mind flashed back to Kim following Travers and Swann into the cathedral – the photograph! He was wearing this blazer.

Down in the lobby the manager's patience was wearing thin. He assumed a rather annoyed tone as he spoke into the telephone for the third time. 'Hello, Madame, hello, there is no reply… Madame.'

The phone went dead, the money had run out.

The manager dealt with the first lady in the queue annoyingly quickly and met Kim's eyes across the desk, readying himself for her question. She looked pensively over towards the stairwell and then towards the lift as seconds ticked by. The manager struggled to hide his irritation. 'Madame, Madame.' His recent lift encounter had made him a little wary, but now the lady appeared to have been struck dumb.

The phone in Room 214 stopped abruptly. The sudden silence increased the urgency even more. Taylor needed more time. He ran his hands over the contours of the blazer. It appeared empty. He slipped his fingers into the inside pocket. The curled, but stiff, edge of a piece of card brushed against his knuckles. He pulled the three-inch square black and white snap-shot from the pocket, laid it on the floor and pointed the Polaroid at it. The camera flashed and whirred into life.

A door closed out on the landing. Taylor fastened his stare onto the door handle, expecting to see it turn. He knew he was pushing his luck. He grabbed the Polaroid and went to replace the photograph in the blazer. It was then that he saw the brief note written in faded handwriting on the back.

They passed each other on the stairway. Travers, holding his newly acquired duplicate key, and concerned about the hotel's loss of his original, didn't give the other man a second look. *Just another tourist on his way out, fiddling with his camera.*

Taylor made a face at Kim as he entered the lounge, high eyebrows and the shape of mouth you make when you whistle. If he could have said anything it would have been: "Phew".

She linked his arm as they strolled back through the lobby. 'That was close.'

The manager was part-way through grilling a young member of staff about the missing key, possibly looking for a scapegoat. He eyed Kim as the couple approached the lift. He smacked the palm of his hand against his forehead emphasising his forgetfulness. His toupee shifted position a little. 'Your coffee, Madame, forgive me, we have had a few problems.'

She smiled. 'Not to worry, I don't need it now.'

Back in their room Taylor hid the stolen key amongst clothing in the depths of his holdall. He slid the Polaroid photograph from his shirt pocket and placed it flat down onto the table. His shake of the head as he looked down at it accompanied a frustrated tone. 'It's not too good. His photo is old and pretty curled up at the edges… I'd no way of keeping it flat.'

The photograph was indeed poor quality, a fuzzy, colour picture of an ancient black and white snapshot, probably taken with an old Brownie box camera. It showed the blue hotel carpet around its edges, whilst in the centre, slightly askew, sat the frozen image of some long ago event.

An out-of-focus face gazed back at them. There was no doubting the identity, handsome, dishevelled, about twenty years old and looking much the same as in the church album wearing his Second World War British Army uniform. That shock of hair, albeit dark and youthful proved conclusively that it was Travers. The heavily bandaged left knee hadn't stopped his grin.

The beaming face was not cast fully towards the camera, but averted towards the full-length painting that he held propped up with his right hand.

Taylor had chanced his luck by trying to memorise the two lines of faded pencil script from the rear of the photo, but was pretty confident that his recollection was a faithful one.

It read:

Dear Mum,

Here's me at Nazareth – not that Nazareth!

Trophies of war! The knee and the picture!

Love from Billy.

FIFTY ONE

TAUNTON'S bright morning sunshine glinted onto a highly polished brass plaque. It was fastened to the brickwork at the side of a black painted front door. The door stood raised up from the pavement by three worn stone steps. Lacey stroked his chin and adjusted his glasses as he read the wording:

Neil Walley BDS (Exeter)

Dental Surgeon

He climbed the steps and pushed the door open entering into a small tidy-looking reception area. The young lady behind the desk greeted him with a welcoming smile.

'Good morning, sir, do you have an appointment?'

Lacey offered his warrant card forwards for the girl to see. 'Detective Sergeant Lacey. I'd like to see Mr Walley please.'

'I'm sorry, I'm afraid Mr Walley is away at the moment. His partner, Mr Middleton, is looking after everything and, as you can imagine, he's very busy.' She raised her eyebrows. 'I gather it's about Mr Bunn.'

Lacey offered a thin lipped nod by way of agreement to the receptionist's deduction and then followed her instructions to take a seat in the adjacent waiting room.

The room appeared recently decorated, cream walls and white woodwork. Lacey sniffed the air, detecting the aroma of a certain red coloured mouthwash above the paint smell, he shuddered.

A throng of magazine-thumbing patients filled every chair leaving Lacey no option but to stand with his back against a wall discreetly studying the various faces, a favourite pastime!

With his briefcase propped against his leg he checked the wall clock: twenty-five minutes past eight. Surprisingly early, he considered, for so many people to be so eager to have pain inflicted upon themselves. He covertly scraped a fingernail down one of his teeth and tried to recall whether he'd brushed that morning.

Lacey evaluated the waiting patients for only a short time, before being ushered into a side room and supplied with tea. Chris Middleton was indeed a busy man, but seemed genuine in his promise to help with enquiries. The young dentist was doing his level best to keep abreast of his hectic workload as he flitted from one room to another; an injection here, a high-pitched whine there, treating up to three different people at the same time. He found a little time between to pop back and answer some of Lacey's preliminary questions.

'Right,' he finally said, 'I can take a breather for a couple of minutes. I've one patient in room two waiting for the anaesthetic to work and my assistant is doing her hygienist thing in room one.'

Middleton washed his hands in the tiny corner basin and sat on the edge of a desk, he went straight into his sentence. 'Yes, Jacob Bunn as you know is, or should I say *was*, a patient here, it's a dreadful business. I actually provided the dental charts for the identification. We all knew Jacob and as you will know he was a good friend of Neil's, I think this has hit him badly. Neil always treated Mr Bunn, with them being such close friends.'

Lacey looked on impassively. 'How long is Mr Walley away for?'

'I can't answer that Sergeant. He took time off after Jacob was abducted. He couldn't concentrate on his work. He is the senior partner, so I've had to soldier on.'

Middleton shuffled uneasily on the edge of the desk. 'When the body was discovered in Staffordshire there was immediate talk in the papers that it was Jacob. I felt sorry for Neil and I knew it was going to be a good while before he would be back at work.'

Lacey pursed his lips. 'They were very close friends?'

'Well, yes,' the dentist confirmed, 'They used to play squash together most weeks at Mr Bunn's gym and I think they were at university together.'

'That would be Exeter University then?' Lacey surmised.

Middleton seemed puzzled. 'That's right.'

'Not much detective work there,' Lacey offered. 'On the plaque outside, BDS Exeter… Bachelor of Dental Surgery, Exeter University.'

Middleton realised he'd seen the plaque so often he'd forgotten it was there.

Lacey now stood gazing through the window, hands behind his back. 'Mr Middleton, you will, of course, know that one of the jobs which falls upon the police is to investigate missing persons.'

Middleton's nodding forehead creased with confusion as he tried to detect where this was leading.

'The forms on which we record the required elements are very detailed and occasionally a missing person turns up as a corpse.'

Lacey turned to face Middleton and continued. 'To cater for such eventualities the details of the missing person's dentist are included on the form. If the corpse is in a poor state, perhaps mangled or burnt, or maybe decomposed we can go straight to the dentist for a dental ID. It saves time you see, cuts out the middle man. No need to worry the next of kin until we are sure.'

Middleton continued to wear his baffled expression as Lacey turned back towards the window and started again. 'I have an on-going missing person enquiry at the moment for a Mr Alan Peter Craine. The form indicates that he is registered as a patient with this practice.'

'Yes, I know the name,' Middleton responded. 'I recall treating him a couple of times, but he was also one of Neil's patients in the main. You know how it is, when someone first comes for treatment they usually always ask for appointments with the same dentist thereafter.'

'I'd like access to Mr Craine's dental records,' Lacey said bluntly as he continued to stare from the window.

In Ghent Taylor's night had been a restless one. He'd been out of bed gazing through the window a couple of times, peering over at the car park and theorising about the photograph.

He was down in the restaurant drinking coffee by nine and actually beat Travers by five minutes. Kim caught up with him at nine fifteen.

'Okay?' he questioned as she took her seat.

She blinked a few times; the worries about her father were evident. 'Yes,' she fibbed as she stole a quick glance over at Travers.

They stretched their breakfast out for an hour until Travers left the dining room and took the stairs up to his room. Another twenty minutes went slowly by in the lounge with failed attempts to find magazines they'd not yet read. The hope was that Travers would stick to his normal routine. Reward came as they spotted him descending the stairs, towel under arm, and heading for the pool.

Taylor and Harding quickly headed outside and across the square to the cathedral. The sun was already hot and several groups of sightseers were clustered about listening attentively to their tour guides. One party, filing in through the cathedral doors, were oblivious to the fact that their number had increased by two.

Some time and thought had been put to this particular visit. 'That painting in the photo is the key to this,' Taylor speculated as they entered. 'It's something to do with religious artwork. We must check everything and cross-reference it.' He gazed around hesitantly at the vast space and then set off along the left-hand side of the building towards the central altar. He caught a glimpse of Kim's hopeful expression as she disappeared from view taking a parallel route down the right-hand side.

It took over an hour to cover the side aisles, to check the countless memorial plaques and the twenty-five chapels radiating off. There were dozens of massive oil paintings, some standing over fifteen feet high. Each one was accompanied with the artist's name, painstakingly inscribed in large black gothic lettering inside its own gilt frame. Taylor and Harding noted the creators of these masterpieces as they carried out their independent surveys.

Rubens and Jan Van Eyck joined the lists along with John Van Cleef and Gaspar de Craeyer. Gerard Van Honthorst and Abraham Janssens were included. The list of art treasures seemed without end.

Taylor cut across the central nave to admire the monumental marble and oak pulpit before getting back to his allotted task.

The colossal stained glass windows were awe-inspiring. The sculptures and sheer scale and quantity of the religious adornments were breath-taking. Each individual chapel was dedicated to a saint, to a previous bishop or to a nobleman who had played a part in the history of the building.

Eventually they met up again in front of the high altar, each with pages of notes. Taylor made a hopeful face. 'Anything?'

'Yes,' she said excitedly. 'Come and look at this, something is different from yesterday, *very* different.'

She led the way over to the right of the altar and stopped alongside one of the side chapels. A lettered plaque on the wall proclaimed the name of its benefactor: Joos Vijd.

She extended her open hand inwards towards an array of age-old oil paintings. These were arranged in two tiers and formed an extensive and complex altar screen. The screen lined the entire breadth of the Joos Vijd Chapel and was made up of a multitude of wonderfully painted panels. A name in eight-inch high, ornate stylised lettering was inscribed in a gilt carved frame. It adorned the wall at the side of this multi-panelled masterpiece declaring the genius responsible:

JAN VAN EYCK

'It wasn't like this when we came in the other day,' she said. 'There are more panels on display.'

Taylor stood back a few yards, quietly regarding the panels. 'Yes, you're right. There definitely weren't these many paintings.'

Kim linked her arm through Taylor's and then pointed at one particular panel that made up a part of the lower left of the screen.

'But that's the really interesting one.'

Taylor's jaw started to drop in amazement. He fumbled in his jacket pocket pulling out the photograph and staring down at it before locking his eyes back onto the panel.

'It's the same… it's the same one,' he repeated 'No doubting it even despite this awful quality snapshot, but how come it wasn't here the other day?'

'It is a folding screen, Monsieur,' stated a thickly accented and cultured female voice from behind.

FIFTY TWO

TAYLOR SPUN around stuffing the photograph back into his pocket. The face that met him caused him some surprise as the voice belonged to a pleasantly smiling elderly lady who stood leaning on a broom.

'It is a *polyptych,*' she said.

Taylor furrowed his brow. 'I'm sorry, a what?'

'A polyptych,' the lady repeated. 'It means, folding altar screen. You see, not all the panels of the polyptych are displayed each day. Only on certain days are they all to be seen as they are today.'

Kim's eyes were uncontrollably drawn to the lady's broom. 'You're very knowledgeable on the subject, Madame.'

'Ah,' the lady gave a mischievous wink. 'Don't read too much into this.' She waggled the broom. 'I have worked in the cathedral for fourteen years. I am still an official guide, but since retiring I mostly help out in the gift shop, usually in my own time. I was an archaeologist and restorer before my retirement.' She waggled the broom again. 'I enjoy helping out with a bit of cleaning. I think of myself as a custodian. The cathedral has been kind to me over the years. It's good to see people such as yourselves showing an interest in our heritage. I saw you here the other day; most tourists spend only a few hours I'm sad to say.'

Taylor made the introductions – first names only. He received a warm handshake in return and quickly recognised the importance of the lady's wisdom on a subject that currently consumed every minute of their lives.

She bowed her head. 'Catherine Swalus, call me Cathy.' She took Kim's hand. 'You are fortunate also with the sunny weather. It's often similar to Britain here in Belgium… rain.'

Taylor's gaze returned to the paintings. 'It's all so incredible, the detail and the colours, so vibrant, it almost glows. When was it painted?'

'Fourteen hundred and thirty-two,' Cathy said. Her voice almost matter of fact.

Taylor shook his head. 'How I wish we could spend more time here, this place is so fascinating, particularly the paintings.'

Kim eyed Taylor suspiciously. She knew his game.

'We're due to return home soon,' he continued. 'I wish you'd got the time to talk to us properly. You are clearly an expert.'

Cathy beamed, 'I can always be tempted with the offer of a cup of coffee. I'm my own boss really… one of the benefits that come from not getting paid much in my retirement days. I know a nice place around the corner. I'll let you treat me.'

Within ten minutes the threesome were settled at a table outside the Brasserie Agrea, just yards from the cathedral. Taylor positioned himself with his back to the street, keeping a watchful eye on the reflection in the café window.

With coffee ordered Taylor was eager to get back to the matter in hand, but could not be too pushy. He paused to choose his words. 'We arrived a few days ago, only a short visit, we've been charmed with the city and particularly the cathedral.' His conscience felt clear with this statement; he was actually telling the truth, despite his additional ulterior motives. 'Perhaps you could tell us a little more about the… polyptych. Is that how it's pronounced?'

'Perfect, yes, I am probably better placed than most people to answer any questions you have about the screen. I have studied its history at length. My book on the subject was published a few years ago.'

After a short, but concise, summary about the construction and history of the cathedral she sat back in her chair. 'Now, I will tell you about the masterpiece of St Bavo, the altar screen, or to use its correct term, the polyptych.' She gave a wry smile as she began. 'It was painted by the most famous of the northern renaissance period painters, Jan Van Eyck, between 1426 and 1432. The painting, as you can imagine, was a huge undertaking. It is, in fact, a complex series of paintings that surround a central painting.

'Officially, the title as a whole is The Adoration of the Mystic Lamb, which is a reference to the central painting. Twenty-four panels in all make up the altarpiece. It is one of the most influential religious works of art in the world. Only certain parts of the polyptych are opened for viewing on certain days. This is why you did not see the particular panel, which I suspect is your main interest, on your first visit.'

Taylor looked at the woman. *How could she know? She must have heard some of the conversation and picked up on their interest from that. She simply could not have seen the photograph.*

Cathy raised her eyebrows as she gave Taylor a long and knowing stare. A glimmer of a smile crossed her lips. 'The panel that is so important to you is called the Just Judges.'

Taylor discreetly patted the outside of his jacket pocket to confirm that the photograph was still there. It was.

'Is that the title of the painting, the Just Judges?' Kim said.

Cathy made a perplexed face. 'I think you know that much. Most people who come to unravel the mystery of the Just Judges at least know its name.'

Taylor settled back onto his seat. 'Tell us about this mystery.'

'Not a problem,' Cathy replied, her frown changing back to mischievous grin. 'I would dearly love for the cathedral to get back the original. Of course the mystery generates a lot of curiosity, so I'm happy to tell you the detail.'

She took another sip at her coffee before getting into what was clearly to be the most enthralling part of the story. 'The altar screen,' she started. 'Has been displayed in the Joos Vijd Chapel of the cathedral since 1432. It has endured an exciting life during that time and there have been many times in the past when it appeared that it would be forever lost. One such interruption to its display seems impossible to correct and I fear that because of this it will always be incomplete.'

Taylor looked mystified at this. 'So, there's something missing?'

Cathy held up the flat of her hand, restraining Taylor from more interruptions and ploughed on. 'In 1934 someone entered the cathedral and stole both the Just Judges panel and the panel depicting St John the Baptist. The thief sent a ransom note to the bishop demanding one million Belgian francs in return for the panels. The note suggested that the St John panel would be returned if a coded advertisement was placed in a newspaper. The bishop did as instructed, and received a baggage claim ticket for the Brussels Railway Station. The St John painting was recovered safely.'

Cathy looked over at the two dumbfounded faces opposite her and then realised that they were ignorant of these facts. 'So, you didn't know anything of this after all?'

Their silent head shaking persuaded Cathy to continue.

'The bishop refused to pay the ransom for the Just Judges panel. A series of other messages were then sent by the thief in an attempt to get the ransom money. Seven months after the theft a local businessman, Arsene Goedertier, was taken ill.' Cathy leaned forward across the table. 'And here, is where the story becomes almost beyond fiction ...' She left a long pause. 'Goedertier somehow realised he was about to die and called for his attorney, proclaiming that he alone knew the location of the stolen painting. He died within minutes of making this admission...' Taylor and Harding hung on her every word as she continued. 'The police investigated and in his home found carbon copies of the ransom messages along with another typed message, ready to be posted. The painting has never been seen since, despite many investigations by police and private investigators from all over the world.'

'So,' Taylor said, taking his chance. 'The painting in the cathedral…?'

Cathy shrugged. '… Is a copy. It was produced for the cathedral in 1945 by a talented Belgian copyist, Jef Van der Veken. Whilst being an excellent reproduction there are several minor, but intentional differences. The authorities told Van der Veken that he must include some discreet changes in his copy. The idea being that future generations would know for certain that this was in fact a copy. He was very good at his work.'

'I gather,' Kim said. 'That the original would be worth a lot of money.'

Cathy agreed. 'Some experts have likened the painting to the Holy Grail in its value. There is no doubting that it would probably fetch upwards of two hundred million English pounds if it were to become available. It is unquestionably the most sought after painting in the world. I know for a fact that the Belgian Government would be on the front row of bidders.'

The pair struggled to hide their surprise. Taylor ran the fingers of his right hand through the hair on his temple and down to the back of his neck. 'So, you are saying the painting is worth more than a Leonardo Da Vinci or a Rembrandt?'

'Oh, yes, unquestionably. Without it the West's greatest work of art will forever remain disfigured. You see now why the cathedral has never broadcast the fact that the panel is a copy. If people want to believe it is complete and intact, as it was in 1432, then that's okay. But when someone has done research and knows something of the truth then we will happily tell the story.'

Taylor sat back in his chair. 'I gather that over the years there have been dozens of gold-diggers trying to unravel the mystery and reap the rewards?'

'Indeed,' Cathy admitted. 'People have written books on the subject and some have come up with crazy ideas as to where the painting is hidden. All theories have fallen flat, and after so long it is now beginning to look as though the painting may have been destroyed.'

Kim leaned forwards, resting both arms on the table. 'So you thought we were yet another pair of gold-diggers?'

'The thought crossed my mind.'

Cathy smiled as she turned down Taylor's offer of payment for her tour guide expertise. 'The coffee and company have been payment enough,' she said, rising from the table. 'I must be getting back.'

FIFTY THREE

'BELGIUM and the big picture,' Taylor said as they sauntered back across the square.

Kim gave him a questioning look. 'What?'

'Remember the little in joke that we overheard at the Brewery? That's what one of them said when Price was outside: "The big picture." He was talking about the painting.'

'Of course, so Price never knew about this part of things.'

They took a route through a few back streets emerging close to the car park of the Belfort Hotel. It was a reconnaissance trip. Swann's car hadn't moved.

Their walk back to the Hotel Harmony took in a longing stare at the window display of a side-street confectionary shop. The purchase of some irresistible chocolate concoctions was unavoidable.

The last leg of their short excursion took them alongside the ancient Belfry and past a group of elderly men. Some sat on the two wooden benches and three or four more stood nearby. This was clearly their regular meeting place, a weekly exchange of gossip and old times all discussed through a haze of cigarette smoke. The men's innocent presence eclipsed a figure, nonchalantly leaning back against the wall, reading a newspaper.

Taylor and Harding sampled their recent purchase, oblivious to the fact that the newspaper was lowered as they passed.

Their over-the-shoulder glance as they climbed the steps to the hotel's front door was rewarded with a clear sighting of the yellow Triumph Dolomite parked squarely in one of the bays. It was a safe bet that Travers was still inside the hotel. A glimpse at the line of room key hooks as the receptionist turned to select their own added some weight to the idea as Travers' hook was empty. The couple were unaware though, that another pair of eyes was also watching keys and in particular, which room key they collected.

'Something must give pretty soon,' Taylor said as they arrived back upstairs. 'It's five o'clock now and I've got to ring Pete in an hour.' He sat down onto the edge of the bed to untie his shoelaces. 'Shall I tell him we're going to the Belgian Police?'

Kim pursed her lips. 'No, we are so close to finding out what all this is about. It's my dad. I just wish I could speak to him.' She gave Taylor a stare. 'It's this man Gorton that has me worried… maybe we can give it another day.'

He returned her stare with a serious look. 'You sure about this?'

She bent forwards and planted a lipstick-staining kiss in the middle of his forehead. 'Yes, she said. 'I'm sure, but I must pop out. I need a few things from the chemist. I'll be back well before you need to make the call.'

Taylor pulled up an armchair near to the window and sat with a mug of coffee perched on the sill as he looked out across the square. He watched Kim's progress from the hotel towards the shops and then out of sight into the maze of side streets.

She arrived at a chemist shop on a corner near a telephone kiosk. Her expression was resolute. She took a fleeting glance around before slipping into the kiosk and lifting the receiver.

The bistro opposite was busy. Most of the tables were surrounded by hungry sightseers. Two men occupied a table near to the door. A plate of sandwiches and two beers rested upon a red and white oilskin table cloth. One of the men made a pointing gesture towards the telephone kiosk and their interest in the food jointly subsided.

Kim's call lasted a full ten minutes. She took a careful look through the grimy window glass of the kiosk before replacing the receiver and stepping out onto the pavement. The door to the chemist's was a matter of yards away. It would be a quick call – soap and deodorant – there could be no time wasting, Taylor wouldn't make that phone call until she was back.

With her purchases in a bag Kim started towards the Harmony but she didn't get far. What caught her eye and stopped her in her tracks stood in the narrow side street on the other side of the road.

The dark blue Mercedes looked unattended, but its boot lid stood upright. She clocked the model immediately, a 280S, the same as Swann's, a common enough model, particularly in Belgium. She turned, half-deciding it was a coincidence, but then swivelled back, bottom lip gripped between teeth – *must check this out.*

A steady stream of pedestrians moving across the entrance to the alleyway obscured her view. She craned her neck, attempting to catch a glimpse of the registration number. She crossed the road, head aloft and on tiptoes, eyes searching.

As she stepped into the alley the car's number plate became legible.

It WAS Swann's car.

Kim took a hesitant left and right look and bit down hard on her lip as she tried to work it out. *There was no one with the car. What was it doing here? Only a short time before it had been parked at the Belfort Hotel! Why was the boot lid up?*

The alley did not have pavements, in fact, little enough space to open the car's doors properly. She glanced behind and then ventured in a little closer. She looked upwards, surveying the expanse of small, handmade age-blackened bricks which made up the walls of the buildings either side. Maybe a clue would present itself, perhaps a sign or a window to look through.

She pulled back her head to take in the full height of the building. There was a sudden flesh-on-flesh *thwack* as the palm of a broad powerful hand slapped down hard onto the back of her neck. Strong fingers dug in, nails piercing skin and gripping like a vice. She struggled, pulled her head forwards, thrashed her arms, tried to scream. The daylight disappeared as a damp cloth closed over her face. She sucked in hard to fill her empty lungs and pulled desperately at the smothering hand.

Her limp body toppled forwards into the boot of the car. A bell rang inside her head, a long unending distorted toll that slowly drifted away as consciousness left her.

A worm of worry had burrowed into Taylor's mind within half an hour and when six thirty arrived he knew his concerns were justified. The six o'clock call to Lacey never entered the equation. Pinning himself down in a callbox for twenty minutes would have been absurd. His bedroom carpet pacing was punctuated with several anxious stints out on the balcony. The crowded square down below had thinned. If Kim was down there he'd spot her.

He checked his watch for the tenth time in as many minutes, almost seven o'clock. His search of the hotel's corridors and downstairs rooms was visibly urgent, even brusque in manner. The need to be inconspicuous was no longer a consideration.

He cornered a hotel porter. 'Have you seen Miss Fry, my partner?'

'No, sir.'

Caution was completely side-lined. He was out and onto the car park, no sunhat, no stupid disguise.

Travers' car had gone. He stared at the space where he'd seen the Triumph a couple of hours before and smacked his fist into the palm of his hand in frustration.

'Shouldn't have let her go off on her own,' he said out loud, and started to run across the square to the Belfort.

Another empty car park space met his gaze, the Mercedes was also gone. Anger boiled inside him. He wanted to kick down the door to room 302 – Swann's room.

He pushed through the revolving doors and advanced on the reception desk.

Composing himself momentarily, he kept the lid on his feelings. 'I have an appointment with Mr Swann, room 302.'

'Oh, I'm so sorry,' the lady replied. 'Mr Swann left early. He checked out an hour ago.'

'You sure?' Taylor demanded, his pleasant facade now history.

'Quite sure,' the lady responded, a little ruffled by the challenge.

'His cases were put into his car for him and he left in a rush, at least an hour ago.'

Taylor turned toward the door before the lady completed her sentence.

His flight across the square to the Harmony approached a sprint. 'Still no sign of her?' he anxiously asked the same porter.

'No, sir.'

He made for the stairs, but halted and turned back to reception.

'Do you know if Mr Travers from room 214 is still booked in?'

The receptionist scrolled through the open page of the hotel diary.

'Mr Travers, yes, he is still with us.' She turned to look at the keys. 'Looks like he's out at the moment though.'

Taylor took the stairs two at a time arriving in his own room breathlessly and making straight for the balcony, fingers gripping the handrail, eyes searching the crowds, willing Kim to appear. His mind raced, assessing the situation, weighing up the facts. *Where had they gone? What would they do next? Where were they holding her?*

He grabbed his holdall from the wardrobe and emptied it on the bed. Spare clothing and paperwork tumbled out. He snatched up their two passports along with his notepad and pushed them into his pockets. A further frantic rummage through the heap produced a black sock, its shape distorted by what it concealed. The rectangular blue plastic key fob bore the wording *Hotel Harmony 214* stamped onto it in red lettering.

'Okay, Mr Travers… if that's your real name, let's have a better look now, and if you happen to drop by whilst I'm there, all the better.'

He pulled the bedroom door closed behind him and dashed down to the second floor. His left hand applied a friendly *rat-tat-tat* to the door of room 214. He tilted his head to one side in a listening pose and clenched his right fist like a huge white hammer.

After a few seconds of silence he pushed the key into the lock.

FIFTY FOUR

IN EXETER Police Station Lacey and Timson sat either side of their office desk. The telephone rested dead centre and save for the occasional glance at the wall clock their eyes were fixed onto it. The only sound came from Lacey's drumming fingers.

Timson got to his feet and stared up at the clock again. 'Quarter to seven Pete… nearly two hours late. Something's very wrong.'

The telephone pinged into life, cutting Timson's sentence short.

'Thank God,' Lacey said, snatching up the phone. 'Detective Sergeant Lacey.'

The voice on the other end was unfamiliar and aggressive. 'Superintendent Farmer here.'

Lacey beckoned Timson over to listen in. Farmer's metallic threatening rasp rose in anger. 'I'm about sick of your interference in matters that don't concern you. I'll warn you once only before getting on to your detective superintendent.'

Lacey settled back in his chair and swung his feet up onto the desk whilst Timson manoeuvred himself to keep within earshot of the conversation.

'What's the problem… sir?' Sarcasm fortified his response – a long pause before the word *Sir.*

Farmer bellowed down the phone: 'I've got enough bloody trouble with the Jacob Bunn murder. I don't need you throwing red herrings about everywhere.'

'You on about the Daniels murder, Superintendent?'

'You damned well know I am Lacey,' Farmer barked. 'Daniels was a paedophile. He's been murdered for that reason and no other. This Gorton bloke that you've been ringing the murder room about has nothing to do with it at all. Daniels was a pervert and whoever killed him should get a medal.'

Lacey took the handset away from his ear and stared at the earpiece as though he was looking Farmer in the face.

'Thought it was worth a mention, sir. I mean the *M.O…* electric carving knife.'

'It's bullshit, Lacey,' Farmer retorted. 'My detectives are investigating REAL leads, so don't contact the incident room again.'

The phone went dead.

Lacey replaced the handset. 'Touched a raw nerve there.'

The bell inside Kim Harding's head restarted its distant echoing. Lights flashed behind her eyes and an involuntarily moan came from the back of her throat as she fought for consciousness. The thick adhesive tape stretched across her mouth and around the back of her neck stifled the sounds into a pathetic mumble.

Her flickering eyelids brushed the damp gritty concrete beneath her face as self-awareness filtered back. Each woolly resounding heartbeat triggered a skull-cracking explosion at her temples. Eventually one eye hauled itself open. The nothingness it perceived prompted a panic level approaching hysteria – utter and total blackness.

She breathed in deeply and slowly, trying to calm herself, and at the same time attempted to pull her arms upwards to remove the tape. A sharp searing pain at her wrists brought the realisation that they were fastened tightly behind her back with a thick plastic security tie. She could feel the pointed loose end sticking into her waist as she moved. She cursed herself. *What a fool. What a silly trap I've fallen into.*

She lifted her face from the stone floor, feeling granules of grit and dirt adhering to her cheeks. A musty dampness and the heavy reek of oil hung in the air, but the absolute and total blackness paled all other perceptions.

The only comfort came as she pulled the aching wrists around to one side and forced her digital watch hard into the belt of her jeans.

For a split second the light in the watch came to life, just a small glowing yellow segment in the dark but good enough to ease her mind. The time was now half past eight. She'd been unconscious for over three hours.

Back in the hotel Travers' room looked like a crime scene. Drawers pulled out, contents strewn onto the carpet. The mattress slung to one side, clothes heaped on the floor. Taylor gathered together a handful of documents and papers. He spread them across the table, pulled out a chair and sifted through.

William Richard Travers clearly left in something of a rush and this time forgot to take his passport. Taylor pocketed it along with a driving licence in the same name.

He then selected the plain white envelope he had opened before. His last attempt to examine its contents were thwarted by Travers' unexpected return to the room. The letter's thick, expensive paper bore a title with the blue and gold embossed crest of *Tinworth and Cordell Solicitors and Commissioners for Oaths of Sherbourne Road, Portland.* It concerned the winding up of the estate of Mrs Elenora Travers, late of Wareham, Dorset. At the age stated in the letter of eighty-seven years Taylor assumed this to be Travers' mother. So, Billy in the old photograph really was *William Richard Travers.*

The letter joined the other documents in Taylor's crammed jacket pocket. He sorted through the remaining papers before giving the table an irritated thump. Nothing gave any clues as to where Kim might be.

He took the stairs back up to floor three, mind working overtime but not yet providing any sensible plan. The sight of his bedroom door hanging partly open, the splintered woodwork and damaged frame, stopped him in his tracks. Fists clenched and ready for trouble he widened the gap and peered inside. The intruders were gone, but the open cupboards and drawers along with the strewn papers and clothing suggested a hasty search. It looked much the same as

Travers' room now did. An overpowering, sweet nutty smell hung in the air, a strange smell, something that evoked a distant memory.

Taylor pushed the damaged door shut, lifted an upturned chair to its feet and settled down at the table concentrating his mind on the facts available.

Whoever was holding Kim, was also now after him. He pulled the notepad from his jacket pocket and started to turn pages. He quickly landed on a particular entry, a particular street name.

Back on his feet his eyes scanned the scattered paperwork, magazines and brochures left by the intruders. He homed in on the one he needed: *A Guide to Ghent*, a small glossy booklet. He went straight to the back page, folded out a twelve-inch square street map and read down the index, stopping at the street name: *Meerhem.*

He stared out across the square with the map flat down on his palm turning it to line up with the road lay-out down below and planned his journey.

Back in Little Stoneleigh Police Station, Farmer's office light still burned. It was unusually late for the superintendent to be working. His overflowing ashtray and the fog of grey cheroot smoke evidenced his stress level. He unlocked his desk drawer and extracted a brown manila card folder. After stubbing out the current cheroot he turned a page.

The light reflected back from the glossy sheen of two black and white photographs, one full face and one profile. The eyes of the full face version stared back with sufficient intimidation to terrorise. The name, *Steven Jeremy Gorton* ran along the bottom edge. A Criminal Records Office serial number also figured. The subsequent pages of the file included the full details of all known crimes committed by the man.

Farmer had seen the file before and so was not keen to leave the sanctuary of his office.

FIFTY FIVE

KIM SHIVERED. Her teeth chattered. The temperature alone was not the cause, fear and shock also played their part.

She writhed and strained in the blackness until, after a colossal effort, she found herself sitting, legs laid out flat in front and back resting against a cold brick wall. The fingernails of her tightly bound hands probed and scratched at the brickwork behind her back. She flinched as she felt the unmistakable texture of human hair, then closed her ineffective eyes and sighed, as she realised it was the wig.

She searched with her toes, sensing more brickwork, a picture forming in her mind of another wall directly in front.

Shuffling forwards a few inches she ran the sole of her trainer against the wall, feeling old plaster or paint crumbling under the pressure. She forced her back hard against the wall behind and drew her knees up tightly. Her legs quivered under the strain as she dug the toes of her trainers down into the floor and tried to stand to her feet. She flexed her wrists into the brickwork behind to gain some additional purchase and slowly shuffled her shoulders upwards against the wall.

She was standing, panting in the darkness, her pounding heartbeats amplifying the searing pain in her skull.

Her trembling searching foot started to deliver a mental picture of the surroundings as it tentatively tapped and felt out each inch of floor space. She was in a brick lined rectangular shaped hole measuring about ten feet long by three or four feet wide. How deep, she did not know.

Her wrists tingled, a stinging pain caused by the plastic tie digging deeply into the thin covering of flesh. She slumped back against the wall resting in the blackness and listened. She could hear the occasional sound of a vehicle, very muffled and infrequent, but definitely the sound of a road.

She hesitantly explored more of the dank blackness using the toes of her trainers, her knees, fingertips and face, until she knew every brick that could be reached. She was lithe, fit and supple. Her regular workouts and judo classes saw to that. But try as she did she couldn't pull her arms under her legs to get them in front. Her wrists were too tightly fastened. She sagged down into a crouching position and rested. Her mouth and tongue had taken on a dried parchment texture and the heavy duty tape had not budged.

She tilted her head upwards, hoping for an outline, a shape or shadow but the blackness remained unrelenting. Her cheek brushed against the wall, the edge of a particular brick felt rough against her skin. She pressed her cheek onto it, rubbing at the tape. It was futile. She rubbed some more, but then stopped and listened. A noise! Not the traffic this time something closer, another sound, a rustling, something above her. A shiver went down her spine as a thought came to mind… *RATS*.

Farmer, still in his office, sat slouched, head lolling down onto chest, his worries about returning home fleetingly allayed by restless sleep. A dozen or more shrivelled cheroot ends lay crumpled in the ashtray.

He twitched into consciousness as one of his two telephones gave half of its full ringing sound before getting into its stride. He was instantly upright, staring at the telephone, eyes like saucers.

'Superintendent Farmer,' he snapped into the mouthpiece, brow contorting as he listened for the response.

'DS Corfield sir, crime squad.'

'Go on.'

'They're in Belgium, Governor. Ghent to be precise. The woman finally slipped up and called her dad. She phoned from a public call box in the city centre. It's taken some time to trace it properly.'

Farmer's face twisted into a baffled expression at the mention of Belgium. 'Go on,' he repeated.

'We checked with the ferry lines and found that they're using a

BMW, and get this Governor,' Corfield crowed. 'It was bought from a dealer in Luton for nine thousand quid in readies.'

Corfield waited for Farmer's response, expecting astonishment and maybe even some praise, but Farmer's silence eventually prompted him to falteringly continue. 'She's using a passport in her maiden name of Fry. I've circulated the details through Interpol to Belgium.'

'What did she say to her father?'

'Nothing to implicate them anymore, but how much more do you want? She was trying to put him at ease, said she'd be back in a few days and everything would be okay. She suggested he should leave home temporarily and move in with his sister.'

'Right, carry on with your enquiries.'

Farmer dumped the receiver back into its cradle. His office chair gave a creak of relief as his backside lifted up. He grabbed his jacket, locked his office door and descended the stairs into the police station enquiry office.

A young constable poured boiling water from kettle to teapot as Farmer passed through on his way out to the car park. The desk sergeant looked up over the top of his newspaper.

'You off now, sir?' he asked, half-standing to his feet, palms flat on the desk in front.

'Yes,' was Farmer's single sharp word as he disappeared through the backdoor He was unaware of the double-handed, two-fingered gesture the sergeant made.

In a rundown Ghent backstreet Taylor pulled the BMW to a halt. The drive had taken him fifteen minutes. He checked the map and contemplated the dilapidated buildings that surrounded him.

Some signs of the day's earlier market were still present, cardboard boxes and bulging bin liners stacked against walls.

Long shadows and darkened corners had now replaced the bright sunlight of earlier. A few pale yellow street lights failed to achieve their purpose in life. A small council-owned street cleaning machine trundled forward, amber light flashing on its roof. The driver, head out of window, manoeuvred the vehicle along, stiff rotary brushes whisking against kerbstones. The machine slowly made its way around the corner and the street became desolate with not another person or vehicle to be seen.

Many of the buildings clustered around the cathedral dated back to the sixteenth century. Here, in the outskirts, derelict mills and factories from the 1800s made up the skyline. The fine lace once produced here seemed worlds away from these titanic, crumbling structures. A few, it seemed, had been given over half-heartedly to small businesses identified by hand painted signs fastened to walls and doors.

Taylor gave a frustrated sigh as he looked up from the driver's window at the cast iron street name plate bolted high up on the side of a building. Another fifty yard crawl brought him to a deserted crossroads. He shook his head and murmured to himself. 'It must be here somewhere.'

In Little Stoneleigh the palm of Steven Gorton's rubber-gloved hand silently pressed the door of the hired Ford Sierra closed. By his reckoning Croft Close was a good place to leave the car whilst he attended to his latest business. He'd done his homework and planned his route. No one would be watching at this hour and the fact that only two of the four street lamps were working proved an unexpected bonus.

He stood with his massive frame concealed in the shadow of a tall privet hedge and analysed the street. The dozen or so houses were probably occupied by retired or professional people. There were no lights on. 'All tucked up in bed.' Gorton mouthed the words.

He crept forwards a few yards, keeping to the grass verge as he studied some of the houses on one side of the street and decided on the best route.

A security light was fastened high up on one wall waiting to catch him as he walked through the gate, *no, not that one.* An estate car stood on another drive, a metal grille behind the back seat… *they have a dog… no not that one.* Tatty wooden gates, flaking paint, a tidy garden, but uneven slabs on the drive, an old Ford Fiesta, rusty and in need of a service. This one will do! Probably an elderly female on her own, husband died or left years ago, no security lights, no dog, perhaps a cat. No problem.

He slipped in though the open gateway, unseen and unheard, taking the path alongside the house and through into the darkness of the back garden. He padded softly across the lawn to where a three feet high wicket fence formed the one minor obstacle between him and the rear garden of 15 Bainbridge Crescent. Easy!

FIFTY SIX

IF KIM COULD have made a joke of her situation it would have been: *That she had got herself into a bit of a hole.* The thought did go through her mind, but she was not in the mood for joking.

She shivered. The sides of her face ached from continually flexing her jaw in an attempt to detach the tape across her mouth; it was not going to work.

It was late now and the distant traffic sounds had died away. She dropped back down onto her haunches, resting her back against the wall and began an exasperated sigh. A noise from above cut the sigh short and triggered a head-cocked listening pose. The rustling sound was back, and this time a soft bump followed it. She hardly dared breathe as she tried to make more sense of it.

A multiple of thoughts went through her mind as she squatted in the blackness. *What were these people going to do, come back and kill her? Or leave her to die? Neither seemed a good option.*

Taylor? What about Doug Taylor? The question went through her mind. *Surely as soon as he realised that she had disappeared he would go to the police.* Her head shook in the darkness. Taylor generally did things his own way and if he reckoned he could find her more quickly himself, then that's what he'd do.

She scraped her face against the wall a little more. A slight rip in the tape finally produced a raised edge where it had peeled away from her cheek.

Strange how the complete blackness allowed the senses to function more acutely! She could picture Taylor's strong handsome features in perfect detail. Thick eyebrows and that near-perfect line from nostril to ear where the six o'clock shadow of dark stubble began. A single tear rolled down her cheek.

She pulled her arms around to her left in what was, by now, a well-practiced manoeuvre and pressed the digital watch into her belt.

The tiny, but comforting glow delivered the time: 00.37.

Taylor must also be in danger, she thought. If Swann wanted her dead then that must also be his plan for Taylor; maybe he had already killed him. The image of Swann back in the brewery came to her. The confident menacing way he held the gun and liked to flick his wrist in a gesture of control.

The faint sound of an engine caused Kim to instinctively jerk her head backwards. She directed an ear upwards and perched on tip-toe to listen. The sound was now closer than the earlier traffic noises and gave away enough for her expert ear to be sure that this was a large car. A rumble of loose cobbles and an additional squeak of brakes preceded a clicking handbrake ratchet. The multiple sounds did more than just hint that the driver had reached his destination. The motor died with a lumpy overrun as the key was turned off.

Kim's heart sank. Taylor was a trained police advanced driver, he wouldn't pull the handbrake up against its ratchet. He'd been taught properly: *Depress the button and pull the handle up noiselessly.*

Another clue came with the clatter of that gas guzzling, out-of-tune engine, it wasn't the BMW. It was Swann's old Mercedes.

A shudder went through her. She stared harder at the blackness above as the distinct bangs of two car doors were clearly made out. Muffled voices came next along with the *click* of a heavy padlock and the dull, deep rolling sound of a considerably sized wooden door on metal runners.

Tight thin strands of weak yellow light materialised about eighteen inches above Kim's head as the feeble glow from a streetlamp crept into the building. Her mind raced as dozens of scenarios were considered. She peered up, blinking at the symmetrical lines, each one the same width as the box she was in and spaced about eight inches apart. Her eyes narrowed as the answer came to her. Now she knew, she knew from the mechanical training that had been a part of her traffic officers' course. She was down inside a garage inspection pit. The streaks of light were filtering in around the edges of the timbers slotted in over the top of the pit.

She cowered into a corner as someone stepped onto the boards causing the lines of light to flicker. Liquid dripped onto her arm stinging the skin. She recoiled as a steady torrent drained through the gaps in the boards and ran down the walls glug-glugging from its metal can. It trickled through her hair, wetting her cheeks and soaking into her clothing. She felt a sharp tingling sensation inside her mouth, where the jaw hinges, the unmistakable tang of petrol.

The pouring sound was different now as the can neared empty, a rapid and higher pitched sloshing. The dregs splashed down onto the concrete floor above before a dull hollow thump ended the sequence with the metal can being tossed to one side.

Kim squinted and instinctively tried to open her mouth against the tape. She wanted to scream. She wanted to scream the bloody building down. She didn't want to burn to death.

The tape that held her mouth like a vice for so many hours had, in an instant softened and transformed. Like a greasy sandwich bag it simply slipped away from her cheeks. The solvent effect of the petrol had dissolved the adhesive, in the same way that it dissolves soft plastics.

She screamed out a full and shrill lung-full of air. It was LOUD… it was CHILLING, but would it buy her some time? Would it stall Swann?

Female niceties would not help Kim now. The petrol soaking her hands and wrists felt slimy where the plastic tie held them behind her back. She screamed some more, jumbling every foul word from every drunk she'd ever arrested together into one ear-splitting sentence. Her backside hit the deck hard as she kicked her legs out and intentionally dropped down. She was on her back now, fingers rapidly scrabbling searching for more of the petrol. She knew she couldn't dissolve the plastic tie, but the slimy feeling showed that some chemical reaction had already started. If she could wet the tiny serrated teeth that held the band together they may soften enough to pull apart.

Her screams intensified, climbing octaves higher. A naked flame now would be enough, there could be no escape. A stinging pain seared through her as petrol crept into the cuts on her wrists caused by the sharp tie. She'd found a small puddle. The sliminess increased as the petrol ate into the plastic.

The tie dropped away and her hands were instantly punching up hard into the heavy timber slats. The boards must each have weighed fifteen kilos, but popped off as if made of balsa wood. The volume and pitch of her screams increased tenfold as the timbers thumped onto the concrete floor. She lunged upwards, hauling herself through the gap in the boards, digging her elbows into the rough floor and dragging her body out onto the edge of the pit.

Framed in the night-blackened garage doorway she saw Swann, right arm brandishing a fiercely burning rag on a two-foot pole. His intentions of sending Kim Harding and the entire building to kingdom come were easily worked out. The flame's orange glow lit his features with the horror of a hideous Halloween mask. The gaping mouth, goggle eyes and crazy-paving forehead exposed Swann's total disbelief. Kim's manic attempts to stall the would-be murderer had, in the short term, worked. He was clearly shaken to the very core by the banshee screams and wild appearance, but a sudden shake of the head indicated a swift return of self-discipline.

Opposite the garage doorway the Mercedes visibly wallowed on its suspension as a figure behind the wheel, eager to hurry Swann, hysterically pumped the accelerator. Blue smoke poured from the exhaust as the revving went well beyond the old engine's danger level. The narrow pavement and a two yard strip of road was all that separated Swann from the passenger side of the car. He shook his head again and lifted his arm to throw the rag as deliberation flooded back. In that same instant he was brightly illuminated in the white bouncing lights of a quickly driven oncoming car. He shielded his eyes from the dazzling lights and staggered off balance.

Even in the split second that this took, Swann's body language clearly spelled out that *he* was now the one in the throes of a lifesaving decision. The oncoming car was being driven brutally and straight at him. He could not dive towards the Mercedes, the car would hit him. He had to dive into the garage, but he couldn't take the rag with him, if he did, he would burn to death along with Kim.

Swann threw the stick skyward, inclining it towards the Mercedes and away from the garage as he hurled himself headlong through the doorway. The flaming rag pirouetted through the air trailing a twisting spiral of black, petrol-induced smoke as the BMW roared up onto the pavement, engine screaming, tyres squealing and punched through the gap between the garage and the Mercedes. Torn from its mountings a wing mirror spun away into the air. A length of drainpipe from the side of the building crashed over the roof of the BMW. Swann thudded heavily face down onto the petrol soaked concrete inside the garage, a sprawling jumble of flailing arms and legs.

Taylor overshot the garage by almost sixty yards as the car came to a shuddering halt with the still blazing rag attached to its roof aerial. His rear-view mirror-glimpse captured the image of Swann leaping in through the passenger door of the Mercedes. He rammed the BMW's gearstick into reverse and gunned the engine, sending the car flying backwards before he wrenched the steering wheel over on full left-hand lock and stamped down on the footbrake. The car spun through one hundred and eighty degrees in a tyre-squealing, vicious J-turn. Taylor's left fist slammed the car into first gear rocketing it forwards after the quickly disappearing Mercedes.

Kim lurched from the garage doorway and went down onto her knees. Taylor banged on the brakes and juddered to a halt well short of the building. His intuition and reasoning were clicking into place – the burning rag, the stench of petrol. He yanked the door handle before the car even came to rest. It flew from his hand with the rapid deceleration and cracked loudly as the metal door stay pulled out of the bodywork.

The rag flopped forwards onto the windscreen, deep orange flames and black smoke. Taylor was out of the car flicking it down onto the road with his bare hand and stamping at it. He kicked it away to safety, snatched the car rug from the back seat and ran over to where Kim stumbled to her feet clutching the doorframe for support. She was a mess and drenched in petrol.

She looked up at him, no tears, a dirt stained face, deep wheals around her wrists, her clothes covered in oil and grime. She trembled as she clung on to him.

'They were going to kill me, burn me alive, to get rid of me.'

'I know, I know, but this is dangerous.'

Taylor's manner was both caring and rational. 'We need to make you safe before we do anything else. You're soaked in petrol.' He sniffed the air. 'This place is like a time bomb.' He unhooked a hosepipe from the wall.

'Okay,' he explained apologetically. 'You're not going to like this.'

'Get on with it,' she gasped as he held the hosepipe above her head.

She threw a look back into the garage as the water cascaded down over her. It was a sizable space containing a mass of old-fashioned machinery. The shape of at least one vehicle could be picked out.

She wiped wet hair from her eyes. 'Isn't that the van over there, the one that they used at the church? The old Citroen.'

Taylor nodded as he finished off the task and then threw the still gushing hose to the ground. 'It will be, yes.'

'How the hell d-did you f-find me?' she stammered as Taylor draped the car rug around her shoulders.

'No time for that now.' He ushered her back towards the car.

They managed a few steps when a dull bump from inside the garage drew their attention back.

'What was that?'

Taylor turned his head in time to hear a second bump. He settled Kim into the front passenger seat but fixed his attention on the garage doorway.

Kim pulled the rug around her shoulders. 'I heard something while I was in there, like a rustling sound, thought it was rats.'

Taylor reached in through the car door and switched on the heater. The bumping quickly developed into a steady repetition. 'That's not rats, there's somebody in there. I'll have to take a look.' He pulled the torch from the glove box. 'That place could go up at any time.'

'Be careful,' she called out, but he was already running back, torch held at arms-length.

The torch beam flashed over the outlines of heavy machinery, tools and welding bottles before landing on the box-like silhouette of the Citroen van. Taylor homed in on the dull *thump-thumping* and cautiously squeezed around to the back of the Citroen.

The light reflected back from a second vehicle jammed against the wall. A muffled voice now accompanied the bumping, a barely audible, contorted murmur as though from the back of the throat. The vehicle jolted slightly with each bump, but as the torchlight moved across it, both the front, and rear seats were empty. Someone was in the boot!

Taylor recognised the car as soon as its yellow paintwork came on show: Travers' Triumph Dolomite.

FIFTY SEVEN

TAYLOR SQUEEZED around to the back of the car and pulled at the boot – locked!

He shone his torch across the littered bench, looking for a jemmy or large screwdriver. The beam settled upon an old wooden handled spade propped against the wall. Ideal!

With the torch lodged to point its beam at the back of the car, he jammed the spade into the slit where the boot lid closed. He wriggled the handle back and forth and pushed the metal blade several inches into the gap. He then pulled upwards with both hands feeling the weight of the car lift on its suspension. The metal of the boot lid started to crumple as his arms quivered with the strain. He bent his knees and adjusted his grip straining upwards like a weightlifter. The alloy lock emitted a creaking groan as it started to tear from the steel mountings and with a loud crack the lid shot upwards. The car settled back down on its suspension.

Under the light of the torch a pair of sickly half-glazed eyes blinked back at Taylor. The man's face and most of his head were bound around tightly with thick grey gaffer tape, distorting his features and creasing the skin. Both cheeks bulged as though the mouth was stuffed. He was inhumanly trussed into a contorted position, bent backwards, wrists and ankles fastened tightly with plastic ties which were connected with a third tie.

The shock of silver hair gave away the man's identity.

Taylor took hold of the edge of the gaffer tape between fingers and thumbs and pinched tightly at it, tearing downwards revealing Travers' face. The bloated cheeks receded to normal as Taylor pulled an orange duster from the mouth.

Travers' eyes rolled. He choked and gagged loudly, head lolling as he gasped at the first proper breath taken in hours.

Kim's outline appeared in the doorway with the car rug pulled tightly around her shoulders.

'Be careful,' Taylor shouted. 'It's still dangerous in here.'

She ignored the well-meant advice and falteringly made her way over. Taylor was busy cutting through the man's bonds with a penknife.

'God… Travers!' she croaked. 'So who was in the car with Swann?'

Taylor cut through the last tie. 'It must be our friend from the brewery, the little bastard who injected you.'

Travers hardly moved from his contorted position. He lay panting, licking his dry lips and slowly trying to straighten his limbs. Taylor pulled him up into a sitting position, lifted him from the boot in his arms like a baby, and carried him out to the BMW.

He placed him down, ashen faced and panting, in the back as Kim scrambled into the passenger seat. She leaned over and dampened the man's lips with a handkerchief soaked from the hosepipe. 'What's going on here?' she said, but Travers just lolled his head incoherently.

Taylor settled in behind the wheel and gave a long sigh. 'Maybe we'll find out…' he gestured with a thumb over his shoulder. 'If he pulls throu…'

The explosion drew the breath from Taylor's lungs stopping him mid-sentence. The garage's giant sized doors burst out onto the road. The windows shattered with a shrill crash of breaking glass as a pyre of orange flame erupted across the street with volcanic violence.

Taylor rammed the car into gear and left a trail of black, wheel-spin tyre marks behind as dense smoke overwhelmed the deserted street.

The distant sound of a fire engine's klaxon reached across the city to the car park of the Hotel Harmony as Taylor pulled in. The quick attendance of the Fire Service had resulted from Taylor's hasty anonymous call from a public phone.

Travers hauled himself into a sitting position for the short journey and remained head slumped down and forearms resting on knees as

Taylor opened the door.

'You okay, can you walk?' Taylor said.

Travers falteringly swung his legs around, accepted Taylor's hand, and placed his feet out of the car. He stood, hesitated, and then slowly made his way forwards towards the entrance.

Kim scraped wet hair from her eyes and stole an intrigued squint at Travers as Taylor held the hotel door open.

'Quite a guy,' she commented.

The receptionist looked up as they entered, his mouth dropping open.

Travers, gripping tightly onto Taylor's arm, tottered forwards. His gaunt grey pallor contrasted starkly with a patch of crimson skin across his left cheek where the tape had been stuck down. The usually neatly combed head of white hair now looked reminiscent of an electric chair victim. His blazer and light grey slacks fared no better, torn and marked.

Kim hobbled behind draped in the car rug, her own dark hair now on display and plastered flat to her scalp. Her tear-stained, mascara-streaked cheeks showed signs of the same crimson blemishes that decorated Travers' face.

Taylor winked at the bemused, open-mouthed receptionist as the trio trouped into the lift. 'Quite a party,' he said as the doors closed.

A temporary repair had been made to the bedroom door during their enforced absence. Taylor sat Travers down at the table and poured two large glasses of whisky. He pulled up a chair opposite.

'What in God's name is going on Travers?' He swallowed half the contents of his glass. Kim headed into the shower.

Travers looked back and sipped slowly, all his faculties now regained. He cleared his throat as he attempted to utter his first words since the start of the ordeal.

'I've got to thank you,' he began. 'There's no doubt that you saved my life tonight. I've seen you in the hotel and I must admit I was suspicious of you both. Such an attractive woman wearing a wig all the time, and you with that hat. I had no reason to believe that you were both involved in all this though.'

Taylor frowned at the thought of the disguises being seen through so easily. He introduced himself with his full police title. 'My friend is also a police officer.' He gave Travers a knowing stare. 'You visited Nazareth Church the night before last with Swann… if that's his real name. You went to a great deal of trouble to steal something from the ceiling of the church.'

Travers made an astounded face. 'How do you know about that?'

'We watched you,' Taylor explained. 'I was impressed with the way you did it. But perhaps now, you'll tell me how all this is connected to the ever rising murder rate in Staffordshire.'

Travers gulped at his whisky. 'Murders, Staffordshire. What the hell are you talking about?'

Taylor took another mouthful and settled an intense stare onto Travers. 'None of us leaves this room until you tell us the entire story and I don't care how long it takes.'

Travers moved his empty glass across the table and gestured with a nod towards the whisky bottle as Kim surfaced from the steaming bathroom.

'From the beginning?' Travers questioned.

'The beginning.'

FIFTY EIGHT

TRAVERS fixed both hands on the edge of the table and stared down as he considered his words. 'The Beginning goes back a long way… all the way to 1944.'

A shake of the head preceded a long sigh. 'I was a soldier with 7th Armoured Division during the Second World War… the Desert Rats. It was September. I'd seen my share of fighting in the desert. We'd had a hard time and I guess we thought we knew it all, but this was different, the weather, the terrain...'

He leaned across the table. 'We'd been set the task of liberating the City of Ghent, but got involved in fierce fighting in and around Nazareth. We suffered heavy losses. Five of my best friends were killed in front of my eyes… a sniper.'

Travers took a deep breath. 'I killed him, but a group of Germans were after me and I took some shrapnel in the knee.' He patted down on his left knee and continued. 'I knew our reinforcements were on the way, but it would be some time before they arrived. Because of my knee I hid in the loft of a damaged villa. Jerry came in looking, but didn't find me. I came across a wooden board wrapped in paper and bound with string like a parcel.'

Kim settled into a chair and rested her clasped hands on the table, eyes wide, taking in the dramatic story.

'The board was the ideal shape and size, so I put it down on the timbers and used it as a bed. I was weak and bleeding, I needed to rest. It stopped me falling through the ceiling. I used some of the string to help make a splint for my leg.

'When the sun came up and shone in through the holes in the roof I saw the board was actually a painting. An old-fashioned scene, men and horses… It was parcelled up with paper and string and even a label. Sometime later our boys arrived; they had no first aid kit so they used the board as a stretcher. It was a bit short, but it did the job.'

Travers rolled his eyes at the thought. 'I'd lost a bit of my kneecap, but could get about within a few days. The old painting stayed with me over the next few weeks and became a sort of joke. I used to have it propped up outside my tent. I even had my photo taken with it for my mum. I gave it to her when I finally made it back home.'

Travers reached into his tattered blazer pocket and pulled out the creased photo.

'I've seen it,' Taylor said and took his photograph of the snapshot from his own pocket. He slid it along the table in line with Travers' original.

Travers' forehead creased as he viewed the two pictures. 'So, that's where my room key went.' He gave a surprised shake of the head before getting back into his stride. 'I'd always intended trying to track down the person the painting was addressed to. I wanted to hand it over, so I tore the label off the wrapping and kept it.

'I was involved for a few weeks helping out the locals getting their lives back to normal. There were half a dozen of us, walking wounded and most of us were tradesmen in civilian life. We decided to make it one of our aims to do what repairs we could to the church. It had been badly damaged during the fighting, particularly the roof, which needed making weatherproof quickly.

'We used whatever we could get hold of to do the repairs, but only the best and sturdiest materials. We weren't particularly bothered what it looked like, but it needed to be a good solid job. We'd almost finished the work when we were told that we were being sent back home. Obviously I couldn't take the painting with me and never imagined it might be valuable. In the rush to finish I used it as part of the ceiling repair. The Vicar was more than pleased with what we had done. They held a ceremony for us, a big party. That was pretty well the end of my war. My injured knee didn't trouble me too much, but it left me with a limp.'

'It didn't stop you getting up that rope ladder,' Kim commented.

'I keep myself pretty fit. I stayed on in the army for several years after the war as a trainer and weapons expert. My wartime exploits never left me, but it wasn't until many years later that I heard any more about Nazareth Church.'

Travers caught sight of his dishevelled appearance in the mirror. He ran fingers through his hair and managed a half-laugh before continuing. 'I read an article in a magazine about the church ceiling and how it remained exactly as we left it. It had become a tourist attraction. Astonishing really, as it was only supposed to be a temporary job. I made plans to go over and see it again, but then my wife died and I suppose I lost interest.

'I heard no more about it at all and then about two years ago my mother died. She'd lived in Wareham, not far from my place. I was the executor and main beneficiary of the will. I employed a local firm of solicitors to see to everything. A legal snag cropped up and I gave the solicitors the go-ahead to employ an expert to sort things out. It was all pretty well wound up when I got a call from this man calling himself Swann.

'Swann explained that he was a private investigator, acting for my solicitors on the will problem. He told me he wished to speak to me on a matter of extreme urgency, and organised a meeting the next day in a pub in Wareham. I couldn't understand why he wouldn't meet me at the solicitor's offices.

'When we met he told me that he'd been going through some of Mum's paperwork and had come across this photograph.' Travers pointed down at his copy of the wartime snapshot. 'He told me that he believed the painting in the photo to be a valuable missing painting. He asked me if I knew what happened to it.'

Travers swilled the amber liquid around in his glass and then emptied it into his mouth. 'Of course I knew… It was part of the ceiling of Nazareth Church. It was the right size to use as one of the supports, so up it went. You couldn't see the painting from below. I put it up the other way and it was partially covered by other materials. Swann suggested that if we could get it down it would be worth a lot of money.'

Taylor leant back in his chair, staring at Travers. 'And you went along with this?'

Travers returned Taylor's stare. 'I didn't go along with it just like that,' he replied, bristling. 'His ideas seemed less than lawful, but he pointed out that if we could recover it without anyone knowing where it came from, then no one would have lost out.'

They both shook their heads at Swann's explanation.

Travers caught their expressions and looked down at the table, eyes half-closed. He now realised that Swann knew much more than he'd let on. The old soldier gave a shrug and held his open palms forwards in his defence. 'Swann explained that no one would ever know where it had been all these years. He said that if it was to turn up in say… America, we could get a decent price for it.

'I had no idea that anyone would be in danger or even that anyone would suffer any loss so, yes, I went along with it. I even planned to make an anonymous donation to Nazareth Church for the repairs and the on-going upkeep of the place.' Travers' brow increased as the serious implications dawned. 'You've already suggested that I was terribly misinformed. If, as you say, someone has been murdered in connection with this affair, it has been done without any knowledge on my part. I'll do anything I can to help you sort this mess out.'

Taylor topped up Travers drink and glided the replenished glass back across the table. 'Carry on.'

'Swann arranged to meet me in Ghent,' Travers said. 'He supplied me with the Triumph and booked my hotel room. He fixed the ferry tickets and even worked out a plan of how we'd actually get the painting down. To be honest, he was clueless, so I took over that part. I went on my own one night to do a recce.'

Taylor was now confident that Travers was being frank about

what had happened. He leaned forwards and poured another inch into Travers' still quarter-full glass before starting on his own empty one. 'But how did you get in?'

A grin spread across Travers' face. 'Couldn't have been easier. I had the key. When we were doing the repairs back in 1944, the Vicar gave me the key to the back door of the church. We could come and go as we liked. I fully intended giving it back, but when the time came for us to leave it was the last thing on my mind. I forgot all about it and it stayed in my rucksack. I kept hold of it all these years. It's a huge thing; I used to keep it on a hook in my kitchen. It was a bit of a talking point.

'The key was one of the reasons I needed to do a recce on the church. I couldn't be sure that it was still the same lock until I tried it. I must say it was breath-taking for me when I shone my torch up on to that ceiling. It was just how I left it all those years ago. I laughed when I saw the old Dubonnet sign we'd used. We weren't sure how that was going to go down, well you know, in a church.'

Kim glanced at Taylor. Her shaking head gave away her incredulity.

'I was confident the painting was still there,' Travers said. 'And I was pretty sure of its location. I planned the recovery operation and Swann came with me on a shopping expedition to get what we needed. Money was no problem to him. He seemed to have wads of cash.

'Swann rented the garage premises where you found me, along with an old van that we used. It was better than the British cars, not so noticeable and we'd got a lot of gear. After we got the painting down we stored it in the garage and then met there to discuss getting it out of the country.

'He'd insisted on me coming in the Triumph. I was standing talking to him in the garage when I was jumped from behind.' Travers rolled his eyes, annoyed with himself. 'I used to lecture and plan for special operations,' he explained. 'We often used chloroform in the early days to overpower people. I knew what it was. I tried not to breathe, but he was a powerful bastard. I was out within seconds.'

Taylor nodded as the puzzle of that sweet nutty smell from his hotel room was answered. He'd learned about chloroform at the police training school. The memory came back to him of the entire class dashing outside to clear their heads when the instructor wafted a few droplets about on a rag.

Travers picked up the story again. 'I hadn't a chance, and the next thing I knew I was trussed up like a turkey in the boot of my car. I couldn't move and was almost choking with that gag in my mouth.'

Kim leaned across the table. 'Did you know that I was in the garage too?'

Travers shrugged. 'I must have been out cold for a while and when I came around I'd got the biggest headache of all time.' He pressed the palm of his hand to his forehead.

Kim stood to her feet and moved around to the back of Taylor's chair. 'Tell me about it,' she empathised.

Travers grimaced. 'I heard the doors open and then voices. I knew something was going on, but then the doors closed and it was quiet again.'

He caught Kim's eye and then ploughed on. 'I guess that's when they brought you in. But it wasn't until they came back and started pouring petrol everywhere that I realised what their plan was. I could hear it and smell it even. I thought my number was up, and then you started that screaming.' He screwed up his eyes. 'God above, I've never heard anything like it. I was in a bad enough situation where I was, but it still scared the wits out of me and I guess it had the same effect on them.'

Kim blushed, 'It gave me a bit of breathing space, just enough as it happened.' She applied her hands to Taylor's square shoulders and squeezed. 'If you hadn't arrived when you did, it would all have been a very different story.'

Travers stared at Kim. 'Has it crossed your mind,' he asked. 'As to why they didn't set the place on fire as soon as they'd dumped you?'

Taylor interrupted. 'They were after me. They wanted the three of us in that garage. They came back to our room to get me, but fortunately I was in the one place they'd never have thought of looking: Room 214… your room. If they could have got rid of us all in one go I guess they'd have thought they were in the clear.'

Kim was now standing by the window, she looked back at Taylor. 'How did you find the garage? It was at least a couple of miles from the hotels.'

'I checked inside the Citroen van when we were watching at the church… remember? I found a rent card inside for the garage and made a note about it when we got back. I figured it might be a lead to their identity. I'd forgotten about it until I was trying to come up with an idea where they might have taken you.'

Kim breathed in deeply. 'I'm glad you did, you certainly cut it a bit fine.'

Taylor turned to face her. 'It was a real struggle to find the street. Most of the street name plates were missing and the map was so tiny. I knew I was close… I turned a corner and there was Swann's Mercedes. I just went for it.'

Travers shuffled forward in his chair as his opportunity for a question arrived. 'Okay,' he said looking at Taylor. 'Now you level with me. What's this business in Staffordshire and murders?'

Travers stayed silent throughout most of Taylor's update, his shaking head giving away his disbelief.

Half past two arrived before all of the events had been recounted. Many pieces of two previously unconnected jigsaws were slotted into place to form one complex story. The bottle of whisky was all but gone.

Taylor ran a finger around the rim of his glass. 'We need to find out where they've gone. I doubt if they're still here. They'll be miles away by now and we haven't a clue where to look. We can't go to the authorities for help. Swann has now got what he came for… he's got the painting, but he's yet to get it out of the country. He can't risk driving across the border with it. Even to an untrained eye it's bound to raise suspicion.'

Taylor finished the last dregs from his glass. 'They must have planned an illegal way out.' He leaned backwards in his chair. 'It can only feasibly be by air. Anything out into the North Sea or the Channel is too risky… radar and coastguards everywhere. Swann is most likely heading towards the South of France, Italy or Spain at a guess, and unless we get a break we've lost them.'

With the conference over Taylor saw Travers to the door. 'Your room is a bit of mess', he warned as the man set off unsteadily along the corridor.

'Can we trust him?' Kim said as Taylor pushed the battered bedroom door closed. 'I mean, aren't you worried he won't disappear in the night?'

Taylor pulled Travers' passport from his pocket and waggled it.

'He won't get far and I must admit I've taken rather a shine to him. I think he's on our side, especially after Swann has tried to kill him.'

'What about Swann? Do you think we're safe here? I mean, he knows our room.'

Taylor shrugged as he flipped the passport onto the table and started to unbutton his shirt.

'He won't come back here.' He looked down at the shirt buttons. 'He must realise he's missed his chance to get rid of us now. He wouldn't take the risk. Mr Swann and his friend are chasing the money.' He took her by the hand. 'Anyway, I need to get to bed.'

FIFTY NINE

THE SPELL of good weather had finally turned. Taylor rolled onto his side and slumbered a little longer, unaware of the fine rain misting the window panes.

Kim, eyes open and wide awake, stared up at the ceiling with yesterday's events racing through her mind. A soft knock on the bedroom door broke her thoughts. The clock showed the time as seven-fifteen. She hopped out of bed and hurriedly pulled on a dressing gown.

Taylor sat up, wary of such an early visit.

'Who is it?' Kim demanded.

'It's Travers, I've thought of something. We need to talk, it could be important.'

Taylor was half out of bed and pulling on his dressing gown before the sentence was finished.

Travers stood a pace back from the door as Taylor opened up. He was smartly dressed and ready for the dining room. The crimson patch on his left cheek and his tired eyes evidenced the fact that yesterday had not been a bad dream. He held a large Belgium road-map book in his left hand.

With a casual nod of the head, Taylor guided him inside and over to the table.

Travers declined the offer of a seat, preferring to stand. He placed the map book down on the edge of the table. 'It's something that's come to mind during the night. A long shot, but it might give us a lead to where they've gone.' He turned to face Taylor. 'You see, I never trusted Swann. I always thought he might double-cross me. I tried to listen in to a phone call he made. It was as we parted company on his first night here. I doubled back and spotted him making a call. He thought I'd gone back to my hotel. I went into the phone booth next to him. I couldn't hear well, but I did make out one word that he repeated. He said it several times and seemed to be spelling it. He sounded unsure about it… confused. He had several goes at it as he spoke to the person on the line before he appeared to understand the word. There was some talk about a meeting.'

'So, what was the word?' Taylor quizzed.

'It threw me at first.' Travers frowned. 'The word was "AS", just "AS". Clearly it puzzled him as well. He repeated it a few times and asked the spelling. I heard him recount it over the telephone, "A, S". There were some directions involved, as though a journey was being planned.'

Travers finished his sentence, expectant of Taylor's next question.

'So, what does it mean?'

'Well…' Travers said with a slight raise of eyebrows. 'You suggested last night that they would need an illegal way out of the country by air?'

Taylor nodded.

Travers looked down at the map. He pushed a finger between its leaves to locate a page with a turned down corner and opened up. The finger moved across the zig-zag of variously coloured depictions of roads, rail lines and rivers and landed adjacent to where the Belgian spelling: *GENT* was inscribed. The finger then moved a fraction to the south west and halted again.

'In 1944 I was here in Nazareth. When I eventually left the district with my other injured comrades we were transported to a place called Asch. It's getting on for a hundred miles due east of Ghent. The roads were in a mess and there were one or two loose Germans about, so it took us several days to get there.'

Travers thumbed through the map to find a second page with a folded corner. 'Asch, you see, was an allied wartime airstrip. We arrived in late December 1944. The airstrip only opened a few weeks before we arrived. It was an advanced landing ground used as the allies were pushing across Europe. We were expecting to be flown straight out, but we were well down the list of priorities. Planes were literally landing as others took off.'

'So, how does this help us?' Taylor interrupted impatiently.

Travers made a hopeful face and stabbed his finger down onto this new page. 'You see Asch is pronounced "Asch", but its Flemish spelling is As… A, S. That's what I think Swann had difficulty with on the telephone.'

They stared down at Travers' fingertip, eyes fixing upon the tiny letters which spelled out in Flemish the location of the village: "As".

Travers turned back to Taylor. The raised eyebrows were now accompanied by tight lips and slight wobble of the head 'It's a gamble,' he said. 'But if Asch Airstrip still exists in some form or other I think they're flying from there.'

At Heavitree Road Police Station in Exeter the few raindrops now falling were as big as marrowfat peas. Lacey looked up from his desk as the droplets struck the window and meandered down, soaking up the dust of the past few weeks. In seconds the drizzle became a downpour blotting out the roar of the morning's traffic rush from below and turning the window into an opaque blur.

The early post had been dumped on his desk in a large slanted heap. He sifted through it as worry piled upon worry. *Why hadn't Taylor phoned last night? There must be a serious reason.*

He pushed most of the heap to one side with a knowing shake of his head. One large brown envelope did catch his eye though. He pulled it out, reading the postal franking mark:

CRIMINAL RECORDS OFFICE NEW SCOTLAND YARD

He pierced the end of the envelope and then drew the razor edge of Exhibit A along its width.

The foolscap sized documents which fell out onto his desk were headed:

FINGERPRINT DEPARTMENT

He pushed his glasses further up the bridge of his nose and smoothed out the slightly crumpled paperwork. Amazement overwhelmed him as he read the given name.

'Fucking hell,' he muttered under his breath, reaching for his telephone. He stabbed at the keypad, but stopped halfway through and replaced the receiver. His eyes narrowed as he reached back to the pile of post again. This time his choice was a standard sized brown envelope. The foreign stamp and postmark caught his attention:

BELGIUM

With surgeon's precision Lacey put Exhibit A to work again. The Polaroid photograph which dropped onto the desk landed right side up.

'Fucking hell squared.' The words were not muttered this time, but shouted with considerable volume. Lacey grabbed the photo, jumped to his feet and headed for the door. The Chief Superintendent's office was his destination.

SIXTY

A TELEPHONE rang in the Enquiry Office at Little Stoneleigh Police Station. The young constable on duty continued to stare out of the window seemingly oblivious to the incoming call as he watched the outside world. Passers-by, umbrellas aloft and heads bent into the downpour hurried along the pavement. The area had not escaped the weather change.

Sudden realisation came that the call on the Murder Room direct line, demanded at least a modicum of efficiency and prompted the constable to lift the receiver. 'Enquiry office,' he announced.

'WPC Hall here,' a female voice said. 'Have you seen anything of Superintendent Farmer? He should have been here for a meeting at half eight.'

The constable looked over at the wooden framed clock above the office fireplace: eight forty-five.

'No, he normally calls in here first as you know. He moans about everything, bollocks everybody, makes a few offensive remarks and then disappears off to your place. He hasn't shown yet.'

'No ideas where he might be?'

'Sorry, can't help. Apparently he was up in his office till late last night.'

Back at the Hotel Harmony Travers had organised a table so that the three could breakfast together. It provided an opportunity to make some last minute plans and with no other leads his hunch about the airstrip at As seemed their only option.

A hasty continental with croissant and coffee followed. The broken bedroom door and early hours dishevelled return had drawn more than a few suspicious stares from staff members. The sooner they could get on the road the better. Last night's action and the need to find Swann before he left the country had also pushed the

"Urgency Thermometer" up many degrees.

Taylor's failed attempts to contact Lacey delayed their departure by an exasperating fifteen minutes. The line to his office just rang without answer.

Belongings were gathered together and packed into the now slightly battered BMW. Hotel bills were paid and eventually the three set off.

Kim's recovery from last night's ordeal was miraculous. She showed little evidence other than sticking plaster around her wrists. She took the front passenger seat and spread the road map open on her lap. Taylor turned on the windscreen wipers and surveyed the rain filled sky. He removed the sunglasses from the top of his head. 'I won't need these today.'

Travers sat in the rear, surrounded by his own belongings which could not be crammed into the overflowing boot.

The windscreen wipers steadily *swish, swished* on fast speed as they battled against torrential rain.

The line of bumper-to-bumper traffic reduced their progress to a crawl through the suburbs of Ghent. The planned route would take them along the E17 towards Antwerp.

Taylor briefly settled his eyes upon Travers through the rear-view mirror. He switched the wipers back to normal speed as the rain eased off. 'This place doesn't show on the map as an airstrip. It might not even be there now.'

Travers leaned forwards between the two front headrests. 'I know it's a long shot, but if it's still there I'll find it.'

As the BMW reached the outskirts of the city, Taylor, Harding and Travers could not have known that four Belgian police cars had just roared across the cobblestones of Sint-Baafsplein square and screeched to a halt outside the Hotel Harmony.

Capitaine-Commandant Roger Schmidt, head of the Ghent Crime Branch, stood hands thrust deep into raincoat pockets inside the open doorway of a certain third floor bedroom. Under his breath he cursed his luck. He had missed his quarries by a mere twenty

minutes.
A fingerprint man started dusting the dressing table mirror of Taylor and Harding's recently vacated room. A uniformed police officer peered in from the corridor cradling his Heckler and Koch sub-machine gun, barrel downwards.

The hotel manager stood with clasped hands and pensive expression alongside Schmidt.

'You say they checked out at about ten?' Schmidt's tone publicised his anger.

Manager, Cedric Peeters, nodded meekly.

'This man from room 214… he left with them?'

More nodding followed.

'Vehicle numbers?' Schmidt snapped

'Yes, yes, I have them both, although Mr Travers' car was not here this morning. They all left together in the BMW.

Six miles outside Little Stoneleigh in the United Kingdom, on a lay-by alongside the A519, forty-one years old Laura Dunning parked her Fiat 500. She locked up and stuffed the keys into the pocket of her jogging bottoms. After a short warm-up routine of stretching exercises and a check of her wristwatch, she set off. It was a remote and rural setting, albeit just a few hundred yards from the ever-roaring M6.

The one hundred feet high embankment down from Laura's parking spot to the motorway had been cut through the Staffordshire countryside twenty-four years before. Over the years a small but fairly dense wood of trees had established itself on the steeply inclined slope.

Miss Dunning always used the same route for her morning four-mile jog, whatever the weather, whatever the day. She crossed the footbridge spanning the M6 and soon got into a steady rhythm. Her route would take her onto the track that led towards the thickly forested expanse known as Trentham Park.

The area had become a haven for walkers, runners and mountain bikers who made good use of the trails which criss-crossed it. Laura knew her route so well that she could probably predict how many paces she would take to complete the four miles.

She hoped to knock up to a minute off yesterday's time. The past few weeks of stifling weather were uncomfortable to run in, and with the first wet day, the cool air was exhilarating. A slow drizzle now replaced the earlier downpour, it was ideal.

The same dog walker she saw every morning gave his usual cheery wave as Laura pounded her *New Balance* running shoes into the stone track. Her breathing had been steady and controlled in those moments before. Now she stood, hands on hips, short, panicky breaths as she took in the horror.

The gruesomely distorted corpse lay over seventy yards away, across the motorway and part way down the embankment. The flapping white shirt with its blood red staining caught her attention, but even from this distant viewpoint she could make out a gaping mouth and twisted limbs.

SIXTY ONE

MIDDAY ARRIVED all too soon in Taylor's mind. The journey had been a slow one. Rain, roadworks and the unending lines of holiday traffic completely destroyed his expectation of an easy drive. In-car conversation was minimal. Too little sleep, too much to think about and maybe too much whisky saw to that.

The road sign he'd stopped alongside read, AS 5K. He swivelled in his seat to face Travers. 'So, where do we go from here?'

Travers looked up the lead grey sky. He paused. 'It's been a long time, forty years or more, but the airstrip was south west of the town. If that dull splodge up there is the sun, then the airstrip should be in that direction.' He pointed over towards the right. 'Perhaps a mile or so.'

Taylor pulled back onto the road and continued towards As, hoping for a turning on the right. When they entered the busier perimeter of the small town a junction came into view. The direction sign showed: Oeleinde 2K. He slowed the car and eyed his mirror for a hint of confirmation from Travers.

Travers studied the sign, recognition spreading across his face. 'Yes, sounds familiar, give it a try.'

In Staffordshire Laura Dunning's lay-by had been closed to all comers. More of that blue and white police incident tape was in evidence. A fluttering length stretched along the entire span of the A519 pull-in, effectively rendering it a crime scene. A uniformed constable struggled against the wind to attach the loose end to a traffic cone.

Cheddar had parked fifty yards short of the lay-by and was half out of the car, untangling his raincoat from the seat belt. Jayne Morrison fought her own battle as she attempted to zip up her flapping windcheater.

'Hi, Gary,' Cheddar shouted over at the constable. 'What have we got?'

The constable made a grab at his black and white chequered cap, slamming it against his scalp before the wind took it.

'Male body, down the embankment, Ched. Lady out jogging spotted it from over the other side of the motorway. I've seen it from on the bridge. It's difficult to get at and I didn't want to disturb anything. Looks as though he's either fallen down from the lay-by or been dumped from a car there.'

'Is SOCO fixed up, Gary?' asked Morrison, pitching her voice against the wind.

'Yes, all sorted, and photographer.'

Cheddar frowned. 'No idea as to who it might be then? I mean, does it look like anyone you know?'

'Nar,' replied the constable. 'Too far away.'

Cheddar made off towards the embankment where a set of concrete steps meandered back and forth down to the level of the motorway. Morrison quickened her pace to catch up.

'Getting a lot of suspicious deaths on our patch of late, Ched.'

'An understatement,' Cheeseman said. 'We'd better have a quick shufty and make sure this one is actually dead. We'll approach from the bottom, so as not to disturb anything.'

It took a full ten minutes to get around to the base of the incline and start the climb up to the flapping bloodstained shirt.

The unrelenting roar of the M6 joined forces with the gusting wind making communication between the pair difficult during the ascent. Morrison struggled to keep her skirt down. A passing motorway lorry driver sounded his horn.

'Git,' she yelled with sufficient volume to overcome the conditions.

They slowly stumbled their way upwards, clutching at branches and roots as they drew closer. After several fairly exhausting minutes and as the traffic noise diminished, they could hear the thwack of the wet shirt striking against cold flesh.

The body had come to rest against the trunk of a tree. The arms and legs were contorted into a hideous arrangement following the violent passage down from the lay-by above. The wind blew the blood stained shirt back, revealing a perfectly circular hole of almost half an inch in diameter to the left of the breast bone. A large exit wound showed in the centre of the back.

The expressionless face stared at nothing through glazed, half-open eyes.

In Belgium the uncertain search for the airstrip persisted. Taylor steered the BMW along narrow, meandering, high-hedged lanes taking them away from the town of As. Their only guide was Travers' fading memory.

With almost two miles behind them the road straightened out. Occasional flashes of level fields and pastures were glimpsed through breaks in the hedges.

Travers' persistent window survey of the passing countryside soon paid dividends. 'Let's have a look around here.'

Taylor nodded at the mirror and pulled into a small passing place on the right.

The three climbed from the car and surveyed a flat grassy field through the roadside hawthorn hedge. The field was populated by a flock of rain-sodden sheep, but in the distance some five hundred yards away a red windsock flapped on its pole. A jumble of antiquated buildings lay clustered nearby.

'That's it,' declared Travers.

Setting off again they took a turning on the right, which common sense dictated would take them in the general direction of the airstrip. After another two hundred yards Taylor slowed the car alongside the mouth of a narrow lane where a hand painted wooden fingerpost sprouted from the roadside turf. The lettering simply read: *Y29*.

A gasp came from the rear seat. Taylor glanced at the rear-view mirror, catching Travers' astonished reaction.

'What is it?'

'Y29,' he said. 'That was the wartime code name for the airbase. It's come back to me. Whoever runs it now must still call it that.'

Potholes dotted the length of the narrow lane and weeds grew down the centre. Taylor slowed to a crawl and then pulled up against a pair of eight feet high, galvanised tubular steel gates. Similar fencing stretched away from either side of the gates which evidently encircled the entire compound. Coiled rusted barbed wire topped the fencing and a ragged Hawthorne hedge added further protection.

A three feet square white board was attached to the gate with *U* bolts, and bore stencilled red lettering in Flemish:

Y29 VLEEGTUIG CLUB

ALEEN LEDEN TOEGELATEN

Taylor eyed the sign, shrugging his shoulders as all three exited the car. 'Flying Club. Keep Out,' he guessed.

A heavy padlock with a thick chain held the gates firmly closed. The earlier downpour had now ceased and a few patches of blue were peeking through an otherwise overcast, windswept sky.

Taylor sidestepped a puddle and stuffed his hands into his pockets. He peered through the bars of the gate at the collection of buildings which lay 200 yards away along a puddle strewn make shift track. The red windsock stuck out horizontally from a mast, there was no sign of life. He closed up to the bars of the gate, staring, as a strong gust unsettled his balance momentarily.

The buildings were an odd assortment, ranging from ageing dilapidated brick constructions to rusting corrugated iron sheds. One, clearly the flying club's current headquarters, appeared more recent than the others. It was wooden and similar in style to an English cricket pavilion.

The largest building, a derelict, three-storey, brick built affair hailed from the World War Two era and was an early form of control tower. Its ground floor had been boarded up years ago and several of the rotting plywood sheets covering its lower windows flapped wildly, threatening to come adrift at any time.

A single, narrow runway stretched away into the distance. Even from their faraway viewpoint it was a patchwork of concrete and tarmac, tufts of grass sprouting from cracks and long overdue for maintenance,

'This could be a wild goose chase,' Taylor surmised as he gazed over at the buildings.

Kim huddled up against his side and linked her arm through his. 'They might have even gone last night.'

Taylor half-agreed. 'Maybe, but I doubt it. Yesterday's events weren't planned for, but might have flushed them out earlier than they intended. I just hope that we're on the right track.'

Travers moved up to the gate. 'We need to locate them to be sure they are going from here. We can't just sit and wait for them in case this is a red herring.'

Taylor frowned in concentration and found himself agreeing with Travers. 'There can't be that many hotels in this one-horse town,' he said. 'We know Swann has loads of cash. If there's anywhere that's half-decent, that's where he'll be.'

He'd hardly finished the sentence before he was back in the driving seat and turning the car around.

SIXTY TWO

TAYLOR drove into the town of As. The place seemed quite small and the definition of "Town" was perhaps a little ambitious. "Large village" might have been more fitting for this cluster shops, cafés, and guest houses which sat along the one main through road.

'Any ideas?' he said looking up at his mirror for Travers' response.

'Long time ago. Lot of changes. Half of this stuff wasn't even built when I was here; most of the older buildings were bombed out.'

Taylor drove slowly as they checked out the car parks and side streets for Swann's Mercedes. Extra care was given to the few hotels and guest houses. The search was thorough, but it drew a blank.

The sighting of a café in the main street reminded the group of their hurried breakfast and so the idea of some lunch was quickly agreed on. Taylor parked in the only available space some fifty yards down from the premises.

As he completed the parking manoeuvre the BBC's World Service news bulletin came through on low volume. The presenter was at pains to give an unbiased interpretation about the furore developing around the English football team's defeat in the World Cup quarter finals. Taylor tweaked the volume up a little. The story centred upon a handball incident by Argentina's, Diego Maradona in the match just two days before. The presenter went on to his next subject:

"Police in Staffordshire are investigating yet another suspicious death with the discovery of a man's body on an embankment adjoining the M6 Motorway. The discovery was made by a young woman out jogging in countryside, six miles outside the town of Little Stoneleigh. Several serious incidents have been reported in and around the area over the past two weeks. These include the disappearance of Exeter policewoman Kimberly Harding and Staffordshire Police Detective Inspector Douglas Taylor. A police spokesman would not comment on any connection between their disappearance and this latest find.

They would not name the victim, but said the discovery was being treated as suspicious."

Taylor switched off the engine, also silencing the radio. Travers' comment was more of a statement than a question: 'What have I got myself into?' No one answered.

Taylor pushed open the café door effectively putting the debate about who the latest corpse might be on hold. It was agreed though, that if this was another murder, Gorton was the likely perpetrator.

A thick smell of roasting beef, garlic and a hint of strong-smelling cigarettes met them as they pulled out chairs. 'I'm going to ring Pete as soon as we've had a bite to eat,' Taylor said. 'I saw a phone box around the corner, there's a lot to talk about.'

A sandwich order was quickly placed, but as it arrived Travers seemed more interested in nail biting. His face hardened in concentration as he focussed on a section of blank café wall.

'What is it?' Kim asked.

'We've tried everywhere in town,' he said. 'But there may just be one place worth a look, if it still exists.' He kept his eyes fixed on the same spot as he hauled the memories back from four decades. 'There used to be a splendid hotel north of the town. The Americans took it over as accommodation for their top brass. If it's still a hotel it's the kind of place Swann would go for.'

Oddly, Taylor made no comment on the idea. His own unblinking stare was now riveted onto something outside in the street. 'Look,' he said nodding slowly out through the window glass and down the road at the BMW.

The other two heads turned.

A large white motorcycle rested on its side-stand diagonally across the rear of the BMW. Thick black lettering on the rear pannier spelled out the word GENDARMERIE. The machine, throbbing on tick-over, effectively blocked the car from moving out.

A gigantic figure clad in the motorcycle leathers and helmet of the Belgian Traffic Police stood against the driver's door. A bulky gun holster and handcuffs were strapped to his side. The policeman pulled a black leather gauntlet from his hand and dropped it down onto the roof of the BMW. He then bent and peered in through the window.

Inside the café the three instinctively sat back in their chairs. They watched as the cop straightened up and slowly turned his head through 180 degrees scrutinising every aspect of the street. He took out a booklet from his breast pocket and flipped through the pages to consult a particular detail. Stepping back, he looked down at the car's front registration plate. He then went over to his motorbike and unclipped the radio's microphone from its bracket near the petrol tank.

Taylor's eyes were still on the policeman. 'He knows something… but how the hell?'

He stared at Travers and instantly dismissed the thought.

Kim blushed and set her lips in a tight straight line. She closed her eyes for a second. 'I'm sorry, it's my fault. I rang my dad. I knew how he was worrying. It was when we were thinking of going to the police. I thought it would be okay. I couldn't get that thug Gorton out of my mind. I knew as soon as I'd done it that I'd made a mistake, and now I've gone and dropped us right in it.'

Taylor shrugged and raised his eyebrows; it was a signal of resignation. He slipped his hand across the table and gave Kim's wrist a squeeze. 'We could be in serious trouble.'

The cop now stood looking away from the café, his broad leather clad back on show and the radio handset held to his mouth. Harding pushed Taylor's hand away and got to her feet. 'I've caused the problem, so I'll sort it.' She turned towards the door.

Taylor's chair tipped over backwards as he quickly raised himself from it. 'What are you doing?'

'I'm going to create a little diversion. 'I'll draw the motorcycle cop away from the car. If it works, meet me around the corner.'

'No way,' Taylor planted himself between Kim and the café door.

'You'll get hurt. These guys carry guns remember.'

'Doug,' she looked up at him, her face paling as if a plug had been pulled. 'I *have* to do this. I've created the problem and I'll sort it out.'

Taylor towered over her. He stretched an arm out across the door barring her way. 'No.'

She tilted her head to one side and rolled her bottom lip between her teeth.

'I mean it, Doug. I'll sort it and no one's going to stop me.' She banged the flats of her hands hard into his chest.

Taylor took a half step backward as the shove shifted his balance. This was a woman who no argument could influence. She lifted his arm like a car-park barrier and walked under it and out onto the street.

The Policeman was now busy trying the BMW's doors. Kim advanced along the pavement towards him.

Taylor gestured over to the waiter with a handful of cash to pay the bill.

Travers watched Kim's progress down the street. He drew his hand up to his mouth. 'God above, what's she up to?'

'I'm not sure,' Taylor said with a shake of the head. 'But there was no way she was going to let me stop her.'

The waiter accepted Taylor's payment, unaware of the unfolding drama and disappeared back into his kitchen.

Kim stalled outside a dress shop in pretence of window shopping. The policeman completed a circuit of the car and returned to the motorcycle to use his radio again. Kim moved in closer, she was now just yards from the BMW and acting out an interest in the items on sale in a DIY store. In reality her eyes were fixed on the policeman's reflection in the window glass.

With all the door handles tried the cop now took to tapping the toe of his boot against one of the tyres as he awaited more information over the radio.

The powerful engine of the Honda VFR 750P ticked over with a steady, soft deep beat as it stood against the kerb, keys dangling from the ignition.

'Oh, God,' Taylor said under his breath as the realisation of what was about to take place began to dawn. Something from that early morning conversation with Kim on the drive from Exeter to Little Stoneleigh, her traffic cop background – BIG BIKES!

SIXTY THREE

KIM LEAPT onto the motorcycle, buttocks bouncing onto the seat in the same instant that her left hand squeezed the clutch lever. The soles of her trainers hit the tarmac, nudging the bike off its stand and then kicked it into gear. The engine note grew to a well-tuned growl as she twisted the throttle. She looked back over her shoulder, eyes narrowing as the growl became a roar.

The cop's expression as his tyre kicking was disturbed, contained a mix of disbelief and horror in equal measures.

Kim paused and then twisted the throttle around to its maximum. The bike launched forwards and the roar became thunder. The front wheel lifted six inches from the road as a blurred forty yards was covered. With a touch on the rear brake and a hard pull back on the front one the bike juddered to a dead stop, its rear wheel lifting high into the air.

The wheel came down with a well-controlled thump. Kim's trainers touched down in unison and held the balance. She stared back over her shoulder and revved the engine into the red on the rev counter.

The young cop was quick. Within seconds he was around from the front of the BMW fumbling to get his gun from his holster. His top of the voice hollering penetrated the engine noise.

'*Stopt, den dief*,' he shouted, running full pelt, gun in right hand.

A mere twenty feet separated the policeman from his motor cycle as Kim opened the throttle again. The front wheel lifted two feet from the tarmac as the bike took off, propelled forwards under ferocious acceleration. An explosive snarl came with the move as half the length of the two hundred-yard long street was covered.

She stamped at the rear brake stopping the machine, slewing it around at an angle to take in the sight of the distant sprinting cop.

Taylor and Travers were out of the café doorway and running for the BMW before Kim began her third wheelie. She wasn't so cruel this time, roaring off well before the policeman was close.

Taylor pointed the remote key at the car, the locks flicked up, Travers dived into the back seat and the engine boomed into life. Taylor sprung the clutch out, the car shot forwards, tyres squealing, accelerating towards the end of the road away from the policeman. Shopkeepers and customers bundled out onto the pavement to see what the commotion was.

Taylor's brief experience of the small town an hour and a half before was enough. He knew that another street ran parallel to the one where they had parked.

He threw the car around the corner as Travers desperately hung on to the back of his seat.

'She sure can handle that motorbike,' he shouted above the engine noise, struggling to steady himself.

'Too right,' Taylor agreed, swinging the car left again into the parallel street. 'But let's hope this is where she wanted us to be.'

Kim was pulling the motorcycle back up onto its stand as Taylor drew alongside her. He shook his head, dumfounded by the display he'd just witnessed.

Kim grinned, stuck out her tongue and then yanked the motorcycle keys from the ignition, tossing them into the air, catching them and stuffing them into her jeans pocket.

They caught sight of the cop as he rounded the far distant end of the road. He'd actually done pretty well.

Taylor pointed the BMW in a vaguely northerly direction out of town. The cop still had a couple of hundred yards to cover before he caught up with his borrowed motorcycle and even then he had no keys. Kim turned in her seat watching the distant figure.

'Hope he doesn't get into trouble.'

'Nice work,' Taylor said. 'But this place is going to be swarming with cops within half an hour.' He frowned as he realised that for the second time he'd made a statement that should have been reserved for a criminal rather than a detective inspector. 'Okay, Travers,' he said, retaking control. 'Where do you think this hotel is? We still don't even know if this is a complete waste of time, something we're fast running out of.'

Travers took another skyward look from the car window. A glimmer of sun was attempting to force through the clouds.

'All I can remember is that it was to the north of the town, so I guess we are heading in roughly the right direction.'

The road straightened out as it left As. They travelled over mile before a large yellow sign came into view on the grass verge with a pointing arrow. *Hotel Résidence Stiemerheide.*

Taylor caught Travers' eye in his mirror and made a questioning face. Travers nodded back.

'Could be, it's the right area.'

Following the sign, Taylor turned the car off the road into a tree-lined expanse of curving driveway and carried slowly on. A glimpse of a building presented itself through the gaps in the trees.

'This is it,' Travers piped up from the back seat.

Taylor pulled the car to a halt opposite a larger gap.

The sprawling, white painted three-storey structure stood squarely in the centre of the grounds. Sharply pitched red tiled roofs and an old bell tower harked back to the seventeenth century when it was built.

A large square of black tarmac at the side of the hotel was sparsely populated with about a dozen cars.

Kim took the binoculars from the glove box and scanned back and forth. She stopped, leant forwards to get a better view and then pointed a finger. 'There,' she said handing the binoculars to Taylor. 'To the left of the red Jag... Swann's Merc. I'm sure of it.'

Taylor focussed in. 'You're right; we're back in the game.' He turned towards the back seat and selected a gear. 'Well done, Travers.'

A skilful three-point turn followed and they were back on the main road. Kim swung sideways in her seat to face Taylor. 'What next then? Like you said, this place is going to be swarming with police any time soon.'

'Hmm,' he mumbled back a desultory agreement. 'But they almost certainly have no idea why we're actually in this region. Chances are after a thorough search they'll be thinking we wasted no time and moved straight on.' Taylor took his eyes momentarily from the road and met Kim's stare. 'We must keep hidden until tonight. Swann won't want to be wasting any more time. Chances are that he's flying tonight.'

Travers leaned forwards, pushing against his seat belt.

'I know the place to hide.'

SIXTY FOUR

THE SOUND of several distant klaxons drifted across the fields, that out of tune warbling, so characteristic of foreign police cars.

Taylor could not better Travers' idea and so the trio were back at the deserted gateway of the Y29 aero club. Travers was out of the car and down on all fours inspecting the hinges of the enormous right hand gate. The far-away noises emphasised the fact that a concentrated search was now underway. The fact that one of the klaxons could be audibly separated from the clamour intensified the urgency of the situation. It was getting closer!

Anxious moments passed as Travers persisted with his examination of gate's hinges. 'Yes, it should work,' he said. 'These gates are heavy. We'll need to use the carjack. You say there's a hacksaw in the toolbox?' his eyes were on Taylor.

In no time Taylor was hunting through the crammed car boot. He quickly pulled out a red plastic box bearing the name *Disley's Tools of Dover* and handed it to Travers. He then dived back in, committed to the more difficult task of unearthing the carjack.

Travers took a hacksaw from the box as Kim helped Taylor reload the boot. The solitary police klaxon continued to grow louder against the background of the more distant ones.

Travers clambered partway up one of the gates and started to saw at the retaining pin fitted through the upper hinge bolt of the gate. The brand new hacksaw blade made short work of the small pin and Travers immediately got to work with the pin fitted to the lower hinge bolt. He carefully picked up the two remnants from the ground and threw them away into the bushes.

Kim knew what was expected of her as she wound the carjack down to its lowest level. She then squeezed the jack's lifting platform under the gate near the hinges on the right-hand side. Taylor now took over, quickly winding the jack handle around. The gate slowly and laboriously started to creep upwards until the hinges cleared the tops of the bolts. The sound of the police car echoed across the fields as it made its way through the narrow lanes.

Travers moved in and set two conveniently discarded bricks underneath the bottom bar of the gate alongside the jack. He then wound the gate down a fraction until it rested on the bricks. With a twisting back and forth action he pulled up the central retaining pole. A loud metal-on-metal squeaking sound reverberated through the entire gate.

Following Travers' shouted instructions the three held the gate at the hinge side and shuffled fingers into firm grips. Eye contact and a nod from Travers commenced the in-unison task and with a couple of grunts of exertion the gate lifted clear of the bricks. They walked forwards with it into the airfield trailing the other gate alongside as that one effortlessly moved inwards on its still intact hinges.

As soon as a car sized gap had been achieved Kim dived into the driving seat. The warbling claxon seemed almost upon them as the BMW lurched forwards a few yards and slammed to a stop. Taylor and Travers strained with crabbed legs and staccato steps to manhandle the gate back towards its original position. They rested it down onto the ground next to the bricks. Taylor slung the toolbox into the still open car boot and quickly got back alongside Travers, shuffling his hands into a solid grip upon the gate.

With adrenaline fuelled, superhuman strength the two men lifted the gate back onto the bricks. They rested for a second and then strained with gritted teeth and white knuckles to raise it until it perched at a slant on top of the hinge bolts.

'After three,' Travers said and started. 'One, two, three.'

A dull metal clang echoed through the gate as its weight thudded heavily down onto the hinge bolts and rested squarely back in its original position.

The klaxon was close now, too close, but another noise added even greater alarm: the whipping, flapping sound of the rotors of a helicopter!

The immense joint effort couldn't even be celebrated with a grin, the police car and now a helicopter saw to that.

Travers chucked the bricks into the bushes and then wiped the mud from his fingers onto the gate hinge bolts where the severed metal pins shone brightly. Taylor crammed the jack and handle back into the boot and banged it shut. The two men leapt into the car and hung on as Kim accelerated away down the track towards the buildings. Her eyes were fixed more on the rear-view mirror than through the front windscreen.

She steered the car in between two of the old buildings. On one side stood the dilapidated wartime control tower and on the other, the single-storey wooden office.

The rotor blades of the helicopter swished and woofed loudly – ALMOST OVERHEAD!

In front of the BMW a ramshackle, open-fronted former hangar, now served as a garage for an old fire engine. The timeworn machine sat solidly on semi-flat tyres with large round rusty headlights like a character from a child's storybook.

Kim frowned as she surveyed the gap between the fire engine on her left and the wooden work bench on the right, definitely too narrow. She instinctively glanced upward through the glass sunroof as the noise of the helicopter pounded closer. She then swung her widening eyes onto the gap ahead and slowly lifted the clutch. A shudder accompanied the rending sound of tortured metal as deep gouges gradually bit into the car's nearside metalwork. The left-hand wing mirror was plucked from its mounting and left dangling on wires. The wooden workbench on the right lifted up on its legs as the BMW's front wing inexorably crunched into it. The sound of splitting wood accompanied the clatter of metal tools falling onto concrete. The last remnant of the right-hand wing mirror, all that remained from Taylor's efforts the day before, was torn from its socket and left swinging on wires like its counterpart.

Kim cut the engine and the three sat motionless, pinned inside the car, its doors jammed tightly against fire engine and bench. Obviously they couldn't be heard or seen, but no one dared move or speak as the helicopter roared overhead.

The helicopter's racket overpowered the police klaxon, but enough of it could still be detected to establish that it was very, very close.

After several pensive minutes the helicopter's chatter drifted away and likewise, the klaxon had gone silent. Taylor wound the sunroof open and struggled out and down over the boot lid. He sidled around to the hangar's entrance and stared through a rusting crack in the corrugated iron sides. Kim and Travers completed their own awkward exit from the BMW and joined him.

Two hundred yards away a police car was now parked against the gates, doors open in exactly the same spot that the BMW had been minutes before. Two bulky uniformed figures stood peering through the gates. After a few minutes one pulled something from his pocket and offered it to his colleague. They hung about smoking for several minutes before getting back into the car and driving away.

A full hour went by before the far-off sounds of police cars ceased and the countryside returned to the silence of their first visit to the airfield.

Taylor checked his watch, five minutes past six. All chances of making that phone call to Lacey were lost. 'Damn,' he cursed under his breath. So much had taken place and a lot more looked possible. The call could have been a lifeline, but now it just wasn't going to happen.

It was some time later when he rubbed at one of the grimy windows of the office. 'A telephone, a bloody telephone,' he said loud enough for Travers to hear.

He checked his watch again, six twenty-five. He grabbed Travers' arm. 'I must use that telephone.'

'Okay, you know best, but we can't let it look like there's been a break-in, they're armed remember. We'll either be shot or off on another chase across the country.'

Travers tried the door. It was solid with a good quality lock fitted. Taylor rechecked his watch. The fingers had advanced little more than a minute.

'This is important, Travers, and it may already be too late.'

Travers trotted around to the rear of the building with Taylor at his heels. He homed in on a transom window.

'This'll do… brace and bit out of the toolbox, small bit, about quarter inch.'

Taylor darted back to the car and delved into the boot for the toolbox, urgency showing on his face.

Kim, startled at the sudden activity and unaware of the conversation was about to attempt to extract the BMW from its jammed position. 'What's going on?' she asked.

'Metal coat hanger, quick,' Travers yelled as he dragged a couple of wooden pallets towards the window.

Taylor tipped the tools out onto the concrete and was quickly twisting at the drill chuck to tighten it onto the bit. He dashed back to Travers, who now stood on the platform of pallets.

'I've been to plenty of break-ins done like this, but never watched it happen before,' Taylor said.

Travers spun the drill and bored into the wooden window frame below the inside catch. Kim ran over holding the metal coat hanger she'd scavenged from one of her outfits in the car.

As Travers made the last few turns Kim plied the coat hanger back and forth until an end came free. She then stretched it out into one long length. She also knew Travers' game.

As the bit pierced the frame Travers tossed the drill to one side and thrust his open hand back at Kim without even looking around. She pressed the hanger down into his palm and watched as he quickly fashioned a bend into one end. He threaded this into the neatly bored hole and made contact with the inside window catch.

Taylor again checked his watch, six thirty-two.

With one deft turn of the wrist Travers flicked the window catch upwards and pressed lightly on the frame. The window jarred forwards, opening two inches, now held only by its bottom catch. Travers poked the coat hanger in through the gap at the bottom and tapped the catch upwards. The window swung open.

Travers moved to one side as Taylor stepped up onto the pallets and without hesitation climbed through the opening and jumped down onto the floor. He grabbed the telephone handset and stabbed out the fourteen-digit number burnt into his memory. The familiar ring tone started its *burr-burr…burr-burr.*

Lacey descended the stairs of Exeter Police Station grim faced. He had waited almost an hour for Taylor's call. It was vital that he spoke with him, but had now resigned himself to the fact that it wasn't going to happen. There was every reason to believe that both Taylor and Harding were in desperately serious trouble and Taylor's failure to ring emphasised this.

The information recovered in the past twenty four hours was astounding and had generated the need for other crucial measures. The news from DC Cheeseman on the latest Little Stoneleigh death added another serious aspect.

Lacey looked miserable and frustrated. He'd even used the stairs on the way down, despite the fact that the lift was now working. He still held a forlorn hope that Taylor might ring.

As he reached the bottom step he fancied he heard a phone on an upper floor, but there were dozens of the damn things in the building and most of them usually rang at the same time.

SIXTY FIVE

LACEY'S DIVE across the desk would have delighted any goalkeeper. His sprint up the stairs must have taken years off him. The gasping voice was hardly recognisable to Taylor, but those breathless words silenced his attempt to be the first to impart information.

'It's Bunn,' Lacey said. 'The man you've photographed outside the cathedral… Swann. It's Jacob Bunn.'

Taylor heard Lacey's wheezing words clearly enough, but couldn't stop himself from questioning them. 'WHAT?'

He paused as he searched for comprehension. 'But the body, the dental identification,' he finally managed.

'Jacob Bunn is no more dead than you or I,' Lacey said. 'It's certainly him, cut his hair and dyed it dark, grown a tash, but no doubting it.'

'Christ, so who…'

'The body is a man named Alan Craine from Taunton'. Lacey explained. 'Mr Craine has been listed as a missing person since the fifteenth of June… that's ten days ago. It seems he had the misfortune to tick all the physical boxes as a body double for Jacob Bunn.'

Taylor took his chance to throw in a question. 'We heard the news on the radio. What's this about another body found near Little Stoneleigh? Is it connected…is it murder?'

Lacey's breath and composure were returning. 'I'll come to that in good time Doug, let's deal with Bunn first. As you know Bunn was a patient of the dentist Walley. I've discovered that Walley and Bunn go back a long way, they were at university together and remained close friends. They played squash together each week. Walley is Bunn's dentist… his practice provided the dental chart identifying the body on Cannock Chase as Jacob Bunn.'

Taylor's stunned silence was understandable.

Lacey delivered more: 'The drug used on Kim, you'll remember, is a dentist's drug. We've searched Walley's surgery this morning. Mr Craine was also a patient of Walley's. It seems that Craine was specifically chosen. He was the same age, height and build as Bunn. He even had the same blood group. He was, as near as damn it, a perfect match, and with his face burnt beyond recognition, the only ID to fall back on is his dental chart. Walley has compiled a completely new chart in Bunn's name, using the current chart for Craine's teeth. He's even aged the paperwork and backdated it all, it's a brilliant forgery. Your pathology experts have quite correctly identified the body's teeth to the dental chart. The only problem is that it was Craine's body and Craine's chart, with Jacob Bunn's name at the top.'

The gravity of Lacey's summary was still sinking in. Taylor took a few seconds to form his question. 'So,' he started. 'How can you be sure of Craine's ID. How do you know it is him?'

'Yes, good point Doug and that's what it really hinges on. You see Craine hasn't always been with Walley's dental practice, so we traced his previous dentist and *BINGO,* they had a copy of his old chart. Quite a few changes over the years but there's absolutely no doubting that it is Craine.'

'There's more Doug,' Lacey said. 'The fingerprint on the syringe is Walley's, so it was him who injected Kim and he's been missing from work since this began. You see Walley has form. He was done for a minor possession of cocaine years ago, but his prints were still on file. He obviously wasn't planning on you and Kim showing up at the brewery.'

Taylor took his opportunity to interrupt. 'Walley is not at work because he's out here with Bunn.'

'That figures,' Lacey said. 'The two of them are up to their eyeballs in this. I've discovered that Mr Craine was on his way for his weekly workout at the gymnasium when he went missing. He was booked in for his normal session but according to the records, he never arrived. It's all there on the Misper form, he'd been a member at Jay's Health and Fitness for ages and that's what originally put me onto it.'

Taylor had gone quiet again. 'You still there Doug?' Lacey said.

'Yes, I'm still here, I'm a bit lost for words.'

Lacey pressed on, 'Bunn's gym has been closed since all this began. We've searched the premises today… gone through all the records. It's beginning to look as though Craine was introduced to the place by Walley and, would you believe it… given twelve months free membership on Bunn's say so.'

'They've groomed him,' Taylor said. 'Walley selected him as an ideal candidate over a period of time. He's even got him to turn up by appointment to be murdered so his body could be used.'

'Correct Doug, exactly how I see it, they planned each detail in advance. Even the Jaguar was pinched whilst the owner Mr Lewis was on holiday.'

'Yes,' Taylor replied. 'You're going to tell me Lewis was one of Walley's patients as well?'

'Nearly right. He works in Taunton, has an office there, he was a member at Bunn's gym, a regular lunchtime visitor. All his details are in the old records, including his address and car registration. He was a regular, so his holiday dates are all recorded. They knew exactly when they could get his car and how long they could keep it before it would be reported stolen; all it needed were false number plates which matched a similar car.'

Taylor looked over at Travers and Harding. They were standing outside, huddled against the open window trying to make sense of the one-sided conversation. He reached over, unlocked the door and indicated with his eyes for them to come in.

Lacey got on with the story. 'The latest body to turn up Doug, is Gorton! Shot through the chest with a 9mm bullet… body dumped a few miles outside Little Stoneleigh.'

Taylor went silent, but not for long. 'I can't say I'm upset,' he eventually said. 'But who's responsible for that?'

'There can only be one suspect with a motive who lives in Little Stoneleigh.'

'Farmer!' was Taylor's single word.

By the time Taylor imparted his side of the story the conversation stretched out for a full twenty five minutes. Lacey would have liked to have chatted a little longer but there were some very serious matters still to attend to.

Kim now turned her attentions to hiding the BMW which remained rammed tightly between the fire engine and the bench. Her noisy attempts to bully it free finally succeeded. Taylor's concerns about the revving and the clouds of tyre smoke were understandable even though the airfield was isolated. She drove the battered car around to the back of the hanger within a copse of trees where it could not be seen.

The flying club's office, a sturdy wooden building, clearly also served as a form of control room. A couple of filing cabinets and some cupboards stood against the walls along with a small sink. On one wall was an electrical panel made up of a multitude of switches with a mass of wiring, it was all rather DIY. A large table took up the centre of the room and this supported a clutter of radio equipment and cabling.

The trio mulled-over the latest revelations for a while as they carefully restored the office to its former self. It was nine o'clock when Taylor pulled the door closed behind him and pressed a flattened palm against it to test that it had locked.

Everything pointed towards a flight from this airfield and common sense hinted at tonight. These were gambles they reminded themselves of constantly. Their loosely stitched together plan was based on these variables and nothing much more. They now needed to explore the other buildings.

The decaying control tower proved favourite as a covert observation point. Travers quickly prised one of the rotted boards from a rear window and climbed in with Kim following.

The upper floors, perhaps originally designed as offices and storage, were not boarded over and what sunlight still existed aided their ascent up a set of debris strewn concrete steps. Shards of glass crunched under their feet as they arrived on the top floor and entered into the old air traffic control room.

This four yard square chamber was perched on the very top of the old brick building and seemed to share some heritage with a large garden greenhouse: The floor to ceiling walls were entirely constructed of iron framed, glazed panels on all four sides. Only a handful of the glass panes had survived intact, the aim of vandals having been perfected over the years. Most of the shattered glass lay on the floor in tiny triangular shaped pieces. The stones and brick ends causing this damage were also strewn about. Rotting wooden desks were fixed beneath the windows with drawers and doors hanging open or missing. Pigeon faeces covered most surfaces in decades-thick clumps.

The slowly darkening sky intensified the desolate surroundings. Travers watched silently from the doorway as Kim pushed her thumb down onto the transmit button of the two-way radio. 'You getting this?' she enquired.

The radio hissed and then responded with a weak and off-key impression of Taylor's voice. 'Receiving, but pretty hopeless.'

She settled down near the window making use of a couple of wooden boxes as a seat. Travers raised the palm of his hand in a temporary goodbye gesture and made his way back down the stairs.

SIXTY SIX

TEDHAM CREMATORIUM Chapel and Cemetery did not usually have night time visitors. A small yellow mechanical digger chugged its way slowly through the neatly laid out walkways. The amber beacon on its roof flashed as the constant note of its diesel engine made easy work against a slight incline.

It was approaching half past ten as the driver pulled in next to the assembled detectives and senior police officers, their outlines picked out by the stark brightness of powerful floodlights.

A multitude of cables snaked away into a large cream-coloured tent pitched nearby to house a humming generator.

The popular choice of dress for the throng appeared to be raincoats. The recent change in the weather after so many glorious weeks made this appropriate. The plain fact existed though, that a smart and respectful turnout was always decreed for such a sombre occasion as an exhumation.

Tradition also prescribed that exhumations were to be completed during the hours of darkness. The official line being: "To prevent undue distress to the public". It may have been more to do with: "Stopping prying eyes".

It had been no simple task for Pete Lacey to arrange the procedure. The paperwork required by the coroner was daunting. The additional health and safety requirements, the equipment, the attendance of cemetery staff, undertakers and crime scene experts, turned the process into a major operation.

The digger driver set to work; the engine note rising and falling with each expertly cut shovelful of earth. In a fairly short space of time a completely symmetrical rectangular slot deepened down into the yellow-brown earth. A sizeable pyramid of the same steadily grew upon an adjacent square of blue plastic sheeting.

'Couple of inches Gov,' the driver shouted over at the Detective

Chief Inspector. 'I can feel it's there. Anymore and I might scratch the varnish.'

A ripple of laughter went around the group at this remark.

A SOCO man clambered down into the grave with a plastic bucket, dustpan and brush to carefully clear the remaining earth from the top of the recently interred casket.

The driver was right, two inches it was. Within less than ten minutes the glossy, deal lid reflected the glare of the floodlights as though it had arrived from the manufacturers that very day. The two council workmen, who were on double pay overtime, grinned broadly as they assisted the SOCO man to finish the job.

The scene was additionally lit with a flashing strobe effect as the police photographer went about his work, recording every detail of the procedure. The engine of the little JCB increased its revs as it hauled the swinging casket out from the hole suspended on thick webbing belts attached to the bucket. It was skilfully placed down at the rear of the undertaker's Mercedes estate.

Old Mr Pedley carried out a cursory examination, brushing away a few of the larger soil deposits from the edges, before giving sons Tom and Andrew approval to: 'load up'.

An entourage of CID officers and coroners' officials in their varying motor cars followed as the vehicle made its way from the graveyard, back to Exeter mortuary. Old man Pedley lit up before even exiting the crematorium gates.

He sat, elbow on the edge of the vehicle's open window exhaling a plume of smoke and chuckling as he considered the irony. Transporting a body *from* the cemetery rather than *to* it was an uncommon journey.

Midnight arrived in Belgium. The Y29 runway showed as nothing more than an inky black line. The moon was playing hide and seek behind quickly drifting clouds and provided little illumination.

Kim's eyes were heavy from the lack of sleep. Her mind wandered back to Heavitree Road nick in Exeter where she first started out as a constable. There was nothing worse than observations: Obs, as all her police colleagues called it. She'd done her fair share of obs as a rookie, sitting in some car, or hiding in a derelict house. It was like watching paint dry. You'd slowly start to drift off and then your head would jerk as it started to loll forwards. All of that and everything in her life before this week seemed so long ago.

The two-way radio hissed and Taylor's distorted voice came through.

'You okay up there?' was what she gathered the question to be.

'Yes, all quiet.'

Four hundred miles due West in Exeter's mortuary an assistant's electric screwdriver whirred as the last screw wound its way up from the lid of the exhumed "casket". Undertaker Frank Pedley had taken every opportunity to enlighten those not familiar with funereal terminology of the correct title of said receptacle.

The casket sat solidly on a white porcelain slab in the post mortem room, glistening wet under fluorescent lights from its recent hosing down. It still showed a few streaks of dark soil and mud against a glossy, new-looking, polyurethane finish. More photographic flashes ensued as the pathologist, in green surgical scrubs, closed up to the slab adjusting his facemask tightly against his nose. Experience readied him for the stench of rotting flesh which would inevitably follow.

The gaggle of suit wearing detectives took up various positions around the room. Nervous laughter and a few tired jokes ensued. It was the typical pretence at indifference which always accompanied post mortems. Raincoats were abandoned in the cloakroom, handkerchiefs pressed to faces and the statutory packet of mints handed around for a second time.

Two drained faces formed part of the throng. Lacey and Timson had already made arrangements with a nearby licensee for a *very* after hours drink. One pint would hit the spot and tomorrow would be both an early and a long day.

There was a sharp *snap* as the seal between lid and casket was broken. The two attendants lifted from each end and then rested the lid down on an adjacent slab.

More camera flashes followed with the accompanying whine as the camera batteries recharged.

One detective retched a couple of times as a miasma of decay enveloped the room.

DI Grainger stepped forwards and with no sign of emotion, scrutinised the ragged, putrefied features. 'Well, well, Mr Sweeney, how nice of you to drop by.' He turned his attention towards the DCI. 'That's a fiver you owe me, Boss.'

SIXTY SEVEN

IN LITTLE STONELEIGH Farmer pushed the key into his front door lock and entered the hallway. He hadn't been so at ease with such an everyday activity a few hours before.

He briefly glanced at himself in the hall mirror, something he did rarely nowadays. A very worried man looked back, dark fleshy pouches beneath the eyes, grey parchment skin.

He slumped into an armchair in the lounge. *Things haven't gone at all to plan*, was one of his thoughts. He stared across at the door, its splintered panelling evoking the full memory of last night's violence and the two hours he'd spent in the darkness in that very same chair, waiting. He relived it all, second by second: *his hand tightly gripping Charlie Price's gun, his senses alert and ready for the murderous house call that he knew would come.*

Gorton was, it has to be said, a professional. He'd made little or no noise, the strips of industrial adhesive tape across the kitchen window pane deadened the breaking of the glass. His climb down to the floor had been silent in spite of his size and the burdens of an electric carving knife in one hand and a heavy revolver in his pocket. He'd convinced himself that Farmer would be fast asleep in a whisky induced coma and was confident that he would: "Make the bastard talk", before torturing him to death. He'd find out where the money was.

Farmer trembled as he recalled the door handle slowly turning and how the vision of Daniels' mutilated body flashed into his mind before he'd pulled the trigger. He physically flinched at the thought.

Gorton didn't even get a chance to see Farmer eye to eye. The bullet smashed through the door and penetrated his sternum. Farmer wanted to go on pumping bullets into the door to make sure he'd killed Gorton. But he'd had time to think about it, thoughts and memories which concentrated his mind. One single shot in the middle of the night he might get away with, several shots were sure to be heard. He knew he must stay calm and shoot again only if it was absolutely necessary. That way he'd get away with it.

If Gorton was still alive and not capable of fighting back, he'd finish him off by strangling him. The length of blue nylon rope lay coiled on the arm of his chair. He'd even switched the electricity off at the mains and hidden the fuses. Oh, yes, he'd thought it out, that would stop Gorton using his electric carving knife.

Farmer struck lucky; his contingency plans were not required. The one bullet killed Gorton immediately. The giant thug made no noise. No cry of pain or last gasp, just a house-shaking dull thud as his ox-like shoulders slammed into the kitchen wall behind.

Farmer's shaking gun hand remained pointing at the door for almost ten minutes before sufficient confidence allowed him to lower it and tentatively view his handiwork.

The struggle to remove the crumpled, bloodied hill of dead flesh proved a monumental task for the overweight, out of condition fifty-five year old. Wrestling the body into his car boot left blood stains, hair and body tissue along with countless other forensic clues. His panic-stricken, poorly thought out disposal of the corpse added even more to the mounting evidence against him, especially when it would be discovered so quickly.

He submitted his official retirement report that very day in a bizarre and futile hope that he'd get away with it. He now knew for sure that the game was up and that a knock at the door would likely come the next morning. He let out a long sigh of desperation. Could there still be time to slip through the net?

The one bonus to come from the disruption to his plans was that he had ended up with far more money than originally agreed on. He'd now got Charlie Price's share, one million three hundred thousand pounds, instead of the measly two hundred and fifty grand they were intending ripping him off with. That huge lump of cash could without doubt buy him out of the predicament if he could get in touch with the right underworld contacts, and he knew plenty of those.

Farmer was one of the few who knew that it was Price who had steadily supplied the tip-offs that led to Sweeney's entire empire crumbling.

Sweeney had been blissfully confident that his trusted old cellmate would get the remaining cash fortune together for one more big drugs purchase. It would be a purchase that would keep him in luxury after Jacob Bunn successfully proved him: "Innocent on all counts".

The change in plan by Bunn to break Sweeney from court when the defence case started to topple proved to be a surprise to the gangster. He didn't know Bunn had it in him. The idea that his "Brief" never intended winning the case, was a concept never to enter his tiny mind.

Sweeney was happy to go along with the idea when Bunn opened his briefcase and handed him the gun. The length of string and plastic bag were Bunn's safeguard to make it look as though an accomplice had lowered the gun down from the roof. Otherwise, if things went wrong with the court escape plan Bunn could have come under suspicion as the supplier of the gun.

"Fire one shot into the ceiling," Bunn told him. "Frighten them… make it look for real. That shot will also be Price's signal. He'll get the car down to the entrance. Only one shot, remember. There are only two bullets in the gun."

Sweeney was equally surprised at Bunn's courageous act in preventing him from putting that one shot into Pete Lacey's head. The barrister's apparently noble deed was not deserving of any medals, though. It was nothing more than a desperate move to keep the plan on track, and ensure that the bullet ended up in the ceiling after all.

It was another shrewdly conceived idea by Farmer putting his police knowledge to good use. "That bullet needs to go harmlessly into the soft plaster of the ceiling," he'd advised. "It will be recovered in good condition and then be matched against the bullet that kills you."

"You", yes he said *"You"*, when he'd explained the plan to Bunn. Bunn had a sharp mind and understood the joke. He knew Farmer was referring to Alan Craine, the body double who would be used as a stooge for himself.

Later, Sweeney predictably turned the gun on Bunn. Both Price and Farmer expected this; hence the reason why there was only ever *one* bullet in the gun rather than the two that Bunn lied to Sweeney about. Sweeney had no idea he was effectively unarmed during his court escape.

Price was ready with his own gun and so more surprise lay in store for Sweeney, especially when his old cellmate appeared to be relishing the idea of killing him. Price showed no emotion as he delivered two swift shots; one in the back as Sweeney turned and attempted to escape and another in the throat. The telephone call delivering this information was the news Farmer had waited over three long years to hear.

Farmer knew all too well that his usefulness would expire along with his retirement. It had sunk in some time ago that Sweeney intended removing all traces of him as soon as that moment arrived. Price advised Farmer of the impending contract on him during an exchange of brown envelopes – money for information. Farmer had been on the take for years. PNC checks, criminal record checks, addresses, ex-directory phone numbers, records destroyed.

So the germ of an idea to kill Sweeney started to grow. If successful the scheme would not only deliver a huge cash hand-out to the main players, but would also ensure Farmer of an extended lifespan.

Charlie Price detested Farmer, but here was a plan destined to reap massive rewards and put all the blame on a fugitive who could never be found.

Craine's involvement was cruel, a completely innocent man, killed so that his death could erase the existence of Jacob Selwyn Bunn.

It was of the utmost importance to Farmer that Bunn should be proved conclusively to be "Dead". He didn't want him coming back to haunt him at some time in the future. The barrister would be able to arrange his own new identity.

The burnt body in the Jaguar would not only match that of Bunn to perfection. It would also be the spark that would mount an international hunt for David Sweeney. The bullet recovered from the femur bone came from the same gun used by Sweeney in court. Sweeney would become the desperate fugitive sought by police for years to come, but also a fugitive who would never be captured.

All hell broke loose when Price shot the 9mm bullet into Craine's chest as he lay tied up in the basement of the Gymnasium. The bullet passed right through and embedded itself into the floor.

"That's no good," Farmer said over the telephone to Bunn. "The bullet needs to stay in the body. Shoot him again through the shoulder downwards. You can't shoot him in the head, you could damage the teeth, and they must remain intact."

Bunn relayed the instructions to Price, who clearly enjoyed the additional work.

Farmer took a second gulp from his glass. A cheroot idled in the ashtray, its wisp of dark grey smoke curling upwards. He looked towards the ceiling for inspiration and calculated his next move. It now all seemed to be about self-preservation.

He thumped the arm of his chair with frustration. If it hadn't been for his clever subterfuge and inside information, there wouldn't have been much of a plan. It was his manipulation of events, his scheming mind with thirty four years of police service which conceived the twists and turns which would throw investigators off track.

A big mistake had been made though. He comforted himself with the thought that it was: *none of his doing*. "Sweeney MUST be cremated… completely disposed of," those were his words to Jacob Bunn. "This is vital. You have to use a public crematorium."

So the bizarre plan was hatched. The mistake in substituting Sweeney's body for Mr Larkin's rather than a body due for cremation was the scheme's ultimate downfall. This eventually led the detectives to Sweeney's body.

"Cannock Chase," was also Farmer's suggestion for the spot to dispose of both Larkin's and Craine's bodies. "The body you steal has to be burnt and the teeth must be smashed," he advised. "No teeth, no face, no fingerprints and therefore no identification," were his instructions. "The other body, Jacob's…" again he added his little joke. "Dump it on the same car park, along with plenty of additional evidence to corroborate it being Jacob. We'll have Exeter and Little Stoneleigh CID running around in circles and getting nowhere. It's my patch I can keep an eye on things from then on and if anyone starts getting too close, I shall intervene."

Farmer also provided the handcuffs… a couple of pairs that he'd managed to steal from HQ stores. "Might just come in handy," he'd advised Bunn. "Just in case we get any unwanted guests somewhere along the line and better than buying them from mail order… too easy to trace."

He really thought he'd covered all the bases… prepared for any eventuality, especially with his other suggestion to Walley. "Put something in from your bag of dental tricks… Knock out drops or similar. I'm sure you've got something that can put someone out cold should the need arise."

Right again, Farmer considered. Little did he realise that this suggestion not only gave Walley the means to quickly stupefy an unexpected visitor (Kim Harding) with an injection. It also provided Bunn and Walley with a solution to a part of the scheme about which Farmer had no idea – the disposal of Bill Travers. The bottle of chloroform had stood on a shelf in the basement of the dentist's surgery since the time when his father started the practice in the

1940's.

Farmer smacked his fist down into the palm of his hand. He'd planned things so well, but his ideas were thwarted when Taylor was placed in charge of the inquiry in preference to one of his *yes men.*

Farmer knew the game was up now. He knew about the exhumation. He guessed it would now have been completed. He knew that the Exeter detectives would know that it was David Sweeney.

He pursed his lips. It wasn't his fault that Taylor had discovered the old man's identity, but why did Taylor and Harding end up in Belgium? Belgium never came into the plan that he knew about. Someone had been keeping something from him.

He tried to push these thoughts to one side as his devious mind schemed yet again. He now had more than enough money to disappear very effectively. He allowed himself a weak smirk as he toyed with the possibility. He could take the money and leave Little Stoneleigh for good. A new life. Perhaps Brazil, where the money could buy him a new identity with no chance of extradition. Ronnie Biggs, the train robber managed it.

He forced another smirk. Perhaps he'd bump into Jacob Bunn.

He eased himself from the chair; it was time to pack what he needed into his car. He wouldn't be taking many personal belongings, just the bare necessities and five plastic boxes loaded with cash.

SIXTY EIGHT

KIM HARDING TOOK a swig from the pop bottle and a bite at a Mars bar. They were items purchased in Dover. *God*, she thought, *even that seems so long ago.*

Her unblinking stare concentrated through the binoculars onto the dark and barely visible outlines of trees and hedges near to the gates, the very limit of her below-the-horizon vision.

The binoculars fell to her chest, swinging from the strap around her neck as she decided on another swig of pop. She quickly stalled the idea as two pinpoints of light briefly twinkled somewhere out in the black landscape. Within seconds, the lights, now brighter and closer reappeared. The vehicle's meandering route, suggested without question, that its destination, via winding high hedged lanes, was the airfield. As the first sign of life since the police car, several hours before, and in view of the time, Kim's pulse increased.

'V… cle approa… ng,' her voice penetrated the static hiss of Taylor's radio.

A full five minutes went by before the car came to a halt at the gates. Kim took up a position against the glassless window and rested the binoculars on one of the rusty cross-bars. She could pick out figures moving about on the other side of the gates – two and a driver still behind the wheel. Even taking account of the distance and poor light Kim had no doubt on the make and model of the car. The identities of at least two of the occupants would not be difficult to guess either.

The glare of the headlights flickered as the gates were pulled open and then brightened as the car drove forward over the uneven ground. A short delay followed as the gates were closed. Distant muffled thumps carried across the field as car doors were closed.

Taylor lay flat against the ground in a clump of bushes hardly daring to breathe as the car drove within yards of him towards the buildings. Its brakes gave a short shrill squeak as it stopped in front of the office. The handbrake clicked up against the ratchet.

From above Kim took it all in, her memory racing back to the garage inspection pit and the thought that these men wanted her, Taylor and Travers dead.

She shook away the thoughts as the driver, Swann, or as she now knew him to be Jacob Bunn, climbed from the driving seat.

Another figure exited from the passenger side. This shorter, stockier man pressed his hands into the small of his back as he straightened up and looked to be in some discomfort. Perhaps the effects of Taylor's metal drainpipe attack were still giving him some gyp. Kim was in no doubt that this was Walley, the dentist she'd fought with back at the brewery, the man who injected her.

The third person, a rear seat passenger, pulled himself from the car and headed toward the office. A tall heavily built man, he delved into the pocket of his flapping raincoat for keys and climbed the two wooden steps to the door.

The other two followed and seconds later the steel mesh-covered window at the front lit up as a fluorescent tube sparked into life. A patch of light spread out onto the gravel.

With no curtains or blinds the activity inside the small building could be scrutinised quite easily by Taylor, thirty yards away in bushes. Kim on the other hand, found that as the men entered the office her line of sight was lost by the acute angle.

Taylor, flat down on his tummy, shuffled for more comfort and watched. He held the radio to his mouth and squeezed the transmit button. Clearly Kim had lost her view and might benefit from an update.

He kept it simple but made a point of adding a radio-handle for the mystery third man. This tiny piece of police protocol, probably one of the few which Taylor chose not to ignore may help simplify any further radio messages.

Taylor's nickname of "Harry" for the third man was not lost on

Kim. The message came through in a rather broken fashion, but she had seen the classic black and white film: *The Third Man* and knew that the main character was named Harry Lime. She shook her head and managed a small snigger in the darkness at Taylor's sense of humour.

Taylor laid his radio down in the grass and propped himself up onto his forearms. He watched Jacob Bunn settled down in a chair next to Walley, as Harry stood talking and checking his wristwatch.

"Twitchy" would be a good word to describe the body language given off by each of the three figures. Bunn got back to his feet and wandered out to the car, eyes heavenwards, head swivelling. He opened a rear door and slowly pulled out a long, rectangular blanket-swathed object.

Taylor took in a steady breath. 'The Just Judges,' he whispered.

Bunn delicately slid the painting from the car and carried it back into the office where he propped it against the wall.

Kim saw Bunn take the painting from the car and watched him disappear from her view back inside again.

Taylor rested his chin down onto his interlinked fingers, sighing with frustration as Harry stepped back outside. He seemed to be carrying something, but the Mercedes blocked his view. Harry struggled down onto his haunches and again became partially hidden between the office and the car.

With his task completed Harry got back to his feet, returned to the office and lifted a radio handset to his mouth.

A distant engine droned; Taylor stared skywards searching for the source. Dark, heavy clouds blotted out any starlight as the noise became louder.

Bunn and Walley were against the window looking upwards as Harry replaced the handset to the table and made his way outside again. He stood in the doorway for a moment, gave a casual skywards glance and then stooped down behind the Mercedes.

The sudden bright glow of a match or lighter from behind the

Mercedes caught Taylor unawares. He blinked as a loud fizzing preceded the snaking hiss of a firework-type rocket shooting up from behind the Mercedes and climbing ever higher into the black sky. The missile burst into a noiseless display of silver balls, and then vanished.

Taylor frowned at the seemingly amateurish performance. He gave an unseen shake of the head in the darkness as a set of red and green wingtip lights appeared in the sky. The engine note of the small plane droned up and down as it headed in, below the clouds and well out of line with the runway. After a few more seconds a central bright white light also came to life.

Harry trotted up the two steps to the office and quickly flipped switches on the control panel.

Kim stepped back from the window. The rocket caught her off guard, but maybe there was more to come.

The runway was short by airport standards and the inky blackness distorted all perception of distance, but now two parallel rows of landing lights were starting to blink into life. One or two were not working and some were yellowy in their brightness, but they did their job. In the instant that they switched on the little plane veered in a different direction and started to line up for a landing.

The engine's hum changed, first slowing then increasing, and then with expert control heading in low. The outline of its wheels and undercarriage could be made out just above the swaying poplar trees.

This would be a hurried and risky landing, no safety procedure, no second chance. The small craft swung about as the breeze caught it. The pilot adjusted the throttle constantly before levelling the wings and then touching the wheels expertly down.

Harry dashed out from the office holding a powerful torch and flashing its beam in a bright, white arching motion. He loped over to Walley handing him the torch and giving instructions. Walley vigorously waved the torch back and forth in the direction of the taxiing plane.

Harry hurried over to a wooden lean-to at the side of the office and disappeared inside. He emerged within moments struggling to haul a small, but heavy looking, four-wheeled cylindrical shaped trailer out towards the plane. The thick rubber hose coiled on the top gave the clue to its purpose.

Taylor quickly understood the situation – a mobile fuel tank. This was clearly intended to be a quick visit.

The plane's engine note cut down and then droned back up as the pilot started to taxi towards the light.

Bunn and Walley joined Harry, their figures picked out against the office light. Bunn, the tallest, stood with the painting propped against his side.

The plane's single engine roared ever louder as it taxied up the remainder of the runway and over a patch of lumpy ground closer to the buildings. The three men gingerly made their way over as the pilot came to a halt and popped open the doors.

Harry started to push at the tail of the plane turning it full circle and pointing it back towards the runway. The pilot gestured a thumbs-up through his open door.

Walley closely followed Bunn taking on a bodyguard-like stance. His arms hung at his sides, his right hand clasping the angular form of a semi-automatic pistol. His head swivelled left and right, looking for trouble as Bunn carried the painting towards the open passenger door.

Kim watched, heart pounding, as the proceedings unfolded below. Her attempts to radio a warning to Taylor about Walley's gun were thwarted by the plane's engine noise. She now knew of at least one gun, and their plan to overpower these desperate men began to look even more dangerous. Memories of the brewery and the lengths to which Bunn and Walley were prepared to go had sharpened her mind. She started towards the stairs; Taylor was going to need help, but where was Travers? He'd got no radio and there had been no sign of him for hours.

Bunn now stood against the plane's tiny rear door carefully sliding the Just Judges into the baggage area. Walley stationed himself six yards back, gun in hand, head swivelling and readying to climb in after Bunn.

Kim crunched across the glass-strewn floor, heading for the staircase and intent on getting involved. Her instinctive final look through the window before she started the descent stopped her in her tracks.

SIXTY NINE

THE BUSHES parted. A figure was out, racing towards the plane, slamming into Walley, hurling him to the ground, gripping him around the throat with one hand, karate-chopping down on the gun wrist with the other. The pistol bounced across the concrete and spun away into the grass. Travers' fists were a blur, steam hammer punches into Walley's face. An attempt to quickly overpower him and payback for that chloroform attack.

Travers' unexpected assault kick-started Taylor into action and flung him into a full-tilt sprint towards the off guard Bunn. The barrister's reaction time was sharp though. He turned, wide-eyed, with the painting balanced precariously half out of the plane and snatched his gun out from a pocket. His finger tightened around the trigger as decisions on targets were made. Travers, an easy first choice, was just yards away.

A loud crack, a flash of flame, Travers lurching, convulsing, slumping flat down, motionless.

Bunn spun on one heel, gun pointing at Taylor and fired off a shot.

Taylor skidded to a halt unscathed and leapt to his left as Bunn lined up for a better aim. An increase in engine revs side-tracked his attention as the plane started to bump away over the rough ground toward the runway. The gunfire had panicked the pilot.

The see-sawing painting jolted Bunn up another gear. He was now running full-tilt alongside the plane, pushing the Just Judges inside with his gun hand and fumbling for a grip on the side handle. His stumbling feet were losing traction. He made a desperate sideways lunge, flinging himself halfway in through the flapping door, with the gun unfeasibly still in his right hand. In a second he swivelled into a sitting position, legs hanging out through the still open door.

With total disregard for the gun Taylor broke into a sprint after the roaring jolting plane, a full pelt race hoping to grab the barrister's feet and drag him onto the tarmac. But the plane had reached the runway and was beginning to gather speed.

Bunn's features contorted with a mixture of hate and panic as he took aim and fired off another round towards Taylor. The shot smacked harmlessly into the ground at Taylor's feet.

Realisation began to dawn on Taylor that the plane was pulling away from him. A sickly smirk spread across Bunn's face as Taylor's pace began to slow. The race was lost.

Bunn levelled the gun at Taylor's diminishing figure from his now stable position as the wings started to take the weight of the plane. He took careful aim. He wouldn't miss this time.

A sudden scouring, grinding noise took over from the engine's roar as the plane's brakes locked its wheels and dug the fat rubber tyres down onto the runway's rough surface. The engine note died as the machine slewed in a violent skid. The tail pulled around in a complete half circle as the pilot desperately fought with the controls to avoid the wheel spinning BMW rocketing out from the darkness. Kim's handbrake-turn and bone jarring braking slammed the car to a stop directly in the plane's path.

The centrifugal force of the spinning aircraft took hold of Bunn and threw him from the doorway like a rag doll down onto the runway.

Kim revved the engine to such a pitch that it could be heard above the deep beat of the plane. She flashed the headlights as if challenging the pilot to try to outmanoeuvre her.

Bunn struggled back to his feet and began a tottering backwards stagger towards the plane. The gun, remarkably still gripped in his right fist waved wildly between Taylor's panting outline and the BMW. A twitch of the head preceded a flash of white teeth as his maniacal snarl and the gun's barrel homed in and steadied on Taylor, the most dangerous threat, the easiest target. The trigger finger tightened.

A roar from the BMW's engine heralded a scream of tyres as Kim lifted the clutch and floored the accelerator. The car jolted forwards a yard, it worked. Bunn swung his aim around and wildly blasted off a shot. The car shuddered as the bullet punched through a rear door. Kim winced, expecting more.

Taylor glared back at Bunn from twenty yards. The barrister had become a dangerous cornered animal, his calm, conceited manner now lost in a desperate fight for survival.

A frantic uncontrolled flailing of Bunn's arms had supplanted the former smug wrist action of the gun hand. It broadcast the level of panic gripping him. Taylor, on the other hand, had slowed and calmed He narrowed his eyes and set his stare upon the revolver. His counting and calculating steadfastly continued. Bunn had fired off four shots, and if that fist still held the same weapon used with the arrogant flick back at the brewery, a five shot, then only one bullet remained. It was a big if and even one bullet could kill.

Bunn stabbed the gun out at arm's length towards the BMW and took more backward steps.

'YOU, you BITCH,' he screamed, his voice piercing high above both engine noises. 'Get that car off the runway or he gets it in the head.'

Kim reversed the car out of the way as Bunn's shrill words tailed off.

Taylor stood frozen. Only his eyes moved as he watched and tried to predict Bunn's next move.

The barrister continued to back away towards the plane, waving his left hand in a beckoning motion. 'Over here Taylor,' he barked. 'Closer… I won't miss you this time.'

Walley scurried across to the plane and struggled in through the door.

Kim's heart raced. She felt helpless as Bunn took more backwards steps to the plane with his gun still directed at Taylor. She set a grim hard stare of hatred on Bunn. If he shot Taylor she would ram the plane. They might all be killed, but what the hell. Something caught her eye, in the distance over by the gate. She could see movement. The silhouette of a big vehicle, large enough to tower over the gate.

The plane's engine note grew louder again as the pilot increased the revs. It blotted out the tearing, rending, screeching as the police lorry bulldozed its way through the metal gates. The vehicle's powerful headlights lit up the landscape as it started to gather speed and crash onwards across the grass, making a beeline for the action. The smaller headlights of several police cars now joined in, jarring crazily up and down as they overtook the lorry across the rough ground. Blue flashing beacons pulsed, klaxons blared.

The pilot revved the engine, franticly gesturing at Bunn to hurry.

Bunn's mouth dropped open as the complex plan crumbled before his eyes. 'Keep coming Taylor,' he screamed, a note of hysteria pitched his voice higher. 'You're my ticket out of here.'

Taylor took a hesitant step forwards, raising his arms above his head, mind racing, weighing up options. Bunn blasted a shot into the air and took more backward steps.

'COME ON TAYLOR.'

Taylor mirrored Bunn's steps. Had Bunn just fired his last shot? He advanced a few more paces, desperately trying to lock his vision onto the revolver, striving for more perspective. Was it the same gun, the five shot, or was Bunn now holding the more common six shot? Bunn waved the gun madly as Taylor tried to fix onto its image. The draught from the propeller played havoc with Bunn's jacket, his trousers flapped against his legs. The barrister took another backwards step and then steadied his aim, hand muscles tightening as his finger pressed against the trigger.

Taylor dropped his hands to his sides and walked forwards towards Bunn. Now he was sure.

Bunn's eyes widened, he jarred the trigger back, the gun's chamber turned over, the hammer lifted and snapped down.

It wasn't possible to hear the *click* over the plane's roaring engine or all the other clicks as Bunn pulled frantically at the trigger and backed towards the plane.

Taylor held up a hand. 'NO… STOP,' he shouted at Bunn.

Bunn didn't stop; he kept on going backwards.

Taylor kept his hand aloft until the last second. He turned his head away when it was too late… as the propeller did its work.

In an instant the barrister was shredded into a mulch of red slivers which flew high into the air and then rained down over a wide area. One of the larger items, the left foot, complete with shoe, succumbed to the pull of gravity as Walley stumbled from the plane, hands in the air. It landed at his feet.

Walley's retching could be heard clearly as the plane's engine spluttered to a stop.

Kim rushed over to Travers, but Taylor beat her to it. He carefully turned him, expecting the worst. Travers, ashen faced, winked up at the pair and even managed a weak smile.

Police vehicles screeched to a halt, some blocking the runway. The plane's headlight picked out six burly, black clad officers. Their shouts, and sub-machine guns, successfully coaxed the pilot, hands above head, out from his cockpit.

Another group, their features indistinguishable against the backdrop of bright lighting, made their way over to where Taylor stood with an arm around Kim's shoulder. A Belgian Police Chief barked out orders to his men. Taylor squinted for perspective as the outline of one man focussed into familiar features.

'Doug,' a voice called out.

Taylor responded, 'Geoff. But how…?'

'Bit of mess you've got here,' Deakin understated.

An ambulance arrived to take Travers to hospital. The bullet had grazed his shoulder, a lucky escape.

When the trip to As Police Station got underway Deakin explained his appearance. 'Farmer suspended me from duty, but Pete

Lacey kept me informed. He wanted me to secretly liaise with you, so I made my way over to Ghent. It's all been a bit of a rush and with you not being able to ring I didn't know where to start looking. Pete got your message through a few hours ago and so I teamed up with the local Police.'

Some time later Taylor found himself standing alongside Police Chief Axel Van Smet in a dimly lit cell corridor at As police station. A rattle of keys preceded a dull *clunk* as the jailer hauled open a grey, steel cell door. The occupant readied himself for visitors.

Leyton O'Neil, an American freelance pilot stood to his feet, his expression pensive.

A tall, slim, thirty-two year old with a tanned complexion and blonde locks, O'Neil could have passed for an Australian life guard. He had learned his flying skills crop dusting in the USA.

No pressure was needed to get the young man talking. He willingly explained how "Mr Swann" approached him back in October the year before. 'I'd been exhibiting the Cessna down at the Shuttleworth Air Show in Bedfordshire,' he said. 'This guy, Swann made me a jackpot offer… just too good to turn down despite the dodgy sounding requirements and the fact that we'd be overweight.'

O'Neil sat back down onto the edge of the cell bench and rested his head in his hands as he described his concerns about Swann's destination of a private airfield near to San Morino.

'Goddamned almost six hundred and forty miles from the tiny airstrip at Westerbroek in the Netherlands where he'd wanted me to fly from. Way beyond the range of the Cessna… even more so with all that weight.'

O'Neil shuffled along the bench as Taylor took up a place next to him. Van Smet lingered in the open cell doorway.

'So, who came up with As… Asch?' Taylor questioned.

The pilot held up his hands. 'Me… my idea. I've used that strip a couple of times. I knew the manager of the club. I guess it's down to me that he's in the slammer too.' He looked around at Taylor and shrugged. 'But As was within the limits at five hundred and forty four miles. It would mean topping up with gas before I took off again, but we never managed that. So even if we'd got off the ground after that bastard started shooting we'd have struggled to make San Morino.' He gave Van Smet a sideways glance. 'I guess he had some alternative plan up his sleeve.' He gazed forlornly at the floor. 'He sure as hell didn't have any alternative plan to that propeller blade, gee, what a mess.'

The aero club manager confessed to his part immediately and handed over one hundred and fifty thousand pounds when the police searched his home a few miles outside As.

A hastily organised debrief got underway in the police chief's comfortable second floor office. Van Smet organised coffee and wasted no time producing a bottle of whisky from his drawer, he was out of milk. The group talked until half past four.

A humorous interlude came when Kim reached into her jeans and pulled out a set of Belgian Police motorcycle keys. Van Smet gave a shake of the head, but managed a smile as Kim handed over.

The Just Judges painting warranted a police armed guard for its transportation to temporary safe keeping in a cell at As Police Station. Along with it went the two cash-stuffed suitcases recovered from the Mercedes. Undoubtedly Bunn and Walley intended piling these into the plane if their plans hadn't been interrupted.

It was light outside and six o'clock before Taylor, Harding and Deakin achieved some rest. A few hours uncomfortable dozing on sofas and armchairs in the police TV room was the best that could be arranged.

SEVENTY

IN LITTLE STONELEIGH the rain clouds had disappeared by the time the day staff arrived at the police station. It came as more of a pleasant surprise than a shock to learn that Superintendent Farmer had at last, decided to retire and would not be making an appearance that morning.

Most people did not know about the recent events and certainly had no idea of Farmer's involvement in such terrible crimes. This knowledge, for the time being was confined to the upper echelons of the Staffordshire and Devon and Cornwall constabularies.

A chatter of excitement went around the station and bets were being laid about who might take Farmer's place. Speculation abounded. Could anyone be a worse boss? A wave of gossip also made an early start as the stories hinging on press reports started to filter in from Belgium. The names of DI Taylor and WPC Harding were mentioned.

One of the more exciting parts of the morning came when Detective Chief Superintendent Ray Burrington entered the murder incident room at half past nine. Lacey and Timson accompanied him, along with other detectives from both Exeter and Staffordshire.

A squad of Staffordshire Police firearms officers waited in their Ford transit in the roadway outside as Burrington placed one of his own men in charge of the murder room. His instructions: 'No telephone calls out until further notice.'

Burrington met DC Cheeseman midway down the stairs. Cheddar gave a respectful nod and handed over a folded foolscap sized document. 'Morning, sir… the search warrant you asked for.'

'Thank you, Mr Cheeseman,' Burrington said, unfolding the paper and looking through the details. 'Any problems?'

'No, sir, the magistrate looked a bit surprised though.'

The relevant address was clearly written at the top of the warrant:

15 Bainbridge Crescent Little Stoneleigh.

Typically, Cheddar grossly understated the magistrate's reaction and his grin could not be concealed from Burrington.

CID officers would often visit local magistrates at their homes during out of court hours. Search warrants need that all important signature to make the document legal. The procedure also required the officer to swear on a bible as to the authenticity of the information leading to the request.

The stories accompanying such requests were often serious and sometimes even exciting. Most magistrates would show more than a passing interest in the identity of the villain under investigation. On this occasion the magistrate could be excused for spilling his tea on the carpet when that name became apparent. The itemised list of offences that Police Superintendent Malcolm Farmer was suspected of, added further astonishment to the Magistrate's face: Murders, firearms offences, theft of money, drugs offences.

Cheddar was delighted and only too pleased to help out when he received the instruction to obtain the search warrant directly from the Detective Chief Super himself.

'You'll need my help to execute this warrant, Boss,' he cheekily added as he handed it over.

The convoy arrived in Bainbridge Crescent within five minutes of leaving the murder room: Three unmarked police cars, the firearms Ford Transit, a patrol car, the special patrol group Transit, a SOCO van and a photographer's van.

Covering the back of the house seemed rather unnecessary. Malcolm Farmer wouldn't have been capable of doing a runner even ten years ago. The Granada took up its usual space on the drive, so why was he not answering the door?

'He never walks anywhere,' Cheddar said. 'He's in all right.'

'MALCOLM,' Burrington shouted up at the windows. 'I know you're in there. You know what happens next, so open up. You have one minute.'

Burrington pulled the cuff of his jacket sleeve back one inch and allowed his wristwatch to accurately dictate the stipulated time.

The order went unheeded. Burrington looked over at the SPG sergeant, heavy steel battering ram cradled in his arms, and gave one slow, closed-eyes nod.

A smile came over the sergeant's face; he loved this bit.

It took two swings of the ram to bash Farmer's front door almost off its hinges. There was no full-scale police rush into the premises as often seen on the TV, no shout of "Armed police".

Farmer sat on the hall floor just beyond the radius of the door, shoulders at a slant against the wall behind and legs splayed awkwardly in front.

The massive opening in his chest cavity was not completely concealed by his drooping head. Shards of white ribcage jaggedly guarded the edges of the blood rimmed hole. The mashed remnants of the vital organs within hunted out the squeamish. A shotgun makes a mess!

A blue plastic box lay by Farmer's side, its heaped contents of banknotes soiled with his blood. Another four boxes remained in the hall waiting to be carted out.

SEVENTY ONE

A TWO HOUR journey from As back to Ghent lay ahead. Police Chief Van Smet wisely decided that the now tattered BMW was no longer roadworthy and could not make the drive under its own steam.

Van Smet took the wheel of the gendarmerie Toyota Corolla with Taylor in the passenger seat, whilst Deakin and Harding shared the rear. A police car transporter followed along behind with the BMW.

News soon came through via Van Smet's police VHF radio of Farmer's death and in no time he patched Detective Sergeant Pete Lacey's telephone call through for a direct link with Taylor on the car's loudspeaker.

'My God, Pete,' Taylor said into the radio. 'I thought we'd finally reached the end of all this. Not suicide then?'

'No,' Lacey replied firmly. 'He'd got boxes of money stacked in the hall, it looks like he was about to load them into his car and scarper. The idea is that someone was waiting for him in the garden… he's opened the door and they've blasted him with a shotgun. It seems they've pulled the door shut and taken the gun.'

'Someone after the money?' Taylor theorised.

'The money was there on plain view Doug, agreed one box is a bit messed up, but it doesn't look as though the person who killed him was interested. They've not touched it, just shot him and pulled the door closed.'

'What about Sadie,' Taylor said. 'Is there any way she's behind it?'

'Well, it's a possibility,' Lacey said. 'We've got the Spanish police making enquires to establish if she's left the country. The pathologist can place the death between eleven last night and two this morning, which fits with a possible gunshot heard by a neighbour.'

The group arrived at Ghent Police HQ at half past three. Teams of detectives were already busy at the Belfort and Harmony hotels. Belgian SOCOs were making painstaking examinations of Bunn's and Travers' rooms. What was left of the burnt out garage premises was also being looked over.

Travers' shoulder had been stitched up and his left arm fitted into a sling. He was transported to Ghent Police HQ and maintained casually that he was: "Okay."

Taylor put forward some reasoned argument in Travers defence. 'He's been foolish, getting involved with this,' he said. 'But he's been nothing more than Bunn's pawn. We certainly wouldn't have got this far if it hadn't been for his help. There's little doubt that Bunn and Walley never intended that he would come out of this alive.'

Van Smet pulled onto the forecourt of the impressive seventeenth-century building that was Ghent Police Headquarters and smiled obligingly at Taylor's words.

Ghent's Chief of Police met them at the doorway. He warmly shook Van Smet's hand and exchanged the pleasantries of old friends who had not met in a while.

A further round of handshakes took place as Van Smet introduced Taylor, Harding and Deakin. The police chief beckoned all to follow as he headed for the lift. Two uniformed officers traipsed slowly behind, carrying the blanket swathed painting.

Taylor stepped into the chief's office and returned nods with a tall, balding middle-aged man who occupied a space at the side of the chief's desk. His smart dark blue suit and expressionless face presented an air of superiority.

The chief held his hand out towards the man. 'Everyone, allow me to introduce Nicholas Van Hive from the Belgian Ministry of Economic Affairs.'

Van Hive graciously turned the corners of his mouth upwards.

Taylor's request that Bill Travers be allowed to take part in the meeting and inspection of the painting raised some hackles. His speech on the issue proved to be short but emotive. He agreed that the war veteran was responsible for some damage to Nazareth Church ceiling, but added that he was also responsible for the original construction of it.

'Yes he did steal the painting,' Taylor said. 'But without him doing so, no one would ever have known of its existence.' He went on to express a notion that Travers' attendance would get to the truth of the story more successfully.

Van Smet ran these factors quickly through his mind and realised that he tended to agree with Taylor's reasoning. The other members acquiesced.

The intercom on the chief's desk buzzed, and a short conversation in Flemish ensued. The chief replaced his telephone. 'A call for you, Mr Taylor. You can take it in my secretary's office.' He gestured towards the door. Taylor got to his feet.

Lacey's voice came on the line. 'Doug… Sadie is in the clear. She hasn't been out of Tenerife. She took an overdose the night before last. She hasn't even been discharged from hospital yet.'

'Is she okay?'

'Yes, she'll be all right, but it blows that theory out of the water as to who killed Farmer. Gorton was the last surviving member of Sweeney's team. So, unless you can come up with any brainwaves we're back to the drawing board and Staffordshire has another unsolved murder.'

There were a few seconds of thoughtful silence before Taylor made a suggestion. 'Have a word with Edward Steele.'

Taylor re-entered the meeting and gave an update on the latest news.

'Your detectives have some work to do,' the chief said sympathetically.

A further telephone call stalled the meeting again. The chief replaced the handset and looked back up at the gathering.

'Our art expert has arrived.'

The secretary's door opened and a figure was shown into the

room. The chief warmly beckoned in the elderly grey-haired lady.

'Let me introduce you, everyone, this is Mevrouw Catherine Swalus.'

Taylor and Harding stood to their feet and grinned.

Cathy's face showed her surprise. 'My friends,' she said with a baffled half-smile.

The police chief seemed bewildered. 'You appear to have met our English detectives.'

Cathy's confused expression quickly changed. 'Detectives? Ah, undercover detectives.' She winked at Taylor.

The Chief beckoned her over towards where the painting stood propped against the wall still swathed in a blanket. The gathering watched in silence as she carefully removed the covering.

Each of the four corners of the painting showed a nail hole, evidence of how it had been fixed into Nazareth's church ceiling. Cathy ran a fingertip over one of the holes, dismissing it as minor damage, she then picked up the panel with both hands; it was heavy for her frail physique.

She gently shook the painting, gauging its weight, before propping it upright against the Chief's desk to take the light from the window. The remarkable colours and hues, the shading and fine detail shone through a patina of age and dust.

Taylor and Harding looked on in silence, consuming their first ever opportunity to see the real article, the reason why they were here, the motivation behind all these events. Before this moment it had only been a blurred image on a tiny Polaroid picture of an even smaller black and white snapshot.

The painting showed a group of noblemen on horseback, all dressed in lavish clothing. The man in the foreground wore a dark blue velvet gown and sat astride a superbly painted white horse. All the figures in the group seemed to be staring at, or were in amazed conversation about whatever was depicted in their line of vision, the central panel, *The Adoration of the Mystic Lamb.*

Everyone in the room had some conception of the history of the polyptych. Even Deakin had managed to swot up on the subject during his crossing.

Cathy felt inside the baggy pocket of her grey knitted cardigan and pulled out a rolled up, seamstress's cloth tape measure. She carefully checked the height and width of the painting, nodding her head as she did so. She took two backward paces and covered her mouth with a hand as she pondered in deep thought.

A frown ridged her forehead as she took hold of the spectacles that hung on a cord around her neck. She pushed them onto the bridge of her nose and knelt down onto one knee.

A hushed silence overtook the room as the expert opened her handbag and produced a silver-coloured jeweller's eyepiece. Removing her spectacles she mimicked a yawn as she pressed the eyepiece into her right eye socket, tightly squeezing it against her eye. She closed her face right up against the canvas until the eyepiece seemed to touch it.

SEVENTY TWO

IN LITTLE STONELEIGH, Cellarbrations off-licence looked closed. The locked front door gave confirmation to this idea. Lacey's face showed his concern. 'I don't like this.'

Cheeseman and Timson needed no prompting and set off the few paces along the side street towards the back alleyway that serviced the rear of the properties.

Finding the gate bolted, Cheddar reached over and undid the catch. It swung open to reveal a small backyard surfaced with an uneven covering of Victorian, diamond pattern pavement bricks. Beer crates, bottles and boxes took up a good deal of the ground space.

Lacey picked his way through the obstacles to join his two colleagues. A row of cream painted rusting iron bars protected the single downstairs window overlooking the yard, the very room that Lacey, Deakin and Timson had occupied during their emotional conversation with Steele a few days before.

The rickety back door bore the same ancient paint as the window bars. A faded, but fictitious *BEWARE OF THE DOG*, sign had been screwed to the woodwork.

Cheddar's heavy knocking produced no answer. He pulled down on the handle and the door opened inwards.

A courteous calling-out of the occupier's name would normally have been protocol for an uninvited guest, but Edward Steele's hanging corpse dispensed with the requirement.

The iron bracket in the kitchen ceiling was a sturdy affair. It had been installed by the Victorians who built the place to support a wooden clothes drying frame. All those terraces had them and evidently it was strong enough to hold the licensee's weight. The green plastic washing line threaded through the bracket and then around Steele's neck had cut deeply into his throat. A bloated crimson tongue stuck out from his mouth mimicking a ghoulish: *up yours mate!* A tiny wooden stool lay near the dangling feet, kicked onto its side on the old red quarry tiles.

In the corner stood the shotgun used on Farmer. Steele had chosen a less messy way to end his own life.

Cheddar reached over and felt Steele's wrist.

'No,' he said. 'Too late… stone cold… several hours ago.'

Back in the police chief's office at Ghent the door opened and a uniformed officer showed Travers to a seat. A white sling cradled his left arm and sticking plaster covered his grazed forehead, no one noticed his limp. The Belgian police officers in the room gave him a look of consternation, but he retained his usual dignified manner, nodding to those present.

Catherine Swalus turned and looked at the new arrival, puzzled by his appearance and unaware of his part in the story.

Van Smet explained: 'This is Mr Travers, the soldier who first discovered the painting back in 1944.'

Travers, the perfect poker player, rarely presented any readable emotions, either through body language or facial expression. A degree of tension within him now seemed apparent though, and this kept the eyes of the group fixed onto him. He appeared mesmerised as he stared over at the painting. This was his own first proper look at it in well over forty years. A smile crossed his lips and at the same moment the very slightest of head shakes.

He jerked back into reality at the sound of Cathy's question.

'Where did you find it?'

His lengthy answer came after a moment of composure.

Cathy listened intently until Travers finished. She then looked up at the assembly of faces.

'Jef Van der Veken,' she said.

The interested expressions of the audience changed to puzzlement.

'Jef Van der Veken,' she repeated. 'The painting is by Jef Van der Veken who, as some of you will know, is the artist commissioned to paint the copy that is now displayed in Ghent Cathedral.' She looked at the bewildered faces before continuing. 'I have no doubt at all. It is superbly executed in a style matching that of Jan Van Eyck so closely that it is brilliant.'

For the first time in their careers, each detective in the room, of whatever nationality, seemed lost for a question. Cathy's bewildering and unexpected statement made the expression: *You could have heard a pin drop,* achievable.

Oddly it was Travers who broke the silence. 'When did Van der Veken produce the copy that is now in the cathedral?'

Cathy looked over at Travers from her squatting position in front of the painting. 'He was commissioned to do the work in 1939, just before the war started and so didn't get to complete it until a few months after the war's end in 1945.'

Travers, deep in thought, looked down at the floor for several seconds. 'I found *that* picture,' he raised an eyebrow towards the panel, '…in September 1944. So, Van der Veken must have produced *it* first. It must have been stored in that attic for a while, but why would he make two copies?'

Cathy smiled mischievously as she stood, and then settled back into her chair. 'Why indeed? And why make such a perfect copy? He had after all been told by the authorities to make the subtle differences to avoid later confusion with the original, should it ever come to light.'

Taylor raised a finger, signalling a question. 'Presumably,' he said. 'Van der Veken worked from photographs of the real Just Judges?'

'Yes,' Cathy replied. 'Without question he will also have had the opportunity to personally examine the original painting in great detail before the theft. He was *the* expert on the works of Jan Van Eyck. He knew how Van Eyck's brush moved. He knew his pallet, his perspective, the depth he gave to his paintings. He carried out most of the necessary restoration on the works of Jan Van Eyck. Even my opinion will be followed up with X-rays and microscopic examination, but I am correct. This is not the original Just Judges.'

The gathering silently, but unanimously accepted Cathy's opinion. She clearly knew her subject.

Taylor posed more questions. 'Why would Van der Veken make a second copy? If he had not included the subtle differences, couldn't he have altered the painting slightly afterwards to make the differences then?'

'Yes, of course he could, but then again, why didn't he paint the differences in the first place? No, this painting was prepared for a reason. It was to be the ORIGINAL Just Judges.'

Cathy had captured her audience. She knew that the people before her were still unravelling her words. She looked over at Travers.

'Tell me again, where did you discover the painting?'

'In the loft of a shell damaged villa on the outskirts of Nazareth.' Travers went over the story in more detail. 'It was parcelled up securely with thick paper and string. There was a label attached to it.'

'A label, a label,' she said excitedly. 'Can you remember what it said?'

Travers shrugged. 'I can do better than that.' He fumbled inside his jacket pocket and pulled something out. 'The only mementos I had were the church door key, and *this*.'

SEVENTY THREE

BILL TRAVERS held an England's Glory matchbox in his hand. He pushed a finger against one end, sliding the tiny blue card drawer open. A piece of several times folded yellowed paper sprung upwards.

Travers unfolded the paper. 'I kept this. My intention originally was to return the painting to its rightful owner. Events took their course and it ended up in the church ceiling. I never told Swann… Bunn… about the label.'

The onlookers shuffled forward in their seats, eager to see the secret of the label.

The faded, carefully written name held a style that looked uniquely 1940's, tall, slim and scrolled in blue fountain pen ink:

Henry Koehn

(Kultur Forscher)

Cathy drew her hand to her mouth. 'Goodness,' she whispered.

She turned to Travers, taking a few seconds to compose herself. If her opinion about the painting had been hard to swallow by any of her audience she now felt vindicated.

'Let me explain things in context,' she said, increasing the suspense. 'The villa Mr Travers has described in Nazareth was owned by Jef Van der Veken's aunt. He used the house as a studio to… how shall I put it… prepare and store certain of his works. For the rest of the time he worked from his studio in Antwerp.'

Kim had listened intently to Cathy throughout and had been impressed. She posed a question: 'It's even more of a puzzle as to why he made two copies. If he mostly worked from Antwerp why was he in Nazareth? There's something about what you said about "certain of his works," what did you say, "prepared and stored, at his aunt's house." Is there something more we should know about Van der Veken?'

Cathy walked back around to her chair facing the room and sat down. She grinned.

'Kim… I made a resolution with myself that if things turned out the way they did, that I would not enter into speculation…' She paused and then slowly skated the label across the glossy surface of the table under her fingertip to position it in front of herself. 'But now that we have this,' she tapped the label. 'I will have to share my theory.'

Another shuffling of chairs seemed synonymous with everyone's interest as they prepared for what seemed destined to be a revelation. Even Van Hive replaced his impassive expression with a curious look.

Cathy began, 'Jef Van der Veken was brilliant at his subject. He could, at a mere whim, take on the style and deliberation of any of the old masters. He could produce a work of art… either a copy of an existing or previously known work, or even a completely new subject matter. He could age the work he produced as he went along. He could make it appear that the painting had not been touched by an artist's brush since the artist himself five hundred years before. When at his most prolific, I would defy any of the art experts of the time to know that the work had been restored.'

'Or a complete fake,' Taylor interjected.

'Exactly,' Cathy agreed.

'Many things have come to light since Van der Veken's death in 1964. Many formerly accepted valuable old paintings that can in some way be traced back to Van der Veken have come under suspicion as not being quite right. Other paintings have been found to have been almost completely over painted, almost certainly by him... and then there was the Renders Collection.'

Mystified expressions seemed to be fashionable as everyone sat silently, waiting for Cathy to explain.

'Emile Renders,' she began. 'Was a Belgian banker who, from the 1920s, amassed an incredible collection of Netherlandish and other paintings. The collection numbered upwards of thirty. It included works by Degas, Van der Weyden, Monet, Hans Memling and many more by some of the world's most sought after artists.' She sipped her coffee. 'You will all be aware of the deeds of the Nazis concerning their theft of valuable works of art during the Second World War. I refer in particular to Reichsmarschall Hermann Goering, who was the chief of all art thieves.'

Every head in the room nodded an agreement as Cathy pressed on with the story. 'Many of Belgium's extensive collection of valuable artworks were taken by the Nazis and the most sought after items ended up in Goering's personal collection.'

A noticeable bitterness now supplemented the tone of Cathy's voice as she reached this part. 'It is a fact that during the Second World War the Nazis took possession of the entire Van Eyck polyptych… all the panels. They effectively stole them from France where they were sent supposedly for safe keeping. The only panel they could not steal was, of course, the Just Judges, which had already been stolen in 1934. The entire altar screen was destined for Goering's collection. Goering wanted the genuine Just Judges so badly that he enlisted a team of Gestapo. They worked full time on the investigation of the original theft in an effort to recover it.'

A further shuffle of chairs accompanied a low murmur of comments.

Cathy patted at the air with her hands commanding silence once more.

'Goering knew of the Renders Collection and he wanted it. He made several offers to Emile Renders to buy the works from him, but Renders greedily, bravely, foolishly maybe, held out, even bartering with Goering, boosting the price. Goering became incensed and issued an ultimatum to Renders, barring him from selling the collection anywhere else. He made veiled threats as to what would happen if he did not supply the paintings.'

Van Hive, eager to know, broke his silence. 'And did he let

Goering have the collection?'

'Oh, yes,' she gave a slow calculated nod. 'Yes, he let Goering have them...' She paused. 'In exchange for three hundred kilograms of pure gold.'

The simultaneous intakes of breath from all present were followed by additional mutterings of astonishment as Cathy held up one hand.

'However,' she said. 'We now know that the paintings of the Renders Collection were not all that they were made out to be. You see Renders was, in fact, a business partner of Jef Van der Veken. Many paintings of the collection were recovered after the war following the Nuremburg Trials. Every one, after close examination, was shown to be the work of Van der Veken. Some were complete works by him. Others contained such fragmentary patches of what they purported to be that to suggest they had merely been restored was, at best, requiring an imaginative mind.'

Taylor sat back in his chair and crossed one leg over from the other.

'So you are saying that Renders and Van der Veken ripped Goering off to the tune of three hundred kilos of gold for some dodgy artwork.'

'Ripped Goering off?' Cathy repeated Taylor's words looking bemused. A ripple of laughter went around the room.

'Ah, yes, I understand, Doug. Yes, ripped him off, well and truly ripped him off.' She stood from her chair and stroked the top edge of the Just Judges panel. 'So, you see, that was the intention of this.' She scanned the faces. 'This would be the final, the best, the most costly, rip-off.' Her eyes turned towards Taylor, she smiled before continuing. '...Of ALL rip-offs. This was to be, as far as Goering was concerned, the real Just Judges back from its travels and waiting to join back once again with the other panels of Ghent's altar screen. It would complete the set for the greedy Reichsmarschall.'

She tapped a finger onto the label again. 'Henry Koehn was an SS special agent tasked with recovering the stolen panel. His flamboyant, important-sounding title of *Kultur Forscher* effectively means, culture researcher.' Cathy placed her elbows on the table and cupped her chin on her hands. She looked back at her audience. 'So *that,* everyone is why we have two Van der Veken copies. The fact that this one,' she held an open hand towards the panel, '…never made it to Goering was down to a sequence of different events… The war moving on quickly… Germany losing… The major battle taking place in the little town of Nazareth rather than Ghent and the forger being separated from his work.' She mused for a few seconds. 'We will never know how the fake would have been delivered to Henry Koehn. Clearly a suggestion that Van der Veken was involved would have raised too many eyebrows, so possibly a third person was to be involved. Maybe Van der Veken's aunt or maybe Koehn himself were part of the rip-off against Goering, we will never know.'

Cathy sat back down in her chair and smiled over at Kim.

Kim returned the smile and then started to clap slowly.

Her solitary clapping was joined within seconds by the rest of the room. There were only eight people, but the applause was eager and genuine even from Van Hive.

Four days passed before the voyage back home got under way. Paperwork, statements, exhibits and photographs saw to that.

Walley faced serious charges in the Belgian courts. The kidnapping of both Kim Harding and Bill Travers along with the attempt to murder them in the petrol swamped garage formed part of his list. He was as guilty as the late Jacob Bunn. The murders on British soil of Sweeney and Craine along further serious crimes, formed part of the catalogue of evil in which he'd played a principle part. It seemed likely that the entire mishmash would eventually be finalised in one place, either Britain's Old Bailey or Belgium's Cour d'Assises.

The pilot, O'Neil, would be facing charges before a Belgium court along with the manager of the aero club. It's doubtful that either would see the inside of a prison cell for long. Both were foolishly dragged along with the proposal of easy money. Neither knew of the evil deeds carried out in order to realise the finances which Bunn used to fund his cleverly thought out perfect crime.

Taylor stood alone against the rail at the back of the ferry. The white wake churned out below him leaving a jagged sweeping curve right back to the slowly disappearing Port of Ostend. The wind caught his hair and the sea spray tingled on his lips.

He shook his head as that phrase: *Perfect Crime* went around in his mind. It had turned out far from perfectly. So much had happened in the past few weeks, so many people affected, so many deaths.

Travers would not be facing any charges. Taylor was firm about that. The old soldier had no knowledge of what had gone before, and who could have imagined what would eventually take place? Bunn clearly never intended for Travers to come out of this alive.

To Travers it was an adventure, a chance to turn the clock back to a time in his life full of excitement, daring and risk. It certainly did that. He was, to use Kim's description: "Quite a guy."

Taylor raised an eyebrow as the thought came to him that the Vauxhall Carlton could still be collecting both dust and parking tickets at Luton Airport. The eyebrow raised a little further with the additional thought that he never did get around to paying that bill at Granville's!

He gripped the handrail. It was dusk and tiny twinkling lights had started to show themselves on the horizon where Ostend had been minutes before. His mind wandered back to Little Stoneleigh, the sleepy market town where nothing much happens.

Taylor thought for a few seconds about Farmer, the police superintendent who raped a young girl and fathered a ruthless gangster son, and then callously conspired to murder him and steal the proceeds of his life of crime.

He shook his head again. Farmer hadn't even known that he was nothing more than a small patch of paint on Bunn's big picture. How apt that Bunn had been chasing around in circles spending Sweeney's cash in an effort to get his hands on what turned out to be a fake painting.

He stared down at the darkening water below and pondered the lengths and depths the players in this game had gone to. How much deceit had been played out since the story began way back in 1934 with the theft of the original painting? How much treachery, trickery and deception? How many lies?

He contemplated the irony of it all and the overriding fact that the whereabouts of the real Just Judges still remained a mystery.

A hand slipped in around Taylor's waist.

'Wondered where you were,' Kim said, raising her voice against the breeze, 'thought you'd jumped ship.'

'No,' Taylor said sliding his arm around her shoulder. 'Back to face the music.'

ENDNOTES

JAN VAN EYCK'S polyptych (pronounced *pol-i-tik)* containing the twenty-four panels collectively known as 'The Adoration of the Mystic Lamb', 'The Ghent Altarpiece' and 'The Lamb of God' was originally displayed in the Joos Vijd Chapel (The 11th Chapel) at St Bavo's Cathedral, Ghent, upon its completion in 1432.

In its long history the polyptych has endured anything but a peaceful existence. There have been occasions when the panels have been separated from each other, sold, resold and reclaimed. More than once it has been almost destroyed by fire.

The six back-to-back panels were sawn apart in order that they could be viewed at the same time, (including the Just Judges).

The First World War saw the splitting up of the collection, which was reassembled again at the war's end when some panels were re-purchased by the Belgian State and the remainder returned under the terms of the Versailles Treaty.

The polyptych enjoyed a short period back home in the Joos Vijd Chapel, but on the night of 10th/11th April 1934 the Just Judges panel and that of John the Baptist were stolen.

The John the Baptist panel was recovered shortly afterwards as part of an elaborate ransom, but the Just Judges panel was not recovered. The troubled times of the polyptych did not end there, as with the outbreak of The Second World War all the other panels were removed to France to keep them from falling into German hands. However, following Nazi pressures the panels were given over to the Germans by the Vichy Government anyway.

The masterpiece was hidden by the Germans in a salt mine in Austria and narrowly escaped being intentionally blown up by them when defeat became apparent. The Allies rescued it on 8th May 1945 and returned to the Joos Vijd Chapel where it was displayed until July 1986 when it was decided to transfer it for security reasons. It was permanently removed to its current home in the de Villachapel, (The 25th Chapel) where it can be viewed to this day.

The Ghent altarpiece, (the polyptych) sadly remains incomplete. Despite the attentions and investigations of detectives and sleuths throughout the world the whereabouts of the Just Judges panel is still an unsolved mystery.

The superb copy of the Just Judges panel by Jef Van der Veken is exhibited together with the other panels of the polyptych. Van der Veken completed this copy in 1945. Van der Veken died in 1964.

The Renders Collection, which is mentioned in the story, was an amazing collection of paintings which had been amassed by businessman Emile Renders.

Hermann Goering forced Renders to sell him the collection and to this day many of these treasures still remain missing.

The Second World War forward landing strip at As (Asch) Belgium, code named Y29 started life as a German Army Air Corps base in 1917. It became a flying school after WW1 and was derelict and grown over by 1924.

In 1944 US forces constructed the advance landing ground code named Y29 at the site. It was the scene of one of the Second World War's most dramatic air battles. It is now used by the Belgium army as a storage depot, the place name being Zuntendaal, a few kilometres from As.

The town of Little Stoneleigh is modelled upon the Staffordshire town of Stone.

Granville's Brasserie, mentioned in the story is a restaurant and music bar in Stone. Permission to use Granville's as a location for part of the story has been kindly given by owner Adam Jones. The real Granville's regularly hosts live music from some of the country's best artists and always provides superb food. The doormen at Granville's are gentlemen.

Johnson's Brewery in Little Stoneleigh was modelled on the old Bent's Brewery of Stone which closed in 1972. Ian and Viv Bradshaw started a microbrewery on the same site in 2008 where they produce fine ales in the traditional manner.

Now that you have read Cathedral of Lies why not look into the stories behind the story. Go to the author's website: **www.cathedraloflies.com** and in the section dedicated to this book (Cathedral of Lies) enter the code given below. It will open secret pages and enhance the experience of reading the book with details and photographs of the places, the buildings, the vehicles and the real events which took place and which inspired the author's imagination. It will also reveal the incredible truth behind this fictional story and all that is known about the missing Just Judges painting. Where is the Just Judges now?

CODE: fact-and-fiction

Remember the code is both case and character sensitive, so don't forget the two mid-word dashes.

This paperback version of Cathedral of Lies is published and available worldwide through Amazon on CreateSpace. The book is also available on Kindle as an ebook. If you have enjoyed Cathedral of Lies please add a review from your Amazon account. Good reviews are the lifeblood of the book and without them little known authors would fail. The positive feedback makes the months and sometimes years of research and writing worth the effort.

About the Author

John Pye is a retired detective from the Staffordshire town of Newcastle under Lyme. During his lengthy police career he was involved in numerous high profile serious investigations including murders, robberies, suspicious deaths and drugs cases. His hobby of writing goes back many years and started with the publication of historical articles for a local newspaper. Cathedral of Lies is the first in the series of the 'Of Lies' Detective Inspector Doug Taylor crime thrillers. All of John's books are available on Kindle and some are additionally produced in paperback by Amazon CreateSpace.

Printed in Dunstable, United Kingdom

74273956R00224